# Bitterroot

James Lee Burke

Simon & Schuster

New York London Toronto Sydney Singapore

SIMON & SCHUSTER
Rockefeller Center
1230 Avenue of the Americas
New York, NY 10020

SIMON & SCHUSTER and colophon are registered trademarks
of Simon & Schuster, Inc.
Designed by Karolina Harris
Manufactured in the United States of America
1   3   5   7   9   10   8   6   4   2
Library of Congress Cataloging-in-Publication Data
Burke, James Lee, date.
Bitterroot / James Lee Burke.
p.   cm.
1. Vietnamese Conflict, 1961–1975—Veterans—Fiction. 2.
Private
investigators—Montana—Fiction. 3. Montana—Fiction. I.
Title.
PS3552.U723 B45 2001
813'. 54—dc21            00-066175
ISBN 0-7432-1402-1

# Acknowledgments

ONCE AGAIN I'd like to thank my wife Pearl and our children Jim, Jr., Andree, Pamala, and Alafair for always being with me.

I'd also like to thank Father Edmond E. Bliven for his insight into the historical and theological nature of Christian baptism.

For Jack
and Shelly Meyer

# Bitterroot

# Chapter

## I

DOC VOSS'S FOLKS were farmers of German descent, Mennonite pacifists who ran a few head of Brahman outside of Deaf Smith, Texas, and raised beans and melons and tomatoes and paid their taxes and generally went their own way. When Doc got his draft notice his senior year in high school, a lot of us thought he might apply for exemption as a conscientious objector. Instead, Doc enlisted in the Navy and became a hospital corpsman attached to the Marines.

Then he got hooked up with Force Reconnaissance and ended up a SEAL and both a helicopter and fixed-wing pilot who did extractions on the Cambodian border. In fact, Doc became one of the most decorated participants in the Vietnam War.

The night Doc returned home he burned his uniform in the backyard of his house, methodically hanging each piece from a stick over a fire that swirled out of a rusted oil drum, dissolving his Marine-issue tropicals into glowing threadworms. He joined a fundamentalist church, one even more radical in its views than his family's traditional faith. When asked to give witness, he rose in the midst of the congregation and calmly recited a story of a village incursion that made his fellow parishioners in the slat-board church house weep and tremble.

At the end of harvest season he disappeared into Mexico. We heard rumors that Doc was an addict, living in a hut on the Bay of Campeche, his mind gone, his hair and beard like a lion's mane, his body pocked with sores.

I received a grimed, pencil-written postcard from him that read: "Dear Billy Bob, Don't let the politicians or the generals get you. I swim with dolphins in the morning. The ocean is full of light and the dolphins speak to me as one of their own. At least I think they do.

"Your bud, the guy who used to be Tobin Voss."

But two years later Doc came back to us, gaunt, his face shaved, his hair cropped like a convict's, a notebook full of poems stuffed down in his duffel bag.

He worked through the summer with his father and mother, selling melons and cantaloupes and strawberries off a tailgate outside of San Antonio, then enrolled at the university in San Marcos. Before we knew it, Doc graduated and went on to Baylor and received a medical degree.

We stopped worrying about Doc, in an almost self-congratulatory way, as you do when an errant relative finally becomes what you thought he should have always been. Doc never talked about the war, except in a collection of poems he published, then in a collection of stories based on the poems, one that perhaps a famous film director stole from in producing an award-winning movie about the Vietnam War.

Doc ran a clinic in Deaf Smith and married a girl from Montana. When he lost her in a plane crash five years ago, he handled tragedy in his own life as he had handled the war. He didn't talk about it.

Nor of the fires that had never died inside him or the latent potential for violence that the gentleness in his eyes denied.

# Chapter 2

DOC'S DECEASED WIFE had come from a ranching family in the Bitterroot Valley of western Montana. When Doc first met her on a fishing vacation nearly twenty years ago, I think he fell in love with her state almost as much as he did with her. After her death and burial on her family's ranch, he returned to Montana again and again, spending the entire summer and holiday season there, floating the Bitterroot River or cross-country skiing and climbing in the Bitterroot Mountains with pitons and ice ax. I suspected in Doc's mind his wife was still with him when he glided down the old sunlit ski trails that crisscrossed the timber above her burial place. Finally he bought a log house on the Blackfoot River. He said it was only a vacation home, but I believed Doc was slipping away from us. Perhaps true peace might eventually come into his life, I told myself.

Then, just last June, he invited me for an indefinite visit. I turned my law office over to a partner for three months and headed north with creel and fly rod in the foolish hope that somehow my own ghosts did not cross state lines.

SUPPOSEDLY the word "Missoula" is from the Salish Indian language and means "the meeting of the rivers." The area is so named because it is there that both the Bitterroot and Blackfoot rivers flow into the Clark Fork of the Columbia.

The wooded hills above the Blackfoot River where Doc had bought his home were still dark at 7 A.M., the moon like a sliver of crusted ice above a steep-sided rock canyon that rose to a plateau covered with ponderosa. The river seemed to glow with a black, metallic light, and steam boiled out of the falls in the channels and off the boulders that were exposed in the current.

I picked up my fly rod and net and canvas creel from the porch of Doc's house and walked down the path toward the riverbank. The air smelled of the water's coldness and the humus back in the darkness of the woods and the deer and elk dung that had dried on the pebbled banks of the river. I watched Doc Voss squat on his haunches in front of a driftwood fire and stir the strips of ham in a skillet with a fork, squinting his eyes against the smoke, his upper body warmed only by a fly vest, his shoulders braided with sinew. Then the sun broke through the tree trunks on the ridge and lighted the meadows and woods and cliffs around us with a pinkness that made us involuntarily look up into the vastness of the Montana sky, as though the stars had been unfairly stolen from us.

Doc handed me a tin plate filled with eggs and ham and chunks of bread he had cut on a rock and browned in the ham's fat. He sat down beside me on a grassy, soft spot and leaned back against a boulder and drank from a collapsible stainless steel coffee cup and watched his daughter standing thigh-deep in the river, without waders, indifferent to the cold, fishing in a pool that swirled behind a rotted cottonwood. He took a tiny salt and pepper shaker out of his rucksack, then removed a holstered .44 Magnum revolver from the sack and set it on top of some ferns, the wide belt and heavy, square brass buckle and leather-snugged cartridges wrapped across the cherrywood grips.

"Fine-looking gun," I said.

"Thank you," he replied.

"Fixing to shoot the rainbow that won't jump in your creel?" I said.

"Cougars come down through the trees at night. They get into the cat bowls and such."

"It's not night," I said.

He grinned at nothing and looked in his daughter's direction. She was a junior in high school, her blond hair cropped short on the back of her neck, her denim shirt tight across her waist when she lifted her rod above her head and pulled her line dripping from under the river's surface and false-cast the dry fly on the tippet in a figure eight.

Doc kept touching his jawbone with his thumb, as though he had an impacted wisdom tooth.

"What are you studying on?" I asked.

"Me?"

"No. The rock you're leaning against."

"The country's going to hell," he said.

"People have been saying that for two hundred years."

"You've been here eleven hours and you've got it all figured out. I wish I had them kind of smarts," he replied.

He left his food uneaten and walked upstream with his fly rod, his long, ash-blond hair blowing in the wind, his shoulders stooped like an ancient hunter's.

❦

FIFTEEN MINUTES LATER I followed his daughter up to the log house that was planted with roses and hung with wind chimes. She stood at the sink, ripping the intestines from a rainbow trout, the water from the tap splashing on her wrists. Her eyebrows were drawn together as though she were trying to see through a skein of tangled thoughts just in front of her face.

"What's the problem with your old man?" I asked.

"Midlife crisis," she answered, feigning a smile, suddenly knowledgeable about the psychological metabolism of people thirty years her senior.

"Why's he carrying a revolver?"

"Somebody shot into our house down in Deaf Smith yesterday. It was probably a drunk hunter. Dad thinks it's the militia or these people dumping cyanide into the Blackfoot. He treats me like a child," she said, her face growing darker with her own rhetoric.

"Excuse me?" I said, trying to follow the progression of her logic.

"I'm almost seventeen. He doesn't get it."

"What militia?"

"They're down in the Bitterroot Valley. A bunch of crazy people who think it's patriotic not to pay their bills. Dad writes letters to the newspaper about them. It's stupid."

"Who's putting cyanide in the water?"

"Ask him. Or his friends who think they're environmentalists because they drink in bars that have logs in the walls."

"Your old man's a good guy. Why not give him a break?"

She scraped the dark and clotted blood away from the trout's vertebrae with her thumbnail, then washed her hands under the tap and dried them on her rump.

"The only person he ever listened to was my mom. I'm not my mom," she said. She walked out the back door with a bag of fish guts for the cats.

I FOUND DOC beyond a wooded bend in the river. He was false-casting his line on a white, pebbled stretch of beach, then dropping his fly as softly as a moth in the middle of an undulating riffle. The light and water on his nylon tippet looked like liquid glass as it cut through the air over his head.

"What's going on with you guys?" I said.

"With Maisey? Just growing pains."

"No, the gun. These militia guys or whatever," I said.

"Wars don't get fought in New York or Paris. They get fought in places nobody cares about. Welcome to the war," he said.

"Maybe I picked a bad time to visit," I said.

"No, you didn't. See, a German brown is feeding right under that overhang. He's thick across as my hand. If I was you, I'd float an elk-hair caddis by him," Doc said.

I hesitated for a moment, then waded into the stream. The coldness of the water surged like melted ice over my tennis shoes and khakis. I pulled my fly line out of the reel with my left hand and felt it feed through the eyelets on the rod as I false-cast with my right, the brightly honed hook of the caddis fly whipping past my ear.

# Chapter

## 3

FAR AWAY, near Fort Davis, Texas, unbeknown to any of us at the time, a man named Wyatt Dixon was being released from a county slam. For the ride out to the railroad track on the hardpan he was chained at the ankles and wrists and waist. His bare feet had been stomped on so that he limped like an old man when he walked from the jail's back door, under armed guard, to the van that awaited him. Inside the van, a three-hundred-pound deputy hooked Wyatt Dixon to a D-ring in the floor, wheezing while he worked, avoiding Dixon's eyes and the grin that shaped and reshaped on his mouth.

Ten minutes later, as the sun was setting behind a low ridge of arid mountains, the van stopped at the railroad track and Wyatt

Dixon stepped out and stood in the hot wind, his red hair lifting like silk, his nostrils dilating with the smell of freedom.

He was lantern-jawed, his eyes as empty and as undefined by color as a desert sky, his skin brown from the sun and clean of tattoos. Four deputy sheriffs pointed their weapons at Wyatt Dixon, then a fifth one methodically unlocked all the manacles on Dixon's ankles and wrists. When the net of chains fell from his body, the men around him involuntarily stepped back or extended their guns farther out in front of themselves.

"That boxcar's gonna take you all the way to Raton Pass, Wyatt," the fat deputy said.

Another deputy threw a sack lunch into Wyatt Dixon's hands. "You ain't got to get off to eat, either. Not in Texas," he said.

"Y'all know where my boots is at?" Wyatt Dixon said, grinning as stiffly as a swath cut in a watermelon.

The freight and cattle cars clanked together, and the wind blew chaff out of the flat-wheeler that Wyatt Dixon was supposed to climb into.

"Better get on it, boy. The mosquitoes out here use soda straws on a fellow," the fat deputy said.

"I'm moving, boss man," Wyatt Dixon said, and limped across the rocks like a man walking on marbles, then pushed himself inside the flat-wheeler as easily as a gymnast.

A cruiser pulled behind the van, and a tall man in a gray suit, wearing a Stetson and shades and a wide, flowered necktie, got out and carried a cardboard suitcase to the boxcar. A badge holder with a gold sheriff's star pinned to it hung from his gunbelt.

"Don't be telling yourself you got a reason to come back," he said, and flung the suitcase into the boxcar.

It burst apart on the floor, spilling out clothes, a white straw hat, a tightly folded American flag, a box of clown makeup, a pair of football cleats, an orange fright wig, and a plastic suction device, like a reverse-action hypodermic, that was sold through comic books to remove blackheads from facial skin.

"Why, thank you, sir. Y'all treat a fellow in princely fashion. God bless America for such as yourselves," Wyatt Dixon said.

"Get this piece of shit out of here before I shoot him," the sheriff said.

A deputy began waving at the engineer in the locomotive.

A few minutes later, when the sun was just an ember among the hills, the freight train made a wide loop on the hardpan and passed in front of the van and the sheriff's cruiser at the crossing guard. Wyatt Dixon stood in the open door of the boxcar, his white straw hat cocked on his head, his American flag flapping from an improvised staff. He drew himself to attention and saluted the men down below, his bare feet discolored like bruised fruit.

ON A FOGGY DAWN, three days later, Doc, his daughter Maisey, and I sat in my truck at the foot of a broad, green mountain that rose into ponderosa pines that were stiff and white with snow that had fallen during the night.

Doc opened the cab door quietly and leaned across the truck's hood and focused his field glasses on the tree line. Then he gestured rapidly at his daughter.

"Here they come," he whispered.

With feigned resignation she took the glasses from her father and looked up the slope toward the spot where he was pointing, her mouth twisted into a red button.

"Lord, you ever see anything that beautiful?" he said.

When she didn't reply, I said, "That's something else, Doc."

The herd of elk, perhaps over one hundred head, moved out of the trees and down the slope, their hooves pocking green holes in the snow, the mist glistening on the bony surfaces of their racks. They fanned out over the bottom of the grade and flowed like brown water across the two-lane road, their numbers and weight and collective mass knocking down a rick fence without any interruption in their momentum or even recognition that an obstacle was in their path.

They swelled into a meadow channeled with wildflowers and grazed into the tall grass by cottonwoods that grew along a copper-colored stream. Their humps were coated with crusted snow, and the heat of their bodies melted the snow and made the entire herd glow with a smoky aura against the sunrise.

"What do you think, Skeeter?" Doc asked his daughter.

"My name is Maisey," she replied.

WE DROVE into Missoula and ate breakfast in a café across the street from the courthouse. Through the café window I could see the crests of the mountains ringing the city and trees bending in a wind that blew down an arroyo. Deer were feeding on a slope above the train yard, and the undersides of their tails were white when they turned their hindquarters into the wind.

I left Doc and Maisey in the café, crossed the street to the courthouse, and went to the sheriff's office. The sheriff had called Doc's house up on the Blackfoot the previous night and had left the type of recorded message that not only irritates but leaves the listener vaguely unsettled and apprehensive: "Mr. Holland, this is Sheriff J. T. Cain. Got a bit of information for you. Eight forty-five, my office. You can't make it, be assured I'll find you."

I took off my hat and opened his office door. "I'm Billy Bob Holland. I hope I'm not in trouble," I said.

"That makes two of us," he answered.

He was a big, crew-cropped, white-haired man, who wore a suit and black, hand-tooled boots. His skin was deeply tanned, his neck and face as wrinkled as a brown leaf.

A folder full of fax sheets was spread open on his desk blotter.

"You recall a man named Wyatt Dixon?" he asked.

"Not offhand."

"He got out of a county lock three or four days ago in West Texas. He left behind a sheet of notebook paper with half a dozen names on it. Also a drawing of human heads in a wheelbarrow. Yours was one of the names."

"Who contacted you?" I asked.

"The sheriff down there ran your name through the computer. You were a Texas Ranger?"

"Yes, sir."

He fitted on his spectacles and peered down at a fax sheet.

"It says here you and your partner were investigated in the killing of some drug mules down in Mexico," he said.

"Rumors die hard," I replied.

He read further on the fax sheet, his eyes stopping on one paragraph in particular. His eyes became neutral, as though he did not want to reveal the knowledge they now held.

He picked up a clipboard and propped it at an angle against his desk. "You're not gonna kill anybody up here, are you?" he said.

"Wouldn't dream of it."

His pencil moved on the clipboard, then his face lifted up at me again.

"You're an attorney now?" he said.

"Yes, sir."

He wrote something on his clipboard.

"You know what bothers me? You haven't asked me one question about this guy Wyatt Dixon," he said.

"A lot of graduates make threats. Most never show up," I said.

He studied his clipboard and tapped on the metal clamp with his mechanical pencil.

"I can't argue with that," he said. "But Dixon did five years in Huntsville before he got picked up in Fort Davis for drunk driving. He did time in California, too. His record indicates he's a violent and unpredictable man. You're not curious at all?"

"I don't know him, Sheriff. If we're finished here . . ." I said.

He tossed his clipboard on the desk. A half-completed crossword puzzle was fastened in place under the spring clamp.

"There's what the press calls 'militia' down in the Bitterroot Valley. I think they're just a bunch of asswipes myself. But your friend Dr. Voss is doing his best to stir them up. Maybe he needs a friend to counsel him," the sheriff said.

"He's not a listener," I replied.

"I've got the feeling you're not, either," he said. He took a gingersnap out of a paper bag and bit it in half with his dentures. But the humor in his eyes did not disguise the bemused, perhaps pitying look he gave me when I rose to leave his office.


DOC'S HOUSE was at the northern end of a valley above the little settlement of Potomac, and you had to cross the river on a log bridge trussed together with rusted cable and drive five miles on a poor road through dense stands of timber to reach it. At night the light played tricks in the sky. Even though the house was located between cliffs and ridgelines, the clouds would reflect the glow of Missoula, or perhaps the bars in the mill town of Bonner, or cities out on the coast. But through the screen window, as I looked up from my bed, I thought I could see distant places upside down in the sky.

Doc said Montana was filled with ghosts. Those of Indians massacred on the Marias River, wagoners who died of cholera and typhus on their way to Oregon, the wandering spirits of Custer and the soldiers of the Seventh Cavalry, whose bodies were sawed apart with stone knives and left on the banks of what the Sioux and Northern Cheyenne called the Greasy Grass.

But I didn't need to change my geography to see apparitions.

When the Missoula County sheriff had read the fax sheets in his folder, his eyes had lighted on a detail he chose not to mention.

Years ago, on a nocturnal and unauthorized raid into Coahuila, I accidentally shot and killed the best friend I ever had.

Today the spirit of my dead friend accompanied me wherever I went. L. Q. Navarro was lean and mustached, with grained skin and lustrous black eyes, and he wore the clothes he had died in, a pinstripe suit and vest with a glowing white shirt, an ash-gray Stetson sweat-stained around the crown, and dusty boots and rowled Mexican spurs that tinkled like tiny bells when he walked.

I saw him at evening inside mesquite groves

traced with fireflies, sitting on top of a stall in a shaft of sunlight on Sunday morning while I bridled my Morgan to go to Mass, or sometimes idly looking over my shoulder while I fished the milky-green river at the back of my property. Whenever the opportunity presented itself, he assured me the purple wound high up on his chest was not my fault.

That was L.Q. His courage, his stoic acceptance of his fate, his refusal to accuse became the rough-hewn cross and set of nails that waited for me every night in my sleep.

WHEN TROUBLE COMES into your life in such a marrow-eating, destructive fashion that eventually you are willing to undergo surgery without anesthesia to rid yourself of it, you inevitably look back at the moment when somehow you blundered across the wrong Rubicon. There must have been a defining moment where it all went south, you tell yourself. Great astronomical signs in the sky that you ignored.

No, you simply took the wrong exit off a freeway into what appeared to be a deserted neighborhood lighted by sodium lamps, or trustingly signed a document handed you by a good-natured bald-headed man, or released the deadbolt on your door so an accident victim could use your telephone.

Doc asked me to meet him and a ladyfriend at a restaurant and bar in the mist-shrouded logging town of Lincoln, high up in the mountains by Rogers Pass. I parked my truck and walked past a dozen chopped-down Harleys into the warmth and cheerful brightness of the restaurant and saw Doc sitting in a booth with a tall woman whose dark hair was pushed up inside a baseball cap.

An empty pitcher of beer rested between them. There was a flush in Doc's throat, an unnatural shine in his eyes.

"This is Cleo Lonnigan. She practices meatball medicine at the Res," Doc said.

"That means I work part time at the free clinic," the woman said. She had dark eyelashes and brown eyes and a mole on her chin. Her high shoulders and slacks and beige silk shirt, one that changed colors in the light, made me think of a photograph taken of my mother when my mother worked in an aircraft plant in California during the war.

Somebody in the bar turned up the jukebox so loud that it shook the wall, then the bartender came from behind the bar and turned the volume down again. A woman laughed in a shrill voice, as though enjoying an obscene joke.

"You see those bikers back there? They think they're nineteenth-century guys who've found the last piece of the American West," Doc said. "What I'm saying is they're actually victims. It's like a bug on a highway facing down an eighteen-wheeler. They're just not students of history, you follow?"

"I'm ready to order. Do you want a steak, Doc?" Cleo said, smiling, obviously not wanting him to drink more.

"Sure. I'll get us a refill," Doc replied.

"Not for me," I said. But he wasn't listening.

I watched him work his way between the tables toward the bar, excusing himself when he bumped against someone's chair.

"Doc's usually not a drinker," I said.

"You could fool me," she said.

So she hadn't known him long, I thought, with more interest than I should have had as Doc's friend.

I heard the door open behind me and saw her eyes go past me and follow three men who had just entered. They wore yellow construction hats and khakis and half-topped boots, and their faces looked pinched and red from the wind. They sat at a table in the corner, one with a red-and-white checkered cloth on it, and studied their menus.

"Those guys are from the Phillips-Carruthers Corporation. It's just as well Doc doesn't see them," Cleo said.

"Why not?"

"They work at the gold mine. They use

cyanide to leach the gold out of the rock,"
she said.

"Near the river?" I said.

"Near everything."

I turned and looked at the men again. One
of them glanced back at me over his menu,
then sipped from his water glass and through
the window watched a truck boomed down
with logs pass in the rain.

"You think Doc's going to be all right?" I
asked.

"I doubt it."

She looked at the expression on my face.

"He's an idealist. Idealists get in trouble,"
she said.

The waitress took our order. I heard more
noise in the bar area and saw Doc talking to
three bikers at a table, his graceful hands extended as though he were holding his spoken
sentences between them.

"Excuse me a minute," I said.

I walked to the rear of the restaurant,
which opened into a darkened, neon-lit bar
area that was layered with cigarette smoke.
I passed Doc without looking at either him
or his listeners and continued toward the
men's room. But I could smell the bikers,
the way you smell a wild animal's presence
in a cage. It was a viscous, glandular odor,
like sweaty leather and unwashed hair and
body grease and testosterone that has dried

and become part of the person's clothes.

Behind me, Doc continued his earnest instruction to his audience: "See, you guys motor on in to Lincoln because you think it's a place with no parameters. The home of the Unabomber, right? A guy who had stink on him that would make buzzards fall out of the sky but who went unnoticed by the locals for twenty years.

"See, what you don't understand is these people are very square and territorial. One time a bunch of guys like you decided to take over a town in the Gallatin Valley on a Saturday afternoon. They started shoving people around in bars, busting beer bottles in the streets, riding their hogs across church lawns, you know, like in the Marlon Brando film *The Wild One*.

"Guess what? In two hours every mill worker, gypo logger, and sheepherder in the county came into town. They parked their log trucks across the roads so the bikers couldn't get out. They broke arms and legs and bent Harleys around telephone poles. Some of the bikers got down on their knees and begged. The townies left enough of the bikers intact to take the wounded into Billings."

I went into the men's room. When I came back out, Doc was still talking. The bikers smoked cigarettes and poured beer into their glasses and drank in measured sips, tipping their ashes into an empty can, occasionally glancing at one another.

One of their girls was watching the scene from the cigarette machine, her arms folded in front of her. She was an Indian, perhaps part white, her long hair streaked with strands of dull yellow. She wore a lavender T-shirt and Levi's that hung low on her hips, exposing her navel. She stared directly into my eyes. When I looked back at her, she tilted her head slightly as though I had not understood a point she was making.

"The waitress is fixing to throw your food out, Doc," I said.

"Go on. I'll be there," he replied, waving me away.

I went back out into the restaurant and sat down across from Cleo. A strand of her hair hung out of her baseball cap across one eye.

"Where do you and Doc know each other from?" I said, glancing back at the bar area.

"A support group," she replied.

"Pardon?"

"It's a group that meets in Missoula. For people who have—" She saw that I was still watching the bar area. "What are you asking for?"

"I'm sorry," I said, my attention coming

back on her face. "You said a support group. I didn't know what you meant."

Her left hand was turned palm down on the table. There was no wedding ring on it. "It's for people who have lost family members to violence. Doc's wife died in a plane crash. My husband and son were murdered. So we attend the same meetings. That's how we met. I thought that's what you were asking me," she said.

The skin of my face felt tight against the bone. The restaurant seemed filled with the clatter of dishes and cacophonous conversation about insignificant subjects.

"I'm sorry. I didn't mean to—" I began, but the waitress arrived at the table and began setting plates of steak and potatoes in front of us. Cleo had already lost interest in anything I had to say by way of apology.

Behind her, the Indian biker girl from the bar walked between the tables, watching me, as though she knew me or expected me to intuit private meaning in her stare.

"Why not get a new cigarette machine instead of putting tape all over it? It not only looks like shit, the cigarettes don't come out," she said to the woman behind the cash register.

"Let me give you some breath mints instead. Oh, there's no charge. Don't they sell cigarettes on the reservation?" the cashier said.

The Indian girl took the last cigarette out of her pack and put it in her mouth, her weight on one foot, her eyes staring into the cashier's.

The cashier smiled tolerantly. "Sorry, honey. But you should learn how to talk to people," she said.

"My speech coach says the same thing. I'm always saying 'blow me' to patronizing white people," the Indian girl said.

She paused by our booth and momentarily rested her fingers on the tabletop and lit her cigarette.

"Your doctor friend is in Lamar Ellison's face. I'd get him out of here," she said, her eyes looking straight ahead.

She walked away, toward the bar.

"Who is *that?*" Cleo said.

"I don't know. But I don't like eating at the O.K. Corral," I said.

I got up from the table and went back to the bar.

"Your food's getting cold, Doc," I said.

"I was just coming," he replied. Then he said to the bikers, "Y'all think on it. Why get your wick snuffed being somebody's hump? I'll check with you later."

I placed my hand under his arm and gently pulled him with me.

"What's wrong with you?" I said.

"You just got to turn these guys around. It's the rednecks who win the wars. The liberals are waiting around on a grant."

"We're eating supper, then blowing this place. Or at least I am."

"You're in Montana. This is no big deal."

He cut into his steak and put a piece into his mouth and drank from his beer, his eyes looking reflectively at the three engineers from the gold mine.

I waited for him to start in on another soliloquy, but an event taking place in the bar had suddenly captured his attention.

Two men and a woman had come in, people who were obviously from somewhere else, their features soft around the edges, their shoulders rounded, their faces circumspect yet self-indulgent and vaguely adventurous. They had taken a booth in the bar, then perhaps one of them had glanced at the bikers, or said something or laughed in a way a biker did not approve of, or maybe it was just their bad luck that their physical weakness gave off an odor like raw meat to a tiger.

One of the bikers took a toothpick out of his mouth and set it in an ashtray. He rose from his chair and walked to their booth, drinking from a long-necked beer bottle, his jeans bagging in the seat. He stared down at them, not speaking, the stench of his body and clothes rising into their faces like a stain.

"Somebody's got to put a tether on those boys," Doc said.

"Don't do it, Tobin," I said.

Doc wiped the steak grease off his mouth and hands with a napkin, the alcoholic warmth gone from his eyes now, and walked back toward the bar.

Cleo rested her forehead on her fingers and let out her breath.

"This was a mistake. It's time to go," she said. She looked up at me. "Aren't you going to do something?"

"It's somebody else's fight," I said.

"How chivalric," she said.

"Doc resents people mixing in his business."

"I'm going to get him out of there if you won't."

"Ask the waitress for the check," I said, and returned to the bar area.

The biker towering over the three tourists wore a leather vest with no shirt and steel-toed engineering boots; his jaws and chin were heavy with gold stubble, his hair tangled in snakes like a Visigoth's. His arms were scrolled with tattoos of daggers dripping blood, helmeted skulls, swastikas, a naked woman in a biker cap chained by the wrists to motorcycle handlebars. The three people in the booth looked at nothing, their hands and bodies motionless, their mouths moving slightly, as though they did not know which expression they wanted their faces to form.

"Excuse me, but you were pinning my friends," the biker said. "Then I got the impression you cracked wise about something. Like your shit don't stink, like other people ain't worthy of respect. I just want you to know we ain't got no beef with nobody. Ain't no biker here gonna hurt you. Everybody cool with that?"

The two men in the booth started to nod imperceptibly, as though their acquiescence would open a door in an airless, superheated room. But the biker was watching the woman.

"You want another beer?" he asked her. He reached out with one finger and touched her lips. "Smile for me. Come on, you got a nice mouth. You don't want to walk around with a pout on it."

Her throat swallowed and her eyes were shiny, her nostrils dilated and white on the edges.

"Here, let me show you," the biker said. He worked his finger into her mouth, wedging it open, forcing it past her teeth, reaching inside her cheek.

"Now, just a minute," the man next to her said.

"You don't want to touch me, Jack. That's something you really don't want to do," the biker said while the woman's saliva ran down his finger.

Doc stepped into the biker's field of vision, raising his hand as a peacemaker might.

"You need to walk outside and get some air, trooper . . . No, no, it's not up for debate," Doc said.

The biker didn't speak. Instead, his left hand, the index finger still wet from the woman's mouth, seemed to float like a balloon toward the side of Doc's head, as though he were about to caress it.

Doc's movements were so fast I was never sure later whether he hit the biker first with his hand or his foot. I saw him spin, then the biker's head snapped back and his mouth exploded in the air. Doc spun again, his foot flying out in a reverse back kick, and I was sure this time I heard bones or teeth snap.

The biker was on the floor now, and I could see spittle and blood on his lips. But his pain and disfigurement were the least of his problems. He was strangling to death.

"Get out of the way!" I heard Cleo say behind me. Then she was on her knees by the biker, pressing his tongue down with a spoon, reaching into his windpipe with her fingers, extracting part of a dental bridge.

I walked outside, past the row of parked Harleys, and removed L.Q. Navarro's blue-black, holstered .45 from the shell on the back of my pickup truck. I dropped the pistol on the front seat and waited for the sheriff's deputies and the paramedics, who I knew would be there momentarily. The sky was black, the mountains steep-sided, the trees suddenly pale green when lightning jumped between the clouds. Down the highway I saw the red emergency lights of an ambulance roaring toward me inside a vortex of rain.

Nailed to a telephone pole was a drenched, wind-torn poster advertising a rodeo in Stevensville, down in the Bitterroot Valley. On the ad was an action photo of a rodeo clown distracting a bull that had just thrown a cowboy into the boards. For some reason the incongruous image of the helpful clown, dressed in vagabond clothes, wearing a derby hat with horns attached to it, would not leave my mind.

# Chapter 4

TWO DAYS LATER I drove west of Missoula, past the U.S. Forest Service smokejumper school, then up a sharp grade between wooded mountains into a long green valley ringed by more mountains. I looked at the map Doc had drawn for me and drove across the Jocko River and followed a dirt road between two bald hills to the gated entrance of Cleo Lonnigan's property.

The morning was still cold. Smoke blew from the stone chimney of her house, and horses were standing in the sun by a barn that was wet on one side with melting frost.

I walked up on the porch and knocked on the door and removed my hat when she answered it.

"I wanted to apologize for speaking ineptly

about your loss. Doc told me about it later," I said.

"That's why you drove all the way out here?" she asked.

"More or less."

There was no screen on the door. She stood perhaps a foot from me but had not asked me in, so that the space between us and her lack of hospitality were even more awkward.

"How's Doc?" she asked.

"The biker didn't file charges, so the cops let Doc slide. I guess getting your face bashed in is just part of an evening out here."

"Pacifists in Montana get about the same respect as vegetarians and gay rights advocates," she said.

"You saved that biker's life," I said.

She looked at me without replying, as though examining my words for manipulation or design.

I fitted on my Stetson and glanced around at the sunlight on her pasture and her horses drinking in a creek that was lined with aspens and cottonwoods.

"Can I take you for breakfast in town?" I asked.

"Doc says you were a Texas Ranger."

"Yeah, before I got hurt. I started off as a city cop in Houston."

She seemed to look past me, into the distance. "I have some coffee on the stove," she said.

Her house was built of lacquered pine, with big windows that looked out on the hills and cathedral ceilings and heavy plank furniture inside and stone fireplaces and pegs in the walls for hats and coats. In the kitchen she poured a cup of coffee for me in a white mug. Out back two llamas were grazing in a lot that was nubbed down to the dirt, and, farther on, up a hill that was still golden with winter grass, a whitetail doe with two fawns stood on the edge of a deep green stand of Douglas fir.

"Are you and Doc pretty tight?" I said, my face deliberately blank.

"Sometimes. In his own mind Doc's still married."

"I don't see Doc in your support group," I said.

"Why?"

"His wife died in an accident. I suspect most people in your group have lost relatives to criminal acts."

"Doc's wife worked for the utility company. They made her fly to Colorado in bad weather. He blames them for her death."

"I never heard him say that," I said.

"Sometimes if you confess your real thoughts, people will be afraid of you," she replied.

But I knew she was talking about herself now and not Doc. He had told me about her husband, a stockbroker from San Francisco who had taken early retirement and bought a ranch in the Jocko Valley six years ago. He and Cleo'd had a six-year-old son. Their lives should have been idyllic. Instead, there were rumors about infidelity and money-laundering back in San Francisco. The husband filed for divorce, accusing his wife of adultery, and won summer visitation rights with his son. He moved to Coeur d'Alene and each June came back to Montana and picked up his boy.

On a July Fourth weekend two years ago, the father's and the son's bodies had been found in the trunk of the father's automobile in the Clearwater National Forest. The automobile had been burned.

"Why are you looking at me like that?" she said.

"No reason."

"Doc told you everything that happened?"

"Yes."

"The people who did it were never caught. That's what's hardest to live with. The only consolation I have is that Isaac, that's my son, was shot before the car was burned. At least that's what the coroner said. But sometimes coroners lie to protect the family."

I picked up my hat off the back of a chair

and turned it in my hands. I didn't want to look at her eyes.

"There's a rodeo this evening in Stevensville. I'd sure like to take you," I said.

THE SUN was setting beyond the Bitterroot Mountains when we walked up into the wood stands that overlooked the arena. The air was cool and smelled like hot dogs and desiccated manure and pitchforked hay. The summer light had climbed high into the sky, and in the distance I could see the humped, purple shapes of the Sapphire Mountains and the shine of the Bitterroot River meandering through cottonwoods whose leaves were fluttering like thousands of green butterflies in the breeze.

"People say you come to Montana once and you never leave. Not unless something is wrong with you," Cleo said.

"It's special, all right," I said. But my attention had shifted away from the softness of the evening to a young woman down by the bucking chutes. She wore suede boots and bleached jeans with a concho belt outside the loops and a T-shirt and a straw cowboy hat that was coned up on the sides; she propped one boot on a white slat fence and watched three wranglers run a bull into the back of a chute.

"You recognize that gal down there?" I said.

"No," Cleo said.

"The biker girl from the bar in Lincoln. She tried to warn us about Doc. She thought he was going to get hurt."

"The one who got in the cashier's face?" Cleo said.

"She said the biker's whole name to me—Lamar Ellison. Like she wanted to make sure I'd remember it and tell somebody else."

"I'd like to forget those people," Cleo said.

"She made me for a cop. Two kinds of people can do that. Jailwise hard cases and other cops."

"Who cares what a person like that does?" she said.

I didn't pursue it.

The girl was joined at the fence by two men in scalped haircuts. They could have been bikers or paratroopers on furlough, but in all likelihood they were simply brain-dead misogynists who daily had to convince themselves of their gender.

A third man, with white hair and a trimmed white beard, joined them. He smoked a corncob pipe and stood very stiffly while he talked to the others, never quite looking at them, his gaze wandering around the arena and the stands, as though the environment around him was subject to his approval.

"I've seen that guy's picture," I said.

"That's Carl Hinkel. He's head of the militia movement here. They have a way of showing up in small towns that can't afford a police force," she said.

A rider climbed down on top of a bull in a bucking chute, working his gloved hand under the bull rope. The bull was rearing its head, blowing mucus, hooking its horns against wood, while the rider tied down his hand with what rodeo people call a suicide wrap. He straightened slightly, humped his shoulders, and clamped his legs tightly into the bull's ribs.

"Outside!" he hollered, his right hand in the air.

The gate to the chute flew open, and the bull exploded into the arena, a cowbell clanging on its neck, its body twisting, hooves slashing at the air, barely missing the two rodeo clowns who stood by the chute behind a rubber barrel.

The bull came down hard on its forequarters, jarring the rider's tailbone, then twisted in mid-stride and reared its head into the rider's face. The rider bounced once on the bull's back, one leg stabbing at the air for balance. Then he was over the side.

Except his gloved hand was caught under the bull rope, the arm bent backward, the rider's body flopping against the bull like a cloth doll's.

A brown balloon of dust rose from the arena as the bull spun in a circle, whipping the rider into the dirt, stomping him under its hooves, trying to hook the rider with one horn.

One of the clowns, a man wearing polka-dot pants, a striped cowboy shirt, firehouse suspenders, football cleats, and an orange fright wig and bowler hat, got in the bull's face, hitting its nose with his hat, actually stiff-arming it up the snout, directing its rage at himself while the other clown jerked loose the flank strap and dragged the rider free of the bull's hooves.

The crowd had risen to their feet, first in horror, then in relief and admiration as they witnessed the bravery of the clowns and the rescue of the rider.

For some reason the scene in the arena seemed to freeze, as in a photograph, but with a wrong detail, one that was out of sync, a flaw in what should have been a tribute to what is best in us. The bull was gone now, through a gate at the far end of the arena. The paramedics were working the rider onto a stretcher. He lifted his hand to the crowd and grinned weakly, his face streaked with dust and blood. The clown who had freed the rider's trapped hand from under the bull rope picked up the rider's hat and carried it over to his stretcher.

But the man who had behaved most bravely,

the clown in the orange wig, never looked at
the downed rider. Instead, he fitted the stub of
a narrow cigar between his teeth and lighted it
and looked up at the stands, smoking, his
greasepaint grin like a fool's at a funeral.

He climbed over the slat fence by the bucking chutes, dropped to the ground, and accepted a can of soda from the militia leader,
the white-bearded man named Carl Hinkel.
He drank until the can was empty, his
Adam's apple working steadily, and crunched
the can in his palm and tossed it into a trash
barrel. Then he studied the crowd again, and
I would have sworn his eyes settled on me.

He walked to the bottom of the stairs that
led to our seats, his cleats clicking on the
concrete, and pointed into the stands, as
though recognizing an old friend.

"Billy Bob?" Cleo said.

"Yes?"

"I think that man's trying to get our attention."

"I don't know any rodeo clowns."

She looked down at the program in her
hand. When she glanced up again, her hand
touched the top of my wrist.

"He's coming up here. Billy Bob, look at his
eyes," she said, staring straight ahead.

They were recessed and wide-set, filled with
an irreverent, invasive light.

He walked up the stairs two steps at a time,

his legs lifting him effortlessly. He stopped at our row and pulled off his fright wig and held it on his heart.

"Why, howdy do, Mr. Holland. Bet you don't know who I am," he said.

"No, I don't," I said.

"Wyatt Dixon. Lately of Fort Davis, Texas. Before that, of Huntsville, Texas," he said, and extended his hand. The wind blew against his back, and I could smell a hot, dry odor like male sweat that has been ironed into a shirt.

I took his hand. It was as rough as a rooster's leg, scaled along the edges, the lines in his palms seamed with dirt.

"You know me from somewhere, Mr. Dixon?" I asked.

"Not me. My sister did, though. Katie Jo Winset was her married name. You call her to mind?"

"I sure do."

"She'd be flattered. Except she's in the graveyard."

"Same one her child's buried in? The one she smothered?" I asked.

He set one cleated foot on the concrete step above him and leaned one arm down on his knee, so that his face was next to Cleo's, his breath touching her skin.

"God bless this country. God bless this fine-looking woman here. Womanhood is the

Lord's most special creation. It's an honor to be here to entertain y'all," he said.

"Thanks for dropping by, Mr. Dixon. Stay in touch," I said.

"Oh, I will. Yes-sirree-bobtail. You'll know when it's my ring, too."

"I'm looking forward to it," I said, and winked at him.

But he didn't ruffle. His lantern jaw seemed to be hooked forward, his eyes holding on mine. Then he jogged down the stairs, his arms cocked at his sides, his football cleats clattering on the concrete, his whipcord body jiggling.

He stopped at the bottom of the stands and counted out several dollar bills to an Indian hot-dog vendor and pointed up at us. The vendor, who was overweight and wore a large white box on a strap around his neck, began laboring up the stairs toward us.

"I can't believe I just listened to that conversation," Cleo said.

The vendor stopped at the end of the row and handed us two fat hog dogs wrapped in napkins, dripping with chili and melted cheese. Wyatt Dixon was watching us from the top of a bucking chute. I stood up so he could see me clearly and pointed to the hot dog in my left hand and made an "A-okay" sign of approval with my thumb and fore-finger.

"I can't believe you just did that," Cleo said.

"Grin at the bad guys and never let them know what you're thinking. It drives them crazy," I said.

"What if they're already crazy?" she said.

# Chapter

## 5

I CALLED the sheriff in Missoula early next morning, then drove in to meet him at his office. When I entered the office, he was standing at his window looking out at the street, dressed in a blue long-sleeve shirt, charcoal-black striped trousers, and a wide leather belt. I realized he was even a bigger man than I'd thought. His arms were propped against the sides of the window, and his back and head blocked out the view of the street entirely.

"I checked on that gal, Dixon's sister, what's-her-name, Katie Jo Winset. Evidently she was a professional snitch. She died of a heart attack while being taken from the woman's prison to a trial in Houston," he said. "Why would her brother want to put it on you?"

"She killed her own child. I got her to plead out. Part of the deal was she had to snitch off some bikers who were muleing dope up from Piedras Negras. If I remember right, one of the mules took Wyatt Dixon down with him. I just didn't remember Dixon's name."

"If Dixon cared about his sister, he should be grateful to you. In Texas she could have gotten the needle," the sheriff said.

When I didn't reply, he said, "She might have skated if she hadn't pled out?"

"I wanted her to fire me and go to trial. She killed two of her other children and buried them in Mexico. Truth be known, I wanted her to hang herself," I said.

The sheriff sat down behind his desk. He wore a black string necktie and there were scars on the backs of his hands. He saw me looking at them.

"I used to drive a log truck. I had a boomer chain snap down on me once," he said. "Mr. Holland, I can't say I'm glad to see you here. I've got enough problems without you people bringing your own up from Texas. This biker, Lamar Ellison, the one your friend Dr. Voss remodeled up at Lincoln? He's been in Deer Lodge and Quentin, both. Your friend's mistake is he didn't kill Lamar when he had the chance."

"Lamar's going to be back around?"

"Don't expect to see him soon at First Assembly."

"Do y'all have a narcotics officer working inside his gang? An Indian girl with blond streaks in her hair?" I said.

"You got some nerve, don't you?"

"I thought I'd ask. Thanks for your time," I said.

"Don't thank me. I wish you'd go home."

I left his office and walked out of the courthouse toward my truck. It was windy, and the sky was blue, and above the university I could see an enormous smooth-sided mountain, with a white "M" on it and pine trees in the saddles and lupine growing in grass that was just turning green.

I heard heavy steps behind me, then a big hand reached out and encircled my upper arm.

"I get short with people. It's just my nature," the sheriff said. "This is a good town, by God. But there's people here with fingers in lots of pies. Dr. Voss hangs with some of those Earth First fanatics and he's gonna get hisself hurt. The same can happen to you, son."

"I appreciate it, Sheriff."

"No, you're a hardhead. Talk with a man name of Xavier Girard. At least if you get broadsided by a train, you can't say I didn't warn you."

"The novelist? His wife's an actress?"

"Maybe it's different where you come from, but most people's public roles hereabouts are pure bullshit. That don't exclude me," he replied.

THE SHERIFF told me that by noon I could probably find Xavier Girard, unless the Apocalypse was in progress, at a low-rent bar down by the old train depot. The last I had read of his escapades was about two years ago in *People* magazine. A photo showed him being escorted out of a Santa Barbara nightclub by two uniformed policemen, the tangled pieces of a broken chair draped over his head and shoulders, a maniacal grin on his bloodied face.

The cutline, as I recall it, had stated something like: "Famed Crime Novelist Takes on Crowd That Boos His Poetry Reading."

I walked into the bar, a long, high-ceilinged place with brick walls, and saw him eating at a table by himself in back. His girth and beard and thick, unbrushed hair and big head made me think of a cinnamon bear. His hands even looked like paws. The bar was full of derelicts, Indians, a few college kids, and a group who looked like they had just bought their Western fashions in the shopping malls of Santa Fe. Xavier Girard watched me approach him as he upended a mug of beer.

"Mr. Girard, my name's Billy Bob Holland. I'm an attorney from Deaf Smith, Texas. The sheriff said I should talk to you," I said.

"Oh yeah? About what?" he said.

"About Tobin Voss." I pulled out a chair from the table and sat down.

He picked up his paper napkin and looked at it and dropped it. "Why don't you just plunk yourself down without being invited?" he said.

"I need some help, sir. If I've intruded, I'll leave."

"You that private detective my film agent hired?"

"Pardon?"

"Got some ID?"

"Are you serious?" I asked.

He thought about it and let his eyes rove over my face.

"I guess that Southern-fried accent didn't come out of Laurel Canyon," he said. "Tobin Voss is on the right side, but he's busting up the wrong people. Over-the-hill meth heads aren't the problem in Montana." Then he raised his voice and looked in the direction of the group dressed in stylized western clothes. "California douche bags buying up the state with their credit cards are a different matter."

"You know a guy named Wyatt Dixon?" I asked.

"No. Who is he?"

"An ex-con from Texas. He seems to be buds with this militia leader, Carl Hinkel."

"If Hinkel had his way, the rest of us would be bars of soap."

"You know this Earth First group?" I said.

"The first line of defense against the dickheads—those are *Los Angeles* dickheads I'm talking about," he said, his voice rising again, his eyes resting on the tourists, "who want to drill for oil in wilderness areas and denude the national forest."

"I see."

"You're not convinced?" he said.

"It's been good meeting you, Mr. Girard. I read a couple of your books. I admire your talent."

He seemed to look at me with a different light in his eyes.

He said, "Holly and I are having some people over tonight. It's a publication party. A collection of essays done by local writers on the Blackfoot. Bring Tobin Voss or whoever you like."

"That's kind of you. Tell me, Mr. Girard, why would a fellow's film agent want to send a private detective after him?"

"Man claims I set fire to his convertible outside the Polo Lounge. But don't put any credence in that. The poor guy's unbalanced. He's trying to set up 900 toll numbers for Charlie Manson and the Menendez brothers."

"This is your agent?"

"Not anymore," he said, his eyes smiling.

"COME WITH US," Doc said to his daughter Maisey that evening.

"Holly Girard looks like melted wax somebody put in the refrigerator," Maisey said.

"I don't want you here alone," he said.

"Steve is picking me up. We're going to the movies. If you don't trust me, then stay home."

"What time are you coming back from the show?" Doc said.

"Maybe you could put an electric monitor on me. The kind that criminals wear when they're sentenced to home arrest."

"How about it with the histrionics?" Doc said.

"How about it yourself, Dad? You're the selfish one. You give up nothing and want me to give up everything."

Maisey's face had the bright shininess of a candied apple. The skin above her upper lip was moist with perspiration, like a little girl's.

Ease up, Doc, I thought.

He looked out the front window at the twilight in the hills and the black swirl of the river as it made a bend and flowed deeper into woods that had already gone dark with shadow.

"We'll be back by eleven. Can you do the same?" he said.

"I don't know. Kids in Missoula fill condoms with water and throw them at each other's cars. Can I give that up for my father's peace of mind? Gee, I'm not sure," she said. She fixed her hair in front of the mirror and looked at her father's reflection and raised her eyebrows innocuously.

I went outside and waited for Doc by my truck. Through the front window I could see him and Maisey arguing bitterly. When he came outside he tried to be good-natured but he couldn't hide the strain in his face.

"They say a father has a few rough moments when his daughter is between thirteen and seventeen. I think it's more like being rope-drug up and down a staircase on a daily basis," he said.

"Who's the kid she's going out with?" I asked.

"He lives up the road. He's a good boy. There's his car now," Doc said.

"Then quit worrying," I said.

WE DROVE into Missoula through Hellgate Canyon and met Cleo Lonnigan at an ice cream parlor on the Clark Fork of the Columbia River. She was outside, at a table by the water, the cottonwoods blowing in the wind behind her. She wore a black dress and pearls and looked absolutely beautiful.

"I called your house. I thought maybe I was late. Maisey said you'd already left," she said.

A network of lines crisscrossed Doc's forehead.

"How long ago did you call?" he asked.

"Just a minute ago," Cleo answered.

"Why is she still at home?" Doc said, then went to the pay phone inside the ice cream parlor before either Cleo or I could speak.

"He's a little wired," I said.

"I think Doc and his daughter should get a divorce," she said.

I saw him replace the receiver on the hook, then walk down the steps toward us.

"Nobody home. They probably took off," he said.

"Sure," I said, glad the conversation was about to change.

He glanced at his wristwatch, his eyes busy with thought. "I'll call from Girard's place," he said.

XAVIER GIRARD and his wife Holly lived in a big log house on a bluff above the Clark Fork. The sun was only a spark between two ridges in the western part of the valley now, but the afterglow rose high into the vault of blue sky overhead, and looking to the north you could see snow-capped mountains in the Rattlesnake Wilderness and, toward Missoula, the maple trees in residential neighborhoods riffling in the breeze and the lights of downtown reflecting on the river's surface.

"Whose money bought this place?" I said as we walked up the drive toward the sundeck of the Girards' house.

"Not Xavier's. He has the reverse King Midas touch. Everything he touches turns to garbage. He went back to Louisiana and built a million-dollar home on the bayou, you know, boy from Shitsville makes good, except he built it in a sinkhole and the foundation caved in and the whole thing slid into the bayou," Doc said.

The guests on the deck and in the living room were writers and university people, artists, biologists and conservationists, photographers, liberal arts students from the East, an editor from Doubleday, a journalist from *Time,* a movie producer from A&E, smoke jumpers, and Xavier Girard's entourage of barroom fans.

An actor from north-central Texas, who wore a suit with no tie, his dress shirt open at the collar, was holding forth at a glass-topped table, his mouth downturned at the corners like a drill instructor's.

He was talking about a casting lunch of years ago.

"See, Dennis is a right good boy and all, but he don't have no understanding of Southerners whatsoever. We was waiting on the food to come out and he started lecturing at me and using profane language and carrying on and getting in my face like he growed up in a vacant lot. So I reached across the table and grabbed him by the necktie and dragged him through the Caesar salad and cut off his tie with a steak knife and slammed him back down in the chair and told him to start acting like a white person for a change. I didn't have no trouble with him after that, but damned if the part didn't go to . . ."

Down below the deck we could hear Xavier Girard, stripped to the waist, pounding a speed bag with his bare fists while his barroom pals looked on admiringly.

It was Girard's wife who was the surprise. I expected her to possess at least some of her husband's eccentricities. Instead, she was either an extraordinary actress or she must have been blind-drunk the night she married him. She seemed to gaze into your eyes with total interest, regardless of the subject of conversation. Her skin was pale, her mouth irregularly shaped, as though her expression and smile were unpracticed, perhaps a bit vulnerable. She wore her dark blond hair in tresses and stood close to the person she was talking to, either man or woman, in a way that seemed sexually intimate yet defenseless.

"You were an Assistant United States Attorney?" she said.

"For a while. In Phoenix," I replied.

"Why'd you quit?" she said.

"I probably wasn't that good at it."

Her eyes probed mine, as though my sentence contained meaning that the two of us should examine together. Then she fitted her thumb and forefinger around my wrist and said, "Will you let me share something with you?"

We walked to the edge of the deck, into the shadows and a layer of cold air that rose from the river. The pines farther up the hill were black against the stars. She wore a purple evening dress and there was a shine on the tops of her breasts. Through the sliding glass doors I could see Doc punching in numbers repeatedly on a telephone while Cleo stood behind him, an exasperated expression on her face.

"I'm concerned for Doc. He's obsessed about this gold mine up the Blackfoot," Holly Girard said.

"Seems like he has a lot of company," I said.

"But people listen to him. He was a war hero. He's got this Byzantine aura of spirituality about him. He could read the phone book and sound like John Donne."

"You think somebody's going to hurt him?"

"How would you feel toward Doc if you had no work and no food in the house and a poet was telling you a trout stream was more important than feeding your family?" she said.

Through the glass door I saw Doc bang the phone receiver down in the cradle.

"Excuse me," I said, and went inside.

Doc widened his eyes at me, his hand still on the phone receiver, feigning a smile.

"I called the theater they were going to. I know the manager. He didn't see her," Doc said.

"Like the theater manager doesn't have anything else on his mind," Cleo said.

"Y'all want to go?" I asked.

"I should have brought my car," Doc said.

"It's all right," I said.

"It's been quite an evening. I just don't know if I can stand any more like it," Cleo said.

I told them I'd see them outside and I went down a hallway to the bathroom. Three women and two men were standing by an abstract oil painting, not far from the bathroom door. Their eyes were bright, their conversation gilded with laughter.

"Is this the line for the bathroom?" I asked.

They stopped talking and looked at me peculiarly, as though I had spoken in another language. Then a woman said, "Holly's inside."

The door was ajar, and I saw Holly Girard bend over a framed mirror that lay horizontally on a marble-topped counter. Her evening dress was backless, and I could see the delicate bones under her skin as she inhaled a chopped white line deeply into her lungs through a rolled dollar bill. She wiped the mirror's surface with her index finger and rubbed her finger inside her gums.

She straightened her shoulders, turned and opened the door, and looked blankly into my face.

"Oh hello, again," she said. "The maid must have misplaced my toothbrush. I had to brush my teeth with my finger. Can you imagine?"

"Right. Can I get out through that far door?" I said, pointing toward the end of the hallway.

"Are you offended in some way?" she asked.

"No, I'm not."

"Then stay," she said, and reached out and encircled my wrist as she had earlier.

"You asked me why I quit the Justice Department," I said. "It's because a Texas Ranger named L.Q. Navarro and I killed a bunch of cocaine and tar mules down in Old

Mexico. I hate the sonsofbitches who sell that stuff, and if I had it to do all over, I'd kill those men again. So I guess it'd be a little hypocritical of me if I prosecuted homicide cases."

The group by the oil painting stared at me with the opaqueness of people caught in a strobe light.

"Don't be that way," Holly said to me, her expression suddenly tender.

I walked down the hall and out the door into the night, the back of my neck flaming with embarrassment.

DOC AND I dropped Cleo at her car by the ice cream parlor, then drove up the Blackfoot River toward his house. We turned off the highway north of Potomac, rumbled across the log-and-cable bridge onto the dirt road, and drove along the edge of a dry creek bed that was white and dusty and webbed with algae under the moon.

Doc kept squinting his eyes through the front window.

"That looks like a fire," he said.

"Where?"

"Through the trees. You see it?" he said.

"No," I said, irritably, and used the electric buttons on the door to roll down all the windows in the truck. "You smell any smoke?"

"None," he said.

"Then for God's sakes, shut up. I don't want to hear any more doom and gloom. If just for five minutes. Okay, Doc?"

We went across a cattle guard and drove down the two-track lane through the meadow behind his house. I had been right. There was no fire in the vicinity. Instead, Doc's yard was filled with emergency vehicles whose flashers lit the front porch of the house and the trees and the pebbled bank of the river and the current that flowed through the boulders with the dull red glow of a smithy's forge.

# Chapter

# 6

A FEW MINUTES LATER I watched the paramedics carry Maisey on a gurney to the back of an ambulance and place her inside. The night air was cold and a paramedic had pulled a blanket to her chin. Her face was turned from me, but I could see a marbled discoloration on her neck, like the shape of a hand. A sheriff's deputy wearing latex gloves came out of the house carrying a vinyl garbage bag that contained Maisey's jeans and torn blouse and undergarments.

Doc climbed into the back of the ambulance with her and looked back at me, his face like I'd never seen it before.

"I'll follow y'all to the hospital," I said.

He didn't answer. A paramedic closed the door and the ambulance turned around in the yard and drove back through the meadow toward the gate and the dirt road. The engine made no sound, and I could hear the grass that grew along the two-track lane brushing against the ambulance's undercarriage.

"Your friend is having a bad night, so I don't hold his rudeness against him," the sheriff said. "But I'm gonna tell you what I told him, and you can repeat it to him in the morning. There were three bikers."

He held up three fingers in front of me.

"One way or another we'll nail them. That means your friend takes care of his daughter and I take care of the law. You hearing me on this?" the sheriff said.

"Yeah, I am, Sheriff. What bothers me is it's the same bullshit I ran on crime victims when I knew the perps would probably skate," I said.

"I don't care for your manner, Mr. Holland, but I'm gonna let that go . . . We talked to the boy she was with earlier. The kids told Dr. Voss they were going to a movie. But that wasn't the real plan. After you and the doctor left, they thought they'd have a little private time together. Except they had a fight at some point and the boy went home. I say 'at some point,' do you follow me?"

"They were in the sack?" I asked.

"Neither one is willing to say that, but that'd be my guess."

"So even if you nail the bikers, their attorney will put it on Maisey's friend?"

"You're a defense lawyer. Do you know an easier client to get off than a sex predator?"

"I couldn't tell you. I don't take them."

"You damn shysters take anybody with a checkbook," he said.

Then he shook his head as though taking himself to task. "Look, back in the 1860s the Montana Vigilance Committee lynched twenty-two murderers and highwaymen," he said. "They bounced them off cottonwood trees and barn rafters all over the state. I guess it could make a man yearn for the good old days. But this ain't them. You tell that to Dr. Voss for me."

Try telling him yourself, bud, I thought as he walked away from me, the thickness of his sidearm showing against the flap of his coat.

I STAYED with Doc in the waiting room at St. Patrick's in Missoula while he paced and hammered one fist on top of the other.

"Slow it down, Tobin," I said.

He stopped pacing, but not because of me. He was listening to a conversation outside the door. Two uniformed deputies were enjoying a joke of some kind, one with coarse edges, a reference to sodomy, a laugh at the expense of a woman.

Doc stepped out into the hall.

"You guys have something else to do?" he said.

"*What?*" one of them said.

"We're all right here," I said, stepping into the deputy's line of vision.

One deputy touched the other on the arm, and the two of them walked back toward the hospital entrance.

"I'll buy you a cup of coffee across the street," I said to Doc.

"I'm going back to the emergency room," he said.

"They told you to stay out. Why don't you let them do their job?"

"You lecture me one more time, Billy Bob, and I'm going to knock you down," he replied.

I couldn't blame him for his anger. He was a good man who loved his daughter, and the two of them had just stepped into the middle of an unending, degrading, and callous process that treats victims and family members as ciphers in an investigative file, rips away all vestiges of their privacy, and often inculcates in them the conclusion that somehow they are deserving of their fate.

I left Doc alone and went outside into the darkness. The maple trees were in full leaf, the night air crisp and tinged with smoke from a grass fire on a hill. Children were rid-

ing bikes on a sidewalk and the sounds of a
baseball game broadcast from the West Coast
came through the open window of an old
brick rooming house. It was a scene from the
brush of Norman Rockwell. But inside the
hospital Maisey Voss was plugged into a
morphine-laced IV, her body strung with purple and yellow bruises that went into the
bone, the fetid breath of her attackers still
wrapped around her face like cobweb.

A few feet away I saw L.Q. Navarro leaning with his back against the trunk of a
maple tree, rolling a cigarette, his down-tilted
Stetson and black suit silhouetted against the
lighted entrance of the emergency room.

*"You don't have anything to say?"* I asked.

*"I'd head for the barn on this one,"* he said.

*"That wasn't ever your style, L.Q.,"* I
replied.

*"Doc fired them bikers up because he cain't
let go of his wife's death."*

*"You don't walk out on your buds,"* I said.

*"He says he didn't like Vietnam? Maybe
dying has messed up my ability to remember
things. I thought SEALs was volunteers."*

I never could win an argument with L.Q.
He twisted the ends of his cigarette and put it
in his mouth and struck a kitchen match on
the butt of his holstered revolver. His skin
and mustache flared in the cupped flame of
the match.

*"This one ain't just about bikers. Why do you think the sheriff pointed you at that alcoholic crime writer and his wife, the actress, what's that gal's name, the one who snorts up coke like an anteater?"* L.Q. said.

*"I stubbed my toe on that one, too."*

*"You gonna keep us here?"*

*"I'll let you know,"* I said.

He drew in on his cigarette and breathed the smoke across the tops of his fingers. His eyes were filled with a black luminescence, the ascetic, lean features of his face even more handsome in death. I thought I saw him grin at the corner of his mouth.

A HALF HOUR LATER Doc Voss joined me outside.

"They moved her upstairs. You want to hear what those bastards did to her?" he said.

"I was a cop, Doc. I've been there," I said.

But he told me anyway. In physiological detail, his voice cracking in his throat, his palms opening and closing at his sides.

"She's alive, partner. A lot of predators don't leave witnesses," I said.

"You're pretty glib for a guy on the sidelines," he said.

I let it pass and looked down the street, away from his angry stare.

He pressed the ball of his thumb into my arm.

"What would you do if she were your daughter? Don't you lie, either," he said.

"Try to get the wrong thoughts out of my head," I replied.

"You and L.Q. Navarro stuck playing cards in the mouths of dead people," he said.

"They tortured a DEA agent to death. They threw down on us first."

"My daughter doesn't count as much as a federal agent?" he said.

"I think you're working on a nervous breakdown, Tobin."

I walked away from him. Down the street a sheriff's department cruiser pulled around the corner and approached us. Inside were the two deputies whom Doc had insulted earlier. One of them sat in back with a handcuffed man whose jaws were bright with gold stubble, his long, tangled hair tied up on his head with a bandanna that leaked blood above one eye. The deputy in back lifted the handcuffed man's chin with a baton, as though displaying a severed head on a plate.

"This is one of the guys who raped and sodomized your daughter. He fell down a fire escape while resisting arrest," the deputy said. "Lamar, you got something you want to say to Dr. Voss?"

"Yeah. My dick in your ear," the biker named Lamar Ellison said out the window.

"The standards in street mutts gets lower every day," the same deputy said, shaking his head. He tapped on the seat for his partner to drive on.

Doc stared at the rear window, his jawbone flexing.

"They got one. They'll get the others," I said.

"It's not enough," he replied.

# Chapter

## 7

MAISEY CAME HOME from the hospital three days later. Doc tied balloons on the furniture in her bedroom and bought teddy bears and stuffed frogs and giraffes and a pink rabbit that was four feet tall and propped them up on her pillows, but his attempt at good cheer and optimism was like wind blowing through an empty building.

Maisey's eyes seemed possessed, haunted by thoughts she didn't share. Her face jumped at sudden noises. Her breath was sour and funk rose out of her clothes. When her father tried to comfort her, she curled into a ball and pulled the bedcovers over her head, spilling the stuffed animals he had bought her on the floor.

Through the doorway I saw Doc sitting on

the side of the bed, his hand on his daughter's back, staring into space. "What are we going to do, kiddo?" he said, more to himself than to her.

The sun was above the mountain now, but the inside of the room was filled with a brittle yellow light that gave no warmth.

At noon Cleo Lonnigan arrived in her truck and fixed lunch and drove into Bonner and bought a cake and a gallon of ice cream. Later she convinced Maisey to put on her quilted robe and fluffy slippers and to sit on the porch with her father while Cleo showed us what she could do with firearms.

She took a holstered .22 revolver off the gun rack in her truck, buckled it on, and set three tin cans in a row against a dirt bluff, then walked back fifty feet and blew each can into the air, then nailed it again as it rolled down the embankment.

"You want to give it a try?" she asked Maisey.

"No. I don't like guns," Maisey said.

"Sure?" Cleo said.

"Yes. Thanks anyway. I just don't like guns. I never did," Maisey said, her eyes slightly out of focus, as though she were thinking of who or what she had once been. The wind blew her hair and made gray lines in her scalp. She stuck her hands inside the sleeves of her robe.

I walked down to the dirt bluff and helped Cleo pick up the cans and place them in a paper sack.

"Good try," I said.

"She's going to need some heavy counseling. I don't think Doc has any idea what they're in for," she said.

"Don't underestimate him."

"You know what victim rape is?"

"The system does it to her a second time?"

She glanced toward the porch, where Doc and Maisey were sitting in the shade. She turned toward the river, so her voice would carry away from the house.

"I talked with the sheriff this morning. Maisey couldn't pick Lamar Ellison out of a photographic lineup," she said.

"What about fingerprints? They lifted prints all over her room," I said.

"Not his. He was released from jail this morning. No charges are being filed."

I let out my breath and looked up at the porch. Doc was petting a calico cat. He scratched its head, then set it in Maisey's lap.

"I wish I had let Ellison strangle to death. I think about putting my hand in his mouth and I want to scrub my skin with disinfectant," Cleo said.

"The sheriff hasn't told Doc?"

"No."

"Why would he tell you first?"

Her throat was red, as though chafed by the wind. "Because I've known the sheriff since my son was murdered. Because Lamar Ellison is a member of the Berdoo Jesters. They were seen at the campground the night before my son died."

She went to the back of the house and dropped the paper sack with the cans in it into a trash barrel, then walked back to her truck. She unbuckled the holstered revolver, threw it on the seat, and slammed the door as though ending an argument in her own mind.

A FEW MINUTES LATER I saw a Jeep Cherokee turn off the dirt road and clatter across Doc's cattle guard and come through the grass behind the house. The Cherokee pulled around by the porch and Holly Girard got out from the driver's side. She picked up a covered dish from the seat and walked up to the steps. A man I didn't know sat in the passenger seat, a camera around his neck.

"I thought you could use some of Xavier's coonass gumbo," Holly said.

"That's thoughtful of you. Where's Xavier?" Doc said.

"Drinking ice water and eating aspirin in the sauna. Guess why?" she replied.

She wore crimson suede boots and tailored

khakis and a white blouse that puffed in the wind and exposed the tops of her breasts. She had on a safari hat, but she removed it and tossed her hair, then I saw the photographer get out of the Jeep and walk down toward the river, as though he did not want to intrude upon a private moment.

"We want Maisey to know she has lots of friends in Missoula," she said.

"Yes, I know she does," Doc said. "How'd you learn about our trouble?"

"Xavier is friends with the police reporter at the *Missoulian*," Holly said.

"Seems like Xavier's friend is more loquacious than he should be," Doc said.

There was silence, then Holly Girard said, "Well, should I put this inside?"

Behind me I heard Cleo Lonnigan open the door and step out on the porch. She looked down on the riverbank, then bit the corner of her lip.

"I just burned something on the stove. The odor's terrible. Here, I'll take that inside for you," she said. "Who's our friend with the camera?"

Holly smiled and stepped up on the porch and put the covered dish in Cleo's hands, her face turned at an angle so that it caught the light.

"He's doing a photo essay on the 'Take

Back the Night' march at the university. I hope you don't mind him tagging along with me," Holly said.

Doc got up from his chair and put a stick of gum into his mouth. He chewed it, his eyes crinkling at the corners, the way he often did when he chose to ignore what was worst in people.

"Come on in and have some cake," he said.

But Cleo remained in front of the door.

"That man's taking pictures, Doc," she said.

Doc turned and looked down the embankment at the photographer, who had now lowered his camera.

"Is that true, Holly?" Doc asked.

"I didn't know he was going to do that. I'm sorry. If you want the film, you can have it," Holly said.

"I think you should leave," Cleo said.

"Excuse me?" Holly said.

"Bad day for photo-ops. That shouldn't be difficult to understand," Cleo said.

"Does this person speak for you, Tobin?" Holly said.

"Why don't all of you stop talking like I'm not here?" Maisey said.

We all turned and stared at her. She wore no makeup, and her face had the bloodless quality of people who have experienced long illness.

"They did it to me, not you. What right have you all to make decisions about what happens around me? You're treating me like a dumb animal," she said.

In the silence we could hear the wind blowing in the cottonwoods and the water coursing around the exposed boulders in the middle of the river. The photographer rubbed the back of his neck, as though he were massaging an insect bite or waiting for a momentary external problem to pass out of his vision. Then he detached the telescopic lens from his camera, got back into the Jeep, and yawned sleepily, waiting for Holly Girard to join him.

AFTER HOLLY GIRARD was gone, I drove down to Bonner and called the sheriff's office.

"You kicked Lamar Ellison loose?" I said.

"At eight o'clock this morning. Right after he ate. He said he couldn't hardly let go of our sausages and hashbrowns," the sheriff replied.

"You think that's funny?"

"You give your damn guff to somebody else. If I had my way, I'd pinch his head off with a log chain."

"Then why don't you do it?"

"Because I don't have victim ID. They put a pillow down on her face. Besides, I don't have bean dip for physical evidence."

"There was DNA in her clothes and on the bedsheets. They took swabs at the hospital," I said.

The line was quiet.

"Hello?" I said.

"It got sent to the lab . . . We don't know what happened to it," the sheriff said.

"Say again?"

"You heard me. I'm coming out there to explain all this to Dr. Voss."

I could feel my hand opening and closing on the phone receiver, my chest rising and falling.

"These bikers, the Berdoo Jesters? Cleo Lonnigan says they may have been involved in her son's murder," I said.

"That's what she *believes*. I like Cleo, but the truth is her husband washed money for the Mob. Maybe she don't like to admit where her wealth comes from. There might even be a mean side to Cleo you don't know about," the sheriff said, and hung up.

I called him back, my hand shaking when I punched in the numbers.

"Rapists who get away with it come back. They increase their power by tormenting the victim," I said.

"Take Dr. Voss and his daughter back to Texas. Let us handle it," he replied.

My ass, I thought.

THE FIRST CALL came the next day. I happened to answer it. In the background I could hear people laughing and a motorcycle engine revving.

"Is this the doctor?" the voice said.

"Who's calling?"

"Thought you might want to know she'd already lost her cherry. So don't make out it's a bigger deal than it was," the voice said.

"What's your name, partner?"

"I just wanted to tell the pill roller his daughter gives good head. I've had better, but she's got promise. If I get horny, I might give her another tumble. Have a nice day."

"You're not a smart man."

The line went dead.

I went into the living room. Doc was rubbing oil into a pair of lace-top boots by the fireplace.

"Who was that?" he asked.

"One of those motorcycle boys."

He rubbed another layer of oil on a boot and turned the boot over in his hands and looked at it.

"You reckon they'll be back around?" he said.

"If they think they can blindside you," I replied.

He wiped the excess oil off his boots with a rag and looked idly out the window, his thoughts masked.

I SPLIT WOOD on a chopping stump in back. The morning had grown warm and I was sweating inside my clothes. It had snowed up high during the night and the newly fallen snow was melting in the trees on the ridges, and there was a dark sheen on the pine and fir needles. I whipped the ax through the air and felt it rip cleanly through a chunk of dry larch. The ax handle was solid and hard inside my hands, and in minutes the ground around the stump was littered with white strips of kindling.

I held the ax blade flat against the stump with my knee and filed it sharp, then attacked another pile of wood.

My head was singing with blood, my palms tingling. I thought I saw L.Q. Navarro up on the edge of the tree line, his coat hitched back of his revolver, and I knew what was really on my mind.

The adrenaline rush that came with the smell of gunpowder and horse sweat during our raids down into Coahuila had the same residual claim on my soul that heroin has on an intravenous addict's. In my sleep I desired it in almost a sexual fashion. It drove me to the grace and loveliness of women's thighs. It made me yearn for absolution and kept me in the Catholic confessional. It made me sometimes sit in the darkness with L.Q.'s blue-black custom-made .45, its yellowed ivory grips like moonlight between my fingers.

I went into the house and showered inside the tin stall and kept my head under the hot water for a long time. There was an old bullet wound, like a putty-colored welted star, on top of my foot, and another on my arm and another on my chest, two inches above the lung. I never associated them with pain, because I had felt only numbness when I was hit.

In fact, the memories they caused in me had never given me trepidation about mortality. Instead, they reminded me of a potential in myself I did not wish to recognize.

I started to comb my hair, but Maisey's robe hung over the only mirror in the room. I removed it and put it on a clothes hanger and hooked the hanger on top of the closet door. The robe was pink and covered with depictions of kittens playing with balls of string. I tried to imagine what Doc was feeling, but I don't believe that anyone could, not unless he has looked into his daughter's eyes after she has been systematically degraded by sub-humans whose level of cruelty is in direct measure to their level of cowardice.

My hair was reddish-blond, like my father's, but there were strands of white in it now, and neither time nor experience had taught me how to deal with the violent legacy that my great-grandfather, Sam Morgan Holland, a besotted drover and gunfighter and Baptist preacher, had bequeathed his descendants.

I had admonished and cautioned Doc, but in truth I felt Maisey's attackers were born for a cottonwood tree.

I DRESSED in fresh clothes and slipped on my boots and went back into the living room. Doc was scraping the ashes out of the fireplace with a small metal scoop and dropping them into a bucket that he covered with a lid each time the ashes puffed into the air.

"The older you get, the more you look like your dad. He was a good-looking fellow, wasn't he?" Doc said.

"Family trait," I said.

He wiped soot off his face with his sleeve and grinned. He waited for me to speak again, reading my expression with more perception than made me comfortable.

"I thought I might go into town," I said.

"What for?"

I cleared my throat slightly.

"If Cleo's not at the clinic, I thought I might invite her to lunch," I said.

"You took her to the rodeo, didn't you?"

"I guess I did."

"You want some advice? Most of us have

fond memories of first love because it was innocent and we didn't exploit it to solve our
problems. Later on we use romance like
dope. Headstones don't keep people in the
grave and neither does getting laid," he
replied. He turned his back on me and
scraped a load of black ash from the fire-
stones and dropped it into the bucket.

"That's a little bit strong, Doc."

I thought he would turn around and grin
again and perhaps indicate some form of
apology.

But he didn't.

WHEN I DROVE into the Jocko Valley the
meadows and hillsides were covered with
sunlight, but the sky in the north had turned
the color of scorched tin, and I could see
lightning pulsing in the clouds above the
ridgeline.

Just as I turned off the main road I glanced
in the rearview mirror and saw a low-slung
red car behind me, one that was coming too
fast, drifting across the center line, as though
the driver were bothered by the fact there
was an obstruction in his path. I remembered
having seen, or rather heard, the same car
earlier back in Missoula, when the driver had
roared onto the I-90 entrance ramp. The car
didn't turn with me and instead kept going

on the main road. A woman in the passenger's seat looked back at me blankly, her hair whipping across her mouth.

I drove through the gated entrance to Cleo's place and stopped by the barn. A bare-chested carpenter, who had the suntanned good looks of a Nordic sailor, was working on the roof. He told me Cleo was not home, that she was with some of her patients.

"At the clinic?" I said.

He slipped his hammer into a loop on his belt and spread his knees on the spine of the roof and pointed to a dirt road that disappeared into trees on an adjoining hill.

"She makes house calls. You'll know when you're there," he said.

"How's that?" I said.

"Some people take care of stray cats. Cleo's special, the best damn woman in these parts, buddy," he replied, almost like a challenge.

I drove back out the gate and up the dirt road into the shade of the trees. Halfway up the hill I saw an unpainted house back in a clearing and Cleo's skinned-up truck parked in the yard.

The yard was littered with flattened beer cans, chicken feathers that had blown from a butcher stump, washing machine and car parts, even a toilet bowl that lay incongruously on its side by an outdoor privy. A trash fire was burning in back of the house, and the wind blew the smoke through the back windows and out the open front door. I stepped up on the porch and saw Cleo in the kitchen, spooning oatmeal out of a pan to three small Indian children at the table.

"Hello?" I said, and tapped on the jamb.

She brushed a strand of hair out of her eyes with the back of her wrist and looked at me through the gloom.

"How'd you know where I was?" she asked.

"Your carpenter."

But she was preoccupied with her work and was not looking at me now.

"Okay, you guys wash your dishes when you're finished," she said to the children. "Can you do that? Your grandmother is going to be here soon. My friend and I are going to wait outside. What are we doing Saturday?"

"Going to the movies!" the children shouted together.

A moment later Cleo and I walked out into the yard. The sun was gone, and a heavy, gray mist was moving across the trees at the top of the mountain and raindrops were striking like wet stars on the dirt in the clearing.

"Their mother is nineteen. *Nineteen,* with three kids. She's in the Missoula jail right now. She gave up glue sniffing for the joys of crystal meth," Cleo said.

"How long has it been out here?" I asked.

"Three years, maybe. The California gangs brought it into Seattle and Spokane, then it was everywhere."

My eyes drifted to her mouth, the mole on her chin, the way the wind blew her hair on her cheek. A middle-aged Indian woman driving a rusted junker that had no glass in the front windows pulled into the yard and went into the house. She nodded at Cleo but ignored me.

"That's the grandmother?" I asked.

"There's a likelihood she'll be a great-grandmother at fifty," Cleo said.

"Take a ride with me," I said.

"Where to?"

"Anyplace you want to go."

She looked at me for a long moment.

"You a serious man, Billy Bob?" she asked.

"You can always run me off."

She looked at the torn shreds of cloud swirling just above the tops of the trees and said, "I'll leave my truck at the clinic. I have to be back there by three."

I opened her truck door for her. When I closed it, my fingers touched the top of her hand.

"Your carpenter says you're special," I said.

Her eyes seemed to reach inside mine, as

they had once before, probing for the secret thought, the personal agenda.

"Eric's gay. That's why he speaks so generously about women," she said.

"My grandpa used to say outcasts and people of color are always a white person's best measure," I replied.

"I think you and Doc really belong here," she said.


WE DROPPED her truck off at the clinic, then drove in the rain toward a café farther up the Jocko that sold buffalo burgers and huckleberry milkshakes. I pulled into a gas station and parked next to a row of sheltered pumps and stuck the gas hose into the tank. Then I saw a low-slung red car at the next gas island and an Indian girl with blond streaks in her hair standing by the back fender while the hose pumped gas into her tank.

She saw me watching her and turned her back and lit a cigarette.

"You got a suicide wish?" I said.

"No, you do, dickhead. Get out of here," she said.

"You're on the job?"

Her face grew heated, her lips crimped tightly together. She ripped the gas nozzle out of the tank and clanked it back on the pump.

Then a red-haired, lantern-jawed man in a yellow slicker and an Australian flop hat pushed open the glass door of the convenience store and walked toward us in the rain, an idiot's grin on his mouth.

"Bless your heart, I been thinking about you all day and you pull right in to the gas pump," Wyatt Dixon said.

"He was coming on to me, Wyatt," the girl said.

"Sue Lynn, Mr. Holland is a lawyer and a respecter of womanhood and a Texas gentleman. My sister, Katie Jo Winset, the one in the graveyard? She said he always removes his hat in the house and he don't never walk around with spit cups, either," Dixon said.

"Did you follow me up to Montana?" I said.

"I'm a rodeo man, sir. Calgary to Madison Square Garden to San Angelo. Can you step over here with me?"

I started back toward my truck. But he situated himself in my path, the taut, grained skin of his face beaded with raindrops. His shirt was unbuttoned to the navel under his slicker, and I could smell the dampness on his body, like the odor of drainwater welling out of an iron grate. Behind him a stump fire was smoking in the mist.

"At night, in a jailhouse, when you hear somebody scream? The kind of scream that's different from any other you ever heard? You know Lamar or one like him has just speared a new fish. Jailing ain't like it was in the old days, Mr. Holland. Folks ain't raising criminals like they used to," Dixon said.

"Step out of my way, please."

"Two thousand dollars and that boy will be in a wood chipper. There won't be no trace of him except a Polaroid picture for your doctor friend to burn in front of his daughter. Me and you has got regional commonalities, sir. For that reason I'm offering you a once-in-a-lifetime bargain." He snapped his fingers at the air, the vacuity of his eyes filling with energy, his lips parted with expectation.

I pinched the bridge of my nose and looked out into the grayness of the mountains and the fir and pine trees bending in the wind.

"Let me see if I can phrase myself adequately, Wyatt," I said. "Every so often a real piece of shit floats to the top of the bowl. I'm not talking about just ordinary white trash like your sister but somebody who should have been strapped down in Ole Sparky and had his grits scorched the first time he got a parking ticket. You following me?"

"I'm fascinated, sir. Your elocution is like none I have ever heard, and I have stood at tent revivals throughout this great nation and have listened to the very best."

"You stay away from me, partner," I said.

After I had pulled the gas nozzle out of my tank and gotten back into the truck, he tapped on my glass, leaning close in to it, his face distorting in the raindrops that slid down it as he stared at Cleo. I wanted to simply drive away, but now I was blocked in by a car both in front and behind me. I rolled down the window.

"What do you want?" I said.

"On Sugarland Farm I learned to read lips from a deaf man. You said 'On the job' to Sue Lynn. You was telling her she's a cop?"

"No."

"I hope you're not lying, sir. It would seriously subtract from my faith in human beings." Then he said to Cleo, lifting his hat, "Good afternoon to you, ma'am. One look at the sweetness of your form and I got to go lift a car bumper."

# Chapter

# 8

WHAT had I done?

I took Cleo back home and drove to the sheriff's office and caught him in the corridor of the courthouse annex.

"You did *what?*" he said, loud enough for passersby to stare.

"Can we go in your office?" I said.

"I'm not sure I want you around here that long."

I felt my face coloring and I looked away from the glare in his eyes and started over.

"I messed up. The question is, can we fix it?" I said.

"This ain't about *we*. You and trouble seem to go together like shit and stink."

"I'm having a hard time with your remarks, Sheriff."

He looked up and down the corridor.

"You blow the cover on an undercover cop, then you drag your sorry ass in here to piss on my rug? You're lucky I don't have you in jail," he said.

"Is she one of yours or not?"

"No. I never heard of her."

"Wyatt Dixon offered to snuff Lamar Ellison for two thousand dollars. That's solicitation of murder."

"Number one, that don't make any sense. Number two . . . There ain't no number two. Just get a lot of gone between you and here, okay?" the sheriff said.

I WENT BACK to Doc's log house on the Blackfoot. Doc and Maisey were out on the riverbank, collecting colored stones to make a rock garden. Maisey lifted up a boxful and smiled at me and carried the stones up the incline. Her jeans were damp on the knees, her skin bright with tan in the sunlight.

But toward evening, when the sun died below the ridgeline, I knew her attempts at cheer would go out of her face and she would sit in front of the television set, her expression disjointed with memories she refused to describe.

"We got another call while you were gone. No voice, just heavy-metal music playing into the receiver," Doc said.

"Maybe it was a crank," I said.

"Sure. Anyway, I had the number changed."

"Doc, I don't want to overstay my welcome. Maybe I'm not much help to you here."

He picked at a callus on his hand, then looked away at the river where it was in shadow between the trees. "Everything I do with Maisey is all thumbs. She sees pity in my face and hides her head under a pillow. How bad can one guy screw up?"

I helped him and Maisey gather rocks, and we laid them out on the sunny side of a spruce tree and spread bagged topsoil between them and planted moss roses and petunias and pansies in the soil.

That evening, at sunset, I walked deep into the woods and squatted by the river's edge and tossed pinecones into a long ribbon of green water flowing between two large round boulders. I glanced up at the ponderosa above me and saw L.Q. Navarro sitting on a thick limb, his face in shadow, a gold toothpick catching the sun's last light.

*"You wanted Doc to tell you to go home?"* he asked.

*"Maybe,"* I said.

"You scared you're falling for that Lonni-gan woman?"

"Did I say that? Did I even think that?" I said.

"She's an angry person."

"Her child was murdered."

"If you ask me, she's working on more than one thorn."

"I'd just like a little peace, L.Q."

"Interesting word choice. What do them big round boulders out there in the river re-mind you of?"

"I'm going into town. You're not coming, either."

"Tell her hello for me," he said.

EARLY THE NEXT MORNING Doc and Maisey drove into Bonner to get the mail, and I washed the breakfast dishes and wa-tered the rock garden with a sprinkler can. The phone rang inside.

When I answered it, a voice said, "Oh, it's the Lone Ranger again."

"Who gave you this number?" I said.

"What do you care? Put the pill roller on."

"He's not here."

He paused, then said, "I made her come."

"If this is Ellison . . ."

"That little twist is lying to you, bubba. She

knows it was consensual. That's why she didn't identify nobody from the mug shots. Ask her what she whispered in my ear when I . . ."

I hung up on him and punched in *69 on the phone, then I called the sheriff.

"Ellison or one of the other rapists is harassing the victim," I said.

"How do you know it's them?"

"I'm not even going to answer that question."

"You can ID the call by—"

"I already tried. The number's blocked."

"Tell Dr. Voss to change his number."

"He did that yesterday."

I heard him take a deep breath. "Tell Dr. Voss to come in and sign a complaint," he said.

"Where's this militia leader live? What's his name, Hinkel?" I said.

"You're jumping me over the hurdles, right?"

"I'm not sympathetic with the problems of your office. You're telling a raped girl and her father, 'Eat shit, you're on your own.'"

"You got a gift, son. Just talking to you gives me the red scours. You should contact the Pentagon, see about a career in biological warfare."

❦

CARL HINKEL'S ranch was outside Hamilton, down in the Bitterroot Valley. Beyond the stone house in which he lived were green pastures dotted with prize Angus, and beyond his pastures were mountains that rose up blue and as jagged as tin against the sky, their saddles and peaks blazing with new snow.

Carl Hinkel's drive was planted with poplar trees, his white gravel walks bordered with rosebeds. An American flag flew upside down in the front yard, the cloth popping in the wind, the chain tinkling against the silver pole.

There was no gate across the cattle guard, but I must have triggered an electronic signal when I entered Hinkel's property, because two men immediately came from behind the house and stood in the driveway, their feet slightly spread, their hands opening and closing at their sides, their bodies contoured with the anatomical distortions of steroid addicts. They wore military boots and undershirts and carried pistols in their belts, and in each of their unshaved faces was a pinched, dark light that seemed to have no relationship to anything in their environment. I nodded at them, but they continued to stare at me with the fixated intensity of people for whom daily life was part of a cosmic conspiracy.

Hinkel emerged from a small stone hut off to the side of the main house, wearing a navy blue shirt and white suspenders and corduroy trousers. He eyed me carefully, smoke leaking from around the stem of the corncob pipe clenched in his mouth. He waved the two men away.

"You were at the rodeo. You have a history with Wyatt," he said.

"I'd like to talk with you about him, Mr. Hinkel. Or, more specifically, about a man named Lamar Ellison," I said.

"Wyatt says you were a Texas Ranger."

"Among other things."

"A Ranger?" he said reflectively. "Well, we'll just have to ask you in, sir."

I followed him into the hut, stooping slightly under the doorway's wood casement. The desk and tables and shelves inside were stacked with clutter. The monitor on his computer bathed the stone walls with a green light. He clicked off the screen so I could not read what was on it.

On the wall were pictures of Douglas MacArthur, A. P. Hill, and the founder of the American Nazi Party, George Lincoln Rockwell. There was also a youthful photograph of Carl Hinkel in uniform.

"You were in the airborne, Mr. Hinkel?" I said.

His eyes had a peculiar cast in them. They

seemed to look at me in a mirthful way, and at the same time analyze each word I had just spoken.

"You asked about this man Ellison. He's been here. But not recently. He won't be back, either," he said, ignoring my question about his military background.

His accent was Tidewater, the *r*'s almost like *w*'s. He sat erectly in his chair at his desk, his entire posture one of ninety-degree angles.

"Ellison is no longer welcome?" I said, and tried to smile.

"I have nothing to say about him."

"Wyatt Dixon offered to kill him for two thousand dollars. That's bargain basement. I have the feeling Wyatt was trying to pick up two grand on a done deal."

"You're offensive, sir."

"Excuse me?"

"I don't share your frame of reference. You presume that I do."

I placed my elbow on his desk and leaned toward him and said, "Psychopaths like Lamar Ellison and Wyatt Dixon and the men who bombed the Federal Building in Oklahoma City? They all seek validation from male authority figures, fraudulent patriarchs who manipulate them for their own ends. They come to you like rats down a mooring rope, Mr. Hinkel."

He looked at me for a long time, his eyelids never blinking.

"You came here to sow discord and violence between two troubled young men," he said. "You use the methods of ZOG well. You may be a gentile but the yellow star is on your brow."

THE EVENING of the next day Doc took Maisey to a movie in Missoula. I called Cleo and asked her to supper, but she had to work late at the clinic and said she would meet me in town, maybe for dessert, at nine o'clock.

I parked my truck by the Clark Fork River and walked back across the bridge toward downtown. The western sky was pink, the mountains unbroken and dark across the horizon. Down below I could see trout feeding on the flies that were hatching in the shadows of the bridge. The air smelled cold and heavy, and the runoff from the melting snow in the mountains had flooded the willows along the banks so that their branches trailed like lace in the water.

I walked farther into town and went into a saloon and café called the Oxford, which claimed to have never closed its doors since 1891. I paid little attention to a waxed, black car across the street, and the three men in suits who sat inside it.

I ate a hamburger and drank a cup of coffee at the counter. Deeper inside the building was a darkened bar area where topless women were dancing on a runway. I finished eating and walked back outside and started to cross the street at the light. The black car pulled to the curb and a man in back opened a door for me. He was sandy-haired and pleasant-looking, and he held up a badge holder for me to see.

"Hop in, Mr. Holland. We'll give you a ride to your truck," he said.

"The Bureau of Alcohol, Tobacco, and Firearms is running a jitney service?" I said.

"We justify our jobs any way we can. Come on, be a sport," he said.

I got inside and closed the door behind me. The two men in front did not turn around. We drove up the street, past an old vaudeville and movie theater that had been turned into a multiplex, and crossed the long bridge over the river. The mountains in the west were rimmed with fire and the air full of birds that swept in and out of the willows on the riverbank.

The agent in back had a folder open on his lap.

"You used to be one of us," he said.

"Yeah, it was a great life," I replied.

"It says here you meddled in a federal investigation down in Texas. That's not true, is it?" He smiled when he spoke.

"No, I don't recall that."

"You always eat supper in T&A joints?" the agent in the passenger's seat asked, without turning around.

"Single man. You know how it is," I said.

"Lamar Ellison hangs out there. Just coincidence you wander in?" the agent in the passenger's seat said.

"Oh, you know Lamar? He raped my friend's daughter," I said.

"My name's Amos Rackley. You know why we're here?" the agent in back said.

"I think I do."

"Good. We'd hate for a well-intentioned person like yourself to hurt one of our people. You understand me, don't you?" the agent named Amos Rackley said.

"Yes, sir," I said.

"I think he's a hard guy," the agent in the passenger's seat said to the driver. The hair on the back of his neck was shaved neatly above his collar, his skin pink, his jawline well defined.

"You talking about me?" I said.

"Your jacket says you were investigated for capping some Mexicans across the border. The Mexican authorities claimed they were wets wandering around in the desert," he said, turning his head so I could hear his words.

I leaned forward in my seat. "I remember

some guys shooting at me down there. It's kind of fuzzy, though. I got hit twice. Maybe that's why my recall isn't as good as it should be," I said.

"He's a fast thinker, too," the agent in the passenger's seat said to the driver.

"That's enough, fellows. Pull in there," the agent named Amos Rackley said. He got out on his side of the car and waited for me to join him.

He put on his sunglasses and stared at the sunlight on the river's surface, then took them off again.

"You see the trout feeding in the shade? You can always see them better with dark glasses on. They cut the glare off the water," he said. He looked at me. "You're not interested in fish?"

"Yeah, I am."

"You got to forgive Jim. He lost some friends in the Oklahoma City bombing," Rackley said.

"A guy named Wyatt Dixon followed me up here. He's bad news," I said.

"You got that right. But that's our worry, not yours."

"Then get him out of my life—"

He raised the ball of his index finger at me before I could continue.

"Jim wasn't the only one who lost friends at Oklahoma City. You quit the Justice Department. You don't have a vote in what we do. If one of our people gets hurt because you've got your nose in the wrong place, I'm going to break it off," he said.

He got back into his car, and the three agents drove away. I stared after them, my face tight and insentient, as though a cold wind had just died and left my skin dead to the touch.

I went to the restaurant where I was supposed to meet Cleo but she wasn't there and she didn't answer her phone, either. I waited an hour, then drove back up the Blackfoot to Doc's house. I went to bed without seeing either Doc or Maisey and dreamed of Texas and a field of bluebonnets in which a white stallion splattered with blood tried to mount a mare that turned and bit him in the forequarters.

# Chapter

## 9

IN THE MORNING I discovered that Cleo had left three messages on Doc's answering machine. The messages said only that she had gotten to the restaurant late and did not explain why. I called her at home.

"It was Lamar Ellison. I'd gone up to the Indian family's house to check on the children. He followed me," she said.

"Ellison? Why's he coming around you?" I said.

"I don't know. I saw him on his motorcycle out on the road. The Indians don't have a phone. I couldn't get back to the house. It was awful," she said.

"Did he do anything?"

"No, he just sat out there in the twilight, looking up and down the road. Then he left."

"I'm coming out," I said.

"No, I have to go to work. I'll call you this afternoon."

"Cleo—"

"I'm sorry. I have to go. I didn't sleep much last night."

"Does this have anything to do with your son?"

"How would I know? I just hope this man Ellison dies a horrible death. I hate him," she said.


I WENT outside and lifted my fly vest and canvas creel off a wood peg on the front porch and put on my hip waders and drove my truck along the dirt road to a spot on the river that was seldom fished. I walked a quarter of a mile through woods and down a soft, green slope where huge gray boulders seemed to grow out of the soil like mushrooms without stems. I waded into the river, which was ice-cold from the melt and lack of sunlight, and fished a deep pool that was fed by a small waterfall.

The days were growing warmer now, and each morning the snow line in the mountain crests was receding and the rivers and creeks were rising and turning from green to copper-colored.

I tied on a royal coachman and coated it

with fly dressing and cast it out twenty-five feet into the riffle at the head of the pool. A rainbow rose from the gravel bed and hit the coachman as it floated toward me, high and stiff and flecked with red hackle on top of the riffle.

The rainbow must have been sixteen inches and should have been mine. But just as I saw the strike, like a flickering of quicksilver on top of the current, and jerked up my rod, I heard the loud roar of a motorcycle out on the dirt road. I cut my eyes in the direction of the road and the fly went whipping past my head into a tree limb and the rainbow's dorsal fin roiled the surface and disappeared.

I saw the rider of the motorcycle pull to the top of a knoll above me and look down at me through the trees. He gunned his engine, the straight exhaust pipe violating the green-gold, pine-scented stillness of the air, reverberating off the boulders on the hillsides and through the gullies that fed into the river.

Then he drove back toward my truck.

I pulled my royal coachman loose from the tree and walked back up the slope toward the road.

The motorcycle driver went past me, looking me full in the face, then turned around a hundred yards down the road. I removed my fly vest and laid it on the hood of my truck and took L.Q. Navarro's .45 revolver out of the cab and put it under the vest.

Lamar Ellison cut his gas feed and let his bike coast to a stop next to the truck. He slid his sunglasses up on top of his head, his eyes wandering over my person.

His body seemed larger in the shadows of the trees, his bronze skin darker. He swung one leg over the motorcycle seat, like a man getting down from a horse, and stood two feet from me. The wind puffed at his back and I could smell reefer in his clothes and hair and an odor like rotted teeth or decaying meat on his breath. I leaned my fly rod against the truck and rested my forearm on top of my fly vest.

"Say it quick," I said.

"I didn't know the guy was a SEAL. I was in the Corps. I'm sorry about his daughter," he said.

"You didn't sound that way over the phone."

He touched at his nose with his wrist and blew air out his nostrils. He glanced up and down the road, and put an unlit cigarette in his mouth, then pulled it back out and stared at it stupidly.

"Other people were listening. It was all flash, man. They got me made for a snitch," he said.

He was bare-chested except for his cracked black leather vest. He inserted his hands in his armpits as though he were cold.

"What were you doing up around Cleo Lonnigan's place?" I asked.

"Looking for you. I got Sue Lynn to call and ask where you was at. Sue Lynn's an Indian broad who digs bikers. I mean, she'll pull a train if she has to."

When I didn't reply he stuck his hands into his pockets, then refolded his arms across his chest and gripped the outside of his triceps.

"I can't go back inside, man. I got the Mexican Mafia and the Black Guerrilla Army down on me. When you're inside, they can reach out anywhere you're at. The Aryan Brotherhood ain't always there. The BGA is. Main pop anywhere is seventy percent boon."

"It's time for you to go," I said.

His lips were dry in the shade, the skin of his face grained with dirt. He shifted his weight and dust powdered around his boots. His eyes were like those of a man trying to figure out how to get inside a bus after the doors have been closed on him.

"Two other guys nailed her first. I'll give them up," he said.

"Are you that afraid of Doc?"

"I want Witness Protection. I talked to an ATF guy. He made fun of me. He said Voss was in the Phoenix Program. He said Voss would find me and cut off my ears and put out my eyes and paint my face."

His eyes were dark green, with cinders for pupils, and now they were wet along the rims.

I lifted up L.Q. Navarro's revolver from under my fly vest and cocked back the hammer.

"You either get out of here now or I'll shoot your sack off. My hope is that you don't believe me," I said.

THAT AFTERNOON I picked Cleo up at her house and we drove toward Flathead Lake to have supper, through ranchland and low hills, along an undulating, boulder-strewn river, into a golden sun. I told her about my encounter with Ellison and the fact that his interest had been in me, not her.

"Why do you believe anything a man like that says?" she asked.

"Because the ATF has obviously jammed him up. Because he's a coward and could hardly hide his fear. I don't think he was lying."

"Why does the ATF care about him?"

"He's mixed up with this militia bunch. Maybe he's dealing guns for them."

We drove through a long, green valley, past the Mission Mountains, whose timbered slopes rose into the clouds. Then I saw Flathead Lake for the first time, so vast it looked like an ocean, its blue water ringed by hills, its eastern shore terraced with cherry orchards. The sun had dropped below the mountains and the air was suddenly cool and touched with rain and the smell of wood smoke, and I looked at the shadow that never seemed to leave Cleo's eyes and squeezed her hand.

"Why'd you do that?" she said.

"You ever read Ernest Hemingway?" I asked.

"A little."

"In *For Whom the Bell Tolls* a Republican guerrilla is about to die on a hilltop in Spain and he tells himself, 'The world is a fine place and well worth the fighting for.' I always try to remember that line when I get down with the nature of things," I said.

We stopped at a restaurant on the eastern shore. It was too cool to eat by the water, but we took a table near the back window where we could see the afterglow of the sun on the hills on the far side of the lake and a steep-sided wooded island where there was a lighted log mansion set inside the trees and a white seaplane was taxiing in a rocky cove at the base of a cliff.

"I might have a chance to buy one of those islands out there," she said.

"You have that kind of money?" I said.

"Not really. But you only live once, right?"

It started to rain out on the lake, and the string of electric lights over the marina came on and Cleo gazed at the boats rocking in their slips, her thoughts known only to herself.

"This is one of the prettiest places I've ever been," I said.

But she didn't seem to hear me.

"I talked with an FBI agent about my son once," she said. "I told him my son was killed on National Forest lands. I thought I could get federal help solving his murder. He called back and said he checked, the body was actually on a state road when it was discovered. I hung up. I couldn't find words to speak. I've always regretted that."

The waitress brought the wine and poured it into both our glasses. Cleo took a sip, ate a piece of bread, then drank deeply from the glass. When she set it down, her mouth was red, her face striped with shadows from the raindrops that ran down the window. Beyond the marina was a motel built on a promontory above the lake. There was a blue neon sign over the entrance and families were eating in a back dining room that was supported by pilings built into the rock.

"You don't have to work tomorrow, huh?" I said.

"No."

"I'm glad."

"Why?"

"Maybe we could do something together," I said.

"You've never been married?"

"No. I have a son, though. He's twenty. He goes to Texas A&M."

"What happened to his mother?"

"She died. She was married to another man when she conceived our son. His name is Lucas. He's probably one of the best string musicians in the state of Texas."

The waitress brought our food and went away. The lake was dark now, and a sailboat was anchored out in the chop, its cabin glowing with an oily yellow light. The back door of the restaurant was open to let in the cool air, and I could hear a band playing at the motel up on the promontory.

"That's Glenn Miller," I said.

"Montana is a time warp," she said.

"So are all good places," I said.

She was quiet for a moment, then she set down her fork and lifted her eyes.

"You're not eating," she said.

"I don't eat much," I said.

"Billy Bob, you have a tendency to stare at people."

"Do you want to go?" I said.

"Where?"

"Down the road. Any place you've a mind. I don't care."

She watched my face, then picked up her purse.

We got into my truck and drove as far as the motel next door. I parked under the porte cochere. Through the lobby window I could see a girl of high school age behind the counter.

"You sure this is what you want?" Cleo said.

"Don't you?"

She didn't answer. She opened the truck door for herself and stepped out in the rain. The neon glow on her skin seemed to disfigure her face. For a moment I thought I saw L.Q. Navarro under the porte cochere, raising his hand in a cautionary way.

Inside the room I turned off the lights and sat in a chair and pulled off my boots with the awkwardness of a man who in reality had never been good with intimacy. A crack of light shone through the drawn curtains and I could see her silhouette as she undressed, a bare thigh, a crinkle in her hip as she pushed her panties down over her knees. The window was open and down below we could hear sounds from the gravel parking lot. I took off my trousers and shirt and walked up behind Cleo and placed my hands on her shoulders and started to turn her toward me. But her attention had been captured by the voices that rose on the wind from the parking lot.

"No! Let me alone!" a little boy was shouting.

"You get in the car, Ty!"

"I'm not going. You can't make me! Get away from me!" the boy yelled.

Cleo held back the curtain, indifferent to her nudity, and stared down at a middle-aged man in a white shirt and tie trying to pull a small boy by his wrists inside an automobile. Cleo's face wore an expression of unrelieved sadness.

"That's the family we saw in the lobby. The kid's probably throwing a temper tantrum," I said.

"I know," she said.

"He's all right," I said.

"I know that. I know that he's all right."

Later, in bed, I tried to pretend to myself that I wanted to give more than I wanted to receive. But I knew the selfishness that was always at work in my life, the heat and the repressed nocturnal longings and the violent memories that made me wake sweating in the false dawn, the dust and blood splatter that flew from L.Q. Navarro's coat the night I shot him, all these things that burned inside me, that made me ache for the absolution of a woman's thighs and breasts and the forgiveness of her mouth and the kneading pressure of her palms in the small of my back.

I buried my face in the smell of Cleo's hair and held her tightly against me and felt my heart twist and a dam break in my loins and all the sound and light in my body enter her womb.

I propped myself up on my arms and looked down into her face. Her stomach and thighs were moist against mine, and I was smiling at her and expected her, at least perhaps, to open her eyes lazily and smile back, her mouth ready to be kissed again. But her eyes were tightly shut, her brow creased with three deep lines, as though I had just made love to a fantasy and she was looking up into a hot sky that was tormented by carrion birds.

And I knew what Doc had meant when he said that neither the weight of headstones nor our heartbreaking and vain attempts at re-creating first love would ever disallow the hold of the dead upon the quick.

THE NEXT NIGHT Lamar Ellison was in a bar up the Blackfoot River, crashed on beer and reds, listening to the country band, talking to Sue Lynn, splitting a pitcher with Hollywood movie types who liked to float the

Blackfoot and the Little Big Horn in safari hats and fly vests that showed off their suntans. Who knows, maybe he'd end up in the movies himself. Hey, look what happened to the Angels when they latched on to Leary and all these middle-class pukes who couldn't wait to fry their heads with Osley purple.

There was Holly Girard over at the bar, her husband, too. Xavier was big shit with the writers' community around here. Big shit in New York and Hollywood, too. European television crews interviewed him in lowlife bars, which Lamar couldn't figure out, because why would a guy who owned a mansion above the river want everybody to see him on camera with drooling rummies?

Had Xavier heard about that rape beef? That doctor, the SEAL, was a writer or poet, too, wasn't he? Man, that wasn't good. Xavier had keys to the right doors and got an artistic buzz or something goofing with bikers and guys who'd been inside. Besides, the guy's wife was a first-rate box of chocolates.

Lamar took the pitcher back up to the bar and stood next to Xavier, nodding at both him and his wife, blowing his cigarette smoke at an upward angle to show the right respect.

"Hey, my man Xavier," Lamar said.

"Yeah, Lamar, what's happenin'?" Xavier said. But his eyes were oblique, focused on the band and the dancers out on the floor, a swizzle stick deep in his jaw.

His wife was even worse, gazing out the door, chin in the air, like her shit should be bronzed and used for paperweights.

"I got some bad press. It was a bum beef, though. The sheriff knew it from the get-go. That's why he cut me loose. I got no bad feelings against that doctor. The dude was in Force Recon. I went to Wal-Mart to buy his book but they didn't have it," Lamar said.

"I don't read the papers a lot, so I'm not real tuned in on it. We're about to boogie, Lamar," Xavier said.

"How you doin', Ms. Girard?" Lamar said, leaning forward so she could see his face.

"I'm quite well," she said. But she didn't turn her head toward him and her eyes were lowered, as though she did not want to see him even on the corner of her vision.

"I'm a big fan," he said.

"Thank you. That's very kind," she replied.

He started to speak again, but she picked up her purse and walked past him to the rest room. She wore a silvery-blue dress that trembled like ice water on her rump.

"Man, she's—" he said to Xavier.

"She's what?" Xavier said, turning toward him.

"Real talented." Lamar watched Xavier sip from his shot glass, then chase the whiskey with beer. The guy must have a liver the size of a football, he thought. How's a drunk fuck like that end up with money and fame and educated broads falling all over him in bookstores?

He felt his irritability growing. "I'm starting to get a big chill here. I do something to you or your lady?" he said.

"No, I just have to go home and write."

"You drink B-52's before you write? . . . Look, I never went asking for no trouble. I'm not a bad guy. You want to see a badass? Check the cowboy in the corner. That's Wyatt Dixon."

"You need to let go of my arm, Lamar."

"I'm paying out thirteen hundred bucks for a new bridge. I didn't press charges against your friend. But I end up on the front page of the fucking newspaper . . ."

"I know what you mean," Xavier said, peeling Lamar's hand loose from his arm. "Those news guys don't know character when they see it."

Then both Xavier and his wife were out the door, and Lamar's face felt full of needles, his ears humming with sound, as though he had been slapped.

HE TALKED awhile with Sue Lynn at the table, even though she had come to the bar with Wyatt. You had to show Wyatt you weren't afraid of him. Not head on, nothing confrontational, just a little signal you didn't rattle. Then he had gone outside and smoked some Mexican gage with two other bikers, swigging off a long-neck beer on top of their scooters, digging the sunset, watching the log trucks disappear up the grade in the dusk, trying to get rid of the vague sense of humiliation he'd felt when the Girards walked away from him like he was wrapped in stink.

But reefer and alcohol together always seemed to cook a terminal or two in his head. When he went back inside and sat down with Sue Lynn, he started talking. And talking. And talking. Without control, as though somebody had shot him up with a combo of crystal meth and Sodium Pentothal.

Then his brain kicked into gear again and he heard his own voice, in mid-sentence, as though waking from a dream, totally unaware of what he had just said.

Sue Lynn was a breed and looked as if she'd been poured out of two different paint buckets, but that didn't explain the whacked-out stare she was giving him now.

"I say something wrong?" Lamar asked.

"Fuck you," she replied.

"Who put a broom up your ass?"

Her eyes were red and glistening, as though she'd had a few hits of gage herself. She pushed back her chair and picked up her beer bottle and went out the door and let the screen slam behind her.

Now Wyatt was looking at him from the corner of the room. How many people in here had any idea what kind of guy was in their midst? They thought Wyatt was one of their own, with his flat-brim cowboy hat and triangular back and narrow waist and small, hard butt inside skintight jeans. But anybody who'd ever been on the yard would scope out a dude like Wyatt Dixon in five seconds.

Lamar winked and gave him a thumbs-up. But Wyatt just looked at him with those colorless dead eyes, his mouth like a purple slit, as though he knew something about Lamar's future that Lamar did not.

Well, eat shit and die, Lamar thought.

Why was everybody either in his face or on his case? A doctor, for Christ's sake, knocks his bridge down his throat. An ATF prick gets his jollies describing how his ears are going to get lopped off. He tries to talk reason to this Texas lawyer and the lawyer points a gun at his crotch. A Hollywood movie star and her rumdum husband blow their noses on him in a public place and Sue Lynn tells him to get fucked.

Maybe it was time to think about losing Montana and heading back out to the Coast. He could almost see himself tooling down the

PCH to Neptune's Net on the Ventura County
line, staying high on the sounds of surf and
salt wind and waves crashing on rocks. Let the
shitkickers frolic with the sheep.

He got on his Harley and bagged it down
the road, leaning into the curves, the roar of
his exhaust flattening against the cliffs on the
roadside. The sun had sunk below the mountains, and the sky was ribbed with strips of
purple cloud. A pickup truck came toward
him out of the dusk and sucked past him in a
rush of cold air, but through the window he
recognized the driver, that damned Texas
doctor he wished he'd never set eyes on.

Did the doctor recognize him? He didn't
need a return performance of that night in
the bar at Lincoln. Lamar watched the truck
disappear in his rearview mirror, then lifted
his face into the wind again, secretly ashamed
of the relief he felt.

He rounded another curve and saw a cottage supported by pilings on the edge of the
river and a white Cherokee parked by the
lilac bushes in front. It was the same Cherokee that Holly and Xavier Girard had left the
saloon in. There were lights on behind the
shades, and smoke rose from a barbecue pit
on the deck above the water.

Maybe the evening still held promise after
all.

Lamar pulled onto a gravel turnaround

against the mountain, killed his engine, and walked back down the shoulder of the road to the Cherokee. He bent down over each tire and sliced off the valve stem with his pocket-knife, then stepped back and viewed his handiwork.

It still needed a little something extra.

He found some rocks under a culvert, heavy and solid and hand-sized for throwing. He heaved one through the front window and two through the passenger windows, then reached inside with his knife and began slicing the leather seats.

That's when he heard Xavier Girard running at him.

It was funny how a celebrity punk thought the real world was like the one he made up in his books. Lamar shifted his knife to his left hand and caught Xavier in the mouth with his right. Xavier went down in the gravel like a sack of grain.

Lamar shook his fingers.

"You must have ate your iron pills today. I think you busted my hand, Xavier," he said.

Xavier didn't answer. He was on his hands and knees now, his mouth dripping blood and spittle, his stomach hanging out of his belt like a balloon full of milk.

"You're done, Xavier. Don't get up. Oh well, I guess this means I don't get a part in one of your wife's movies," Lamar said.

He pulled Xavier the rest of the way to his feet, then propped him against the side of the Cherokee and drove his fist into Xavier's stomach, just below the sternum.

Xavier fell to his knees and vomited, then pressed his forehead against the gravel, gasping for breath, his back shaking.

"See you around. By the way, I read one of your books in the joint. I thought it sucked," Lamar said, and started back toward his Harley.

But Xavier's hand caught the calf of his leg, then he wrapped both arms around Lamar's thigh.

"You want a little soft-shoe? 'Cause this time I'm gonna take out all your teeth," Lamar said, and cocked back his boot.

Holly Girard seemed to float out of nowhere, holding a nickel-plated revolver with both hands, the tiny bones in her hands whitening behind the cylinder. Her dark blond tresses hung on her cheeks and her mouth was as red and soft-looking as a strawberry that he would have loved to burst against his teeth.

He stepped back from her, his palms raised upward. Three or four other people had walked out of the cottage behind her.

"It's over as far as I'm concerned. Your old

man shouldn't have dissed me. You want to call the heat, I understand your point of view," he said.

That ought to leave a fishhook or two in her head, he thought.

But when he looked at her eyes, then at Xavier and the other people from the cottage, he realized they never heard him, that the loathing and disgust they felt for him was so great they viewed him as they would a voiceless obscenity trapped under a glass bell.

He walked away, toward his motorcycle, his hobnailed boots crunching on the gravel. When he turned around they were gone, back inside the cottage, probably dialing 911.

So what? He was probably better off in the can than back on the street. He fired up his Harley and roared down the asphalt.

Home was a one-room block house made of railroad ties and an open-air tin shed where he sometimes repaired motorcycles. But it was on the Blackfoot, right upstream from a bar that was surrounded by pine trees, and he could cross the water on a cable-hung walk-bridge and shoot deer and bear up a canyon just above the old railroad bed. This spring he had killed a black bear and had hung it by its hind legs from an engine hoist to dress it out, then had gotten drunk and let the meat spoil. The bear still hung in the shed, coated with blowflies, its smell rising up against the tin roof of the shed as the day heated.

He sat on the edge of the bed in the darkness of his cabin, stripped to the waist, and smoked a joint and drank a quart bottle of beer, then lay back on the pillow and went to sleep. Tomorrow was another day. The same sun would rise on the jail as on the river. You just stayed on the hucklebuck, man. It didn't matter where you did it.

In his dream he thought he heard the weight of the black bear swinging slightly from the engine hoist in the tin shed, then he awoke and realized someone was in the room with him.

A chain locked down across his throat, the links binding and cutting into his skin. Lamar pried at the chain with his fingers, but the dark figure who stood above him fitted a pipe over the boom handle, as a professional logger would, and squeezed down the boom, tightening it until saliva ran from both corners of Lamar's mouth.

Lamar heard the rattle of liquid inside a tin container, then a splashing sound on the floor. The unmistakable sharpness of paint thinner climbed into his nostrils. A match flared in the figure's hands and just briefly in the illumination Lamar saw a face that was both strange and familiar at the same time.

The fire spread under his bed in seconds. He thrashed his legs, twisting his head back and forth, and beat his fists against his own skull.

The fire swelled over him in a cone, and inside the flames he thought he heard a sound like blowflies and he saw himself, for just an instant, hanging upside down over a bright fissure in the earth he had long ago convinced himself did not exist.

# Chapter

# 10

❦

WITH THE CLARITY OF VISION and singleness of purpose that seemed to characterize everything Sheriff Cain did, he arrested Doc Voss the next afternoon and lodged him in the county jail.

I went into the sheriff's office without knocking. He lowered the newspaper he was reading and looked at me over his spectacles.

"You grow up in a hog lot?" he said.

"What makes you think you can get away with something like this?" I said.

He took his feet off his desk. "Let's see if I understand you correctly," he said. "Putting a friend of yours in jail on a murder warrant is somehow outside my job description?"

"On what evidence?"

He yawned sleepily. "On a previous occasion he almost killed the victim in a bar. The victim later raped the suspect's daughter. The suspect, that's Dr. Voss I'm talking about, was in the Phoenix Program in Vietnam and probably did things to human beings that would make most people vomit. If you were still a Texas Ranger, who'd you be looking at?"

"Because he was in Vietnam doesn't make him a murderer. What's the matter with you?"

"Did I mention that a bone-handled skinning knife with the doctor's fingerprints on it was found at the crime scene?" the sheriff asked.

I wanted to speak, to say something that would refute his words, but my throat was suddenly dry, my palms damp and stiff and hard to close.

"Shut the door after you leave," the sheriff said.

"Ellison was in Doc's house. He took the knife then. Were his prints on the knife?" I said.

"No."

I rubbed my forehead, trying to think.

"Look, Maisey said at least one of the men who raped her had gloves on. That was Ellison," I said.

"Good. Dr. Voss's defense attorney can say all that in court."

"Ellison was a snitch. His own people wanted him dead. Talk to the ATF," I said.

"I classify most of those federal boys as A.A. Which means I leave them alone," he replied.

I looked at him incredulously. "You're saying the feds are drunks?"

"Arrogant Asswipes. Now go piddle around on the trout stream or visit your friend up in the holding tank or whittle some shavings outside under a tree. To tell you the truth, son, my estimation of the Texas Rangers has plummeted."

I went out of his office, my ears ringing. But I couldn't let go of his remarks. I opened his door again and went back inside.

"I'm representing Dr. Voss. He's not to be questioned unless I'm present. I'm going to hang this case around your neck," I said.

"Damn, I wish you would. I hate this job," he said, and picked up his newspaper again.

IT WAS SATURDAY and Doc's bail would not be set until his arraignment Tuesday afternoon. I rode the elevator up to the jail section of the courthouse with a deputy sheriff and waited in a small interview room until the deputy brought Doc down the corridor in handcuffs and an orange jumpsuit.

"How about it on the cuffs?" I said to the deputy.

"They stay on," he answered, and closed the door on us.

"I'll get you out Tuesday, Doc," I said.

Doc stood at the window, looking down on the maple trees along the streets. "How bad is this going to be?" he asked.

"You know that knife I gave you?"

"Yeah, I couldn't find it the other day."

"It was in Ellison's cabin. With your prints on it."

"That's not good, is it?" He lifted his manacled wrists and propped them on the windowsill. The hills north of the train depot were green and domed against the sky and clumps of whitetail were grazing on the slopes. "Take good care of Maisey, will you?"

"Doc, you didn't do it, did you?"

He started to answer, then stared out the window silently. His ill-fitting orange jumpsuit looked like a clown's costume on his body.

BY MONDAY AFTERNOON I had read the homicide investigators' reports on Lamar Ellison's murder and had retraced Ellison's movements of Friday evening back to the tavern on the Blackfoot. I had also managed to interview a bartender at the tavern, Holly and Xavier Girard, and a biker who'd been at the table with Sue Lynn and Ellison.

The biker's name was Clell Miller and he ran a welding business in a tin shed on the west side of Missoula. He was shirtless and wore black goggles up on his forehead, and sweat ran down his torso into the underwear that was bunched out over the top of his jeans.

"What were Lamar and Sue Lynn talking about?" I said.

"It didn't make no sense. Lamar was stoned. Something about kids," he said. "Look, man, I don't want to speak bad of the dead. The Mexican Mafia had a hit on the guy. He ratted out some people inside. So maybe they cooked him. That's their style. They'll Molotov a guy in his cell."

"You think Wyatt Dixon might have lit up his life?" I said.

He shut down the valves on the acetylene torch he had been using. He wiped the sweat and soot off his face with a rag.

"I ain't said nothing about Wyatt Dixon. I ain't even told you he was there."

"That's right. You haven't said a word about him. Where'd you get the Confederate flag on your wall?" I said.

"At the Indian powwow in Arlee. What do you care?" he said irritably.

"Is Wyatt a bad dude?"

"I know what you're trying to do, man. This all started 'cause your friend's daughter pulled a train. The way I heard it, she invited them guys over and couldn't get enough. Flush it any way you want, chief, you either beat feet or I'm gonna fry up some Texas toast."

He popped his welding torch alight.

WHEN I GOT BACK to Doc's place I saw an old sedan parked in the trees, down by the river. Its windshield and headlights had been removed, the body sprayed with gray primer, and two large numerals were painted in orange on the driver's door.

The back door of the house was open. I walked inside and saw Maisey in her bedroom, lying on her side, her back to me. The Indian girl named Sue Lynn sat on the mattress beside her, stroking Maisey's hair. The plank floor creaked under my foot, and Sue Lynn's face jerked toward me.

"What are you doing in here?" I said through the doorway.

"I came to see about the doctor. Is he going to be all right?" she said, standing up now.

"He's in the county jail, charged with murder. Does that sound all right?" I said.

"Don't talk to her like that, Billy Bob. She came here to help," Maisey said.

"She's buds with Ellison's motorcycle pals, Maisey," I said.

"What do you know?" Sue Lynn said.

"I think you're here for self-serving reasons," I said.

"Then sit on this," she replied, and raised her middle finger at me.

She tried to stare me down, then her eyes broke. She hurried out the far bedroom door into the living room and kept going, through the front screen and down the slope toward the riverbank. I went after her.

"Listen to me," I said. "I used to be a lawman. I think the G put you inside the Berdoo Jesters. You know who set fire to Ellison, don't you?"

She was standing in the shade of the trees, and her dark skin was freckled with the sunlight that shone through the canopy.

"You should have kept the doctor away from Lamar in the bar up at Lincoln. You wouldn't listen to me. This is all on you," she said.

"What's your last name?"

"Big Medicine."

"You're a Crow?" I said.

"How did you know that?" she said.

"One of the scouts for Custer at the Little

Big Horn was a Crow Indian named Big Medicine. The scouts wanted to sing their death song before they rode into Sitting Bull's village. Custer accused them of cowardice and fired them. They were the only survivors of the massacre."

She began backing toward her automobile, her eyes fixed uncertainly on mine, as though I possessed omniscience or some form of magic. Even though the air was cool in the shade, there was a bright chain of sweat around her throat.

"The car belongs to a stock-car driver. It doesn't have lights. I have to get it back to the junkyard before sunset," she said.

"Wyatt Dixon is a dangerous man. Don't let those federal guys use you."

She felt behind her for the handle on the car door, then a moment of resolve, perhaps even cautious trust, seemed to form in her face.

"Say I do know some government fucks? Why would they be asking me if Lamar and the others have been in Kingman, Arizona?" she said.

"The men who blew up the Alfred P. Murrah Building in Oklahoma City hung around there at one time or another," I said.

Her lips moved silently, as though she were repeating the words to herself, as though the enormity of their connotation would not come into focus behind her eyes.


AN ATTORNEY FRIEND of Doc's filed a *pro hac vice* petition on my behalf, which would empower me to represent Doc on a one-case basis without passing the Montana bar exam. On Tuesday afternoon Doc was released from the county jail on a two-hundred-thousand-dollar bond.

When we walked outside the sun was shining on the hills and the air smelled of freshly mowed grass and raindrops striking on warm cement.

"How about I buy you a dinner?" I said.

"Where's Maisey?"

"At the house."

"She didn't want to come with you?"

"I don't know much about these things, Doc, but I think rape is like theft of the soul. You've got to give her some time."

"Sure," he said, his eyes averted, his face empty. "Let's get some dinner."


THAT EVENING, at a university gathering, Xavier Girard gave a reading from his newest novel, one that some believed might win him his third Edgar Award. Students and faculty and local writers filled the room. Sitting in the middle of the audience was a man in skintight jeans and cowboy boots and a long-sleeve polka-dot shirt buttoned at the wrists. He wore women's purple garters on his upper arms. He did not remove his wide-brim hat, even though the people behind him kept clearing their throats and leaning to the side to see around him.

He had arrived early, with an effeminate, long-haired youth whose smirk at his surroundings and flaccid muscle tone and lack of posture were in exact contrast to the hatted man's obvious physical power and lantern-jawed concentration.

The audience loved Xavier Girard. He was generous in spirit and irreverent toward stuffiness and convention. He was egalitarian and humble and acutely aware of propriety and language in the presence of women. He wore his own success and fame like a loose garment, and at signings charged books on his own account when a student or clergyperson could not afford one. If he drank too much from the thermos of cold vodka by his elbow, his sin was a forgivable one, the alcoholic flush on his face a mask for the pain that only a poet felt.

His mouth was slightly bruised, his lip still puffed from his fight with Lamar Ellison, but his voice resonated through the room. He read the dialogue of his characters in peckerwood and Cajun accents; his eyes seemed to look directly at every one of his listeners, the iambic cadence of his descriptive passages like lines from a sonnet.

But when his eyes fell on Wyatt Dixon's, they held there, narrowing, the way a hunter's might when he sees an unexpected presence in a woods and realizes the nature of the game has just changed.

During the question and answer period that followed the reading, Wyatt Dixon's square, callus-edged hand floated into the air.

"Yes, sir?" Xavier said.

Dixon stood and removed his hat. "You, sir, are obviously a great writer and believer in the land of the free and home of the brave," he said. "In that spirit, can you tell me what is wrong with Americans running a gold mine on the Blackfoot River and providing jobs for other Americans?"

The room was silent. A couple of people turned and looked in Dixon's direction, then glanced away.

"We don't need cyanide in the river. Does that answer your question?" Xavier said.

"It surely does. I'm glad that's been explained to me. Thank you very much, sir," Dixon said. "Sir, could I ask you—"

A woman librarian picked up the microphone from the podium and, her lips brushing against the mike's surface, hurriedly said, "Mr. Girard will be signing books at the table in the back. In the meantime, everyone can help himself to the punch."

After the line had thinned out at the refreshment table, Wyatt Dixon and his young friend filled their cups. Except Dixon did not drink his. He smelled it, inhaling the strawberry bouquet and seltzer water approvingly. Then he removed his hat and dipped his pocket comb into the bowl and combed his hair in a wall mirror.

While people stared at him openmouthed, he fitted his hat back on and got in the line for a signed book.

"Just make it out to my friend Carl Hinkel, a Virginia gentleman and patriot," Dixon said.

"I can't do that," Xavier said.

"I can see you are a man of your convictions. Just sign your name and I will treasure it always. Sir, I'd also like to shake your hand."

Xavier rose and placed his hand inside Dixon's.

"It was good of you to be here. But you shouldn't try to jerk people around," he said, then his mouth stiffened involuntarily when Dixon began to squeeze.

"Lamar Ellison and me shared the same house inside Quentin," Dixon said. He continued to grin, his vacuous eyes staring into Xavier's. "On the West Coast, people inside call a cell a 'house.' You don't know that, 'cause you ain't never been inside. So that ain't to be held against you. But you might brush up on the details for your next book."

"Let go of my hand," Xavier said, his words spaced out, as he tried to retain any dignity the situation would allow him.

"You didn't set fire to my bunkie, did you, Mr. Girard? Just 'cause he busted out a window in your car and laid open your lip? You can't do that to a Berdoo Jester, sir," Dixon said, his hand catching fresh purchase.

The blood had drained out of Xavier's face. He felt with his other hand for a weapon, for the thermos on the book table, but Dixon pulled him forward, off balance.

"I don't mean to mock you, sir, but for a man who has just warmed up all these women's secret parts, your eloquent vocabulary has flown like a flock of shit birds off a manure wagon," Dixon said.

Xavier's knees were buckling now, tears running without shame down his cheeks.

Suddenly Dixon released him.

"Somebody get a mop. This man has done wet hisself," he said.

He picked up his cup of punch, and, with

one gartered arm across his young friend's shoulders, walked out of the room.

THE NEXT MORNING I heard the story from the owner of a local bookstore who had come out to see Doc and Maisey. At noon I drove to the sheriff's office and was told where I could find him.

I parked my truck in the leafy shade of cottonwoods on the Clark Fork, only three blocks from the courthouse, and walked down the embankment to the water's edge. The sheriff was casting a Mepps spinner in a high arc out into the middle of the river, letting it swing taut in the riffle before he began retrieving it. In the sunlight the scars on the backs of his hands looked like thin white snakes.

I went through the account about Wyatt Dixon's behavior at the university reading. He waited for me to finish, reeling in his line, casting it out again, then said, "I know all about it."

"Why's a guy like Dixon care about this gold mine up on the Blackfoot River?" I asked.

"Carl Hinkel uses these morons to run various kinds of scams on the government."

"What kinds of scams?"

"Hinkel finds old mining laws on the books

that allow him to file mineral claims for next to nothing. Then he starts bulldozing the mountain away and washing the rock with cyanide. The tree huggers go apeshit and hammer their tallywhackers on their congressman's desk till the government buys out the claim and makes a millionaire out of a pissant who wouldn't recognize gold if you pulled it out of his teeth and stuck it up his nose."

"I think Dixon wants to put suspicion for Ellison's death on Xavier Girard," I said. "He knows Doc didn't do it, and he figures eventually you're going to be looking at him for the murder."

"In other words, just about anybody in Missoula County could have killed Lamar Ellison except your friend?"

I hesitated before I spoke again. His physical size was huge, his level of tolerance unpredictable.

"You told me you'd like to pinch Ellison's head off with a chain. You drove a log truck. Whoever killed Ellison knew how to use a boomer chain," I said.

"Son, there's three categories of stupid. 'Stupid,' 'stupider,' and 'stupidest.' But I think you're establishing new standards. Did the doctor have to use forceps on your head to get you out of the womb?"

"You'd love Texas, Sheriff."

"That's not a compliment, is it?"

"Search me," I said, and walked back to my truck.

Behind me, I heard his nylon line zing off the reel, his metal lure rattling through the shining air.

AN HOUR LATER I answered the phone at Doc's house.

"I ain't ever seen a place this beautiful, Billy Bob. I cain't wait to hit the stream," the voice on the other end said.

"Lucas?"

"Yeah. We're at Rock Creek. We need directions out to Doc's place."

"*We?*"

"Temple and me. My drilling rig shut down. You said to come out if I could get some time off."

I tried to remember the conversation but could not. My innocent, wonderful, talented, and vulnerable son, why did you have to come here now?

"Temple's with you?" I said.

"Yeah, what's wrong?"

Temple Carrol was the private investigator I relied on in my law practice. But she was a lot more than that, and our relationship was one that neither of us had ever been able to define.

"I didn't tell her to come up here," I said.

"Since when do you have to tell her anything?"

My head was throbbing.

"Lucas—" I began.

"Maisey called her. So did Doc. He said Maisey's real messed up in the head. Who are these guys who raped her?"

"You stay out of this stuff, Lucas."

"I'm gonna put Temple on the phone. Thanks for the welcome to Montana," he said.

# Chapter

## II

❦

TEMPLE STOOD in the dusk by the side of
the Ford Explorer she drove, her face obviously fatigued by the long drive from Deaf
Smith and now my ineptness in her presence.
Temple had been a gunbull in Angola Prison
in Louisiana, a patrolwoman in Dallas, and a
sheriff's deputy in Fort Bend County in
Southeast Texas. She had chestnut hair and
dressed like a tomboy and had never lost the
baby fat on her hips and arms. Her level of
loyalty was ferocious. But so was her demand
on the loyalty of others.

Lucas had already unloaded his things and
was pegging up a tent among the trees by the
river.

"Maisey and Doc didn't tell you I was coming up with Lucas?" she asked.

"No. But I'm glad you did," I said.

"I'm going to check into a motel in Missoula."

"There's room inside."

She shook her head. "Where's a good place to eat?"

"There's a truck stop in Bonner. I'll go with you. Then we'll come back here and you can stay the night."

She thought about it and yawned, then said, "You involved with somebody here?"

"Why do you think that?" I said, my eyes slipping off her face.

"Just a wild guess."


EARLY THE NEXT MORNING I smelled wood smoke and bacon frying outside, and I looked through the window and saw Lucas squatting by a fire ring he had made of stones next to the river's edge. He dipped a coffeepot into a creek that flowed into the river and sprinkled coffee grinds into the water and set the pot to boil on the edge of his fire. I walked down to the bank and squatted next to him.

"That creek water's got deer scat in it," I said.

"The animals drink it. It don't bother them," he said. He grinned and wedged the blade of his pocketknife into a can of condensed milk.

He was as tall as I, with the same hair and wide, narrow shoulders. But he had his mother's hands, those of a musician, and her gentle looks.

"It's good to have you here, bud," I said.

"How could anybody figure Doc for a murderer? What kind of law they got up here, anyway?"

"Doc's a complicated man."

"What's that supposed to mean?"

"He killed a lot of people in the war, Lucas."

I could feel his eyes on the side of my face.

"You saying maybe he done it?" he asked.

"I try not to study on it. The way I figure it, the guy who died had it coming."

I heard him clear his throat, as though a moth had flown into it. He lifted the bacon in his skillet with a fork and turned it over in the grease, his eyes watering in the smoke.

"Sometimes things come out of you that scare me, Billy Bob," he said.


I PICKED UP Temple at her motel in Missoula and we drove to the courthouse and walked down the corridor to the sheriff's office.

"Let me talk to him alone," she said.

"Why?"

"Woman's touch, that sort of thing."

"You think I already tracked pig flop on the rug?"

"You? Not a chance."

She left his door partly open, and I could see inside and hear them talking. I soon had the feeling the sheriff wished he had gone to lunch early.

"How does anybody lose a bag full of bloody and semen-stained sheets and clothing? You drop it off at the Goodwill by mistake?" she said.

"We think the night janitor picked up the bag and threw it in the incinerator," the sheriff said.

"So then you conclude there's no physical evidence to prove Ellison stole Doc's knife. Which allows you to arrest Doc for Ellison's murder. What kind of brain-twisted logic is that?"

"Now listen—"

"You pulled in two other suspects for Maisey's rape. Their fingerprints were at the crime scene. But you didn't charge them."

"One guy was a part-time carpenter. He worked on that house before Dr. Voss bought it. The other man was at a party there. A couple of witnesses back up his story."

"You know they did it."

"Help me prove that and I'll lock them up. Look, you're mad because your friend is not easy to defend. The knife puts him inside Ellison's cabin. He stopped at a filling station a mile down the road and filled his tank with gas a half hour before the fire started. He had motivation and no alibi. When we picked him up and told him somebody had burned Ellison to death, he said, 'I should give a shit?' You were a police officer. Who would you have in custody?"

"I'd start with Wyatt Dixon. Why do you allow a psychopath like that in your town, anyway?"

"Say again?" he said.

"Back home our sheriff is a one-lung cretin who couldn't go to the bathroom without a diagram. But he'd have Wyatt Dixon pepper-Maced and in waist chains five minutes after he hit town."

"Yeah, I heard about the way you do things down there. We sent a bunch of our convicts from Deer Lodge to one of your rental prisons. We're still paying off the lawsuits. Now, look, Missy—"

"Say that again?"

"Sorry. I mean Ms. Carrol. You and Mr. Holland aren't married, are you? You two seem to make a fine match," the sheriff said.

"I'll be back later."

"Oh I know. Yes, ma'am, I surely know," he said, two fingers pressed against one eyebrow.

TEMPLE AND I walked outside into the sunshine. The maples on the courthouse lawn were puffing in the wind, and a long procession of bicyclists in brightly colored Spandex outfits was threading in and out of the traffic.

"Who was the kid with Dixon? The one at the literary reading you told me about?" Temple said.

"You got me. Why?"

"We need to find a weak link. What's the deal on this Indian gal?" she said.

"Her name is Sue Lynn Big Medicine. I think she's working for the ATF."

"What's their interest?"

"Guns, maybe. Or the Alfred P. Murrah Building."

"The Oklahoma City bombing?"

"Sue Lynn asked me why the feds would want information on people who have been in Kingman, Arizona."

Temple widened her eyes.

"That puts a new perspective on things," she said.

"I don't buy it," I said. "This trouble is local, and it has to do with money."

"It always has to do with money. Or sex and power," she said. "Who's this woman you're involved with?"

IT WASN'T HARD to get the name of the kid who had accompanied Wyatt Dixon to Xavier Girard's literary reading. The reading had been intended as a library fund-raiser, and everyone attending had been required to sign the guest book and give his mailing address at the door.

The name above Wyatt Dixon's was a woman's. The name below was Terry Witherspoon.

Temple used her cell phone to call a friend in the sheriff's department in San Antonio. He ran the name through the computer at the National Crime Information Center in Washington, D.C., and called us back. Temple listened, then thanked him and clicked off her phone.

"If it's the same kid, he was in a juvenile facility in North Carolina," she said.

"What for?"

"His records are sealed."

Terry Witherspoon lived in a knocked-together shack on a dirt road notched out of a hillside high above the Clark Fork River.

I parked in a clearing among the pines and waited for the dust to blow away before we got out of the truck. Out in the trees we could see a great, rust-streaked, ventilated iron cylinder set up on a rubber-tired trailer. A huge gray hunk of raw meat was hung inside the front of the cylinder, crawling with flies, stinking of putrefaction.

"What's *that?*" Temple said.

"A bear barrel. Fish and Game uses them to trap black bears when people complain about them."

"Billy Bob, there's something in there," she said.

A cinnamon bear, one weighing perhaps two hundred and fifty or three hundred pounds, had climbed into the back of the barrel, lured by the odor of meat, and an iron gate had slammed down behind it, trapping it so it could not turn around or go either forward or backward.

In a railed dirt lot behind the shack a lean, bare-chested kid, with ribs etched against his skin, was throwing a long, single-bladed pocketknife into a fence post. His brown hair grew over his ears, and he wore horn-rimmed glasses and a mocking smile at the corner of his mouth.

"You Terry Witherspoon?" I asked.

His glasses were full of reflected light when he looked at us.

The smile never left his mouth. "Who wants to know?" he said.

"We're investigating the death of Lamar Ellison," Temple said. She opened her private investigator's badge holder, then closed it.

"Yeah?" he said, almost enthusiastically. The knife's blade hung from the tips of his fingers. Hardly glancing at his target, he whipped the knife sideways, flinging it end over end into the fence post, where it embedded solidly into the wood and trembled like a dinner fork.

"What's the story on the bear?" I asked.

"It's been getting into my trash. I called the game warden. They brought out the barrel," he replied.

"When are they going to pick it up?" I said.

"They didn't say. Maybe if it gets thirsty in there, it won't come back when they turn it loose," he said.

His face was flat and his glasses wobbled with light.

Temple studied a folded-back page in her notebook. "Wyatt Dixon talk to you about killing Lamar Ellison?" she said.

His face seemed to soften. "Wyatt hasn't hurt anybody. If I was you, I wouldn't be talking about him that way," he said.

He pulled the knife from the fence post and walked back into the center of the lot. He stood at an oblique angle to the post, concentrating, the knife blade dripping from his fingers. His mouth pursed slightly before he flung the knife again. This time the handle caromed off the post.

"You go to the university, Terry?" I said.

"I'm thinking about it. Or I might take up rodeoing."

"What were you down for in North Carolina?" I asked.

He grinned and pushed his glasses up on his nose. "Littering," he said.

"Did you guys make Ellison for a snitch? Because if you had knowledge of what was going to happen to him, you've become an accessory," Temple said.

"Y'all are local cops who went down South and learned your accents?" he said. He pitched his head at his own joke.

"You seem like a smart young guy, Terry," I said. "Wyatt's been down at least twice. He'll probably go down again. You want to be his fall partner?"

"Y'all have a TV camera hid out in the bushes? I'd like to say hello to my mom," he said.

Temple looked at me, then began punching in numbers on her cell phone.

"Who you calling?" Witherspoon asked.

She didn't reply. She spoke into the cell phone and clicked it shut.

"Fish and Game will be here in a little while," she said. "You're right, Terry, I'm not a local cop. That means I really wish you'd wise off again so I can rip that grin off your face and shove your puny little ass into that bear barrel."

He pitched his head again, clearing his hair off his glasses, then cocked the knife over his shoulder and parked it solidly into the fence post. When he walked over to retrieve it, his profile jiggled with laughter.

THAT NIGHT I heard a vehicle grinding through the field behind Doc's house, then a rattling sound like rocks under the vehicle's fenders and a thud down in the trees by the river. I unlocked the front door and walked barefoot out on the porch. It was cold and the valley and cliffs were lighted by the moon, and I could see a sports utility vehicle high-centered on a sand spit in the river, the current riffling around its tires. A man waded from the driver's door toward the front of Doc's property.

The man stumbled and fell in the water but held aloft the square-shaped gin bottle he carried so it did not break on the rocks. He splashed up on the bank, his clothes and thick hair dripping with water and moonlight. Just before he tumbled into the grass and passed out I saw the bandaged hand and feral and besotted face of Xavier Girard.

I closed the door and slipped the bolt and went back to sleep and hoped the sun would rise on a better world for all of us.

# Chapter

## 12

AT FIRST LIGHT I looked through my window and saw him on all fours, cupping water out of the river and sipping it from his palm. When I walked up behind him, he turned his head slowly, as though he were in pain. His face was gray with hangover, his eyes the color of iodine.

"How'd I get here?" he asked.

Smoke from Lucas's breakfast fire was blowing through the trees out onto the darkness of the water. Upstream I could see Lucas standing in the middle of the riffle, false-casting a dry fly under the overhang.

"Looks like you might have wanted to wash your Jeep," I said. I found a clean cup in Lucas's rucksack and filled it with coffee from the pot on the fire, then squatted down next to Xavier and handed it to him. "How's your hand?"

He looked at the dirty elastic bandage that hung from his fingers like strips of mummy cloth. "It doesn't feel good to be my age and wonder if you're anybody's punch," he said.

I shifted my weight on one haunch and picked up a small, flat stone and flipped it with my thumb into the current. "Why'd you come out here, sir?" I said.

"I don't rightly remember. It probably made a lot of sense last night," he said.

His face was dripping with river water and he blotted his mouth and forehead on his sleeve. His eyes were puffed, as though they had been stung with bees, his breath as dense as sewer gas.

"Have you ever thought about hitting one of those twelve-step meetings?" I said.

"They're full of drunks," he said.

"I guess that's a possibility," I said, my gaze focusing on nothing.

He sat on a rock and held the coffee cup to his mouth with both hands. He tried to drink but couldn't swallow. He pressed the back of his wrist to his forehead. His fingers were shaking.

"I talked with Holly about starting up a defense fund for Doc. She said it was none of our damn business," he said. The river was still in shadow, and he stared upstream at Lucas false-casting in the riffle, as though the image of a young man in hip waders silhouetted under the lighted canopy of the forest was a reminder of someone he might have known long ago.

"Maybe she has her reasons," I said.

He pitched the coffee from his cup into the rocks. "You see a gin bottle around here?"

"It's over there, in the grass."

He walked over to the bottle and picked it up and tightened the cap on it, then tilted it sideways, measuring its content.

"I'd better go now," he said.

"Come back anytime."

"Holly worries about finances. I've gone belly-up on a couple of deals. She always thinks we're going to take on legal liability. That's why she's a lot more conservative than I am," he said.

"Makes sense," I said.

"Forget I was here, will you, Mr. Holland?"

"No problem," I said, and watched him walk to his Jeep Cherokee, his fingers spidered around the square edges of the gin bottle. When he drove into the sunlight, grinding the gears, the skin of his face seemed to shrink at the hard, bright, lonely reality of the day that awaited him.

LATER, I drove out to see Cleo at her place
in the Jocko Valley. When I thumped across
the cattle guard I saw Cleo's gay carpenter
arguing with three men in a maroon Cadillac
convertible. The carpenter wore a leather
tool belt and no shirt; a ball-peen hammer
hung loosely from his right hand. Farther up
the dirt drive I could see Cleo standing on the
porch of her house.

I got out of my truck and walked toward
the convertible. It wasn't hard to make the
men inside. They wore slacks with knife-
blade creases and sport shirts unbuttoned at
the top to show off their gold chains and
chest hair, and radiated a visceral self-satis-
faction. Their stares were invasive, vaguely
contemptuous, devoid of all empathy. The
man in back was eating the last of a hot dog.
When he finished, he wiped the mustard off
his mouth with a paper napkin and let the
napkin blow away on the grass.

The carpenter grinned at me as I approached
the convertible. He flipped the hammer into
the air and caught it again and slipped the
handle through a loop in his belt. His skin was
bronzed and his hair gold from the sun.

"These fellows are just leaving. Cleo's up at
the house," he said.

"I see," I said.

"They didn't like the welcome they got,"
the carpenter said.

I looked the carpenter flatly in the face. Don't crowd them, bud, I thought.

"Catch you later," he said to me, and walked back toward the barn where he had been working.

The driver of the convertible was a muscular, handsome man, with smooth skin and black hair that he combed straight back. He wore a bright yellow golf shirt, and when he had drawn his car abreast of me, he said, "You got a problem, too?"

"No, I don't think so," I replied.

"Your truck's in the road," he said.

"Just pull around on the grass," I said.

"Why you looking at me like that?" he said.

"You're Nicki Molinari."

"You know me from somewhere?"

"I used to work for the G. Your picture would float across my desk from time to time."

"Sorry the recognition isn't mutual. Now please move your fucking truck out of the fucking road."

"What's your business with Cleo, Nicki?"

"Where you get off calling me by my first name?"

"You're a famous guy. No offense meant. I heard you were doing a nickel in Terminal Island."

The man in the passenger seat started to

get out. But Nicki Molinari raised his hand.

"Here's your lesson for the day, whatever your name is," he said. "If that broad is your regular pump, I feel sorry for you. Second of all, I'd better not see you again."

He eased his transmission out of park and drove around my truck, across the cattle guard, and onto the county road. When I pulled into Cleo's yard, she walked down the steps toward me, but her eyes were still on the convertible that was now disappearing over a rise.

"What's with the greaseballs?" I said.

"You know them?"

"Every DEA agent in the country knows who Nicki Molinari is. You didn't answer my question. Why are they here?"

"They claim my husband owed them money."

"What did you tell them?"

"To get out."

"Why would your husband owe them money?"

"I don't care and I don't want to know."

"These aren't guys you just run off."

"I just did. I stuck a gun in his face. He looked bad in front of his men, so he tried to give Eric a hard time. You want to come in or not?"

"I thought you might want to go to lunch."

"I can fix something if you're hungry," she

said, her voice flat, disinterested, her eyes lingering on the dust cloud left by Nicki Molinari's convertible.

"This isn't quite what I had in mind, Cleo."

"What?" she said, her attention refocusing itself on my words.

"No, I'm not hungry. I thought you might be. Maybe I should go."

"Will you just come in, Billy Bob?" she said, and pulled me by the arm, either out of irritation or conciliation, I didn't know which.

A chrome-plated .44 Magnum revolver rested on a table in the hallway.

"Just a minute," she said, and picked up the revolver and entered the den and opened a felt-backed glass gun cabinet where at least two dozen antique and modern pistols were hung. She flipped open the cylinder on the Magnum and dumped the cartridges into her palm, then fitted the Magnum on its hooks and closed the glass doors.

"What a collection," I said.

"They were my father's. He was career Army. He wanted a son."

"He taught you to shoot?"

"I taught myself. You want a roast beef sandwich?"

"Sure," I said.

On the way out of the den I saw on top of a bookcase a framed photograph of a little boy.

He wore a cowboy hat and sat atop a Shetland pony. The pony was eating out of a bucket, and the little boy's legs were too short to reach the stirrups. The boy was holding on to the pommel as though he were frightened by the distance to the ground.

I followed Cleo into the kitchen.

"Why so quiet?" she asked.

Greaseballs in her front yard, her suppressed rage and grief over a murdered child, compassion for a rape victim and destitute Indians, a personality that blew hot and cold with the moment. I couldn't begin to express my thoughts.

"My son's staying out at Doc's. I'd like for you to meet him," I said.

But she made no reply.

I stood next to her at the drainboard. Through the window the Douglas fir trees on the hill crest looked hard and perpendicular against the sky. I placed my hand on her back. "You have to be at the clinic this afternoon?" I said.

"Not really."

"You have any other commitments?" I said, touching her hair.

"I have a lot of chores to do," she said.

I nodded and took my hand away.

"You interrogated me, Billy Bob. I don't care for it," she said.

"Nicki Molinari is a dope dealer and a degenerate. He not only kills people, he has them taken apart."

"You don't have to tell me that. My husband brought him to our house. He used our phone to have a chippy delivered to his motel."

It was not a time to say anything else. In fact, I was tired of playing the fool's role. I picked up my hat and left. When I was driving back out the front gate, I saw her in the rearview mirror, standing in the doorway, her dress blowing across her thighs.

I WENT BACK to Doc's and found Lucas sitting on the front steps, playing his guitar. It was a Martin HD-28, one I had given him for his birthday. The lightest touch of the plectrum on the strings resonated out of the box with the deep, mellow quality of sound that might have been aged in oak.

"Here's one I bet you don't know," he said. Then he began to sing,

> *"I'm an old log hauler,*
> *I drove a big truck.*
> *I shot the pinball machine,*
> *But it caused me bad luck.*
> *All I ever made*
> *On a pinball machine*
> *Was four katty-corners,*
> *Then I'd miss the sixteen."*

He rested his arm across the top of the Martin, careful not to scratch the finish with the button on the cuff of his denim shirt.

"That's one of them old ones," he said.

"Really?" I said, trying not to smile at what he considered old. "Where is everybody?"

"Doc and Maisey had a fight. I don't know where he went, but she took off with some high school boy. Does Maisey act kind of funny for a girl who's been raped?" he said.

"How's that?"

"The way she was dressed and acting. Hoop earrings, fire-engine makeup, one of them bras that—" His eyes went away from mine, as they always did when he felt he had to protect me from his generation's knowledge of the world.

"That what?" I said.

"It don't exactly signal a guy to keep his big-boy in his britches."

"That's how it works, Lucas."

"What works?" he asked.

"Rape victims want to show they still have control. So they try to fly back through the candle flame."

He seemed to study the thought, his fingers chording without sound on the neck of the guitar. "An Indian gal was looking for you," he said.

"Sue Lynn?"

"She didn't say. She has blond streaks in

her hair. What's the deal on her?" He threaded his plectrum through the strings at the top of the guitar neck and adjusted his straw hat and gazed abstractly at the river.

"Why?" I said.

"No reason. She said she liked country music. I was showing her some chords."

"I'd leave her alone."

"She seemed pretty nice."

"She hangs with some bad dudes. Why not keep things simple and enjoy the trout fishing?"

He fed a stick of gum into his mouth and nodded his head slowly, as though humbly agreeing with a profound statement.

"That's how come you been milking through Doc's fence?" he said.

I walked on inside the house and hung my hat on a wood peg and poured a glass of iced tea in the kitchen. Through the front door I could see him putting his guitar inside its case, tucking the cloth strap around its edges, gum snapping in his jaw, his eyes bright with a thought he couldn't handle. He got up from the porch step, the guitar case still open, and came inside.

"I didn't mean to say that."

"I asked for it."

He grinned and spun his hat on his finger. "Who am I to argue with superior minds?" he said.

TEMPLE CARROL had been told the juvenile file on Wyatt Dixon's knife-throwing friend, Terry Witherspoon, had been sealed. But there was another avenue. Temple had written down the name of the small town in western North Carolina where Witherspoon had been convicted, and I called the sheriff's department in the county seat there and asked to talk with any officer on duty who handled juvenile cases.

My call was transferred to a detective named Benbow.

"Terry Witherspoon's a suspect in a murder investigation in Montana?" he said.

"Not exactly."

"Sounds a mite vague, Mr. Holland. Regardless, his records were sealed a long time ago. For all I know they were destroyed when he reached legal age."

"You know him?" I asked.

"I wish I didn't."

"Give me a thread," I said.

"You say you were a Texas Ranger?"

"Yes, sir."

I waited.

"Then you know the rules. Wish I could help," he said, and hung up.

But half an hour later he called back.

"I can't tell you anything about the records

the court has sealed. We clear on that?" he said.

"You bet."

"But I can tell you about suspicions I have that never became part of a formal investigation. A year ago we had a bomber hid out in these mountains. I think Terry was bringing him food. I don't have any evidence to prove that. But I've known Terry since he was seven years old, and he's the meanest little shit I ever came acrost."

"He's hooked up with terrorists?"

"The cause will find Terry, not the other way around. A farmhouse was broken into not far from the caves where this bomber was hid out. The owner and his wife probably came home and surprised the intruder. He tied them both to chairs and stuffed gags in their mouths. Then he cut the woman's throat and shot the man."

"You think Witherspoon did it?"

"The FBI still hasn't caught the bomber. Whoever was feeding him knew every cave in this county. I think the same guy killed the two people in the farmhouse. We have a small population here. To my knowledge, we've produced only one kid around here the likes of Terry Witherspoon. You know what kills me about this stuff, Mr. Holland?"

"What's that?"

"The only job this simpleton ever had was

boxing up groceries at a supermarket. We'll spend our careers getting a net over a box boy."

"You know why he came out to Montana?"

"He said he wanted to be a mountain man in a whites-only nation. Is it true you can buy Montana T-shirts that say 'At Least Our Cows Are Sane'?"

THAT NIGHT, outside a small settlement near the Idaho border, a truncated man with arms that were too short for his torso was carrying everything he owned out of a clapboard house and packing it into his automobile. The moon had just risen above the hollow where the man lived, and the crests of the mountains were black against the sky and the hard-packed dirt road in front of the house wound like a flattened white snake under the railroad trestle, past other dilapidated houses, out to the four-lane highway the man planned to drive full-bore all the way to the Cascades and Seattle.

The man's name was Tommy Lee Stoltz, and he wore a black cowboy hat mashed down on his ears and engineering boots with double soles and heels and thick glasses that made his eyes look like large marbles. Tiny blue teardrops were tattooed just below the corners of his eyes so that he appeared to be in a state of perpetual mourning. The night air was cold but he was sweating inside his clothes and his heart raced each time he heard automobile or truck tires on the dirt road.

Why had he ever left Florida? He'd had a good life dry-walling, hanging in open-air bars down on the beach, getting ripped on beer and cheap weed that was smuggled in from the islands, and opening up his scooter on Seven-Mile Bridge. Even that one-bit he did on a road gang in the Keys wasn't bad. The winter days were beautiful, and the fish was fresh and deep-fried and, if you wanted it, the Cubans on the serving line at the stockade would heap shitpiles of black beans and rice on your plate.

It was in California that his luck did the big flush, over a union card, locked out of the Operating Engineers because he couldn't pass a tenth-grade arithmetic test. Then he got evicted from his hotel in Santa Monica and had to sell his scooter and move into South Central. A Crip shoved him down a stairs. Two Bloods listened to him ask directions to the bus line, then roared at his cracker accent, and tossed him from a fire escape into a Dumpster filled with rotting produce.

Screw that. If he had to live in a toilet, he might as well go native and enjoy it. So he got in on the next Los Angeles riot. The gang-bangers, the illegals, the pipeheads, the out-of-work peckerwoods like himself, everybody on the South Side was burning out the Koreans, looting liquor stores and pawnshops, pulling business types out of their cars and robbing them and busting bottles over their heads, all of it on TV, helicopters swirling overhead while the cops stood behind their own barricades and watched. It was like going apeshit in a war zone, except the other side wasn't allowed to shoot back. There was definitely an upside to slum life and social protest, Tommy Lee told himself.

But after five days of watching the city burn, the Army finally moved in, setting up sandbags and machine guns, herding looters into six-bys. Guess who they nail?

Because he was white, that was it. Three dozen cannibals are running out of the appliance store, carrying TVs and stereo players on their heads, and here he comes, tripping through the broken glass, trying to heft a huge microwave out the window for this black broad who promised she'd haul his ashes if he scored something nice for her kitchen, and *whop,* he gets a baton right across the spine.

Then lands on all fours and watches a .25 auto spill out of his pocket onto the sidewalk.

Next stop, San Quentin, the beaner and melon picker capital of America. Where a short white dude with fishbowl glasses and a hush-puppy accent is anybody's portable pump.

That's when he met Lamar Ellison, out on the yard, Lamar wearing mirrored sunglasses, eyeballing the cannibals, cleaning his nails with a toothpick. "I can put you with the AB, Tommy Lee. They're righteous dudes and they look after their own. You'll walk on water, my man," Lamar said.

You couldn't mistake the AB out on the yard, clanking iron, their bodies glowing with stink, sweat popping on their tattoos, their shaved heads wrapped with blue and red bandannas to show their contempt for the Crips and the Bloods.

Three years in Quentin and not one black dude or East L.A. bean roller ever put a hand on him. No one stole cigarettes or scarf out of his house, and the worst wolf in the joint would emasculate himself before trying to put moves on him in the shower. Business types thought they had respect? Unless you'd been in the Aryan Brotherhood, you didn't know the meaning of the word.

The downside was the nature of the dues. The AB was for life.

He was going to miss Montana. Next week Merle Haggard was playing at the Mule Palace up in the Jocko Valley. Man, he'd like to see that, the Hag, an Okie by way of Bakersfield, who'd done two and one half years at Quentin and was still a legend there, bigger than Cash or Paycheck, living proof you could wear state blues and still reenter the world and get sprinkled with starshine.

He threw the last box of his belongings into his car and went back into the house to unscrew all the lightbulbs, remove the toilet paper roll, and tear out the elk rack the last tenant had left nailed above the living room door.

But no matter how he tried to occupy himself or stay in motion, he could not shake a recurring image out of his head.

It was the Voss girl. With her face pressed down under the pillow, her body writhing, her fists striking at his chest. Why had he let Lamar talk him into busting a sixteen-year-old girl, one who'd dime them all as soon as she could get to a phone?

But secretly he knew the answer. He'd been afraid of Lamar. And not only of Lamar, but of Tommy Lee's father, who'd been a gunbull in the Georgia penal system, of people who made fun of his sawed-off torso, of guys who rode with the Jokers and Outlaws and Angels and Banditos and kept him around like a pet, a motorized goof they sent for cigarettes and beer and sometimes cheap rock down in Boon Town.

In fact, Tommy Lee could not remember when he had not been afraid.

But Lamar had gotten his. Big Time. Soaked in paint thinner and flame-roasted from head to foot like a burned burrito. Man, he didn't want to think about it. Nor about the fact the girl's father was out on bail, a doctor who was some kind of government-trained killing machine.

A doctor who kills people? The illogic of it hurt his head.

Time to slide on down the road, he thought. He stuffed two lightbulbs into his jeans pockets and hefted a box of canned goods on one shoulder and the elk rack on the other and pushed open the front door and stepped out into the coldness of the night.

A hatted figure was standing at the corner of the house, holding a revolver in two hands, the barrel pointed at the ground.

"Who is that?" Tommy Lee said.

There was no answer. The hatted figure raised the revolver at arm's length and aimed, the knees squatting slightly into a classic shooter's position.

Tommy Lee knew that somehow he could make words come out of his mouth that would show the hatted figure he was no threat to anyone, that in the big scheme of things his worst offenses were only those of a motorized goof, a harmless, good-natured little guy the swinging dicks took care of. What did this guy in the hat want? Why didn't the guy say something? Tommy Lee's skin felt as if it were being peeled off his face.

He couldn't keep his thoughts straight. In his mind he saw the farm in Georgia where he had grown up, a girl who had asked him to dance with her at a high school prom, a red molten sun descending into the Gulf of Mexico. He wanted all these things back in his life and would pay any price to return to them. If he could only make that happen, he would correct all the wrongs he had done and make amends to every person he had ever harmed.

If only the hatted figure with the shadowed face would please point the revolver somewhere else.

He had almost formed the sentence that would contain all those thoughts when the pistol barrel exploded with light and sound and the copper-jacketed round punched a neat hole through the right lens of his glasses and blew a single spurt of blood out the back of his head onto the grass.

# Chapter

## 13

SHERIFF J. T. CAIN knocked on Doc's door early the next morning.

"Where were you last night?" he said.

"Here," Doc said.

"All night?"

"Yeah, I was here all night."

"Doing what?" the sheriff said.

"Sleeping."

"You vouch for that?" the sheriff said to me.

"What's this about, Sheriff?" I said.

"Nothing much. Another dead man. Step out here, please," he said to me.

I followed him to his car. The sun wasn't up yet, and fog rose off the boulders in the river and hung in the trees. The sheriff stood with his hands on his hips, his cowboy hat slanted on his head, his wide red tie clipped to his shirt.

"That man in there didn't leave the house last night?" he asked.

"To my knowledge, no."

"To your knowledge, huh? Take a ride with me."

"What for?"

"You defense lawyers spend too much time in your office. I want you to see the handi-work of our shooter."

I got into his car and we rode west of Missoula, up the long grade toward the Idaho line. The mountains were green with Douglas fir, the crests tumbling higher and higher against a salmon-colored sky. Then the Clark Fork dropped away in the canyons below us and finally disappeared from view altogether.

We went through the little town of St. Regis, then turned off the four-lane under a train trestle and entered a hollow traversed by a  dirt road that was dotted with clap-board houses on each side. The yards were strung with washlines and littered with de-bris, like a scene out of Appalachia.

The sheriff had said very little during our journey.

"See all that old growth timber up there? That's the way it used to be everywhere," he said. "We didn't have cyanide in the river and runoff from the clear-cuts destroying the spawning beds. We didn't have no Aryan Nation or Christian Identity or militia people coming in here from Idaho, either. You know why they like it up here in the woods?"

"They're cowards. They fear blacks and Jews and locate in places where they'll never have to face them on equal terms."

He turned his head and stared at me and almost drove us off the road.

"Damn, son, you may have more sense than I give you credit for," he said.

The coroner had been late in arriving at the crime scene and was just finishing his work. Two paramedics were waiting by the road with a gurney. An empty black body bag lay unzipped on top of it.

The impact of the round had blown Tommy Lee Stoltz off the porch and into the yard. A roll of toilet paper from the box of groceries he had been carrying had bounced down the steps and rolled back under the porch into a pool of brown water. Stoltz lay on his back, staring at the sky, his shattered glasses crooked on his face. The right lens was embedded in the eye socket, coated with blood.

The sheriff from Mineral County stooped under the front door and walked out on the porch and looked at me and Sheriff Cain. He had a broad stomach and red face and graying blond hair and mustache. He wore a

sheep-lined vest and a blue baseball cap with
the letters MCSD on it.

"Who's he?" he said to Cain.

"An ex–Texas Ranger along for the ride.
What have you got?" Sheriff Cain said.

"A neighbor heard the shot and looked out
the window and saw somebody in a hat and
a long coat with a chrome-plated pistol. We
didn't find any brass, so the shooter picked it
up or he was using a revolver. I don't think
we'll get much from ballistics. The exit
wound and the splatter tell me that round's
way up on the hillside somewheres. This one
of the guys you pulled in for questioning in
the Voss rape?"

"Yep," Sheriff Cain said.

"Where was the girl's father last night?"

"He says he was at home," Sheriff Cain
said.

"You believe him?"

"I haven't decided," Sheriff Cain said.

"J.T., you quit running these morons into
my jurisdiction," the Mineral County sheriff
said.

"You folks got a lot more room over here,"
Sheriff Cain said.

The Mineral County sheriff lit a pipe and
smoked it out on the road while the paramedics loaded the body into an ambulance. I
was beginning to look at Sheriff Cain in a
new light.

"Why'd you introduce me as an ex-Ranger and not as Doc Voss's attorney?" I asked.

"I felt like it. What do you think Stoltz got hit with?" he said.

"Something big. Probably with a jacket on it."

"A .44 Magnum?"

"Maybe."

"Dr. Voss has got one registered in his name."

"There're .44 Magnums all over this state." And in my mind's eye, I saw the heavy, chrome-plated revolver that Cleo Lonnigan had used to threaten Nicki Molinari at her house. "You really figure Doc for this?"

The sheriff squinted at the sun breaking over the top of the hollow and chewed on the end of a toothpick until it was flat.

"Whoever killed Stoltz just wanted him dead. The person who killed Lamar Ellison wanted him to suffer first. I think we got two different perpetrators," the sheriff said.

"I think you're an intelligent man."

"Your friend ain't off the hook. Come on, let's eat breakfast. I been up since four. I got to find me another job. This morning my old woman told me I'm the reason our grandkids are ugly," he said.

"Doc didn't kill Ellison, Sheriff."

"How do you know?"

"He would have made Ellison fight for his

life. Then he would have cut him from his scrotum to his throat."

"That'll make a fine defense, won't it?" he replied.


FRIDAY EVENING Lucas walked up from his tent on the river and took a shower in Doc's house and was combing his hair in the mirror when I inadvertently opened the bathroom door on him. His cheeks glowed with a fresh shave and his back was white and cuffed with sunburn around the neck.

"Where you headed, slick?" I asked.

"To see Merle Haggard. He's playing at a place called the Mule Palace. You ever been there?" His words were hurried, as though he wanted to distract me from an impending question.

"No, I've never been there. Who you going with?"

"Sue Lynn Big Medicine."

"Tell me, bud, did you come all the way up here to see how much grief you could get into?"

"Since you're already pissed off at me, can I share something else with you?"

"What might that be?" I said.

"I need to borrow your truck," he replied.

Ten minutes later I watched him shine his boots on the porch and slip them on his feet and walk back down to the tent and put on a long-sleeve white cowboy shirt embroidered with roses and his wide-brim cream-colored straw hat, with a scarlet cord around the crown, and climb into my truck and start the engine.

But before he could get out of the yard I waved my hand to stop him. He wore mirrored sunglasses, and I could see my reflection bending down toward him, distorted, a bit comical, the constant deliverer of rhetoric that was meant to compensate for my years of absence as a father.

He waited for me to speak. When I didn't, he said, "What was you gonna say?"

"Nothing. Y'all have a good time."

"Say, you couldn't let me have a ten-spot till I cash a check, could you? Tickets are twenty-five dollars," he said.

I ate supper with Doc and Maisey, then took a walk along the river and threw pinecones into the current and watched them float downstream into the shade. I saw L.Q. Navarro sitting in the fork of a cottonwood tree.

*"Quit picking on that Indian gal,"* he said.

*"She keeps company with people you wouldn't spit on, L.Q. Don't lecture at me."*

*"You got a way of getting upset when that boy takes up with minority people."*

*"That's a dadburn lie."*

*"Then leave him alone."*
*"All right, I will. Just stop pestering me."*
*"Where you goin'?"* L.Q. said.
*"None of your business."*

I walked back to the house and called Temple Carrol at her motel in Missoula.

"You like Merle Haggard?" I asked.

TEMPLE picked me up at Doc's and we drove back down the Blackfoot highway toward Missoula. The sun was still above the mountains in the west, but the bottom of the canyon was already in shadow. When the wind gusted, the leaves of the cottonwoods and aspens along the riverbank flickered like paper against the copperish-green tint of the current.

"Your hot water bottle occupied tonight?" Temple said.

"Pardon?"

"Your girlfriend, the one who works at the clinic on the Reservation."

"I haven't seen her."

"A friend ran her name through NCIC. He got a hit."

"Cleo?"

"Her ex-husband was mobbed up with a gangster named Molinari on the West Coast."

"I know all about it," I said.

"Good," she said, and didn't speak again

until we reached the top of the long timber-lined grade that fed into the Jocko Valley.

The concert was being held outdoors on the edge of the Flathead Indian Reservation. The sun had just gone down behind the mountains, and the hills were plum-colored and the floor of the valley a dark green under a light-filled sky that gave you vertigo when you looked directly up into it. The air was heavy with the cool smell of water in irrigation ditches and the pine trees that were in shadow on the hillsides and the faintly acidic warm odor of mules and horses penned outside the viewing stands. To one side of the stage, concessionaires were grilling sausages and hamburgers on open pits and selling beer and soda pop out of galvanized horse tanks swimming with crushed ice. Merle Haggard had just walked out on the stage with his band, and the crowd on the cement dance slab was shouting, "Hag! Hag! Hag!"

Temple and I sat midway up in the stands. Her cheeks were as red as a doll's, her mouth like a small purple flower, her face glowing with the perfection of the evening. But it was obvious her thoughts were far away.

"I came up to Montana because Doc asked me to. But maybe I should head back to Deaf Smith," she said.

"I need you here, Temple," I said, my eyes looking straight ahead.

"I'm not convinced Doc's an innocent man," she said.

"Guilty or innocent, we still defend him."

"Let me put it another way. You've got a girlfriend with Mob connections. She also has an obsession about this biker gang, the Berdoo Jesters."

"The sheriff told you this?"

"Don't worry about who told me. If you want me to work with you, you'd better haul your head out of your ass."

A drunk cowboy in front of us heard the last statement and turned around and grinned.

"How about saving it till later?" I said to Temple.

"Fine," she replied, and sipped from her soda can, her throat streaked with color.

I touched her on the top of her hand in hopes she would look back at me. But she didn't.

The crowd out on the dance slab was hard-core working class: truck drivers, horse wranglers, waitresses, gypo loggers, Indian feed growers, bale buckers, 4-H kids, women who drank beer with one hand and smoked with the other while they bumped rumps, petty criminals scrolled with jailhouse art, barroom strippers dancing for their own gender with undisguised erotic joy, a group of fist-fighting drunks charter-bused from a saloon, and three Indians who kept squatting down below eye level to inhale huge mouthfuls of white smoke off a crack pipe.

Then I saw my son dancing with Sue Lynn Big Medicine, like kids from the early fifties. She wore a black cowboy hat and a denim shirt with the sleeves cut off at the armpits and black jeans that were dusty in the rump. She danced close to Lucas without actually touching his body, her blond-streaked hair hanging to her shoulders, her chin lifted in the air. With each beat in the music she raised one booted foot behind her, her Roman profile opaque, the brim of his hat touching hers when he leaned over her, his shadow like a protective screen between her and the glare of the world.

"You going to talk to me at all?" I said to Temple.

She finished her soda and set the empty can between us. She seemed to concentrate on the stage. "Was Haggard really in the pen?" she said.

"Yeah, Quentin or Folsom."

"I don't think he's the only graduate here. Take a look at that bunch by the side of the stage," she said.

Three head-shaved, bare-chested young men, wearing laced, steel-toed boots and bleached jeans without belts, were drinking canned beer and watching the dancers from the edge of the cement slab. Their skin was

jailhouse white, emblazoned with swastikas
and red and black German crosses, their torsos plated and tapered with the muscle devel-
opment of dedicated, on-the-yard bench
pressers. Each wore a stubble mustache and
goatee, so that his mouth looked like a dirty
hole leering out of the whiteness of his face.

"Is that Carl Hinkel with them?" Temple
said.

"That's the man. The George Lincoln
Rockwell of the Bitterroot Valley."

Then two other men walked from the rest
room area and joined them. One was a slender kid with glasses and a crooked smile on
his mouth, an ever-present facial insult that
allowed him to offend others without giving
them sufficient provocation to tear him
apart. His companion had large, wide-set
teeth and virtually colorless eyes and wore a
flowered green shirt with purple garters on
the sleeves, a polished rodeo buckle against
his corrugated stomach, and new, stiff jeans
that were hitched tightly around his genitalia.

Temple was watching my face.

"What's wrong?" she asked.

"That's Wyatt Dixon. I can't think of a
worse time for that guy to show up."

Dixon had seen Lucas and Sue Lynn out on
the dance slab. He put a cigar into his mouth
and popped a kitchen match on his thumbnail and cupped the flame to the cigar in the

shadow of his hat. He stood duck-footed, smoking, an amused light in his face, and watched Lucas and Sue Lynn dance. Then he walked out onto the slab, his shoulders pushing aside anyone who chanced to move into his path.

When, as a father, do you intervene in your son's life and perhaps steal his self-respect? I'd never had an answer to that question.

"I'll be back," I said to Temple, and walked down the wood stairs onto the cement slab.

Dixon stood inches from Lucas and Sue Lynn, his back to me, saying something I couldn't hear. But I saw the heat climb into Sue Lynn's face and the bewilderment in Lucas's.

"You want to talk to me, Mr. Dixon?" I said.

He screwed his head around, his cigar clenched in his teeth, his profiled right eye like a clear glass bubble.

"I declare, people from all walks of life has shown up here tonight. It ain't accident you and the boy favor, is it?" he said.

"How about I buy you a beer?" I said.

"No, thank you, sir. I aim to dance. Sue Lynn don't mind. She and me has bellied up before in what you might call private-type situations."

Lucas's hat was pushed back on his head and his hands hung awkwardly at his sides.

There were red circles, like apples, in his cheeks.

"What's with you, man?" he said to Wyatt Dixon.

"I'm a great admirer of womanhood, son. I respect every part of their God-made bodies, and this 'un here done won my heart a long time ago. Now go over yonder and sit down and drink you a soda pop. Ask your daddy to tell you about my sister, Katie Jo Winset. Her fate was a great Texas tragedy."

Dixon reached out with two forked knuckles toward Lucas's nose, but Lucas stepped backward and slapped Dixon's hand away, disbelieving the insult to his person even as it took place. Dixon smiled and glanced toward the purple glow on the hills, breathing in the heavy fragrance of the evening, then lowered his hand between Lucas and Sue Lynn and fastened it on Lucas's scrotum. That's when Lucas hit him.

The blow knocked Dixon's hat off his head, but the grin never left his face.

"I still got your package in my hand, boy. You want, I can tear it out root and stem," he said.

I swung my fist into Dixon's ear but it was like hitting stone. He turned his head slowly toward me, his ear bleeding, his right hand tightening on my son's genitalia.

"I'm gonna come for you, Mr. Holland.

You'll smell me in the dark, then you'll feel my hand fasten on you, and the next day you'll be somebody else," he said.

I swung my fist into his mouth and felt the edges of his teeth cut into my skin. Then his friends were upon me.

The fight rolled through the concession area. I can't describe what happened with any certitude, because since I have been a young boy anger has always affected me in the same way whiskey does a drunkard. I would hear whirring sounds in my ears, then I would be inside a dead zone filled with shards of red and yellow light, a place where I felt neither physical pain nor any form of moral restraint.

I remember being knocked into the side of a horse tank, of hearing hooves thudding inside the livestock pens, then picking up a shaved wooden pole, about four foot in length, and smashing it into the face of a man who had a swastika tattooed between his eyes. I kicked a man who was on the ground, hard, in the spleen, and again in the head. Women were screaming, an overweight rent-a-cop was flung into a water puddle, and I swung the wood pole like a baseball bat and saw blood fly against the canvas side of a tepee and saw the man I'd hit fall on his knees and weep.

But it was Wyatt Dixon I wanted. As in a dream, I flailed at my attackers, but the source of my rage stood on the edge of the fray and grinned, adjusting the garters on his sleeves, one ear leaking a scarlet line down his jawbone.

The rent-a-cop struggled to his feet from the water puddle, wheezing for breath, his uniform flecked with mud. The strap on his revolver had popped loose and the checkered handle protruded loosely from the holster, the heavy, brass-cased rounds fat and snug inside the cylinder.

I pushed someone out of the way and reached for the revolver. Then I heard horse's hooves and suddenly the side of an enormous buckskin mare knocked me senseless into a rick fence.

I stared up from the ground at the silhouette of the rider. He was huge, the backs of his hands traced with scar tissue, his face a mixture of pity and incomprehension.

"I ain't playing with you, son. I'll whip you with a blackjack if I have to," he said.

Then I felt the world come back into focus and saw Temple and Lucas bending down toward me, touching me with their hands.

"Why, how you doin', Sheriff?" I said to the man on horseback. "You like Merle Haggard?"

# Chapter

## 14

❦

MY WRISTS were cuffed behind my back, and I was put in a holding cell at the county jail, where I stayed, without being booked, until early the next morning.

Sheriff Cain walked down the corridor behind a trusty who was wheeling a food cart from cell to cell. The sheriff picked up a Styrofoam container of scrambled eggs and tiny sausages and a cup of coffee and a cellophane-wrapped plastic fork from the tray and set them on the apron of the food slit.

"Them three skinheads you whacked with that pole are still in the hospital," he said.

"Gee, I'm sorry to hear that," I replied.

"I was gonna ride in the parade last night. I was really looking forward to it. Somebody should glue warning labels on you. You're a traveling shit storm."

"Do I get out of here?"

"You got a bloodlust, Mr. Holland. I seen it in your face."

"I don't apologize for it."

"Then I hope you can live with it, 'cause it'll plumb eat you up. A federal agent wants to talk with you. When he's done, I'll kick you loose," the sheriff said, and walked away heavily, like a man who knew his knowledge of the world would never have an influence upon it.

I sat down on the bench in the cell and drank from the Styrofoam coffee cup. Amos Rackley, the ATF agent who had told me he'd break my nose off if I put it in government business again, walked to the cell door and propped his arms across a horizontal iron plate, then removed them and dusted off his sleeves.

His face was smooth-grained and handsome, his sandy hair neatly parted. He took a ballpoint pen from his shirt pocket and kept clicking the button on top with his thumb.

"Can you explain to me what your son is doing with Sue Lynn Big Medicine?" he said.

"Dancing, the last time I saw her."

"You were an officer of the federal court. You know how our operations work. You know the danger that certain individuals are exposed to. Where's your judgment, man?"

I set the Styrofoam cup down on the bench and stood up. My khakis and leather jacket and boots were powdered with dust, my body sore and stiff all over from the fight at the concert.

"Y'all are still after the Oklahoma City bombers. You don't care about the rape of a teenage girl. You don't care about the assault on my son's person. You lost friends in the Murrah Building and I can understand the feelings you have now. So I don't want you to take it personally when I tell you to go play with your pencils and stay out of my life."

He bit his lip and looked down the corridor at nothing, then fixed his eyes on me again.

"You know what I wish, Mr. Holland? That I could forget who I was for just ten minutes and stomp the living shit out of you," he said.

TWO NIGHTS LATER Doc was in Missoula, buying groceries, when an electric storm rolled up the Blackfoot canyon. Bolts of lightning crashed on the ridges above the house, bursting ponderosa trees into small fires that flared and died in the rain. Then the storm passed and the rain stopped and black clouds sealed the sky, flickering with lightning that gave no thunder. Just above the river, the mountainsides were hung with mist, the air sweet with smoke from woodstove pine.

Bears had been in the garbage before sunrise that same day and had pushed against the windows with their paws, trying to slide the glass. Now a sow and two cubs came down out of the trees on the far side of the river and waded into the shallows and crossed the deepest part of the current by jumping from boulder to boulder until they lumbered belly-deep into the water on the near side and walked dripping up the bank past the garden.

Maisey went into the bathroom and undressed for her shower, then heard the garbage cans rattle. She rubbed the moisture off the window glass and looked out at the log barn and saw the bears ripping the bungee cords off the garbage can tops and pulling the vinyl bags out with their teeth. One of the cubs dug into a split bag and flung the garbage backward through his hindquarters.

She got into the shower and stayed under the hot water until her skin was red. When she toweled off, the window was clouded with steam and she thought she saw a bear's paw push and flatten against the glass. She wrapped the towel around her head and approached the window, leaned one way and then the other in order to see outside, then used her arm to wipe a swath through the moisture on the glass.

The face of a young man stared back at her. He wore glasses and his eyes traveled the length of her nakedness and his mouth formed a red oval as though he wanted to speak.

From the living room I heard her scream, then the sound of feet running outside. I pulled Doc's sporterized '03 Springfield from the gun rack and went out the front door and around the side of the house. Dry lightning jumped between the clouds and the valley floor turned white. I saw a slender man run past the barn, toward the river.

I slid a round into the chamber and locked down the bolt, wrapped the leather sling around my left arm, and put the Springfield to my shoulder. I aimed through the iron sights, leading the target just slightly, waiting for lightning to leap between the clouds again.

Maybe he had seen me, because he seemed to know that someone had locked down on him. He jumped a rock fence like a deer, then zigzagged across a field, glancing back once as though a round was about to nail him between the shoulder blades. When the clouds pulsed with lightning I saw the reflection on his glasses, his brown hair, his body that was as lithe and supple as a young girl's.

I swung the rifle's sights ahead of him and fired a single round that whined off a rock into the darkness.

The running figure disappeared into the trees.

Maisey came out on the porch in her robe, the towel still wrapped on her head.

"He was at the bathroom window. He was watching me take a shower," she said.

"Did you recognize him?" I asked.

"The glass was steamed over. I saw him for just a second."

"Maybe he just wandered in off the highway," I said, my eyes avoiding hers. I ejected the spent shell from the rifle and pressed down the rounds in the magazine with my thumb and slid the bolt over them so the chamber remained empty, then propped the rifle against the porch rail and traced the footprints of the voyeur from the bathroom window back to a rick fence he had climbed through by the barn.

A fuel can lay on its side by the bottom rail of the fence, leaking gas into the mud.

I called the sheriff's department. A half hour later a tall, overworked deputy with a black mustache walked with me out to the fence and looked down at the can and then at the house. His breath fogged in the dampness of the air.

"He didn't come here to borrow gas. The can's almost full. He was watching the girl through the window?" he said.

"Yes."

"It looks like he was going to torch your

house and got distracted. I'd say you're lucky."

"I don't think the Voss family feels lucky, sir," I said.

"No offense meant. Some people around here would have shot him and drug his body through the door. Who do you think he was?"

"Y'all got a file on a kid from North Carolina by the name of Terry Witherspoon?"

WEDNESDAY MORNING Doc answered the cordless phone in the kitchen, then handed it to me and walked out of the room.

"I'm trying to figure out what your idea of a relationship is. I'm sure the problem is mine," Cleo's voice said.

"I'm sorry?"

"Just for a minute, can't you lose that obtuse attitude?"

"I haven't called you? That's what we're talking about?"

"What do you think?" she asked.

"I figured I'd struck out."

"Maybe you decided you'd just find another chickie and cut a new notch on your gun."

"I don't think that's a real good thing to say, Cleo."

"Then maybe we need to have a serious talk."

"What do you call this?" I said.

"Come to the house."

"I have an appointment at the sheriff's office."

"Screw your appointment," she said.

"I'm going to hang up now. Good-bye, Cleo."

I eased the receiver down in the cradle, my skin tingling, as though I had just walked through a cobweb.

DOC WAS BOARDING an Appaloosa and a thoroughbred for a neighbor. I went outside and propped my forearms across the top rail of the rick fence that enclosed the horse lot and began to shave an apple with my pocketknife. The barn was made of ancient logs that were soft with decay. Through the open back doors I saw both horses walk out of the pasture, through the cool darkness of the barn, their hooves powdering dust in the air, sawing their heads as they approached the fence.

I quartered the apple and fed pieces to each of them with the flat of my hand. Inside the barn, his pinstripe suit and ash-gray Stetson slatted with sunlight, I saw L.Q. Navarro perched atop a stall, idly spinning the rowel on a Mexican spur.

*"You're getting sucked in, bud,"* he said.

*"With Cleo?"*

*"I'm talking about these skinheads and bik-
ers. Doc was trying to shut down that gold
mine. Now he's charged with murder and
you're rolling in the dirt with a collection of
tattooed pissants whose mothers was probably knocked up by a spittoon."*

*"I didn't have much selection about it,
L.Q."*

*"That's what we told each other when we
was blowing feathers off them Mexican drug
mules."*

*"Anything else you want to tell me?"*

He flicked the rowel on the spur and lifted
his eyes.

*"I'd sure like a couple of ice-cold Carta
Blancas,"* he said.

I WENT BACK UP on the front porch,
where Doc was trying to tie a blood knot in a
tapered leader. But it was obvious he could not
concentrate on the task at hand. He squinted
at the tippets, missed threading a nylon tip
through a loop, then gave it up and dropped
the leader on top of a cloth creel by his foot.

"Can you show me all the information you
have on that mining company?" I said.

"What for?"

"They have a vested interest in seeing you
jammed up."

"I remodeled Lamar Ellison's face in that

bar. I got my daughter raped. I thought I was through with free-fire zones. Instead, I carried one back from Vietnam."

"Don't put this on yourself, Doc."

"That stuff you want is out in the barn. You can burn it when you're finished," he said.

I spent the next two hours rooting through the cardboard boxes that Doc had stuffed with news clippings and documents on extractive industries in Montana. File folders filled with aerial photographs showed miles of clear-cuts and once-virgin wilderness areas that had been turned into stump farms or chemical soup. Networks of creeks that fed the upper Blackfoot River looked like gangrene in living tissue. The cumulative damage wasn't just bad. It numbed the mind.

The corporation name that recurred again and again was Phillips-Carruthers, old-time union busters whose goons had once loaded Wobblies onto cattle cars and transported them in 115-degree heat into the Arizona–New Mexico desert and left then locked inside without water for two days. Those who didn't die or end up in Yuma Territorial Prison as syndicalists thought twice about trying to shut down a Phillips-Carruthers mine again.

How far would a bunch like this be willing to go in order to get Doc off the board?

I heard the tinkling sound of roweled spurs on the plank floor of the barn and looked up and saw L.Q. Navarro peering over my shoulder.

*"There's a story in there about Woody Guthrie and his buds going up against that company in 1947,"* he said.

*"These are the guys we love to hate. It's too easy, L.Q.,"* I said.

*"John D.'s hired thugs killed my grand-mother at the Ludlow Massacre in 1914. Wasn't no mystery to it,"* he said.

*"The bad guys are a lot slicker today,"* I said.

*"They ain't no slicker, son. The good guys are just dumber."*

I started to smile at his joke, but then looked at his face. He was staring out the back of the barn at the thoroughbred and Appaloosa in the pasture, an unrelieved glint of sadness in his eyes. The horses were grazing next to a ribbon-like stream that wound through Indian paintbrush and harebells, tearing at the grass, their tails switching across their rumps.

*"What are you studying on?"* I asked.

He shook the moment out of his face. *"Remember when we chased that bunch of coke mules across the sand flats? We painted red flowers all over those stovepipe cactus. We took a rum flask out of a dead man's pocket and had a drink and poured the rest on his face. You miss it sometimes?"* he said.

"*No,*" I replied.

L.Q. pulled his Stetson down over his brow and turned away from me to hide the gentle reproach in his eyes. When I looked at him again he had gone.

I don't miss it. I know I don't, I said to myself as I walked back toward the house, like the alcoholic on his way to the saloon, denying the nature of his own insatiable desires.

"Talking to yourself?" a voice said from the porch.

"Oh, hi, Maisey, I didn't see you there," I said.

"No kidding?" she said. She wore makeup and khakis and sandals and a low-cut embroidered white peasant blouse and looked older than her years. She picked up an oversize can of beer that was wrapped in a paper bag. She salted the top and drank from it.

"Where's your old man?" I asked.

"In town."

"Early in the morning for a cold one, isn't it?"

"Billy Bob?"

"Yes?"

"Mind your own business. By the way, Lucas said to tell you he was going down to the Milltown Bar with Sue Lynn Big Medicine to see about a job in the band. You want a beer?"

THE MILLTOWN BAR was a legendary clapboard blue-collar anachronism squeezed between river shacks and railroad tracks and a sawmill at the southern tip of the Blackfoot Valley.

Lucas had no trouble getting a four-night-a-week slot in the house band. Besides guitar, he could sing and play banjo, mandolin, fiddle, Dobro, and stand-up bass. Also, he didn't bother to ask the bar owner how much he would be paid.

It should have been a fine morning for Lucas. It wasn't. This was the first time he'd seen Sue Lynn Big Medicine since the fight at the dance up in the Jocko. But she didn't act the same anymore. She seemed disconnected, her gaze lingering on his only momentarily, like somehow the fact she was two years older had suddenly become important.

Outside the bar, while he fitted his guitar case into the backseat of her car, he said, "Something wrong, Sue Lynn?"

"Not in a way you can do anything about," she replied.

"I see. There's a problem, but I'm too young or dumb to understand it?"

"Your father doesn't want me around you. He's probably right."

"That's just Billy Bob. You watch. He'll be taking us out to dinner."

But he might as well have been talking to the wind. She started the car, and they drove along the highway, past the sawmill, through the willow-lined streets of Bonner. The car had no windshield and Sue Lynn's hair kept whipping in her face.

He looked at her Roman profile, the coffee-and-milk color of her skin, a threadlike white scar on her cheek, the soft purple hue of her mouth. He wanted to touch her, but her silence and the roar of the gutted muffler against the asphalt fed his irritation and ineptitude.

"Why do you drive a junker like this, anyway?" Lucas said.

"Because I live in a junkyard. Because the government tells me what I have to do. Because I don't have choices about my life," she said.

Her hands had tightened on the wheel. When she looked over at him her eyes were blazing.

"Pull over," he said.

"No!"

"Stop acting like you got to talk in code. It's a real drag, Sue Lynn," he said, and grabbed the wheel so that the car drove across the opposite lane onto a flat turnaround above a sandy beach that flanged the Blackfoot River.

"I made a mistake. I shouldn't have gone to the dance with you. Wyatt Dixon and Carl Hinkel and their friends are animals. They'll tear you in pieces," she said.

"Back home their kind are a dime a tote sack."

"You're just a boy. You don't know what you're talking about."

She got out of the car. He thought she was going to kick the door, but instead she stared silently at the river, the wind blowing her hair in her face, a look of regret in her eyes that he couldn't explain.

"I'm sorry for getting mad. I like you a lot, Sue Lynn. But I ain't no kid and you got to stop talking to me like I am one," he said.

"I'm not who you think I am, Lucas. I'm not a good person," she said.

She walked down a footpath to the beach. Five college boys in swim trunks were sitting in the shadow of a huge egg-shaped rock, drinking beer and sailing a red Frisbee out on the river for a mongrel dog to retrieve. Each time the dog brought back the Frisbee, one of the boys would give it a piece of hamburger bun.

Lucas caught up with Sue Lynn by the water's edge. The Frisbee sailed like a dinner plate past her head and landed far out in the current. The dog splashed into the water and swam after it. Its back was lesioned with mange, its ribs etched against its sides.

"What gives you the right to be saying you're no good? That's like telling folks who believe in you they're stupid," Lucas said.

"I'm going to drive you back home now," she said.

"Billy Bob give me two tickets to the Joan Baez concert at the university," he lied.

"I'm glad I met you, Lucas, but I'm not going to see you again."

"That's a rotten damn way to be," he replied.

"One day it'll make sense to you."

"Right," he said.

The dog had just returned the Frisbee to one of the college boys and was trying to nose a piece of bread out of the sand. The dog was trembling with exhaustion, the wet hair on its hindquarters exposing the emaciated thinness of its legs. The college boy flung the Frisbee through the air again. It plopped on top of the riffle and floated downstream.

"Just a minute," Lucas said to Sue Lynn.

He waded into the river and picked up the Frisbee and walked to the shade of the rock, where the college boys were sitting on blankets with an ice chest set among them. They were suntanned and hard-muscled, innocently secure in the knowledge that membership in a group of people such as themselves meant that age and mortality would never hold sway in their lives.

"This dog's wore out. If you want to feed him, why not just do it? Don't make him drown hisself to get a little food," Lucas said.

One of the boys propped himself up on his elbow and squinted into the sun with one eye.

"You think that up all by yourself?" he asked.

"It's five of y'all, one of me. I know what you can do. But don't torment a dumb animal," Lucas said.

One of the other boys removed his sunglasses and started to his feet, sand sifting off of his body. But the boy who was propped on one elbow put a hand on his friend's arm.

"You got a point. Why don't *you* feed him?" he said, and tossed a sack of lunch trash to Lucas.

Lucas started up the trail, then knelt and gave the dog a half-eaten weenie.

"Hey, buddy, what's your name?" the college boy yelled after him.

"Lucas Smothers."

"How about throwing our Frisbee back, Lucas Smothers?"

Lucas sailed it through the air, then picked

up the dog under the stomach and put it into the backseat of Sue Lynn's car.

Sue Lynn had watched it all without saying a word. Now she was staring at him with a strange light in her face, pushing her hair out of her eyes, tilting her chin up as though she were having a conversation with herself.

"What's wrong?" he asked.

"Nothing," she said.

"I'd better get home. Billy Bob gets in trouble if I ain't around."

"You want to drive?" she asked.

"I don't mind."

They headed up the highway, following the Blackfoot, through timbered canyons and meadowland, through sunlight and shady areas where springwater leaked across the asphalt. The dog was already sound asleep on the backseat. Sue Lynn moved closer to Lucas and took his right hand off the steering wheel and held it in hers.

When he looked over at her, her gaze was focused straight ahead, her eyes sleepy with thoughts he couldn't fathom.

Tell me women ain't a puzzle, he thought.

# Chapter

## 15

THE NEXT DAY I drove to a Catholic church in Missoula's university district. The chapel area was empty, the confessional booths stacked with furniture. A secretary in the pastor's office told me I could find the pastor at his home down the street. I walked a block under maple trees to a tan stucco house with a neat yard and tulip beds and saw a tall man in an undershirt and black trousers up on the roof.

"Can I help you?" he said, peering down through an overhang of maple leaves.

"I'd like to go to Reconciliation," I replied.

"You have a problem with heights?"

I climbed the ladder and joined him in a flat, sunless place where he had hung his tool bag on the chimney and was eating his lunch. The blueness of the sky overhead looked like a river through a gap in the canopy of the maple trees, as though the earth were turned upside down and we were viewing a riparian landscape from high above.

The priest's name was Hogan and he offered me a sandwich from his lunch sack. He talked politely for a moment, then realized the origin of my awkwardness with the ritual that Catholics today call Reconciliation.

"You're not a cradle Catholic?" he asked.

"I was baptized by immersion in a fundamentalist church when I was a child. I became a convert after the loss of a friend."

"You want to tell me what's bothering you?"

"I went to bed with a woman. It was self-serving act, impulsive and badly thought out," I said.

"I'm getting the sense things didn't turn out as you planned."

"That's an understatement, sir."

"I'm not quite sure what we're owning up to here. You mean you acted lustfully or you feel you've used somebody, or you simply regret getting involved with the wrong person?"

"How about all of the above?"

"I see."

"I've done this previously. For reasons that mask a more grave sin in my past."

"I'm not sure I follow," he said.

In the silence I could hear the maple branches sweeping against the roof.

"I accidentally shot and killed my best friend. I did this while we were killing other men. His death is with me morning and night. His specter never leaves me," I said.

The face of the priest remained impassive, but he lowered his eyes so I could not see the sadness in them.

"Is there anything else you want to tell me?" he asked.

"No, sir."

He placed one hand on my shoulder. "You all right, partner?" he said.

"Right as rain," I said, hoping he would not hold my lie against me.

THAT AFTERNOON a waxed, black car drove through the field behind Doc's house and parked in front, the sunlight wobbling like a yellow flame on the tinted windows.

Amos Rackley, the ATF agent, got out of the passenger seat and knocked on the door with his fist, rattling a picture on the wall. He wore shades and a dark suit that seemed to contain and intensify the heat and energy in his body. His gum snapped in his mouth and his jawbone was slick with perspiration.

When I opened the door, he said, "It must be the genes."

"What?"

"Your family. Like a stopped-up commode that keeps overflowing on the floor. First I have trouble with you. Now your kid."

"What are you talking about?"

"We sent somebody to ring the doorbell at a certain Indian gal's house. Guess who answers the door?"

"Lucas?"

"Not wearing shirt or shoes. With long red scratches on his back. I'm surprised he took time to zip his fly."

"You guys should have had jobs at Salem in 1692. You would have fit right in," I said.

"You listen, you arrogant prick . . ."

But he was so angry he couldn't talk. He took the gum out of his mouth and stuck it on a post and opened a folder full of eight-by-ten photographs. They showed blood-streaked people being lifted from rubble, a woman crying with a dead child in her arms, a white police officer giving mouth-to-mouth to a black man on a stretcher.

"That's the Alfred P. Murrah Building, motherfucker," he said. "I'm betting my career this shit goes back to Hayden Lake, Idaho. But you and now your son have decided to factor yourself in, either because you've got cooze on the brain or you just can't stand to let things alone. So why don't we just walk out in the woods here, you and me, and see what develops? I can't tell you how much I'd enjoy that."

I stepped out on the porch. The day was bright, the wind cold on my face in the shade.

"My son has nothing to do with your investigation. His interest in Sue Lynn Big Medicine is romantic. You were that age once. Why don't you show a little empathy?" I said.

"That's a great word coming from a disgraced Ranger who killed his own partner. I changed my mind about you, Mr. Holland. I wouldn't dirty my hands fighting a man like you. You turn my stomach."

When he drove away I could feel my eyes filming, the ridgeline and ponderosa and cliffs distorting into green and yellow shapes. I wanted to turn and see L.Q. standing by the barn or down in the shade of the cottonwoods by the river or perched atop a rail by the horse lot.

"*L.Q.?*" I said.

But there was no reply except the wind in the trees.

TOWARD EVENING Maisey and I saddled the Appaloosa and thoroughbred that Doc boarded for his neighbors and rode them up a switchback logging road in the hills behind the house. In the distance we could see old clear-cuts and burned stumps along the sides of the Rattlesnake Mountains.

"I overheard what that Treasury agent said to you this morning, Billy Bob. Why'd you let him get away with that?" she said.

"He lost his friends in Oklahoma City. He can't do anything about it, so he takes his grief out on others. That's the way it is sometimes."

"My father says under it all you're a violent man."

"I have been. That doesn't mean I am today."

"The sheriff called this morning. He wants to talk to my father again."

"What for?"

"The third man who raped me is dead. I'm glad. I hope he suffered when he died," she said. Her face was narrow with anger, her mouth pinched with an unrelieved bitterness.

"Maisey, I can't argue with your feelings, but—"

"Don't say anything, Billy Bob. Just please don't say anything."

She turned her horse away from me and rode into the shade, then dismounted and began picking huckleberries and putting them into her hat, even though they were green and much too sour to eat.

Down below I saw the sheriff's cruiser pull into the yard.

I RODE the thoroughbred down the hill and took off my hat and looked at the greenness of the country and grinned at the sheriff and waited for him to explain the cloud in his face.

"I don't care to look up at a man on horseback," he said.

I got down from the saddle and hung my hat on the pommel and tied the reins to the porch railing. I let my hand trail off the thoroughbred's rump, my eyes fixed on the sheriff's.

"Where was the good doctor yesterday afternoon?" he said.

"I don't know. Ask him," I replied.

"I would. If I could find him." The sheriff stood by the open door of his vehicle, his face cut by light and shadow, the wind flapping his coat. "The third suspect in Miss Voss's rape was pulled out of a river two days ago in Idaho. He had chest waders on and was submerged standing up in the bottom of a pool like a man with concrete boots on."

"Sounds like an accident to me," I said.

"Except he wasn't carrying no fishing gear, never owned a fishing license, and was never known to fish. Also, most sane people don't wear chest waders in July."

"Well, we'll all try to feel as bad as possible about his passing, Sheriff."

"I love to hear you talk, Mr. Holland. Every time you open your mouth I'm convinced this is indeed a great country, that absolutely any little dimwit can become an attorney. Tell Dr. Voss to call me before I come out here and put him in handcuffs."

I watched his cruiser drive across the field behind the house, then disappear down the dirt road. A half hour later my head was still pounding with his remarks. I called him at his office.

"Did you bother to check out this kid Terry Witherspoon?" I asked.

"The voyeur? Yeah, I did. He says he never looked in Maisey Voss's window and was never on her property."

"What did you expect him to say? Did you lift any prints off that gas can?"

"Lab work on peeping Tom complaints? Yeah, we got time for that. When we ain't busting up crack labs and trying to keep them goddamn Crips out of here."

"I really don't like being your straight man, Sheriff."

"Son, you were born for it. Lord God, I wish you people would move to Los Angeles," he said, and hung up.

TEMPLE CARROL picked me up at Doc's house the next morning, and we drove into Missoula for breakfast. She wore khakis and scuffed boots and a yellow pullover, and because of her short height she steered with her chin tilted slightly upward. She was one of those women whose contradictions made both her admirers and her adversaries misjudge her potential.

Her eyes were a milky green that changed color when she was angry, as though dark smoke swam inside them, and she had a distracting habit of chewing gum or piling her hair on top of her head while I talked to her, as though she were not listening. Then I would discover days later she could repeat a conversation back to me, word for word, and accurately correct my own memory of it.

She kick-boxed on a heavy bag every day at a gym in Deaf Smith and could touch the floor with the flats of her hands. She was often dirty from work in her garden, the seat of her shorts grass-stained, her hair full of leaves, her body glowing with sweat and the smell of crushed flowers. She cared nothing for other people's opinions, thought politics were foolish, kept guns all over her house, and fed every stray animal on the west side of the county. Anyone who mistook her eccentricities for weakness and crossed a line with her did so only once.

As I looked at the pinkness of her skin, the baby fat on her arms, the way a strand of her chestnut hair kept blowing in her eye, I wanted to touch her, to place the back of my hand on the heat of her cheek, to rest my arm across her shoulders. As she drove along the river, through the blueness of the morning, her profile and the angle of her mouth contained all the innocence and loveliness of a high school girl waiting to be kissed, and I felt ashamed of my own impulses and all the times I had been cavalier about her loyalty and friendship.

But try as I might, I always did or said the wrong thing with Temple Carrol.

"You have a reason for staring at me?" she said.

"Sorry," I said.

"I get the feeling you're in a confessional mood about something," she said.

"Excuse me?"

"I was jogging by the campus yesterday. I happened to see you on the roof of a house with another man."

"Really?" I said.

"The postman told me that's the home of a

Catholic priest. Are we using the clergy again
to rinse out our latest affair?"

"How about some slack, Temple?"

"I'd like to break your damn neck," she
replied, and gave me a look. "I interviewed
your Dr. Pisspot yesterday. You can really
pick them."

"You did what?"

"I went out to Cleo Lonnigan's house.
God's gift to the Red Man. She seems to
think she glows with blue fire."

"You shouldn't have done that."

"She thinks those bikers killed her child.
That makes her a viable murder suspect. By
the way, I wouldn't waste my energies being
protective of her. She seems to put you on a
level with the Antichrist."

"I shouldn't have gotten involved with her.
It was my fault. She's not a bad person."

"I don't think you're chivalric, Billy Bob.
You're just real dumb sometimes," she said.
When she looked at me the milky green color
of her eyes had darkened but not with anger.
The depth of injury in them, like a stone
bruise down in the soul, made me swallow
with shame.

FIVE MINUTES after I returned to Doc's
the phone rang in the living room.

"Hello?" I said.

"Where have you been?" Cleo Lonnigan's voice said.

"Out."

"Then why don't you get a message machine?" she asked.

"Because it's not my home."

"Did you send that nasty little bitch up to my ranch?" she said.

"What did you say?"

"*Ms.* Carrol. Is she house-trained?"

"You keep your mouth off her, Cleo."

"Do you think you can take a woman to bed and then just say, 'Drop dead, I'm busy color-matching my socks right now'?"

"Good-bye, Cleo. You're an amazing woman. I hope I never see you again," I said, and gently hung up the phone.

I went outside so I would not have to hear the phone ring when she called back.


I WALKED through the cottonwoods and aspens on the riverbank. The river was in shadow under the canopy, but the sun had risen above the ridge and the boulders in the center of the current were steaming in the light. I saw L.Q. Navarro squatting down on his haunches in the shallows, scraping a hellgrammite off the bottom of a rock with the blade of his pocketknife. The bottoms of his

suit pants were dark with water, his teeth
white with his grin. He threaded the hellgrammite onto a hook that hung from a fishing
pole carved out of a willow branch.

*"The last couple of days been hard on your
pride?"*

*"You might say that."*

*"Next time that ATF agent smarts off, you
bust his jaw. I never could abide them federal
types."*

*"What am I going to do with Cleo Lonni-
gan?"*

*"Get out of town?"*

*"That's not funny."*

*"It wasn't meant to be."*

Then his attention wandered, as it often did
when I imposed all my daily concerns upon
him. His hellgrammite had slipped off the
hook in the current, and he waded deeper
into the water, into the shade, and lifted up a
heavy rock from the bed and set it down on
top of a boulder and scraped another hellgrammite from the moss-slick underside.

*"Hand me my pole, will you, bud?"* he
said.

I picked up the willow branch he had
shaved clean of leaves and notched at one
end for his line and walked into the stream
with it. The current, filled with snowmelt,
climbed over my knees and struck my geni-
tals like a hammer. The sunlight had gone

and the tunnel of trees suddenly seemed as cold as the grave.

I realized L.Q. was looking beyond me, at someone on the bank. Then L.Q. was gone and in his place a huge hatch of pink and dark-winged salmon flies churned over the current.

"You always get in the water with your clothes on, Mr. Holland? Hand me your stick and I'll pull you out," Nicki Molinari said from the bank, his cigarette smoke leaking like a piece of cotton from his mouth.

# Chapter
# 16

NICKI MOLINARI wore leather hiking shorts rolled tightly around his thighs, alpine climbing shoes with red laces and heavy lugs, and a purple polo shirt scissored off below his nipples. A nest of scars, like pink string, was festooned on his skin between one hip and his rib cage. On his left hand was a sunbleached fielder's glove with a scuffed baseball gripped inside the pocket.

His eyes searched up and down the tunnel of trees, as though he heard voices in the wind.

"Were you talking to somebody out here?" he asked.

I saw his convertible parked in the sunshine. His men were nowhere around.

"What do you want?" I asked.

"That skank up in the Jocko Valley owes me seven hundred grand. I'll pay you a ten percent finder's fee if you can get it out of her."

"The skank is Cleo Lonnigan?"

"The language I use offends your sensibilities, that's too bad. Her husband was the business partner of some associates of mine. He stiffed them, they stiffed me. I ended up in Terminal Island. The shorter version is I got cluster-fucked eight ways from breakfast and that broad is living on a horse ranch bought with my money."

"Not interested," I said.

He flipped the baseball into the air and caught it.

"You want to play catch?" he said.

"No."

He grinned and tossed the ball at my face so that I had to catch it or be hit.

"See, you can do it," he said. "Come on, I got another glove in the Caddy."

"How about getting out of here?" I said.

"I thought you might have a sense of humor."

I walked past him, into the sunlight, and handed him his ball. I heard him follow me.

"What do you have against me?" he asked.

"You hurt people."

"Oh, you heard the stories, huh? I leave body parts in garbage grinders, throw people off roofs, stuff like that? It's DEA bullshit."

"I don't think so."

"Were you in the service?"

"No."

"I was in Laos, at a place where these sawed-off little guys called the Hmongs grew a lot of poppies. Me and about four hundred other guys. We got left behind. Why do you think that happened?"

"I don't know."

"Yeah, you do. You worked for the G. If you like government mythology about wiseguys, that's your business. What I do in five years don't add up to five minutes of what I seen in Vietnam. That includes dope getting flown out of the Golden Triangle on American planes."

"How'd you get out of Laos?"

"Play catch with me and I'll tell you the whole story," he said.

"Nope."

"Were you in the sack with Cleo?"

"You're out of line, Nicki."

"There's my first name again. I love it. I did some boom-boom with that broad, too. It was like curling up with an ice cube. Tell me I'm wrong."

He bounced the baseball up and down in the pocket of his glove, studying its scuffed surface, his mouth down-hooked at the corners.

THAT NIGHT I dreamed I saw Doc Voss standing waist-deep in a stream, under a yellow moon, his skin prickled with cold. Then his fly line stiffened in the riffle and the tip of his rod bent almost to the water's surface, trembling with tension.

He wrapped the line around his left forearm, so tightly his veins corded with blood, and horsed a long, thick-bodied brown trout through the shallows onto the gravel. He slipped a huge knife from a scabbard on his side and stooped over the trout and inserted the knife point into the trout's anus and slit its belly all the way to the gills.

Doc lifted the trout by its mouth and the unborn roe fell in a gush of heavy pink water from the separated skin in its belly and glistened on the rocks at Doc's feet. He looked up and grinned at me, but I hardly recognized him. His face had become skeletal, his eyes lighted with the moon's reflection off the river.

"Where are your waders, Doc?" I said.

He turned and walked away from me, the blade in his hand glowing with white fire.

I woke from the dream and went into the kitchen and opened a drawer where Doc often stuffed his shopping receipts. It took me a minute to find it, but there it was, crumpled up at the back of the drawer, the carbon of a bill of sale from Bob Ward's Sporting Goods.

"What are you doing in there?" Doc said behind me.

"I saw this receipt a week ago. For a pair of chest waders," I said.

"So?"

"Where are they?" I asked.

"I returned them," he replied.

"Without the receipt?"

"What are you saying, Billy Bob?"

"Did you drown that man?" My voice caught in my throat.

"Somebody else got to him first. Turn out the light when you go to bed," he said.

ON SUNDAY I went to Mass at the Catholic church by the university, then drove out on the Clark Fork west of town in a sun shower and sat on an enormous flat rock that slanted into the water. The river was wide, the color of green-tarnished copper, and cottonwoods dotted the banks and there were blue mountains in the distance. Upstream, a radio was playing gospel music in a parked pickup truck, and for just a moment I was nine years old again, at a camp meeting in the Winding Stair Mountains of eastern Oklahoma. The preacher had just lowered me backward into the river, and when the coldness of the water struck my lungs I opened my eyes involuntarily and looked upward at the lacy green canopy of the heartwood trees overhead and at the blue dome of sky and at the autumnal light that broke around the preacher's silhouette as though it had been poured from a gold beaker.

Then he lifted me from the water, my mouth gasping for air. When I walked with him toward the bank, where my father waited for me, the world did not seem changed but re-defined in a way I could not explain at the time. The sky was joined to the rim of the earth; the trees fluttered with red and gold leaves all the way to the hazy outline of the Ozarks, and there was a cool, fecund odor of silt and ponded water and disturbed animal nests blowing out of the shade. Then a huge woman with a black-lacquered big-bellied Gibson hung around her neck commenced singing "I Saw the Light."

The preacher was as lean as a scarecrow. He spoke in tongues and clogged on the wood stage, a Bible cupped in his hand, while the congregation clapped and shouted with a thunderous rhythm that made the ground shake. The pitch of their voices was almost orgasmic, filled with joy and visceral release. Even my father, who ordinarily was a sober and reticent man, picked me up with one arm and danced in a circle.

It was a moment that others might parody

or ridicule, but I'll never forget it. After my father and I had gotten into our pickup truck and were preparing to leave, the preacher leaned his head through the passenger's window. His hair looked like it had been cut with sheep shears; his face was as long as a horse's, his skin as rough as a wood shingle.

"You wasn't scared, was you?" he asked.

"No, sir," I lied.

"The papists got seven sacraments. We ain't got but one. That's why we really let 'er rip. You're river-baptized, son. From here on out, you take your church with you wherever you go, earth and sky and water and spirit, all of it burned forever into your soul. You ain't never got to be afraid," he said, his dark eyes bursting with certitude.

"WHAT are you doin', slim?" a voice said behind me.

I turned and looked up at Temple Carrol, who stood on the down-sloping rock, her thumbs hooked in her back pockets.

"How'd you know I was here?" I asked.

"I saw you leaving the church, so I followed you."

"What's on your mind?" I said.

She sat down, just a little higher on the rock than I was, her knees pulled up before her. She wore brown jeans and loafers and white socks and she crossed her hands on her knees. "Was I too hard on you the other day?"

"Not in the least," I said. I picked up a pebble and tossed it into the current. The rock we sat on was pink and gray and dappled with the sunlight that shone through a cottonwood. I could see her shadow move next to me, then her fingers lifted a wet leaf off my shoulder and let it blow away in the breeze.

She moved her foot slightly and hit me in the thigh with the point of her shoe.

"Your feelings hurt?" she said.

"I thought I'd give you a couple of days' rest. Don't turn it into a production."

Her foot moved and punched me again.

"Hey," I said.

She poked me in the knee.

"Temple—" I turned around and looked directly in her face.

"What?" she said. Her hands looked small on top of her knees.

"With regularity I say the wrong things to you. I just don't want to do that anymore," I said.

"Come on, get off your butt. I'll buy you lunch," she said, rising to her feet, brushing the rock dust off her rump.

She seemed casual, pushing back her hair, looking at the trees puff with wind. But I could see her watching me out of the corner of her eye.

"Where we going?" I said.

She took a breath and cleared her throat and lifted her blouse off her skin as though the day were warm.

Because she stood higher on the rock than I, we were suddenly the same height. I looked at the milky greenness of her eyes and the color in her cheeks and the roundness of her arms and the way her mouth became like a small flower whenever there was an extended silence between us.

"Temple?" I said.

"Yes?"

"Where we going?"

She smelled like rain and leaves and there was a scent of raspberry soda on her breath. Her mouth was inches from mine and I saw her chest swell, the pulse quicken in her throat. Then she slipped on the rock and her weight fell against me.

Her hair touched my face and I felt her breasts and stomach and the tops of her thighs against me, and her ribs and the taper of her hips were like a gift suddenly placed in my palms when I helped her regain her balance. For just a moment, her mouth parted and her eyes looked into mine in such a way I never wanted to separate from her.

"It's real slippery here," I said, my face burning.

"Yes," she said. "Did you want to go to the

restaurant on the river. The pizza place?"

"Sure. That's a grand place," I said. "I'll be right with you. I dropped some change a minute ago."

She walked back up the rock through a stand of birch trees that were white-trunked and stiff and arching slightly in the wind, while I pretended to hunt for coins down below, my back turned to her to conceal a problem involving a form of male rigidity that made me wonder at my level of maturity.

MAISEY AND DOC VOSS'S Sunday evening began with an argument in the barn over a parrot, one Doc had just brought her from the pet store.

"You don't keep birds in cages! I don't want it!" she shouted.

"Then take it back. Or go feed it to an owl," he replied.

"That's a cruel and stupid thing to say!"

They insulted and shouted at each other and slammed doors all over the house, breaking a bottle of milk in the sink, stepping on the cat's tail, briefly pausing in opposite parts of the house to refocus their anger and then find the other and reopen every wound possible.

While her father kicked an empty bucket over a fence in the yard and ground the starter on the truck, only to find, after starting the engine, that he had a flat tire, Maisey locked herself in her bedroom and changed into black panties and a black silk bra and loose khakis and a white blouse that exposed her navel and cleavage, and put on hoop earrings and rouged her cheeks and lipsticked her mouth and went to work on her eyes with liquid eyeliner and mascara and eye shadow.

When she flung open the bedroom door she looked out the front window and saw her father's truck lights disappearing in the dusk. A strange sense of disappointment and abandonment flooded through her, although she could not explain the sense of desertion and fear that she felt.

She telephoned Steve, the boy down the road, and lit a cigarette over the sink and opened one of her father's bottles of beer and drank it on the front porch while she waited for her friend, her heart pounding without explanation.

The evening sky had turned yellow with dust and wind whipped the trees on the ridge above the house, and she could smell the rain that floated like a lavender vapor on the hills to the north. But whatever portent the evening held, whatever misadventure might wait for her down the road, she told herself she would shape and master it, that the martial energy beating in her temples would vanquish all the adversaries that invaded her sleep and degraded her person, that were made incarnate in the waking day by the sting of her father's words and the way he tried to control her.

*That's* what he couldn't understand, she thought. Every word of chastisement he used was like the probing fingers and tongue and phallus of the each of the faceless men who had raped her. It had never been so clear to her. Why couldn't her father see it? She wanted to scream the question in his face.

She and Steve drove in his car to a nightclub in Missoula, on a street that had once housed bordellos, then workingmen's bars, before it had been absorbed into the gentrification of the town as the town lost its blue-collar ways and gave itself over to art galleries and boutiques.

But there was still one nightclub on the street that shook with noise every night of the week. When Maisey and Steve walked to the entrance, the foothills had turned red in the sun's afterglow, and the bowl of sky above the valley was filled with plumes of yellow and purple cloud, as though they had been scoured out of the valley floor, and the dust that blew in the wind was cold and mixed with rain and as hard as grains of sand against her skin.

But even though a storm threatened the valley, the evening was nonetheless a grand one, and the smell of the air was so good and clean inside her lungs she didn't want to disconnect from it.

Maybe she and Steve should just drive out on the river someplace, maybe watch the deer drift down out of the trees to drink, maybe just eat hamburgers in a brightly lit restaurant full of family people and go to a movie afterward.

No, that's exactly what her father would want her to do, the kind of anal-retentive agenda he might as well write out on a clipboard for her.

She hesitated at the doorway. Men who wore motorcycle boots and gold earrings and leather vests without shirts stood at the bar, knocking back shots with beer chasers, their arms blue from the wrists to the armpits with tattoos. But young women, not much older than she, were in the club, too, and a rock 'n' roll band was belting it out on the stage, and three college boys who looked like football players were taking a breath of air at the entrance, grinning good-naturedly at her.

She smiled back at them, as though they were all old friends, and went inside, with Steve in front of her, his shirt hanging out of his pants, his flip-flops slapping on the floor, his face as trusting and vulnerable as a fawn's. But the football players never even glanced at him. Instead, she felt their eyes light on her mouth and rouged cheeks, her blouse, which hung on the tops of her breasts, the crease in her exposed hips when she walked. Unconsciously she slipped one hand in her back pocket to cover the elastic edge of her panties, which she believed had worked its way above the beltline of her khakis.

She and Steve sat in back, and when he was in the rest room she used her forged ID to order him a draft beer and a vodka collins for herself.

"There're some biker guys at the bar, Maisey. One of them just barfed in the washbasin, then mopped the puke off his mouth on the roller towel, and went back outside like nothing happened," Steve said when he came back to the table.

"Thanks for describing that, Steve," she said.

"Why'd you want to come here? It's full of losers," he said, surveying the other tables.

"Stop staring at people," she said.

"I wish I hadn't left you alone that night. I wish I'd had my father's .357. My father says the welfare system is producing armies of subhumans that are moving into the Northwest."

His presumption that he was responsible for her fate, that his presence could have prevented it, infuriated her and somehow diminished the level of injury that had been visited upon her. Steve twisted around and hooked one arm on the back of his chair and stared at the bikers as though he were visiting a zoo.

"Steve, until somebody puts his penis in your ass and comes in your mouth, don't tell me about subhumans," she said.

"That's sick," he said.

"I think if you say another word I'm going to slap your face," she said.

"Excuse me for telling you this, your attitude not only sucks, you look deeply weird in those clothes and that Frankenstein make-up," he said, and got up from the table and went through the front door onto the street.

The noise from the bandstand seemed to envelope her. She was alone now and suddenly regretted the rashness of her words. She looked around to see if anyone was watching her. But the people at the other tables, the crowd at the bar, the couples on the dance floor, were all involved with themselves and their drinks and their own conversations. It was dumb to think anyone cared what Maisey Voss was doing.

Through the open front door she saw Steve's car drive away, the neon glow from the nightclub rippling across his profile.

She would have to call her father for a ride home. She couldn't bear to think about it. She opened her purse and took out the money for another vodka collins.

The vodka was both cold and warm inside
her at the same time. She chewed the cherries
and orange slices on her molars and drank
the sugar and melted ice in the bottom of the
glass and went to the bar and ordered another drink and watched the bartender while
he made it. A biker's arm brushed hers, but
before she could react the biker turned and
apologized, then resumed his conversation
with his girlfriend, as though Maisey were
not there.

The bartender wrapped a napkin around her
drink and set it in front of her. She began
counting out the money from her purse to pay
for it but the bartender said, "Man down at
the end's already got it."

"Which man?" she said, looking past the
bikers into the haze of cigarette smoke.

But the bartender only shrugged and
walked away.

She drank her vodka collins at the table
and tried not to think about the phone booth
in the corner, the one she would eventually
walk to, almost like entering a Catholic confessional, where she would shut herself inside
and drop the coins into the slot and admit to
her father she couldn't get home by herself.

But the three college boys she had passed at
the entrance were using it. Their upper torsos
looked huge in their short-sleeve workout
jerseys, and she decided the boys were part of

the group she had seen running plays in pads
and sweat shorts on the university practice
field by the river.

Somehow their presence made her feel
more at ease. In spite of their size there was
nothing aggressive or mean-spirited about
them. In fact, their buzzed haircuts, the
youthfulness in their faces, the shine of
cologne on their freshly shaved jaws, made
her think of country boys back home who
could twist a steer into the ground by its
horns but who wouldn't get on a dance floor
at gunpoint.

One of them nodded at her, then turned his
attention back to his friends.

"You want another drink, hon?" the waitress asked.

"Yeah. Let me pay you now, though,"
Maisey said.

"That's a new one," the waitress said.

After Maisey finished her drink, she went
to the rest room. When she came back, the
waitress was picking up her empty glass and
setting down another vodka collins on a napkin.

"Who paid for this?" Maisey said.

"Some guy at the bar," the waitress replied.

"Which guy?"

"Honey, this is a dump. One of these bozos
buys you a drink, marry him," the waitress
said, and walked away, her short skirt swish-

ing across the tops of her fishnet stockings.

Maisey slid another cigarette from her pack, then realized she didn't have matches to light it. Her face was hot, her ears humming with the noise in the room. The electronic feedback in the band's speaker system was beginning to affect her like fingernails on a blackboard. She took a long swallow out of her glass and felt the coldness of the vodka flow through her like wind blowing across snow.

One more drink and she would call her father. By that time his silence and the depression he would wear like a mantle on the long ride home, the acknowledged failure of their relationship that would almost form a third presence in the car, the echoes of all the insults they had hurled at each other earlier, would be lost in fatigue and the ennui that always followed their arguments and the residual numbness of the vodka that now nestled in her system like an old friend.

A boy in his early twenties, in beltless khakis and a pressed, long-sleeved denim shirt with a pair of glasses in the pocket, was standing by her chair now. He held a green and gold can of ginger ale in his hand, and the wetness of the can dripped through his fingers. His eyes crinkled at the corners.

"Can I help you with something?" she asked.

"I heard you talking and I knew you were

from the South. I'm from North Ca'lina. So it was me bought you the drinks. Did you mind I did that?" he said.

She tried to sort through what he had just said. Behind him, on a revolving bar stool, sat a man in a white, wide-brim Stetson and a cowboy shirt that rippled with an electric blue sheen. He was watching her and the boy with the naked curiosity of an animal.

"Say again?" Maisey said.

"I didn't want to offend you by buying those drinks without asking, but you're really a pretty lady," the boy said.

"Who's that man watching us?" she said, then realized her anxiety had made her seek reassurance from a stranger whose features disturbed her for reasons she didn't understand, like someone who belonged inside a drunk dream.

"That's Wyatt. He wants me to rodeo with him, but I think I'm gonna study aeronautical engineering at the university."

"Aeronautical engineering at the University of Montana?"

"I haven't made up my mind. I might study religion or forestry instead. You want to dance?"

"I have to go home."

"Another vodka collins is coming. You got to stay for the drink. It's bad manners if you don't stay for the drink."

"Your friend is using his hand for a cod-piece. Who are you?" she said, her head spinning.

"I'm the guy bought the drinks," he replied, and wrinkled his nose.

She gathered up her purse and rose from the table and walked toward the front door, realizing, as the blood rushed to her feet, that she was drunk.

Outside, the air was cold, the wetness of the street glazed with yellow light. She walked toward the main thoroughfare, although she had no idea what she intended to do. The door of a parked car opened in front of her, and one of the football players stepped out on the sidewalk and grinned at her.

Then he was joined by his two friends. They towered over her, like trees. No matter which direction she turned, she could see nothing but the size of their chests and arms, the necks that were as thick as fire hydrants, the tautness of their grins.

"I want to catch a cab. Can I get one on Higgins?" she said.

"We'll take you home," one of the boys said.

"No, that's all right. I have money for a cab," she said.

"Come on, get in back. You shouldn't be out on the street by yourself," the same boy said.

His face seemed to come into focus for the first time. He had bad skin and his crewcut hair was peroxided. A tiny green shamrock was tattooed on his throat.

"I'm going now. Let me get by," she said.

But one of the other boys placed his arm around her shoulders. He inflated his bicep against her, like someone spinning the handle of a vise to show its potential, and the testosterone smell of his armpit rose into her face.

"Let go of me," she said, her eyes looking between their bodies at the backs of a couple who were walking in the opposite direction.

"There's a lot of street people around here, Maisey, guys with dirty things on their minds," the first boy said.

How did he know her name? she thought.

They were pressing her inside the car now, not all at once, not in a violent fashion, just with the proximity of their size, almost as though they were her attendants, as though they knew her and what she thought and what her history was and what she deserved from them.

She was halfway in the car now, and the boy with peroxided hair leaned close to her face, blocking out all light from the street, his breath sweet with mouth spray.

He raised one finger to his lips. "Nobody's out here. Just us, Maisey. Don't act like a kid," he said.

She got her hand inside her purse and felt it close on a metal nail file. His right eye suddenly looked as big as a quarter, as blue and deep as an inkwell.

But a pair of high-beam headlights pulled in behind the boys' car. The three boys stood erect, their heads turning. A car door opened, and a figure walked out of the headlights' glare, and Maisey could see the physical size of the three boys somehow deflating, like air leaking from a balloon.

"That's my friend. Y'all shouldn't be bothering her," the boy who had bought her the drinks said.

But the football players, if that's what they were, were not looking at the boy who'd said he was from North Carolina. Instead, they stared at the man in the wide-brim white hat and blue silk shirt who stood behind him, his hands curled inward, simian-like, toward his thighs.

"We got no quarrel with you, buddy," the boy with peroxided hair said.

"That's right, you don't," the man in the hat said. "That's why you little farts are gone."

Maisey looked on in disbelief as her three tormentors walked away.

"We'll get you home safe," the boy from North Carolina said.

"I can get a cab," she said.

"Those guys will come after you when me and Wyatt leave. They're always causing trouble here'bouts. Is your name Maisey?" he said.

"How did you know?"

"I heard that guy use your name, that's all," he replied. He held the door open for her, his face suffused with goodwill. Maisey looked back at the nightclub. One of the football players stood just inside the entrance, cleaning his nails with a toothpick. She got into the car.

The man named Wyatt sat in back and the boy, who said his name was Terry, started the engine. The car was red, low-slung, high-powered, with a stick shift on the floor, and Terry drove it full out, tacking up on the curves as they headed toward Bonner and the Blackfoot River, dropping back in front of a semi so abruptly the car shook on its springs.

But even though he drove too fast, she began to feel all the evening's fear and apprehension and self-condemnation go out of her chest.

"What'd you say your last name was?" the man named Wyatt said.

"Voss. Maisey Voss," she said.

"You related to a doctor by that name?" Wyatt asked.

"He's my father."

"I read about him in the paper. Man named Holland live with y'all?"

Maisey turned in the seat. "Billy Bob Holland does," she said.

"I declare. Now that's a fellow I admire. He was the lawyer for my sister, Katie Jo Winset. Ain't this world a miracle of coincidences?" Wyatt said.

"I don't understand," Maisey said.

"A sweet thing like you don't have to." Wyatt leaned forward, his arm propped on the back of her seat, his eyes close to hers. "You like Terry?"

"Pardon?"

"He likes *you*. He gets that possum grin on his face and I know what he's thinking about."

"Lay off it, Wyatt," Terry said.

Wyatt's hand lay close to her shoulder. The nails were clipped and clean, the fingers as pale and thick and gnarled as turnips. The back of his ring finger touched her skin. She felt herself jerk, as though she had been burned with a piece of ice.

"Mr. Holland got a young'un up at Dr. Voss's place? A boy named Lucas?"

"Yes," Maisey said, looking straight ahead now, watching a lighted gas station slide behind them in the darkness.

"You know who I am, don't you?" Wyatt said at the back of her head.

"No."

"You ever go to Sunday school?"

"Yes."

"Then you know it's a sin to lie."

"Give it a rest, Wyatt," Terry said.

The inside of the car became very quiet. Maisey forced herself to turn and look in the backseat. Wyatt was staring at Terry, his head tilted slightly. Terry glanced in the rearview mirror, his eyes like two marbles caught inside the glass.

"I'm gonna pull in for gas," Terry said.

"You do that," Wyatt said.

"Wyatt?"

But Wyatt only grinned and didn't answer.

"Wyatt?" Terry said again.

"Lend me your comb. This beautiful girl has made me sweat inside my hat," Wyatt said.

Terry pulled off the highway into a truck stop and parked the car by a gas pump. He got out and put the nozzle into the gas tank and began cleaning the windows. He seemed to study Wyatt's face through the glass.

"You want me to pay for it?" Terry asked.

"No, I'm going in. Maybe get us some fried pies. Other supplies, too," Wyatt said, as though coming out of a trance. He smiled in a knowing way at Terry and pushed Maisey's seat forward and got out of the car.

Terry watched him enter the truck stop,

then he pulled the gas nozzle from the tank and clanked it back on the pump and got into the car. Through the truck stop window he watched Wyatt pay for the gas, then return to the counter and exchange a dollar bill for silver and go into the men's room.

Terry chewed on his lip, his eyes busy with thought.

"What are you doing?" Maisey said.

"Don't worry about it," Terry said, and started the car and burned rubber onto the highway.

They roared through Bonner, passing the lumber mill and a church and a school and rows of company houses with birch trees in the yards. Terry poured on the gas at the edge of town and the tires squealed on the curves above the Blackfoot River.

"Slow down," she said.

"Don't be telling me what to do, Maisey," he said.

"Where are we going?"

"To your house. Where you think?" he replied.

"I didn't tell you where I live."

"Yeah, you did. You just don't remember."

He had his glasses on now and he was breathing through his mouth, like a fish on land, his cheeks and neck bladed with color.

"You were the man at my window," she said.

"I'm taking you home now. That's all you should care about. Then I'm going back for Wyatt. You don't realize what you've made me do."

"Made you do *what?*" she asked.

"Things just don't work out for me," Terry said, and hit his fist on the steering wheel. "I just don't know why. They just never work out. I'd like to tear somebody apart right now."

He squeezed the floor shift knob tightly in his hand and passed a camper on the double stripe, whipping back into the proper lane an instant before an oncoming log truck crested the hill in front of them. He shot the finger at the truck's headlights.

# Chapter
# 17

AFTER TERRY WITHERSPOON had dropped Maisey off and she had told Doc of the events of the evening, I thought he was going to go after either Witherspoon or Wyatt Dixon or the three football players at the nightclub.

Or at least lecture Maisey on her recklessness.

"Wyatt Dixon went into the rest room with a handful of change? That's when this kid Witherspoon decided to bag it down the road?" Doc said.

"Yes. Was the older man going to buy—" Maisey began.

"Come on into the kitchen," Doc said.

"What is it?" she said.

"You didn't eat supper," he said, and re-

moved two steaks from the freezer and un-
wrapped them from butcher paper at the sink
and began thawing them with hot water.
"Why don't you help me slice a few potatoes
and we'll cook some hash browns?"

Maisey looked at him curiously.

"You're not mad?" she asked.

"Not at you, Maisey. Never at you," he
replied.

She placed a chopping board on the
counter top near the sink and began peeling
an Idaho potato, pausing to glance at her father's profile, as though seeing him for the
first time.

NICKI MOLINARI didn't give up easily. I
saw him in downtown Missoula the next
morning, coming out of a sporting goods
store. He carried a tennis shoe box under his
arm.

"You saved me a trip out to your place.
Come out to the ball field with me. It's right
down by the river," he said.

"No thanks," I replied.

"You want this guy Wyatt Dixon out of
your hair? Or maybe you'd like him climbing
your investigator, what's the lady's name,
Temple something? Give it some thought,
Mr. Holland."

He got into his convertible and drove away.
I tried to ignore what he had said, but he

had planted the hook. I drove my truck down to the ball diamond by the Clark Fork and parked behind the stands and walked toward the third-base line. Nicki Molinari was hitting grounders to three other men out on the diamond, splintering the ball low and hard across the grass.

Two people were sitting on the top row of the otherwise empty stands. The man lifted his hand in recognition, but the woman with him kept her gaze fixed on the field, her face as hard-planed as refrigerated wax.

Nicki Molinari tossed his bat to another player and walked toward me.

"What are Xavier and Holly Girard doing here?" I asked, nodding toward the top of the stands.

"He's writing a book about me. I got stock in her new movie. It's being shot on the Blackfoot. Why, that bother you?" Nicki said.

"You said something about my investigator, Temple Carrol."

"Yeah, I want my seven hundred large back from the skank. That's Cleo Lonnigan to you. You're not interested in a finder's fee, I can shake and bake Wyatt Dixon for you or anybody else who might be giving you a hard time."

"Why'd you mention Temple?"

"Dixon almost tore out your son's package.

What do you think he'd do to a woman?"

"How do you know all this stuff, Nicki?"

"Ah, my first name again. It's my business to know."

"Good. Stay out of mine," I said, and turned to leave.

He caught up with me and placed two fingers on my arm. They were moist with perspiration. He looked at my face and took his hand away.

"It's not my purpose to be enemies with you," he said. "We got a, what do you call it, a symbiotic relationship. You see that big guy out by second base? He works for me. He's incontinent and blows gas in crowded elevators and thinks Nostradamus is a college football team. But he's got a talent. Know what it is?"

"He kills people?"

"He's a great second baseman. We were on the same team at TI. In a playoff game nobody could figure out how I was wetting down the ball. I didn't touch my face or hat or belt, but my curve was jumping out of the catcher's mitt. Know how I did it?"

"No."

"We'd whip the ball around the infield. Frank out there had a hole cut in the pocket of his glove and a sponge inside it. He'd be the last infielder to handle the ball. When it came back to me it looked like it'd been through a car wash." Nicki smiled, his dark eyes dancing on my face.

"What's the point?"

"Everybody has a function. You put the right people and the right functions together, everybody wins. Help me out, man. I don't want to sell Cleo's debt."

"Sell it?"

He gave me a look. "You're sure you were with the G? Yeah, sell it. Discount it, twenty cents on the dollar. But the guys who buy the debt are not like me. They recover all the principal and all the back vig, plus interest on the vig. You want me to draw you a picture? Think about guys who carry tin snips in their glove compartments."

I left him standing there and got back into my truck. The baseball field was green, the base paths blown with dust, the outfield bordered by the cottonwoods and aspens that fringed the river. High above it all sat Xavier and Holly Girard, artists whose interests were wedded to those of an ex-convict war veteran who played baseball in the middle of a Norman Rockwell setting and probably helped Hmong tribesmen grow opium in Laos.

What had the sheriff said, something to the effect that most people's public roles were pure bullshit? I wondered if he should not be given an endowed chair at the local university.

I BOUGHT French bread and cheese and sliced meat at a delicatessen and picked up Temple Carrol at the health club in Hellgate Canyon where she had started working out on a daily basis. We drove to a picnic ground in a grove of cedar trees by the river, and I fixed lunch for us at a plank table in the shade while she leafed through her notebooks and file folders and went over the edited transcriptions of her interviews with anyone she thought to be connected to the death of Lamar Ellison.

"I interviewed Sue Lynn Big Medicine," she said.

"Yes?"

"She was in the saloon up the Blackfoot with Lamar Ellison just before he was killed. She's hiding something." Temple had not changed from her workout. She wore pink shorts rolled up high on her legs and a gray workout halter and she kept lifting her hair off the back of her neck and pushing it on top of her head with one hand while she flipped through her notes.

"Hiding what?" I said.

"This is what she told me: 'Lamar would have blackouts when he mixed alcohol and reefer. Don't ask me what he talked about. He didn't make sense when he was stoned.'

"So then I asked her why she even bothered to mention the fact that Lamar'd had a blackout. She goes, 'Because you wanted to know what he was talking about the last time I saw him. I'm trying to tell you I don't know what he was talking about. What do you expect from a guy who had shit for brains even when he was sober?'"

"Could I see the folder you have on her?" I said.

As an investigator and researcher, Temple had no peer. If at all possible, her interviews got on tape. Then she would transcribe the tape onto the printed page and go through the person's rambling statements and attempts at obfuscation and highlight sentences and phrases that were part of patterns.

She never asked a question that required only a yes-or-no response, which forced the subject, if he was dishonest, to search in his mind for ideational associations that would mislead the interviewer. Usually in that moment the subject's eyes went askance. However, if the subject was a pathological liar, his eyelids stayed stitched to his forehead and he leaned forward aggressively, an angry tone of self-righteousness threaded through his answer.

Temple maintained that the first response out of the subject's mouth was always the most revealing, even if the person was lying.

She said nouns went to the heart of the matter and adverbs showed manipulation. Honest people erred on the side of self-accusation and took responsibility for the evil deeds others had visited upon them. Sociopaths, when they had nothing at risk, told stories about themselves that made the mind reel and the stomach constrict, then a moment later tried to conceal the fact they had been raised in an alley by a single mother. One way or another, Temple's highlighter found it all.

The transcription of her interview with Sue Lynn Big Medicine was two pages long.

"She uses the words 'blackout' and 'stoned' six separate times," Temple said. "The impression I get is that Ellison went outside the bar, smoked a lot of reefer with some other bikers, then came back in and told her something that made her skin crawl. You got any idea what it might be?"

"No," I replied.

"Why would she want to hide it from us?"

"She's working for the G. She wants to be careful about what she says. What else do you have on her?" I asked.

"She was arrested on the edge of the Crow Reservation for armed robbery of the mails."

"What?"

"She went into a general store with three or four other Indians. One of them pulled out a gun and robbed the owner of fifty dollars and a quart of whiskey. But the general store was also a post office. The Indians were charged with robbery of the mails, which is a federal offense. Sue Lynn's case is still pending."

"So that's the hold the Treasury agents have on her."

"Here's the rest of it. One of the guys she was arrested with was Lamar Ellison's cell mate in Deer Lodge."

"They had the perfect person to plant inside the militia."

"There's one other detail, but I don't know if it has any bearing on the fact she's a government informant. Two years ago her little brother disappeared from a Little League ball game in Hardin, Montana. A month later his body was found in a garbage dump outside Baltimore."

"How old was he?"

"Ten," Temple said. "This is a pissed-off young woman."

"She's seems to be a mixed bag, all right," I said, spinning my hat on my finger. "Her little brother was found dead in Baltimore?"

"He'd been strangled. No clues, no leads." When I didn't speak, Temple said, "Your boy's in the sack with her?"

"Celibacy isn't a high priority with most kids today."

"I wonder who their role models were," she said.

She got up from the table and gazed through the cedar trees at the river. Downstream, college kids were riding bicycles back and forth across an old railroad bridge that had been converted for pedestrian use.

"Why do you act like that, Temple?" I said.

"Because sometimes I feel like it. Because maybe I just get depressed digging up grief and misery in people's lives."

"Then warn me in advance."

Her lips started to shape a word, but no sound came out of her throat. Her eyes were fixed on mine now, an expression in them that was somewhere between anger and pain and the love that teenage girls sometimes carry inside them as brightly as a flame. I put my hands on her shoulders, and when she raised her face, unsure of what was happening, I kissed her on the mouth. I felt the surprise go through her body as tangibly as an electric shock.

She stepped back from me, her eyes wide, her cheeks coloring.

"Go ahead and hit me," I said.

Instead, she averted her eyes so I could not read whatever emotion was in them and packed all her notebooks and file folders in her nylon backpack and walked toward my truck, the backs of her thighs wrinkled from the picnic bench.

And once again I was left alone with the

beating of my own heart and my confused thoughts about Temple Carrol and the certainty that I had succeeded once more in making a fool of myself.

LATER, I had the oil changed in my truck, then called the sheriff at his office.

"Do you know a hood named Nicki Molinari?" I asked.

"He and a bunch of other greasers own a dude ranch down by Stevensville," he replied.

"It doesn't bother you to have these guys on your turf?"

"We've had gangsters here for years. They'd like to get casino gambling legalized and turn Flathead Lake into Tahoe," he said.

"I saw Molinari with Xavier and Holly Girard this morning," I said.

"That's supposed to be skin off my ass?"

"You pointed me at the Girards when I first met you. It was for a reason."

"So go figure it out and stop bothering me," he said, and hung up.

I drove out to the Girards' home on the Clark Fork. My visit was to become another reminder that it's presumptuous to assume a common moral belief governs us all.

ℐ

I SMELLED alcohol on Xavier Girard when he answered the door. But he wasn't drunk, at least not so that I could tell. In fact, his thick hair had just been barbered, his eyebrows trimmed. His shoulders were straight, his demeanor casual and nonexpressive. If his mood could be characterized at all, it was a bit melancholy and perhaps resigned.

"Am I disturbing you?" I asked.

"I was writing."

"Can you give me ten minutes?"

"Come in," he replied.

I followed him into a spacious office with cedar bookshelves that ran from the floor to the ceiling. The windows were arched and looked out on wooded hills and a red barn down below and a pasture that was full of Appaloosa and quarter horses.

The wall was covered with framed book reviews, all of them sneering indictments of his work. The centerpiece was a legal form initiated by the censor at the Texas State Prison in Huntsville, stating Girard's last novel had been banned from the Texas penal system because the dialogue made use of racial and profane language and encouraged a disrespect for authority.

The convict whose copy of Girard's novel had been confiscated was in the Ellis unit, awaiting execution.

On the shelves above Girard's desk were his

two Edgar Awards, in the form of ceramic busts of Edgar Allen Poe, and a display of arrowheads and pottery shards and a collection of .58-caliber oxidized lead minié balls and rusted case shot.

"This is Civil War ordnance. You dug this up in Louisiana?" I said.

But he wasn't listening. I thought I heard voices through the wall or perhaps the ceiling.

"What could I help you with?" he asked.

"Nobody's looking at you for the murder of Lamar Ellison," I replied.

"Are you?"

"He vandalized your vehicle and punched you out just before somebody boiled his cabbage."

"You want a drink?"

"No."

"You don't really think I killed Ellison, do you?" he asked.

"Probably not."

"Then why are you here, Mr. Holland?"

"The sheriff's got you and Ms. Girard on his mind. I just don't know why."

"If that's all, I'd better get some pages ready for my editor," he said.

I could hear a knocking sound, like a headboard slamming into a wall, and a woman's voice mounting to a barely suppressed shriek. I felt the skin draw tight on my face. Xavier's eyes lifted toward the ceiling.

"You wanted to say something?" Girard asked.

"No, not really."

"People have different kinds of relationships, Mr. Holland. It doesn't mean one is better than another."

I nodded, my eyes averted.

"I'll let myself out. Thanks for your time," I said.

"Sorry. It looks like the landscaper has you blocked in. I'll find him. He's out back somewhere."

So I had to wait ten minutes for the landscaper to move his vehicle. But at least the sounds from upstairs had stopped. As I turned around in front of the garage, Nicki Molinari came out the front door of the house barefoot and headed for my truck, gesturing at me to stop. His hair was wet on his shirt collar.

"Say it," I said.

"Don't drive out of here with your nose in the air. You got the wrong idea about what's going on here."

"You were bopping the guy's wife while he was downstairs," I said.

"He's a marshmallow and a drunk. Besides, we didn't know he had come home."

"Take your hands off my truck, please."

"I checked you out, Mr. Holland. You killed your best friend. I knew your kind in

'Nam. A ROTC commission and a cause stuffed up your butt, except it's always other guys who get turned into chipped beef."

"You should have put your shoes on, Nicki," I said.

"What?"

"You stepped in dog poop."

He stared down at the brown smear his toes had left on the cement.

I drove away from the house and up on a rise above the river and got out of my truck and looked down at the cottonwoods below, the words of Nicki Molinari ringing in my ears. I wanted to go back to the Girards' house and kill Nicki Molinari, literally blow him all over the grass. In the old days I could have done it and sipped a cup of coffee while I reloaded. I wondered if L.Q.'s ghost would ever let me rest.

# Chapter 18

THE NEXT MORNING I received a phone call from the sheriff.

"That kid, Terry Witherspoon, the one you think was watching Maisey Voss in her bathroom? He's in St. Pat's Hospital. Somebody tossed him out of a car," the sheriff said.

"Why are you telling me?"

"Maybe the girl would like to know. A crime victim's day don't always come in court," he replied.

"Who did it to him?"

"Maybe he'll tell you. He was wearing lipstick and rouge when the paramedics brought him in. Why would queer bait want to be looking at a young girl through a bathroom window?"

"I think Wyatt Dixon is AC/DC. Witherspoon is his boy."

"Our worst problem around here used to be pollution from tepee burners. We even had a whorehouse over in Wallace, Idaho. It's sure nice to have you new folks around, Mr. Holland," he said.

"How should I interpret that? You're really a cryptic man, Sheriff."

"Thank you," he said, and hung up.


WHEN I ENTERED Terry Witherspoon's room he was standing by his bed, putting on his shirt. His elbows and forehead were barked and one eye was clotted with blood.

His face jerked when he saw me, as though he feared I might be someone else.

"Wyatt was going to rape Maisey the other night, wasn't he?" I said.

He put on his glasses and crinkled his nose. A sun shower had burst on the hills rimming the valley and the hills were green and shining with light, but it was not a good day for Terry Witherspoon. His face was pinched with resentment and shame, like a child who had been unjustly punished.

"You did an honorable deed, Terry. It takes a standup guy to 'front a dude like Wyatt Dixon," I said.

"He's picking me up. You'd better not be here when he does," he said.

"Free country," I said.

"It used to be. Before the likes of y'all took over," he replied.

"Who's this 'y'all' we're talking about?"

"Liberals, muff divers, tree huggers, the people who are ruining everything."

"You want to be a hump for Wyatt the rest of your life?"

"Don't call me a hump. I'm not a hump."

"You only listen to people who denigrate you, Terry."

"Do what?"

"You grew up being dumped on. So in your mind the only people who really know you are the ones who run you down. A guy like me tells you you're standup and you blow me off."

He looked out the window, down onto the sidewalk.

"He's coming. Get out of here," he said.

"You like Maisey?" I asked.

He looked at me silently, as though there were a trick in the question.

"Ellison and his friends already put their mark on her soul. Give her a break. Stay away from her," I said.

"I'm not good enough?" he said, his glasses full of light.

"Back in North Carolina you broke into a house and tied two people to chairs and shot the man and cut the woman's throat. They'll stand by your deathbed one day, kid. Count on it."

His jaw dropped and his breath went out of his mouth as though I'd punched him in the stomach. Then I saw his attention shift to the doorway. I turned and looked into the face of Wyatt Dixon.

"Why, I be go-to-hell if it ain't the counselor again, right in the midst of it all. Counselor, every time I see you I'm put in mind of a shithog ear-deep in a slop bucket. Search me for the explanation. By the way, did you know that boy of yours pulled a skinning knife on me this morning?"

He let his grin hang, his eyes dancing with delight at the expression on my face.

I DROVE BACK to Doc Voss's place on the Blackfoot but Lucas wasn't there.

"You know where Sue Lynn Big Medicine lives?" I asked Maisey.

"Lucas said by a junkyard in East Missoula," she replied. "You saw Terry this morning?"

"*Terry?* You're on a first-name basis with this asswipe?" I said. She was sitting on the porch step with a book splayed open on her knee. Her calico cat was flipping in the dust by her feet. She squinted her eyes at me in the sunlight.

"That's his name, isn't it?" she said.

"Don't let that guy get near you, Maisey."

"I wish you wouldn't tell me what to do."

"Don't any of you kids have any judgment about the people you associate with?" I asked.

"Your problem is with Lucas, Billy Bob, not me. Please change your tone of voice."

There's no feeling quite like being corrected by a sixteen-year-old girl.

I drove back down the Blackfoot and into East Missoula, a community of trailers and truckstops and low-rent casinos, where the poor and unskilled watched the world they had taken for granted disappear around them. It wasn't hard to find the junkyard where Sue Lynn lived. Cars that had been crushed and flattened by a compactor were stacked in layers on a knoll above the highway, and the windowless gray-primed stock car she drove, with orange numerals on the doors, was parked by an old brick cottage with a sign over the porch that read SALVAGE.

Sue Lynn and Lucas were on their hands and knees in the backyard, working on what I thought was a rock garden. Then I realized the design was far more intricate. They had laid out a circle of stones, with two intersecting lines inside it. One line of stones was painted red, the other black. In the middle of the cross was a willow tree.

Now Lucas and Sue Lynn were working each of the quadrants with trowels and sprinkling them down with a water can and planting purple and white and pink pansies into the mixture of mulch and black soil. The mongrel dog Lucas had saved from drowning in the Blackfoot River was nosing his snout into the dirt, his tail wagging, his hair matted down with the medicine Lucas had smeared on his mange.

I squatted on my haunches outside the circle of stones and took off my hat and put a peppermint stick in the corner of my mouth.

"It looks real good," I said.

"It's an Indian prayer garden. The willow is the Tree of Life. One part of the cross is the red road. That's the good way in this world. The other one, the black road, that one's not so cool," Lucas said.

"Wyatt Dixon said you pulled a knife on him."

"He's full of shit. I took out a pocketknife to peel an apple and he made some kind of wise-ass remark about it," Lucas replied. "Why's he want to think I'd pull a knife?"

"So he can kill you, son." I felt my gaze break at the content of my own words. I also realized I'd never called Lucas son before.

"Maybe he'll get a surprise," Lucas said.

"Don't talk that way," I said.

"Should I leave?" Sue Lynn said.

"How are you, Sue Lynn?" I said.

She pressed the roots of a petunia into the damp soil and didn't answer. She wore cutoff jeans and a halter, and the tips of her hair were wet with perspiration and there were sun freckles on the tops of her breasts.

"Who owns this place?" I asked.

"My uncle. He did time in Marion," she replied.

"As joints go, that's real mainline."

"I told you once before I don't get to choose where I live."

"You ever read *Black Elk Speaks* by John Neihardt?" I asked.

"I never heard of it," she replied.

"You should. This prayer garden is in his book."

"My grandfather was a Crow holy man and you're an asshole, Mr. Holland," she said.

"Come on, Sue Lynn," Lucas said.

I got to my feet and put my hat back on. The hills across the river were velvet green and rose abruptly into the sky and ponderosa pine flowed from the crests down into the arroyos.

"My apologies to you, Ms. Big Medicine. Y'all have a fine day," I said, and walked back to my truck.

I saw Lucas running to catch me before I got out on the highway. I winked at him and gave him the thumbs-up sign.

THAT NIGHT Lucas played at the Milltown Bar. The tables and dance floor were filled, the crowd happy and drunk and raucous. When Lucas came to the microphone to sing his first song of the evening, his eyes were watering from the cigarette smoke and the heat of the stage lights that shone upward into his face. He clicked the floor switch with his boot and the banks of white lights died and cooled, and he clicked a second switch and four overhead flood lamps wrapped with tinted cellophane came on and bathed the stage with a soft reddish-blue glow.

He blotted the sweat out of his eyes and the room came into focus, then he looked down into a face that made him twitch inside.

"During your break I'd like to compare notes with you on Sue Lynn. She can really rise to the occasion if you can get down past that wore-out part," Wyatt Dixon said.

THE NEXT EVENING Doc and I attended a town meeting hosted by the Phillips-Carruthers Corporation at the Holiday Inn in Missoula. The crowd was a hostile one.

Things had not been going well for Phillips-Carruthers. The previous day a famous female country singer had agreed to visit the mine site. Perhaps because of the fact she chain-smoked cigarettes and looked as if she had just been blown through the doors of a beer joint, the mine operators thought they had a sympathetic vehicle for their message. Also, like most greedy and obtuse people, they believed news media existed for no other purpose than to promote their business interests. Hence, they arranged for both print and television journalists to be at the mine site when the singer was escorted from a company helicopter to the water processing shed that supposedly neutralized any contaminants that might leak into the ecosystem.

On camera, a smiling company executive filled a drinking glass from a tap and offered it to the singer.

"It's as clear as spring water, ma'am. I'd give it to my grandchildren," he said.

"Thank you, sir. But I don't care to have nuclear-strength spinach growing out of my lungs," she replied, and smiled sweetly at him.

Probably due to the influence of a PR person with a brain, tonight the mine operators played over the heads of the audience and made use of their hostility. There was no shortage of fanatics and professional naysayers in the crowd, people who wore their eccentricity like a uniform and loved conflict and acrimony so they would not have to contemplate the paucity of significance in their own lives. The mine operators paraded workingpeople in front of the microphone, both men and women who spoke sincerely about their dependence upon the mine for their homes and livelihoods. You could almost feel the mine executives praying under their breaths for a catcall from the audience.

But it didn't happen. The audience was respectful, the occasional dissenting moan in a listener hushed by those around him. Then Carl Hinkel, the militia leader from the Bitterroot Valley, rose from his chair in the third row and gave the mine operators what they needed, a dignified presentation that belied his agenda, that mixed patriotism and blue-collar attitudes with positive economic statistics and Montana traditions.

He wore a western-cut sports coat with pads on the elbows and a maroon shirt and a flowered tie and charcoal slacks. His beard was freshly clipped, his shoulders straight, his corncob pipe cupped in his palm. His Tidewater accent, empty of anger or malicious intent, was both foreign and intriguing to the audience. Their faces seemed to be reconsidering all the impressions they had previously formed about him.

"You're not going to spike this guy's cannon?" I said to Doc.

But Doc just looked at his feet.

"The Earth was put here for a purpose, to nurture and sustain us. The minerals we take from the ground are like the vegetables we grow on our farms. They're all gifts of the Lord," Hinkel said. "It seems to me a terrible arrogance to reject that gift. I don't mean to offend anyone here. I love this state. I think it's our charge to be good stewards of the land. I appreciate the opportunity you've given me to speak here tonight. God bless every one of you, and God bless these working folks who need their jobs."

When Hinkel sat down, no one rose to rebut him. A long-haired kid in a fatigue jacket with a feather dangling from one earring stood up and made a rambling speech about Native Americans and wind power and the timber industry and missile silos east of the Divide. People's eyes crossed with boredom. Carl Hinkel now seemed like Clarence Darrow.

"Say something, Doc."

"Fuck it. If they need the likes of me for a leader, they're not worth leading," he replied.

The sky was still bright when the meeting broke up and the audience drifted outside. The clouds were mauve-colored in the west and the rain blowing in the canyon at Alberton Gorge looked like spun glass against the light. I could smell the heavy, cold odor of the Clark Fork and the wetness of the boulders in the shadows along the banks and the hay that someone was mowing in a distant field. The riparian countryside, the purple haze on the mountains, the old-growth trees that were so tall they looked as if they lived in the sky, were probably as close to Eden as modern man ever got, I thought. But this wonderful part of the world was also one that Carl Hinkel and his friends, if given the opportunity, would turn into a separate country surrounded by razor wire and guard towers.

People who should have known better had stopped to chat with him. He was obviously a strong man physically, and he demonstrated his strength by picking up a plump little girl of ten or eleven and holding her out at arm's length.

"Excuse me, Mr. Hinkel," I said.

"Yes?" he said, turning toward me, his eyebrows raised.

"I keep having trouble with Wyatt Dixon. I don't think he does anything without your permission. The next time he bothers my son, I'm going to be out to your place and kick a nail-studded two-by-four up your sorry white ass."

"I'm afraid I don't know who you are," he said.

"Oh, really?"

"I'm sixty years old, sir. It seems to me you embarrass your son and degrade yourself. But if you wish to physically attack me, do it and be done," he said.

The conversation died around us and every person on the motel's grass swale and tree-shaded driveway was now staring at me. Carl Hinkel waited, then put his pipe into his mouth and drew a thumbnail across the top of a match and lit the tobacco in his pipe bowl and gazed into the distance.

My face was red with shame. I turned and walked away, unable to believe my own vanity and stupidity.

I heard Doc at my elbow.

"You're going about it the wrong way, bud. These guys don't fight fair," he said.

"Tell me about it."

"My father always said God loves fools. Join the club. Don't worry. They're all going down," Doc said. He cupped his hand around the back of my neck like a baseball catcher mothering a pitcher who had just been shelled off the mound.

I turned and looked into his face.

"All going down?" I said.

I GUESS I had misjudged Doc's potential. Or at least Wyatt Dixon had.

The next night he was at home in the small log house Carl Hinkel had given him to use on the back of Hinkel's property. The moon was up and from his window he could see the lines of cottonwoods along the Bitterroot River and the monolithic shapes of the mountains against the sky and the thick stands of timber that grew into the canyons. A star shower burst above the valley and Wyatt Dixon wondered if the tracings of light across the darkness of the heavens were a sign, perhaps an indicator that an enormous historical change was at hand for him and his kind.

Or perhaps he thought nothing at all.

The night was cold, but neither cold nor heat had ever had an appreciable effect on him. He wore only a nylon vest over his skin when he walked down to the river with a cane pole and a can of worms and bobber-fished in an eddy behind a beaver dam. Two nights earlier he had spread the surface of the water with cornmeal, and now, in less than five minutes, he hooked what was at least a twenty-five-inch bull trout. He let the trout swallow the treble hook, down the throat and into the belly, so there would be no chance of its slipping off, then he horsed it onto the bank and picked it up by the tail and swung it like a sock full of wet sand and bashed its brains out on a rock.

As he walked back to his house he saw car

lights through a stand of lodgepole pine on the neighbor's property, but the lights disappeared and he gave them no more thought. He slit the belly of his fish under an outside faucet and raked out the guts and threw them to one of Carl's cats, then he scrubbed his hands clean under the faucet and threaded a stick through the trout's gills and mouth and went inside his house.

Just inside the doorway a piece of bronze wire glistened once on the edge of his vision, then looped over his head and tightened around his neck, squeezing tendon and artery, shutting off air to his lungs and blood to his brain.

He lost both his sight and his consciousness as though he were watching a red-black liquid slide down the lens of a camera.

When he awoke his head snapped upward, like that of a man rising from a coffin, and the room, with all its familiar gunracks and deer and elk antlers and assortment of western hats and Indian blankets on the furniture and logs burning in the woodstove, came back into focus, everything in its right place, even the plastic suction device on the kitchen table that he used to clean impurities from the pores of his facial skin.

He realized he was seated in a chair and the wire loop that had razored into his flesh was no longer around his throat but on the floor by his foot and he saw that the loop had been fashioned from guitar strings. But his arms had been pinioned behind the chair and his wrists crossed and taped together, and his calves were secured to the chair's legs with wide strips of silver tape from his ankle to the knee. He looked at the intruder who sat on a straight-back wood chair no more than three feet from him.

"Howdy do, sir? My name is Wyatt Dixon. What might yours be?" he said.

"You don't know?" the intruder said.

"My guess is you're Maisey Voss's daddy. If that be the case, I'm honored to meet a decorated soldier such as yourself. That Bowie knife on your hip could saw the head off a hog, couldn't it?"

"You were going back into the men's room at the truck stop to buy rubbers?" Doc said.

"That's not a fit question to be asking a man, sir."

"You planned to rape my daughter."

"Some weight lifters or football farts, I don't know which, was trying to get into her pants. Excuse the language I use to describe what could have been a repeat scene for your poor little girl. But that's what happened, sir."

"What I don't understand about you is that evidently you're a brave man. Cruel people are almost always cowards. How would you explain the discrepancy, Mr. Dixon?"

"I can tell you are Mr. Holland's friend. You both are natural-born orators. Your speech is filled with philosophic content that is far beyond the understanding of a rodeo cowboy."

Doc got up from his chair and walked to the butane cookstove that was set in a small curtain-hung alcove that served as a kitchen. He turned the butane on and listened to it hiss through the unlit jets, then turned it off.

"It won't give you no satisfaction," Wyatt Dixon said.

"Why not?" Doc asked.

"'Cause you'll have given me power. 'Cause I'll live in you every morning you get up. Ask them who run Old Sparky at Huntsville Pen. They don't never eat breakfast alone."

"That doesn't apply to you?"

Wyatt Dixon's silky red hair hung in his eyes like a little boy's. He shifted his weight on his small, hard buttocks and wet his lips.

"There's people that's different. We all know each other, though. It's a bigger club than you might think," Wyatt Dixon said.

"I think you've convinced me, Mr. Dixon."

"I don't rightly follow you, sir. But I have to say I'm in awe of your military background. You had Lamar Ellison spotting his drawers."

"I'm glad to hear that," Doc replied.

The woodstove was inset in an old stone

hearth. Doc picked up two chunks of split pine from the woodbox and opened the stove's doors and threw them on the fire. Then he opened the damper on the chimney and watched the flame bloom inside the stove's iron walls.

All the while Wyatt Dixon watched him as though he were a spectator rather than a participant in the events taking place around him.

"Cut me loose and give me a knife and let's see how it shapes up. I'm making a bona fide gentleman's offer to you, sir," he said.

But Doc had walked past Wyatt Dixon's line of vision and was now at the cookstove again, where this time he reached behind it and ripped a length of flex pipe from a steel container. Suddenly the smell of butane filled the room.

"I can see you are a man of purpose, sir," Wyatt Dixon said. "Was you in that bunch over there that would slip into a village and cut people's throats in their sleep and paint their faces yellow so their folks would get a major surprise at daylight?"

When Doc went out the door and closed it behind him, Wyatt Dixon was staring at the fire in the woodstove, his face whimsical, as though an idle and insignificant thought were hovering in front of his eyes.

But whatever passions had driven Doc as a Navy SEAL had become little more than ashes on a dead fire. He came back into the log house and screwed down the valve on the butane tank and opened the windows and filled a plastic bucket in the sink and threw the water on the flames in the woodstove. Smoke billowed up into the room.

Wyatt Dixon watched him with a bead in his eye, his hands opening and closing behind him.

Doc flung the bucket at the sink and walked back outside, leaving the door open behind him.

But just as he started his truck he saw Wyatt Dixon walk out of the door, strands of silver tape hanging from his wrists, a splintered piece of chair leg still bound to the calf of his leg. His silhouette seemed haloed with light and smoke.

"You don't have it in you, sir. Know what that means? I own you. You and yours. If I've a mind, I'll split your little girl in half and take the bones out of the Holland boy. Once more please pardon my language, but, sir, you done fucked with the devil hisself," he said.

# Chapter

## 19

"HE'S A SATANIST?" I said to Doc the next morning.

"I don't know what he is," he replied.

"What have you done, Doc?"

The sun had not broken above the ridgeline and the house was in shadow. Doc picked up his uneaten breakfast and threw it out the back door.

"I'm going into town. You want to come?" he said.

"No," I said, my anger as thick as a walnut in my throat.

I walked down to Lucas's tent on the river and crouched down and pulled open the flap. He raised his head up from his sleeping bag.

"Anything wrong?" he asked.

"Doc stoked up Wyatt Dixon. I think you should go back to Deaf Smith."

"Why?"

"He made a threatening statement about you and Maisey."

"Fuck him."

"I had a feeling you might say that. Excuse me for waking you up."

"Joan Baez is playing at the university to-morrow night," he said.

I waited for him to go on.

His eyes shifted off mine. "I told Sue Lynn you give us two tickets. Can you let me have forty dollars?"


I WENT BACK into the house and opened the Missoula phone directory and began the long process of trying to contact a federal agent for whom I had no business card. Finally I reached a Treasury Department switchboard in Washington, D.C., and after three transfers was able to leave my name and number.

Then I went to Bob Ward's Sporting Goods and bought a .38 revolver with a two-inch barrel and a clip-on holster and a box of cartridges.

By that afternoon I had heard nothing back from my inquiry at the Treasury Department.

I called the *Missoulian* and asked for the classified ad department.

"Is there still time to get a two-column boldface in tomorrow's paper?" I asked.

"Yes, I think we can do that. What do you want it to say?" a woman replied sweetly.

" 'Amos Rackley, Please Get in Touch. Urgent.' Sign it 'Billy Bob Holland.' "

"That's it?" she asked.

"No. Let me make an addition," I said.

THAT EVENING I picked up Temple at the airport. She had been called back to Texas to testify at a trial and I had not seen her since I had impetuously kissed her in the picnic grounds by the river. When she walked off the plane I felt that the best friend I had on earth had just come back into my life.

"Anything happen while I was gone?" she asked.

"A little bit. Doc garroted Wyatt Dixon with Lucas's guitar strings and taped him to a chair and came within an inch of blowing up him and his house with butane gas."

"You're making this up?"

"I wish Doc had finished what he started."

"Say again?"

"Dixon said he might take Lucas's bones out. Those are the words he used," I said, and felt myself swallow.

Temple put her suitcase into the bed of my truck and got into the cab. I started the engine and drove out on the highway. The hills across the river looked low and humped in the sunset and the sky was dull gold and flecked with dark birds. I felt her watching the side of my face.

"Don't be too hard on Doc," she said.

"He wants it both ways. He whips a rope on these guys, but he's not willing to go to the tree with them."

"You better hope he doesn't."

We didn't speak for several moments. Then I said, "Do you want to have supper?"

"I ate on the plane. Another time, okay?" she said, and smiled wanly.

"Sure," I said, and pulled into the parking lot of her motel on East Broadway, not far from Hellgate Canyon, which had been named by Jesuit missionaries after they saw the litter of human bones left from the Blackfoot ambushes of the Flatheads.

She hefted her suitcase out of the truck bed and yawned. The wind was cool and the light had gone pink on the trees that grew along the crest of the canyon and I could see white-water rafters bouncing through the rapids on the river.

"Can you come in a minute?" she said.

"Sure," I said, and walked behind her into her room.

She set her suitcase down and shut the blinds and closed the door and turned on the lights. She sat on the edge of her bed and looked into space for a moment, and I could see the fatigue of the trip seep into her face.

"Maybe I should come back tomorrow," I said.

"No, stay," she said, and pulled off her loafers and unscrewed her earrings and set them on the nightstand. Then she took a breath and smiled and let her eyes rest on mine. "It's been a long day."

"I guess it has," I said, and saw an ice bucket and two drinking glasses on the desk. "I'll get a couple of sodas if you like."

"No, that's all right," she said, and lifted her large shoulder bag onto her lap. "A friend of mine got ahold of Carl Hinkel's sheet. I thought we should go over it."

"Hinkel's sheet?"

"Yeah. This guy recruits ex-cons like Lamar Ellison and Wyatt Dixon over the Internet. He was a college professor once, can you believe that?"

"You wanted to go over Hinkel's sheet?"

"You'd rather not do it now?"

"Hinkel's a bucket of shit, Temple. Who cares what his history is?"

"I just don't believe I've come back to this," she said.

THE NEXT MORNING was Saturday and I went into town by myself and ate steak and eggs in a café by the rail yards, then took a walk across the Higgins Street Bridge and along the river by an old train depot that was now used for offices by an environmental group. The walkway by the river was still deep in shadow, the runoff loud through the cottonwoods and willows. I didn't hear the car that pulled off the bridge and drove down a ramp and stopped behind me.

Out of the corner of my eye I saw a car door open and a crew-cut blond man in a suit suddenly running at me, his arm outstretched. I turned and ripped my elbow into his face and felt the bone break in his nose.

He cupped his hands to his face and an unintelligible sound came out of his mouth. His white shirt was splattered with blood and his eyes were filled with pain and rage. His hand went inside his suitcoat and closed on the butt of an automatic pistol.

I grabbed his wrist with my left hand and tore my .38 from its clip-on belt holster and slammed him against the front of his car and wedged the .38 into his mouth, my hand still gripped on his wrist. He gagged on the two-inch barrel and I pushed it deeper into his throat, bending him back against the car.

Blood and spittle ran from his mouth and I heard the automatic fall from his hand onto the cement.

Then someone pressed a pistol against my temple.

"Let Jim go, Mr. Holland," Amos Rackley said.

"Kiss my ass. You take that gun away from my head," I said.

"You're not in a bargaining position," he replied.

"Watch this," I said. I fitted my left hand on the throat of the man called Jim and shoved the .38 deeper into his mouth and cocked the hammer with my thumb, the cylinder actually clacking against his teeth now. "You take your piece away from my head or I'll empty his brainpan on the hood."

Rackley lowered his gun. I released the man named Jim and stepped away from him.

"You fucking lunatic," Rackley said.

"You jump out of cars at people and pull guns on them, this is what you get," I said.

"What do you call this?" he said, and reached into the backseat of his car and shoved the morning newspaper at me. It was folded back to a red-circled classified ad that read, "Amos Rackley, Please Get in Touch. I Don't Feel Like Cleaning Up Your Mess—Billy Bob Holland."

"I think you're deliberately letting Wyatt Dixon and Carl Hinkel stay in circulation so they'll lead you to other conspirators in the Oklahoma City bombing. In the meantime they're hurting innocent people."

"You just assaulted a federal agent," he replied.

"There're must be twenty spectators watching this from the bridge. I wonder what they'll have to say about who assaulted whom. You want to get a news reporter down here?"

"You're threatening me?"

"It's not a threat, Mr. Rackley. You point a gun at me again and I'll pick your cotton."

He tossed the newspaper at my face. The pages broke apart in the wind and blew down the walkway. His fellow agent cleared his mouth of blood and spat it on the cement, then bent over and retrieved his automatic and replaced it into its holster. There was a large red knot on the bridge of his nose.

"I'm sorry I hurt you," I said.

"Blow me, Gomer," he replied.

I slipped the .38 back into its clip-on holster. I saw his eyes travel to the holster's position on my belt.

"It's unconcealed. I don't need a permit for it. Welcome to Montana," I said.

THAT NIGHT I took Temple to the Joan Baez concert at the university. The auditorium was packed, the air stifling. But the crowd didn't care. They were wild about Joan. George McGovern was in the audience and she introduced him as an old friend. She was sweating in the lights, her clothes sticking damply to her skin. Finally she touched her wrist to her brow in desperation and said, "I have to be honest with you. I've never been so hot in my life. Sweat is actually running down the backs of my legs."

A man in the balcony stood up, cupping his hands to his mouth, and shouted, "That's all right, Joan! You're still beautiful!"

The crowd roared. Her humor and grace, her sustained youthfulness and lack of any bitterness, and the incredible range of her voice were a conduit back into an era thirty years gone. For two hours it was 1969 and the flower children still danced barefoot on the lawn at Golden Gate Park.

But seated in the second row, in the seat next to the right aisle, was a man in a domed white hat with an Indian band around the crown and garters on his sleeves. In the glow of the stage lights his face looked as smooth as moist clay, clean of all imperfections, flat-bladed, the jaw hooked, the eyes fascinated, like those of a visitor in an alien environment.

He never applauded nor did his facial expression ever change from one of bemused curiosity. At intermission he remained in his chair, his rectangular posture like stone, so others had to labor to get around him.

"L.Q. Navarro used to say there are two Americas," I said to Temple.

"How's that?" she said, watching the musicians regroup on stage.

"One bunch wants good things for the world. The other bunch thinks the Earth is there to be ground up for profit. The cutting edge for the second bunch are guys like Wyatt Dixon."

"Are you telling me he's here?"

But just at that moment the man in the domed white hat went out the fire exit and let the metal door slam behind him.

"I just miss L.Q. sometimes," I said.

The lights went down and Joan Baez came to the microphone and introduced her niece. Temple was whispering to me behind her hand, something about the song "Silver Dagger," when I realized Cleo Lonnigan and her gay carpenter were seated three rows in front of us. Cleo had happened to turn and look up the aisle, and suddenly I was staring into her face.

I started to wave, then thought better of it.

"What's wrong?" Temple asked.

"Nothing," I replied.

But Temple followed my eyes to Cleo.

"Oh, it's Dr. Bedpan," Temple said.

"Come on, Temple," I said.

"Is she still staring at us?"

"No."

"Good. I was worried. I thought it was she who was rude and needed correcting."

Temple gazed benignly up at the stage.

At the end of the concert the audience brought Joan back on stage three times. The auditorium was sweltering now, the air fetid with body odor. After Joan left the stage a final time, someone opened a side door and the auditorium was suddenly flooded with cool air. I put my hand on Temple's arm and steered us for the exit.

Too late.

Cleo Lonnigan stood solidly in our path.

"Was Little Miss Muffet whispering about me?" she asked.

"Muffet?" Temple said.

"I'm sure you get my meaning," Cleo said.

"Shut your mouth, Cleo," I said.

"Hey, Cleo, let's ease on out of here," Eric, Cleo's carpenter friend, said.

"I'm sure that's just part of Dr. Lonnigan's regular pillow talk. She doesn't mean anything by it," Temple said to me.

"Look at me," Cleo said.

"Oh, I don't think so," Temple said.

"If you ever whisper behind my back or try

to ridicule me in public again, you'll wish you were back waiting tables or whatever you did before somebody let you in a junior college."

I put my arm around Temple's shoulders and almost forced her out the door.

"Would you get your arm off me, please?" Temple said, flexing her shoulders, her neck flaring with color.

"I apologize for that in there."

"You actually went to bed with her? It must be horrible remembering it."

"Why don't you ease up, Temple?"

The sky was green, the evening star glittering like a solitary diamond over the mountains in the west.

"Billy Bob, don't you see it?" Temple said.

"What?" I said, confused.

"It's that woman in there, or it's me, or a female DEA agent, or an old girlfriend from high school. We're just Valium. You're married to the ghost of L.Q. Navarro."

THAT NIGHT dry lightning rippled through the thunderclouds that sealed the Blackfoot Valley. The wind was up and the trees shook along the riverbank and I could see pine needles scattering on the surface of the water. I walked through Doc's fields, restless and irritable and discontent, a nameless fear trembling like a crystal goblet in my breast. The Appaloosa and thoroughbred in Doc's pasture nickered in the darkness and I could smell river damp and pine gum and wildflowers and wet stone and woodsmoke in the air, as though the four seasons of the year had come together at once and formed a dead zone under clouds that pulsed with light but gave no rain. I wished for earsplitting thunder to roll through the mountains or high winds to tear at barn roofs. I wished for the hand of God to destroy the airless vacuum in which I seemed to be caught.

My heart raced and my skin crawled with apprehension. It was the same feeling I'd had when L.Q. Navarro and I had waited in ambush for Mexican tar mules deep in Coahuila, our palms sweating on our weapons, our wrists tingling with adrenaline. We washed the salt and insects out of our eyes with canteens and could hardly contain our excitement, one that bordered almost on sexual release, when we saw silhouettes appear on a hill.

Lucas was still not back from the concert. I drove to East Missoula and parked in front of the brick cottage where Sue Lynn Big Medicine lived with her uncle. As I walked up to the porch I thought I heard voices behind the building.

"Is that you, Lucas?" I said into the darkness.

"Oh, hi, Billy Bob," he replied, walking toward me. "Something wrong?"

"I'm not sure. What's Sue Lynn doing?"

"She says a prayer to all the Grandfathers. Those are the spirits who live in the four corners of the universe."

"A prayer about what?"

"People got their secrets," he replied.

"What's *that* supposed to mean?" I said.

"She carries a big load about something. It don't always hep our love life."

"Come home with me," I said.

"She'll drive me. Everything's cool here."

"Did you see Wyatt Dixon at the concert?"

"Nope."

"He intends to do us harm, Lucas."

"He'd better not come around here. Sue Lynn's uncle was in the federal pen for cutting up a couple of guys on the Res."

"I can see this is a great place for a prayer garden. You're not moving in with this girl, are you?" I said.

"Quit calling her a girl. You worry too much, Billy Bob," he said, and hit me on the arm.

The innocence in his smile made my heart sink.

I DROVE BACK to Doc's place but found no release from the abiding fear that an undeserved fate was about to be visited upon someone close to me. The house was lighted and smoke flattened off the chimney and I could smell bread baking in the kitchen. Maisey played in front of the fireplace with her cat, the goodness in her young face un-diminished by the violence the world had done her. Doc had an apron tied around his waist and was carrying two bread pans with hot pads to the plank table in the center of the kitchen. He had already laid out jars of blackberry and orange jam and a block of butter and a cold platter of fried chicken and a pitcher of milk on the table, and for just a moment I saw the tranquillity in his expres-sion as he became both mother and doting father, and I was sure the bloodlust he had brought back from Vietnam had finally be-come a decaying memory.

But for some illogical reason I kept remem-bering a story, or rather an image, related to me by my grandfather about the death of the gunfighter John Wesley Hardin in the Acme Saloon in El Paso in 1895. Hardin was the most feared and dangerous man in Texas and may have killed as many as seventy-five men. In the Acme he was drinking shot-glass whiskey and rolling poker dice out of a leather cup. He inverted the cup and clapped the dice on the bar and said to a friend, "You got four sixes to beat."

That's when he heard a revolver cock behind him. A split second later a lawman named John Selman blew Hardin's brain matter on the mirror.

"You make me think of an ice cube sweating in a skillet. You worried about something?" Doc said.

"You rolled the dice for all of us, Doc," I replied.

"I'd change it if I could."

I paced up and down. "Did I get any phone calls?"

"Yeah, you did." He started slicing bread, the knife going *snick, snick, snick* into the plank table while I waited.

"From whom?"

"Cleo Lonnigan. She says you and Temple Carrol caused a scene at the concert."

"Is she crazy?"

"Yeah, probably."

"I appreciate your telling me that now."

"This bread is special. You want to try it with some jam?" he said.

An hour later, however, Doc's spirits died with the appearance of the sheriff's cruiser in the front yard, its emergency lights flashing.

"Step out here, Mr. Holland," the sheriff said.

"What do you want?" I asked.

"Are you hard of hearing?"

I walked out on the porch. Under the

shadow of his hat the sheriff's face looked as hard and bloodless as a turnip.

"Where were you two hours ago?" he asked.

"In East Missoula. Talking with my son."

"Cleo Lonnigan says you were on her property, up the Jocko."

"She's delusional."

"You're under arrest for assault and battery. Put your hands on the banister. No, don't open your mouth, don't think about it, just do what I tell you," he said.

I leaned on the porch railing and felt his hands travel over my person.

"Who is he supposed to have assaulted?" Doc said behind me.

"Go back inside, Dr. Voss. If there was ever a double-header giant-size pain in the ass, it's you two. You better hope that man don't die," the sheriff said, and hooked up my wrists and turned me toward his cruiser.

"Which man? Who are you talking about?" I said.

"That homosexual carpenter you beat the shit out of with a piece of pipe, one with an iron bonnet on it. Why didn't you just run his head over with a tractor wheel while you was at it?"

"This is insane," I said.

"Tell that to Cleo Lonnigan. She wants

your head on a post, Mr. Holland. You'd better be thankful I got to you first," he replied.

I TRIED to reason with him from the backseat of the cruiser as we headed toward the
county jail. When we passed through East
Missoula I craned my head to catch a glimpse
of the salvage yard where I had left Lucas
with Sue Lynn.

"Listen to me, Sheriff. I can't be in jail. Wyatt Dixon threatened both my son and Doc's
daughter. That woman's lying. I couldn't
have been up the Jocko. Stop and talk with
Lucas."

"Shut up, Mr. Holland," the sheriff replied.

I kicked the wire-mesh screen. "You're a
thick-headed old fool, sir. I'm an attorney. I
don't beat up innocent people with metal ob-
jects. Use your judgment, for God's sake," I
said.

"You hurt my vehicle, I'm gonna pull on a
side road and take your bark off," he said.

In the holding cell I yelled down the corridor, demanded to use the phone, and shook
the barred door against the lock. Finally a
sleepy, overweight turnkey walked down the
corridor and looked into my face.

"You want something?" he asked.

"To use the phone."

"It's out of order. We'll let you know when it's fixed," he said, and walked away.

At three in the morning the sheriff came down the corridor with a wood chair gripped in his hand. He set the chair in front of my cell and sat in it. He removed an apple wrapped in a paper bag from his coat pocket and began paring the skin away with a pocketknife.

"I checked with your son. He confirms your story," the sheriff said.

"Then kick me loose."

"Not till I tell Cleo she made a mistake. What'd you do to her, anyway?"

"You're keeping me here for my own protection?" I said incredulously.

A long curlicue of apple skin dangled from the sheriff's knife blade. "Let's see if I can remember her words. Something like 'I'd better not see that sorry sack of shit before you do.' You think she meant anything by that?"

"Where's my son?"

"Safe and snug in his tent. The Voss girl is with her daddy. You don't need to worry about them."

"Let me out of here, sir."

"I hear Carl Hinkel told you he was sixty years old outside that town meeting at the Holiday Inn. Made everybody think you was picking on an old man."

"I've had better moments."

"He's fifty-three. He isn't no military hero, either. He was kicked out of the Army for running some kind of PX scam in Vietnam. You know how you can tell when Carl Hinkel is lying? His lips are moving."

The sheriff split the apple longways and hollowed the seeds out of the pulp and stuck one piece into his mouth and speared the other half on his knife blade and extended it through the bars. "You got a good heart, Mr. Holland. But I suspect you was off playing pocket pool when the Lord passed out the brains."

Later, I lay down on a bench at the back of the cell and rested my arm across my eyes and tried to sleep. But I found no rest. L.Q. Navarro stood in the gloom, his arms folded, one foot propped backward on the wall, his eyes lost in thought.

"*Want to share what's on your mind?*" I asked.

"*Wyatt Dixon's gonna pay you back by hurting somebody close to you he don't have no connection with hisself.*"

"Who?" I asked.

"*He's a cruel man. He's got womanhood on the brain. You figure it out.*"

"*He's seen me with Cleo. Maybe it was Dixon who busted up her carpenter.*"

"*Good try, bud,*" L.Q. replied, and looked toward the window as a clap of dry thunder rolled through the mountains.

The light was turning gray outside and the storm clouds of last night now looked as if they were filled with snow. A trusty walked by my cell door with a mop and bucket in one hand.

"Get the turnkey down here," I said to him.

# Chapter
# 20

❦

TEMPLE WENT to the health club for her workout at six that morning. She couldn't believe the change in the weather. The temperature had dropped perhaps forty degrees and the fir trees at the top of the canyon were powdered with snow. She went up to the Nautilus room on the second floor of the club and did stomach crunches on a recliner board and watched through the window as a gray curtain of rain and mist and snow moved through the canyon, obscuring the cliff walls, smudging the trees, leaving only the emerald green ribbon of the river inside the mist.

The parking lot was white now and she could see the curlicues of car tracks on the cement and her Ford Explorer parked by the river. A low-slung red automobile pulled up on the far side of it, as though the driver could not decide whether to park. Then the mist and snow swirled over the lot and her vehicle faded and disappeared inside it.

She finished her workout and showered and dressed in her khaki jeans and a warm flannel shirt and her scuffed boots and put on a cotton jacket with a hood and began to tie it with a drawstring, then accidently pulled the plastic tippet off the string. She dropped the tippet into her shirt pocket and hung her workout bag on her shoulder and walked to her vehicle.

She shut the Explorer's door and started the engine. The windows had frosted and she turned on the heater and felt the coldness of the air surge into her face. While she waited for the engine to warm and the air vents to dry the moisture on the windows she pushed in the cigarette lighter so she could soften the plastic tippet and mold it back on the drawstring of her hood.

For just a second she saw a man's face under a hat brim in the rearview mirror, then the face slipped out of the glass and a pair of arms and gloved hands seized her neck and upper torso. Her attacker's strength was incredible. He lifted her over the seat and into the back as though she were stuffed with straw. Then he fitted his forearms on her neck and began to squeeze.

But the cigarette lighter was still in her hand and she reached backward with it blindly and felt the heated coils bite into his skin. An odor like animal hair burning in a trash barrel struck her nostrils. Even with the blood flow to her brain shutting down she held the lighter tightly against his flesh. She expected him to give up, his arms to fling her from him, but instead his body trembled and grew more rigid as he ate his pain and tightened his hold on her neck and crushed her head into the point of his chin, a grinding sound like a wood saw rasping against metal issuing from his throat.

The defroster was forming an oval-shaped clear area over the steering wheel now and Temple could see snow crystals blowing horizontally above the river. She could see college kids in bright winter clothes climbing a zigzag trail to the top of the mountain, their scarves whipping in the wind. She could see orange cliffs and trees and a solitary ball of tumbleweed bouncing across the land toward her vehicle. Her right hand went limp and she felt the cigarette lighter drop from her fingers, then the vision in her left eye clouded over and one side of her body went dead and she saw the tumbleweed bounce once over

the hood of her vehicle and slap wetly against
the defrosted clearing on the window glass
like an angry man stuffing a cork in a bottle.

WHEN SHE AWOKE, her eyes were bound
and she was being carried under the thighs
and back by someone with arms that were as
hard as oak. Her head was pressed against
his chest and she could hear the whirrings of
his heart and feel the rise and fall of his lungs
as he carried her through trees and across
ground that was littered with leaves and dead
twigs.

She tried to raise her hands, then realized
they were taped at the wrists and the tape
was wound around her body. The man carrying her knelt to the ground and placed her
on pine needles and leaves that were cold
against her skin where her shirt had pulled
out of her jeans. She could hear a river down
below, roaring through a canyon or perhaps
over rocks, and she could smell the coldness
of the water and the clean odor of new snow
in the wind. Then she heard a shovel bite
into the earth and she swallowed with a type
of fear she had never experienced before.

"Why are you doing this?" she asked.

But her words were lost in the sounds of
the river. She heard a second shovel chopping
at the ground, the metal clanging against

rocks, scraping back soil into a pile, the way someone might use an Army entrenching tool, and she knew two people were now digging her grave.

She tried to sit up, but a large hand restrained her, pressing her back onto the ground. The man lowered his face to hers, and she felt his breath on her skin and she knew his eyes were examining her mouth and nose and hair, like a curious animal investigating prey he had stumbled upon in a den. One finger traced a mole by the corner of her mouth, then his knuckle moved up and down her jawline, and she was convinced she had never been touched by a more brutal hand. It was sheathed in callus, as though the tissue had been rubbed with brick dust or burned and hardened with chemicals. The pads of the fingers had the texture of emery paper.

His thumb brushed her lips and his nail played with her teeth, then he pried them apart and inserted a rubber hose in her mouth.

"No, don't be trying to spit it out, now. That ain't smart. No-sirree-bob," the man's voice said.

But she did it anyway, spitting the hose out as well as the unwashed taste of his hand.

"You motherfuckers," she said, turning her head, trying to sight her words on his face.

"A profane woman brings discredit on her

gender. Please do not use words of that nature to me again. I declare, this world has done become a toilet," the man said.

He fitted his hands under her arms and dragged her into a depressed, rocky place that caused her heels to drop abruptly into the hardness of the ground. Then the two diggers began burying her alive, flinging spadeful after spadeful of dirt onto her body.

She was amazed at how little time it took for her feet, then her calves and thighs and stomach and chest and arms to be weighted and encased with dirt and rock that seemed to hold her as solidly as cement. One of the diggers stopped work and dropped his shovel on the ground and knelt down and removed a strand of hair from the edge of her mouth.

Then he touched the hose against her teeth, and this time she opened her mouth and took it.

The diggers went back to work, and she felt the dirt strike her cheeks like dry rain and the earth close on her face. The noise of the river and the voices of the diggers disappeared, as though effaced from the surface of the world, and the only sound she could hear was her own breathing through the hose and the thump of large stones being dropped into place on top of her.

She tried to think of the farm where she had lived as a little girl down by Matagorda

Bay. The pasture was carpeted with blue-bonnets in the spring, and a family of owls lived in a desiccated red barn behind the house, and at sunrise she would look through the window and see the owls gliding out of the woods to a hole in the barn roof, where they squeezed inside and disappeared just as the pinkness of the morning broke across the countryside. She came to associate the owls' flight into darkness with the fine beginning of a new day.

She thought of Gulf storms and the way the rain marched across the bay and danced on the watermelons in her father's fields. She saw the windmill ginning in the breeze and water pumping into the horse tank and the hard blueness of the sky and the moss straightening in the live oak that shaded one side of their house. She saw a sky writer spelling out the name of a soda pop, banking and climbing straight up into the dome of heaven itself, laying out white smoke one thick letter at a time. Then the letters lost their rigidity of line and broke into curds, like buttermilk, and her father told her that was the wind blowing across the top of the sky, and she wondered how wind could blow in a place where no trees grew.

She thought of all the earth's gifts that lived in the air, the smell of sea salt on a hot day, the way clouds transformed themselves when you lay in the grass and looked up into the heavens, the ozone that lightning gave off, the clatter of palm fronds, the red and gold leaves that cascaded out of the trees in the fall.

In her mind's eye she saw the mother owl returning from the woods again, gliding on extended wings toward the hole in the barn roof, its stomach gorged from feeding all night. The return of the owl always meant the beginning of a new day, didn't it, one filled with promise and expectation? But this time the owl didn't squeeze back through the hole in the roof. Instead, it flew directly at her face, its talons open.

It grew in size and shape and texture, its wings leathery, enormous in breadth now, flapping in the sky, blocking out the sun. The flapping sound was so loud now it droned in her ears and made the earth around her head tremble.

So this is the way it comes, she thought, and she gagged on her own saliva and felt the hose slip loose from her mouth.

That's when a pair of hands pried a flat stone loose from above her forehead and wiped the dirt from her face and pulled the tape from her eyes and removed a sliver of rock from her tongue.

"Billy Bob?" she said.

Then she was being pulled from her grave

by each arm, like a crucified figure being lifted from a cross.

"You're going to be all right, lady," the sheriff said. "Don't worry about a thing. We'll have you at the heliport and into St. Pat's in ten minutes."

She stared into the sunlight and at the silhouettes above her and at the humped shape of a helicopter by a stand of ponderosa that grew out of rock. "Billy Bob?" she said.

"Yes," I said.

But she looked down at the river bursting against boulders in the channel below us and at the iridescent spray on the canyon walls, then at the snow melting on the fir trees and the brown hawks wheeling in the sky and the long green roll of the northern Rockies and she could not find any other words to speak.

# Chapter

# 21

‹❧›

THE SHERIFF sat with me in the waiting
room at St. Patrick's Hospital. He watched
me walk up and down.

"I'll bring Dixon in. You got my word on
it," he said.

"Then what?" I said.

"She's never heard his voice before. I'll find
a half-dozen other peckerwoods and do a
voice lineup."

"She marked him with the cigarette lighter.
That should be enough."

"It's a start. Why don't you relax? You re-
mind me of a lizard panting on top of a hot
rock."

"You'd better get him off the street, Sheriff."

"I think your mama put you outdoors before the glue was dry, son. I really do," he replied.

A half hour later, after the sheriff had gone, Temple walked out of the emergency room. Her clothes were wrinkled and grimed with dirt, her hair in disarray.

"Give a girl a ride?" she said.

"You okay?"

"Sure," she said.

"Let me talk to the doctor first," I said.

She stepped close to me and leaned her forehead against my shoulder. I could smell the damp odor of earth and decayed leaves in her hair and clothes. "Take me home, Billy Bob," she said.

I opened the truck door for her and drove down Broadway toward her motel. The sky was blue, the snow melted from the trees now, the streets glistening and wet in the sunshine. It was a beautiful day, but Temple's eyes were disconnected from the world around her.

"Say it again. How did y'all find me?" she said.

"Somebody at the health club saw a man drive your Explorer away. I called the sheriff and he put an APB on it. A highway patrolman called in and said he'd seen a vehicle like yours headed west through Alberton Gorge. The sheriff got a helicopter and we took off."

"You could see the Explorer from the air?"

"Yeah, that's about it."

Her gaze was turned inward, as though she were adding up numerical sums.

"If they'd parked the Explorer in the trees, y'all would have flown right over me," she said.

"I guess we would have," I said.

She took a breath and pushed her hair back off her forehead.

"I don't think I'm going to sleep for a long time," she said.

I walked with her into her motel room, then left while she showered and changed. I drove down to a fast-food restaurant and ordered fried chicken and french-fried potatoes and a milk shake to go. When I returned to the motel, Temple opened the door on the night chain, her .38 hidden behind her leg.

"It's only me," I said, and tried to smile.

She slipped the chain and let me in and placed her revolver on a table by the door. She had put on makeup and a fresh pair of jeans and a blouse with flowers on it, but her eyes would not meet mine and her breath hung in her throat, as though the air were tainted and might injure her lungs.

"Don't you want to eat something?" I asked.

"Not now."

"Those tar mules down in Coahuila set a field on fire with me in the middle of it," I said. "I would have burned to death if L.Q. hadn't pulled me up on his horse. I still have nightmares about it. But that's all they are, nightmares."

She sat down on the edge of the bed and looked into space.

"Why did they give me the air hose? Why did they want to keep me alive?" she said.

"To make both of us suffer."

"I spit it out the first time. The second time I let him put it in my mouth. That bastard won, didn't he?" she said.

"No. They're cowards. Their kind never win," I said.

But my words were useless. She squeezed her temples and lowered her head, her eyes shut. I sat beside her and placed my arm around her and felt her back shaking, as though an incurable coldness had invaded her body.

I STAYED with Temple until she fell asleep, then I covered her up and left a note to the effect that I would return later in the day.

I drove west of town, through green pastureland and small horse ranches with new red barns and white fences, then up the dirt road that led to Terry Witherspoon's shack above the Clark Fork River. I parked in the clearing and banged on his door and looked in his windows, then walked around back.

A trash fire was burning in a rusty oil barrel. The thick curds of black smoke rolling from it were laced with an eye-watering stench. I found a rake in a toolshed and kicked the barrel on its side and combed out the contents.

In the tangle of wire and cans and tinfoil he hadn't bothered to separate out from his ignitable trash were plastic bottles of motor oil, animal entrails and strips of fur, and a blackened roll of pipe tape.

I went back into the toolshed and hunted in the corners and under a molded canvas tarp and in a huge wood locker box full of tractor parts. Then I pushed over a stack of bald tires and found an Army surplus entrenching tool that had been propped inside, the blade still locked in the right-angle position of a hoe, the tip scratched a dull silver from fresh digging.

Just as I went outside I saw Witherspoon walk into the clearing, a wood rabbit with a bloody head hanging from his belt, a .22 bolt-action rifle over his shoulder. A bone-handled skinning knife in a scabbard was stuck down in his side pocket. For just a moment he looked like a nineteenth-century illustration in a Mark Twain novel.

"What do you think you're doing?" he asked.

"Tearing your place up. You couldn't bring yourself to get rid of the E-tool, could you? You're a mountain man. A mountain man needs all his equipment," I said.

"Stay away from me," he said.

I slapped him across the face, so hard the light went out of his eyes and his glasses swung from one ear. He peeled his glasses off his head and stared at me in disbelief.

"Go ahead. Throw down on me," I said.

"You've got a gun in your belt."

"That's right," I said, and slapped him again. My handprint was bright red on his cheek and there was spittle on his chin. "Where's Wyatt?"

"I don't know. Why don't you go to his house instead of coming here?" he said, his eyes blinking in anticipation of being hit again.

"Because he's not going to be there. Because he's not as stupid as you are."

I ripped his rifle from his shoulder and whipped it by the barrel against a pine trunk. The stock snapped in half and spun crazily, like a splintered baseball bat, out into the trees.

Then I headed for Terry Witherspoon again.

"Wyatt's at a rodeo in Billings. Carl flies him to all his rodeos," he said hurriedly. Involuntarily his thumb hooked over the bone handle of his knife.

I hit him with my fist and knocked him on the ground. Then I knelt over him and knotted his shirt in one hand and pulled the .38 from my belt and gripped it by the barrel, the butt curved outward, like a hammer.

"Does it make you feel powerful to bury a woman alive, Terry?" I asked.

"I didn't do it," he replied.

"Do what? Say what you did not do. How do you know what I'm talking about?"

His words bound in his throat and his eyes looked at mine and filled with genuine terror.

"I didn't do whatever you're talking about. I been here. I don't have a car. I can't go anywhere."

I dropped the pistol to the ground and drove my fist into the center of his face, then released his shirt and clenched my hand on his throat, pinching off his air, and raised my right fist again.

On the edge of the clearing, his Stetson and striped black suit cut by a shaft of sunlight, I saw L.Q. Navarro looking at me, his gold toothpick between his teeth, his lips pursed as though he were witnessing a spectacle that offended moral paradigms he considered mandatory in his friends.

I pulled Terry Witherspoon to his feet and shoved him toward the woods and kicked him in the tailbone.

"Get out of here," I said.

"I live here," he said, his breath hiccupping in his throat.

"That doesn't matter. Get out of my sight until I'm gone."

He backed away from me, hooking on his glasses crookedly, then turned and hurried into the forest, the dead rabbit coated with dust and blood, swinging stiffly against his thigh.

I drove back into Missoula and used a pay phone to call the sheriff at his office. There was no answer. I called the 911 dispatcher.

"It's Sunday. He's not in his office today," she said.

"Give me his home number."

"I can't do that."

"This is about an attempted homicide. I'll give you my number. I'll wait by the pay phone."

"Sir, you'd better not be jerking people around," she replied.

But she pulled it off. Five minutes later the pay phone rang.

"Go up to Terry Witherspoon's shack on the river. There's a roll of half-burned pipe tape by the trash barrel in back. Get there before he finishes destroying it and I bet it'll match the tape that was used to tie up Temple," I said.

"You tossed his place?" the sheriff said.

"No, I tossed Witherspoon."

"I think you just managed to blow it for everybody. It's Sunday. I have to get a hold of a judge and a search warrant."

"I need directions to Nicki Molinari's dude ranch," I said.

"You're about to start a second career, son. Convict cowboy over at Deer Lodge. The place is full of smart asses who got their own mind about everything. You'll fit right in," he replied.


BUT ACTUALLY I didn't need the sheriff's directions to find the Molinari ranch. Previously the sheriff had mentioned it was outside Stevensville, twenty-five miles down in the Bitterroots. On Monday, I drove to Stevensville and stopped at a barbershop in an old brick building on the main street and went inside. Two barbers were cutting hair while a third customer, an old man with his trousers tucked inside his boots, read a newspaper, his elbows on his knees, his face scowling with disapproval at the news of the day.

"Could you tell me where Nicki Molinari lives?" I asked.

Both the barbers turned their backs on me and went on snipping and combing hair as though they hadn't heard me. The customers in the barber chairs cut their eyes at me, then looked straight ahead.

But the old man had lowered his newspaper and was staring at me with the intensity of a hawk sighting in on a field mouse from a telephone line. His skin looked like it had been cured in a smokehouse, his clothes soaked in a bucket of starch and flat-ironed on his skinny frame. A cross was embroidered with gold thread on the pocket of his white snap-button shirt, and there were choleric blazes in his throat, as though heat were climbing out of his collar.

"You a pimp?" he asked.

"Sir?" I said.

"I asked if you're a procurer, one of them that brings women out to that greaser's ranch." His accent was Appalachian, West Virginia or perhaps Kentucky, a wood rasp being ground across a metal surface.

"No, sir. I'm an attorney."

"Is there a difference?" he said.

"Thanks for y'all's time," I said, and went back out on the street.

But the old man followed me out on the sidewalk. The Sapphire Mountains rose up behind him, their green slopes the texture of velvet, the crests strung with clouds.

"What's your business with that gangster?" he asked.

"As you imply, sir, it's my business."

"No, it ain't. He's my neighbor. I run a church. Now I got a shitpot of criminals and whores swimming naked in a pool within view of our services."

"I guess what I aim to do is mess up Nicki Molinari's day any way I can."

When he grinned he showed two teeth that stood up in his gums like slats.

"Drive straight toward the Sapphires. The China-Polish hogs are mine. The Cadillacs and the naked whores throwing beach balls on the lawn are his," he said.

THE RANCH owned by Nicki Molinari and his friends looked out of place, out of sync with itself, as though it had been designed and put together by someone who had toured the West and wasn't quite sure what he remembered about it.

The house was Santa Fe stucco, with shady arcades and tile walkways and big glazed urns spilling over with flowers. An antique freight wagon sat by the driveway, as though announcing a historical connection to the past. A half-dozen horses, their backs rubbed with saddle sores the size of half dollars, stood listlessly in a lot that was nubbed down to the dirt, while rolled hay lay humped and yellow in the fields. A swimming pool the color and shape of a chemical green teardrop steamed in the cool air next to a new log barn that housed no animals or farm machinery but an enclosed batting cage with an automatic pitching machine inside.

I pulled into a gravel parking area on the side of the house. Molinari shut down the pitching machine and opened a door in the batting cage and came toward me, dressed only in tennis shoes and knee-length socks and cutoff sweatpants that were hitched tightly into his genitalia.

"Am I gonna have trouble here?" he said.

"Call somebody if you feel uncomfortable," I replied.

"If I call anybody, it'll be for an ambulance. You're starting to be a nuisance."

"You bashed Cleo Lonnigan's carpenter. I got picked up for it. While I was in jail, a friend of mine was buried alive by Wyatt Dixon."

His eyes fixed on mine, as though reading significance in my words that only he understood. He scratched at a pimple on top of his shoulder.

"I'm sorry about the carpenter, but it's not on me. Cleo is sitting on money that don't belong to her. I told you, the people her husband stiffed give out motivational lessons nobody forgets. Her husband didn't learn that lesson, either, and it got him and his kid killed," he said.

He squeezed the pimple until it popped, then brushed at his skin.

"Save the shuck for your hired morons. My friend and I took your weight. That means if Wyatt Dixon comes around my friend again, I'm going to be out to see you," I said.

"Right," he said, and looked off into the breeze. His skin was olive-toned and looked cool and taut in the sunshine. "You want to hit some in the cage?"

"No."

"Don't go, man. What do you think of Xavier Girard as a writer?"

"Why?"

"Because he's writing my life story. Because I've told him stuff I don't tell everybody."

"What stuff?"

"You asked me once how I got out of Laos. I rode out on the skid of a helicopter. Except I pushed another guy off the skid. A GI. At five hundred feet." His eyes left mine, then came back and refocused on me again. His face seemed to energize, as though the answer to all his questions lay within inches of his grasp. "After you capped your friend, that other Texas Ranger, you saw a shrink?"

I wanted to simply walk away, to pretend I was above his inquisition and his criminal level of morality. He waited, his face expectant. A woman with dyed red hair came out of the house and got into a convertible with a bright white top and began blowing the horn at him.

"Shut up that damn noise!" he yelled at her, then turned back to me. "How'd you get that guy off your conscience?"

"I didn't. I never dealt with it. I feel sorry for you," I said.

"You never dealt—" he said, then stopped and pressed his fingers in the center of his forehead, his mouth open slightly, as though he were fingering a tumor or perhaps recognizing a brother-in-arms.

THAT SAME DAY Carl Hinkel drifted his single-engine plane on currents of warm air above the Bitterroot River and landed on a freshly mowed pasture at the rear of his ranch. As soon as Wyatt Dixon stepped from the passenger door, he was arrested by two sheriff's deputies. But before they could cuff him he peeled off his T-shirt and shook it loose from his hand like a stripteaser on a stage. The veins and tendons in his upper torso looked like the root system in a tree.

"Please notice I am burned from the neck all the way down one shoulder," he said, lifting a thick pad of grease-stained bandages from his skin. "I am placing myself at y'all's disposal, with hopes you will take me to a hospital. It is civil servants such as yourself a rodeo cowboy must turn to when he don't have enough sense not to drop a red-hot car muffler on his face."

He held his right hand in stiff salute against his eyebrow.

The voice lineup consisted of an escaped Arkansas convict who was being held in the county jail, a toothless cook at the transient shelter, a sheriff's deputy from Sweetwater, Texas, an insane street preacher who spent the day shouting at traffic in the middle of town, and a university speech therapist from Oklahoma whose voice sounded like wire being pulled through a hole in a tin can. Together, they represented a cross section of mushmouth and adenoidal Southern accents that would have probably caused Shakespeare to burn his texts and rewrite his plays in Cantonese.

But the lineup was not like one shown in television dramas. Neither the city police nor the sheriff's department had a stage, and the latter did not even have an interview room large enough to accommodate the six men who were to take part in the voice identification. So the sheriff recorded Wyatt Dixon and the five other men on cassettes and numbered each cassette one through six. Each man read the same statement into the microphone: "This world has done become a toilet."

Then Temple sat in the sheriff's office, a notepad on her knee, and listened to the cassettes, one at a time, while I sat behind her.

She was attentive, motionless, her head lowered slightly, while the sheriff played the first four. Then he put the fifth cassette into the machine and hit the play button. The voice was Wyatt Dixon's, but without dramatic emphasis, devoid of the manufactured and startled tone that characterized his speech. Temple raised her head, as though she were going to speak, then she motioned the sheriff to play the sixth tape.

"There ain't no hurry. You want me to play any of them again?" the sheriff asked.

"Number two and five," she said.

"Yes, ma'am," he said.

She listened again, then nodded, her lips crimping together.

"It's number two," she said.

The sheriff slapped the back of his head and blew out his breath.

"No?" she said.

"You just picked out my deputy," the sheriff said. He looked at me, his cheeks puffed with air.

"Don't say what I think you're fixing to," I said.

"I got to kick him loose. Terry Witherspoon got rid of the pipe tape you called me about. There are no latents in Ms. Carrol's vehicle. Three or four people over in Billings are willing to swear Dixon was at the rodeo when Ms. Carrol was abducted," he said.

"Which people in Billings?" I asked.

"A prostitute and Carl Hinkel and a couple of ex-convicts. He don't hang out with your regular civic club types."

"Talk to them about the consequences for perjury. Bring in Witherspoon. Put him in a cell full of Indians and blacks and lose his paperwork," I said.

"Come on, Ms. Carrol, I'll walk you to your car," the sheriff said, ignoring me.

"I can manage, thank you," she replied.

"Don't misinterpret the gesture. I'm just going across the street to buy my grandson a birthday present. Counselor, one way or another I'm gonna put Wyatt Dixon and this Witherspoon kid out of business. But in the meantime they'd better remain the healthiest pair of white trash in Missoula County. We clear on this?"

"Not really," I said.

He hooked on his glasses and studied the calendar on his desk.

"You got about three weeks before Dr. Voss goes to trial for Lamar Ellison's murder. Why don't you turn your attentions to your profession and quit pretending you're still a lawman?" he said.

"Don't you dare speak down to him like

that. He was a Texas Ranger. In the old days he and his partner would have fed Wyatt Dixon into a hay baler," Temple said.

The sheriff flexed his dentures and tried to obscure his face when he fitted on his hat, but he could not hide the embarrassed light in his eyes.

THAT NIGHT Lucas returned late from Sue Lynn's house. Through my bedroom window I saw him build a fire by his tent and squat next to the flames and slice open a can with his pocketknife and pour the contents into a skillet. I put on a coat and walked down to the riverbank and sat on a stump behind him without his hearing me.

"Lordy, you give me a start!" he said when he saw me.

"Guilty conscience?" I said.

He stirred the corned beef hash in the skillet and sprinkled red pepper on it. "You was born for the pulpit, Billy Bob," he said.

"Go back home, Lucas."

"I've done fell in love with Montana. I'm thinking of transferring up here to the university."

The woods were dark, the larch trees shaggy with moss. An animal, perhaps the cougar that had been getting into the pet bowls, growled somewhere on the other side of the river. Lucas shifted his weight and stared into the darkness, one knee crimping into the pine needles on the ground, his young face and long-sleeved cream-colored shirt painted with the light from the fire. I looked at the innocence in his face and his refusal to show fear, and felt again my old inadequacy as his father.

But before I could speak, he said, "You believe in hell, Billy Bob?"

"I can't rightly say."

"Sue Lynn thinks she's going there."

"What has she done that's so terrible?"

"She has this nightmare all the time. It might make sense to you, but I sure cain't cipher it out."

THE WORLD of Sue Lynn Big Medicine's sleep seemed more a collective record of her people than a dream. There was no historical date on the scene nor many particular names associated with it, but the season was summer and the hills above the river were treeless and golden in the heat, the water down in the river basin milky green, tepid to the touch, the surface flecked with cottonwood bloom.

The column of soldiers came out of the south, the razored blue peaks of distant mountains at their backs. They wore gray hats that were damp and wilted in the heat and blue blouses and trousers with yellow stripes on the legs, and the pommels of their saddles were strung with wooden canteens that clunked against the leather. The soldiers' blouses were sun-faded and stiff with salt, puffed in the hot wind, and their trousers so dark with sweat against their saddles that the soldiers looked as if they had fouled themselves.

The Crow scouts rode at the head of the column with an officer who was dressed differently from the rest. His boots were polished and flared at the knees, his trousers skintight, his yellow hair longer than a woman's, his hat festooned with bird plumes. The sun danced on the nickel plate of his English Bulldog revolvers. An ethereal light seemed to glow in his face, and he breathed the wind as though the chaff and dust in it were simply the embellishments on a grand day in history that was of his own manufacture.

The Crow horses pitched their heads, the nostrils dilating, the eyes protruding like walnuts, then they whirled in circles, fighting against the bit as though snakes lay in the golden grass that grew up the slope of the hill. The cottonwoods on the river were empty of birds, the buffalo briefly visible on the horizon, then gone. Magpies clattered in an arroyo, pulling shreds of meat from the exposed ribs of an elk that had already been butchered and skinned with stone knives.

The wind changed and a familiar odor struck the noses of the Crow scouts, a dense mixture of woodsmoke, horses hobbled among shade trees, animal hides curing over fires piled with willow branches and wet leaves, and churned mud flats that were now green and slick with feces in the sun.

The Crow were the first to reach the crest of the hill. What they saw in the valley below them turned them to stone.

The wickiups along the river and up the arroyos numbered in the thousands. These were all Sioux and Northern Cheyenne, the enemies of the Crow, but for just a moment the scouts wished the Crow were part of the assemblage, too, because surely the red people now had enough numbers to drive the white men back across the mountains to a place in the East where all the white man's diseases and his greed and his treachery came from.

The officer who was different from all the others joined them, his face impassive, his profile motionless against the hard blue background of the sky. His hair hung in ringlets on his shoulders, and he wiped the dampness off his throat with a kerchief and raised himself slightly in the stirrups, the leather creaking under him, in order to form a better view of the valley.

The Crow waited, not speaking, their faces as flat and empty of emotion as potter's clay. They had long ago learned not to speak to the officer unless he addressed them first. His anger was of a quiet kind that burned just below the skin, but his capacity for cruelty was legendary. The kitchen tent had been converted to a workshop where the officer indulged his hobby of stuffing the animals and birds he shot while his men ate cold rations. A soldier who stole a dried apple from a supply wagon was shaved bald and not allowed to mount his horse for one hundred miles. Three deserters were forced to kneel, then were shot to death at point-blank range.

Another officer, this one young, the exposed skin of his chest emblazoned with a V-shaped patch of sunburn, rode forward from the column, posting in the saddle.

"Sir?" he said, sweat running through his eyebrows.

But the officer who was different, whom the Indians called the Son of the Morning Star, did not answer.

"Sir?" the younger officer repeated.

"What?"

"What are your orders, sir?"

The Son of the Morning Star pulled off his fringed gloves and rubbed the tips of his fingers against the heel of his right hand, as though enjoying the feel of the oil in his skin.

"Why, young man, I'm very glad you asked that. I think I'm going to take an elk's tooth off a squaw's dress today," he said.

The younger officer let the focus go out of his eyes to hide his recognition of the senior officer's implication.

Big Medicine, the spokesman for the Crow scouts, glanced at his friends, then backed his horse away from the crest until he was abreast of the Son of the Morning Star.

"We go down there?" Big Medicine asked.

"They're ours for the taking, my painted friend," the Son of the Morning Star said.

"We go down there, in that valley, we sing death song first," he said.

"Then you are cowards and you do not belong on this hill. Be gone from my sight," the Son of the Morning Star replied.

But the three Crow did not move. The Son of the Morning Star was scribbling in a book filled with blank pages. He tore a page with a single line on it from the book and handed it to a messenger.

"Can you read what that says?" he asked.

"Yes, sir. 'Hurry—bring packs,'" the messenger replied.

"Take these cowards back with you. They dishonor sacred ground," the Son of the Morning Star said.

The Crow scouts looked at one another again, then rode their horses in file past the senior officer, their eyes straight ahead, the coup feathers in their hair stiffening and flattening in the wind.

But Big Medicine reined his horse and turned it in a circle and pulled a heavy, cap-and-ball Army-issue revolver from a holster strapped across his chest. He clenched the revolver by the barrel and flung it spinning down the hill.

"The Shyelas hate Son of the Morning Star for all the women and children and old ones he killed on the Washita. You will take no button off a squaw's clothes today. Instead your spirit will travel the Ghost Trail without ears to listen or sight to see," he said.

If the senior officer heard, he gave no sign. His posture in the saddle was regal, his thoughts already deep in the battle that was about to take place. The Crow disappeared down the slope, through the golden fields of yellow grass, out of history, while the long column of sweat-soaked soldiers rode past them toward the senior officer and the crest of the hill and the panorama of sky and cottonwoods on a lazy green river and thousands of deerhide wickiups that teemed with families who never thought they would be attacked by a military force as small as the one now flowing over the hill's crest.

But the next events in Sue Lynn Big Medicine's dream broke with history and reason.

Even though she was a Crow, she was inside the encampment of Sioux and Northern Cheyenne and saw the attack through their eyes rather than through her people's.

The soldiers rode down the valley with a recklessness that the Indians could not believe, firing pistols and rifles from their saddles into the wickiups, splitting their column down the middle to encircle the Indians as though they were about to round up livestock. She heard toppling rounds whirring past her head and saw the stitched deerhide on the wickiup she had just exited pop and snap on the lodge poles that supported it.

She raced back inside and saw her ten-year-old brother sitting on a buffalo robe, holding the flat of his palm against his mouth. He removed his hand and stared at it and at the circle of blood in the center of it, then looked at her and grinned and put his fingers to the small hole in his chest. She sank to both knees in front of him, while bullets from the soldiers' guns tore through the wickiup, and held both his hands in hers and watched the focus go out of his eyes and the pallor of death invade his cheeks.

When she rose to her feet the streaks of blood on her hands felt as hot as burns. She wiped the blood on her face and hair and went outside into the swirl of dust from the soldiers' horses and the running of people from the wickiups. Up the slope she saw the officer the Indians called the Son of the Morning Star. Many of his men were down now, running for the hilltop behind them, their horses gut-shot and writhing in the grass, but the Son of the Morning Star was still mounted and only yards from the edge of the village, the bit sawed back in his horse's mouth, while he fired one ball after another from his revolvers.

But his courage or his devotion to killing Indians or his grandiose belief in himself, whatever quality or vice had allowed him to remain unscathed in years of warfare, suddenly had no application in the maelstrom he had ridden into. His men, mostly German and Irish immigrants from the slums of the East, many who had never heard a shot fired in anger, were now forming a ragged perimeter on the hilltop, their noncommissioned officers screaming orders at men whose hands shook so badly they could hardly throw the breech on their rifles.

The Son of the Morning Star rode after his men, firing back over his horse's rump to cover their retreat, his heels slashing into his horse's ribs, his face filled with rage, as though history were betraying him. Then the Indians surged out of the encampment, with arrows and bows and coup sticks and Spencer and Henry repeaters and steel hatchets and stone axes and bundles of fire they dragged on ropes behind their horses.

The squaws ferreted out the wounded who tried to hide in the cattails along the river and mutilated them with knives. The wind was blowing out of the south, and the fires climbed up the hill where the surviving soldiers were kneeling in the grass and shooting down the slope. Many of the soldiers had carried whiskey in their canteens and now had no water. The dust and smoke swirled over them, and down the hill they heard the screams of their friends inside the burning grass, saw blackened shapes trying to rise like crippled birds from the flames. Some of the soldiers on the hill inverted their pistols and discharged them into their mouths.

Inside it all the Son of the Morning Star fired his nickel-plated revolvers at the Indians, who now had broken through his perimeter and were clubbing his men to death with stone axes, cracking skulls and jawbones apart as if they were clay pots. The Indians swept across the top of the hill, and the Son of the Morning Star fell to one knee, like a medieval knight giving allegiance to a king, an arrow quivering in his rib cage. The squaws thronged up the incline, their throats warbling with birdsong.

In the dream Sue Lynn Big Medicine was in their midst and saw the Shyela and Sioux women bend over the fallen officer and pierce his eyes and ears with bone awls. But it was not enough price to exact from him, she thought, not nearly enough, and with a knife made from rose-colored quartz and elk antler she stooped over the fallen officer and pulled loose his belt and unfastened the top button of his trousers and pulled the cloth back from the whiteness of his stomach.

Her hand slashed downward with the knife. When she had finished, the Son of the Morning Star seemed to stare into her face with his destroyed eyes, seeing her inside his mind, discovering only now the level of enmity in which he was held by his adversaries. Then with the other squaws Sue Lynn forced the bloody burden in her hands down his throat. From the bottom of the slope she thought she heard the screams of a soldier burning to death inside the grass, then realized, her eyes tightly shut now, her temples thundering like a thousand drums, it was her own voice bursting from her chest, breaking against her teeth, keening into a sky that had already filled with carrion birds.

LUCAS BROKE two eggs on top of the corned beef hash, then divided the pan with a spatula and put half his food in a tin plate for me.

"Sue Lynn says the Indians gelded Custer and suffocated him with his own scrotum," he said. "That's not in history books, is it?"

"Not to my knowledge."

"How come she's in a dream like that?"

I picked up a pebble and tossed it into the river.

"I was never big on psychoanalysis."

"Billy Bob, analyzing is a full-time job with you. You see a flea on a possum's belly and you got a take on it."

"I think Sue Lynn killed somebody."

The smile fell away from his lips and he stared at me with his mouth open. Out in the darkness I heard an animal's roar, and this time I knew it was a cougar's.

# Chapter

# 22

❧

EARLY THE NEXT MORNING Maisey looked through the front window, sipping coffee in a house robe, her face quizzical.

"What are you looking at?" I asked.

"Not much. Xavier Girard throwing pine-cones at the chipmunks," she replied.

I walked outside into the coolness of the morning, under the vastness of a purple, rain-scented sky that had not been touched yet by the sun. The sound of the river was loud through the trees, the riffle blackish-green in the shadows, the air sweet with the smell of woodsmoke and wet pine needles.

Xavier stood by the bank, his back to me. He wore a nylon vest and plaid flannel shirt and baggy jeans, and his neck was cuffed with sunburn and his hair freshly cropped.

When he turned around, I hardly recognized him. The alcoholic flush and dissipated lines were gone from his face. He grinned with the easy composure of a man who had just been given a new lease on life.

"Can I help you?" I asked.

"I took your advice and started hitting some meetings. My sponsor said I needed to come out here and tell you that," he said.

"Well, I appreciate that," I replied, not knowing what else to say.

"I hear you had a talk with Nicki Molinari."

"Yeah, I happened to be in his neighborhood."

"He's quite a guy."

"That's one way to put it," I said, my sense of discomfort starting to grow.

"I guess you don't think much of me. I mean, letting the guy get in the sack with my wife."

"I don't remember much of that afternoon, sir," I said, studying a spot of the riverbank.

"Nicki's free ride is over. I've learned in the program I don't have to take bullshit off greaseballs or anybody else."

"I didn't know AA worked like that."

"It's a great life. Everybody ought to try it," he said.

"You bet," I said, and glanced at my watch. "Well, big day ahead. All the best to you."

I walked back into the house, then looked through the window at his Jeep Cherokee bouncing across the field toward the dirt road.

"Was he drunk?" Maisey asked.

"He says he's out of the saloons."

She waited for me to continue.

"It's no accident a lot of saloons have revolving doors," I said.

THE TRUTH was I didn't care what Xavier and Holly Girard or Nicki Molinari did with their lives. The truth was I had even stopped worrying about Doc. The truth was I could not get the sadistic injury done to Temple Carrol by Wyatt Dixon and Terry Witherspoon off my mind, done to her in all probability with the approval of Carl Hinkel.

I put my rucksack and fly vest and fly rod and creel into my truck and picked up Temple at her motel and took her for breakfast at a truck stop in Lolo. Then we drove deeper into the Bitterroot Valley, up a dirt road through meadowland to a canyon with a roaring creek and a chain of deep-water pools at the bottom. A trail followed the creek up a steady incline, winding under cliffs and the ponderosa that grew out of rock, until the creek and a series of falls were far below us. Then the trail leveled out in a box canyon filled with birch trees and we came out on the creek again, and sat on a table rock just above a pool that was so clear you could see the cut-throat and brook trout ginning in the current, ten feet below the surface.

I had known Temple most of her life. She hid her pain, rarely complained, and never accepted defeat. But now she had the same detached cast in her eyes that I had seen in Maisey's after Maisey was gang-raped. I flipped a dry fly at the head of the pool and hooked a small cutthroat, then wet my hand and released it and gave the rod to Temple.

"Cast it over on the other side. There's usu-ally a fat one hanging under the bank," I said.

She was sitting against a birch tree with her knees pulled up before her. The rock was mottled with lichen and the leaves overhead flickered against the sunlight.

"I'll just watch," she said.

"I tried to get Lucas to go back to Deaf Smith. You wouldn't consider that yourself, would you?"

"I'll pass, thanks," she said.

I laid down my fly rod and sat next to her. I put my hand on her shoulder and brushed a lock of hair off her forehead. When she looked into my eyes I could read no meaning in them.

"What are you thinking, Temple?" I asked.

But she didn't answer. She leaned her head back against the tree and watched a bighorn sheep that stood on a ledge high up on the canyon's far wall. Her complexion had the glow and smoothness of a newly opened rose. I rested my hand on top of hers.

"Do you think of me as a victim, Billy Bob?" she asked.

"No, I don't."

"Then you don't need to worry about me."

Her nylon backpack was propped against a huckleberry bush. The flap had fallen open and inside I could see the blue-black finish and pearl-handled butt of her .38 revolver.

"You aim to kill Wyatt Dixon, don't you?" I said.

"You think of me as a friend or you think of me with guilt. But you don't think of me in other ways," she said, ignoring my statement.

"You're not fair," I said, and took my hand from hers.

She rose to her feet and gathered up her backpack by its straps and stepped off the rock onto the trail.

"I'm going to walk back now. It's pretty out here. Don't worry about this stuff. It's not your fault," she said.

And with that she slung her backpack over one shoulder and strolled back down the trail, her chestnut hair freckled with the sunlight that shone through the canopy, the clash of color in her jeans and pink tennis shoes somehow reminiscent of the little girl who lived inside her and who I'd learned could sometimes break my heart.

MY GREAT-GRANDFATHER, Sam Morgan Holland, the drover and drunkard and gunfighter turned saddle preacher, had kept a journal that told of the herds he had swum across the Red River and chased through mesa country and stream bottoms in electric storms on the Goodnight-Loving and Chisholm trails, his armed encounters with the Dalton-Doolin gang in Oklahoma Territory, and his love affair with the outlaw woman, the Rose of Cimarron.

But he wrote mostly about the abiding anger inside him that never allowed him to rest, that made him sit sleepless on the side of his bed in a patch of moonlight, his palms aching to hold his twin Navy Colt revolvers. In Wichita and Newton and Abilene, while prostitutes watched from the balconies of saloons, he lighted up the street with the flashes from his revolvers and filled the night with thunder and the smell of cordite and for just a moment felt he had righted the world and driven evil from his own breast by taking the lives of others who were worse men than he.

How did a man who had always been inclined for the cloth, who was basically decent and honorable, allow himself to be branded with the mark of Cain?

He did it at Little Round Top and Kennesaw Mountain and the Battle of Franklin, and learned it was easy. You just had to convince yourself, or be convinced by others, that your enemy deserved his fate and keep your mind free of empathy and moral restraint before you did it.

I ATE SUPPER early that afternoon, out of a tin plate and a cup from a GI mess kit, sitting on a stump down by the river, so I would not have to talk to anyone before I left Doc's house. But Doc caught me before I drove away.

"Where you going with L.Q.'s pistol?" he asked.

"Target shooting."

"You don't have enough room around here?" he said.

"Tag along if you like." I focused my eyes at a spot in empty space.

"You go ahead. Stay out of trouble. Don't follow my example."

"Wouldn't dream of it," I said.

I DROVE DOWN to Hamilton and went past Carl Hinkel's ranch to a farm road that wound down to the Bitterroot River. I parked my truck among cottonwoods in an empty campground and walked downstream until I was at the back of Hinkel's property. I stepped across a barbed-wire fence that ran down through a slough into the river and walked up a boulder-strewn, wooded incline until I was slightly above the log house where Wyatt Dixon lived. I could hear the muttering of a chain saw on the far side of the house.

The sun was still above the Bitterroots, but the pine trees on the incline were deep in shadow, the boulder I stood behind cool and damp to the touch. The light on the fields was soft, almost like a green vapor hanging over the grass, and Wyatt Dixon, stripped to the waist, his jeans so tight they looked stitched to his skin, walked into full view and went to work on a log he had propped across sawhorses, lopping it into segments for firewood.

The wind was in my face, the distance about seventy yards.

I took L.Q. Navarro's .45 revolver from my belt and steadied it with both hands on top of the boulder and sighted on Dixon's back.

His skin was taut and brown, etched with vertebrae, his biceps pumped as he worked, his silky red hair creased in the wind.

Walk away, I heard a voice say inside me.

*L.Q.?*

I looked around me in the shadows, among the pine trunks and the boulders that grew out of the humus like the tops of toadstools, but L.Q. was not there.

I pulled back the hammer on full cock and fired.

The .45 jerked upward from the rock, the report flattening in the wind.

I saw water jump in the river on the far side of Wyatt Dixon, and I knew the round had carried high and to the left.

My heart was thundering now. I fired a second and third time, the butt of the .45 raking finely against rock dust, the pleasant cordite smell of burned power in my face. But Wyatt Dixon moved about unawares in the roar of the chain saw, the rounds missing him by inches. My hands were sweating on the ivory grips now, the air damp and tannic inside my lungs. When I fired again I thought I heard the round knock into wood.

This time Wyatt Dixon paused, as though a foreign object might have invaded his environment. He looked away at the river, the cottonwoods and aspens bending in the breeze, the mountains on the western side of the valley and the clouds that were now filled with a purple and gold sheen. Then he bent to his work again, his saw ripping a spray of white pulp out of the log.

I was sweating inside my clothes. Bile rose out of my stomach and I could smell the sourness of my own breath when I breathed into my palm. I pulled back the hammer with my thumb a fifth time.

Walk away, the voice said.

Yes, I thought. This time, yes.

I stepped back from the boulder, my temples pounding, my ears almost deaf from the four rounds I had discharged. I eased the hammer back down with both thumbs and shoved the pistol into my belt and walked back through the trees, stepping across a creek drainage, mounting a small hill that should have brought me out above my truck and the campground on the river.

Instead, I walked right into two of Amos Rackley's Treasury agents.

They were set up behind a rock, like picnickers, a lunch box opened in front of them, with sandwiches placed on paper napkins next to their thermos and cell phone and binoculars.

"What do you think you're doing, asshole?" the blond, crewcut man named Jim said, chewing a small bite of sandwich. He wore khakis and a checkered shirt and a tan

cap with a green fish on it. There was a
blood-filled bump on the bridge of his nose.
He and his partner wore identical sunglasses.

"Me?" I said.

"Dixon did a mind-fuck on you, huh?" Jim
said.

"Is Wyatt around here? That's why you
guys are here?" I said.

"You haven't had the pleasure," Jim said to
his partner. "This guy's a real wit."

I took a breath and widened my eyes. My
face felt sweaty and dilated in the breeze.
"Tell me if my reasoning is messed up. You
don't care if somebody pops Ole Wyatt or
not. You know you can't turn him, so he's of
no use to you."

"You ought to ask Amos for a job. He's always looking for new talent," Jim said.

I dumped my spent brass in my palm.

"Give him this for me, will you?" I said,
and bounced the casings off the rock in front
of them. "It's great seeing you. Keep up the
good work."

Jim bit into his sandwich and turned to his
friend. "This guy was an Assistant U.S. Attorney," he said. The friend grinned and
looked at his nails.

# Chapter

## 23

❦

I WAS STILL WIRED when I walked into an old brick Catholic church on the north side of Missoula early the next morning. The day was cool and misty, and the pillared interior of the church, whose ceilings were painted with celestial scenes, seemed to enclose an unnatural, smoky blue light. The few parishioners in the pews were elderly, traditional people from another era who said rosaries and probably attended Mass daily and confessed sins that were largely imaginary to a priest who fought to keep from nodding off. I felt like an intruder in their midst.

I knelt in the back of the church and prayed to be relieved of the anger that still throbbed in my wrists and left my mouth as dry as paper and my thoughts like shards of glass. A young priest in a cassock entered the center booth in the confessional and I followed him and knelt in the adjoining booth and waited for him to slide back the wood cover on the small screened window that separated us.

"I should confess early on I know another priest here in town but I chose not to go to him," I said.

"Why is that?" the priest asked.

"I'm ashamed."

"There's no shame when you take your sins to God."

"I tried to kill a man yesterday, Father. He was unarmed. I shot at his back four times."

The priest started to turn, to look through the screen at my face, but instead lowered his eyes and remained motionless. I could hear the soft rise and fall of his breath.

"What you're telling me is very serious," he said.

"This man did something truly evil to a friend of mine," I said.

"With respect, I have to stop you there. You don't bargain in a sacramental situation."

"He buried her alive."

I saw him press his forehead with the heel of his hand.

"Listen, do you plan to make another attempt against this man's life?" he said.

"I'll do him no harm except in defense of myself or another."

I could see a thin sheen of perspiration along his jawbone and a lump of cartilage working below his ear. He waited a long time before he spoke again.

"If you have not been honest with me, the absolution you receive here will be of little use to you. That said, you are forgiven of your sins," he said. Then added, as I rose from the kneeler, "You must put away your violence, sir. You will never have peace until you do. Until that day comes, a minister such as I will be only a seashell echoing the wind."

His words clung to me like a net when I walked out into the sunlight.

I WALKED from the church down to the river and sat on a shady bench and watched the sun burn the mist off the hills. The siltation caused by the snow melt had settled out of the river and the water was now a dark green again, undulating smoothly over the submerged boulders in the deepest part of the river, the trout rising on the edge of the shade for the first fly hatch of the day.

I had less than three weeks to prepare Doc's defense. When all else failed, a hard-nosed criminal lawyer could always put the police on trial. But that was not only unwise in the case of Sheriff Cain, who was an intelligent and decent man and also well liked, a defense strategy deliberately based on destroying people's faith in their legal system was a little bit like burning down all your neighbors' houses in order to save your own.

Who had really killed Lamar Ellison? I had an idea, but my speculations were of no value. I believed Lamar Ellison and his two cohorts were sent by Carl Hinkel to Doc Voss's house to rape his daughter. But all three rapists were dead now and I would probably never get Hinkel into a courtroom. Hinkel was like the drunk who runs a red light at ninety miles an hour and fills an intersection with mayhem and carnage and disappears back into anonymity. Regardless, as much as I disliked him and the xenophobic mentality that was characteristic of his kind, I did not think he was behind Ellison's murder.

I tried to think through the tangled web Doc and I had wandered into the night he went up against the bikers in the bar at Lincoln: gold mine interests on the Blackfoot River, Cleo Lonnigan's belief that Lamar Ellison's biker gang had murdered her child, Nicki Molinari's insistence that Cleo Lonnigan had stolen money from him, Xavier and Holly Girard's involvement with Molinari, the kidnapping and murder of Sue Lynn Big Medicine's little brother, the fanatical dedication of the ATF agents who wanted to avenge the deaths of their friends and colleagues in the Alfred P. Murrah Building.

I wondered what it would be like to line up childhood photos of all the above-mentioned people. Would it tell us something about the influence of the world on each of us? Probably. But the lesson was too depressing to even think about.

"I have a bone to pick with you," a voice said behind me.

"Oh, hello, Ms. Girard," I said, removing my hat and rising from the bench.

She wore shades and a white suit and high heels and white stockings and carried a shopping bag from a fashionable store by its paper straps. She sat down and crossed her legs and lit a cigarette with a silver lighter.

"Do you mind?" she asked.

"No," I said, not quite sure if she was referring to her cigarette or her sitting down uninvited.

"God forbid, my prayers have been answered. My husband has stopped drinking. He has also gone crazy. I think he gets some of his ideas from you and Doc Voss," she said.

"I doubt it."

"He wants to stop production of my picture. He says more publicity about the Blackfoot will cause it to be overrun by tourists.

He says he's going to rat-fuck Nicki Molinari. Do you think that's an advisable activity?"

"I wouldn't know, Ms. Girard. To tell you the truth, I don't care, either."

She removed her sunglasses and let them rest in her lap. In the shade, or perhaps because of her makeup, her eyes had the color of lilacs. They roved over my face thoughtfully, then she smiled in that unrehearsed and vulnerable way that seemed totally foreign to everything else she did.

"I've made a bad impression on you twice now," she said.

"How's that?"

"When you caught me inhaling a substance I could do without. Then Xavier told you of a foolish moment I had with Nicki Molinari."

"I don't guess I remember any of that very well."

"You're quite a guy, Tex. I could cast you in a minute, if you're not too ambitious. Don't pay too much attention to Xavier while he's sober. He thinks better when he's drunk," she said, and pinched me on top of the thigh when she got up to leave.

WHEN I GOT BACK to Doc's house Maisey was waiting for me on the front porch.

"What's wrong?" I said.

She handed me a folded piece of notebook paper. "This was pushed in under my screen," she said. It read:

*Dear Maysy,*

*I saw Mr. Holland shoot at Wyatt. Wyatt was running a chain saw and couldn't hear the shots. So I told him what I saw. You need to get away from Mr. Holland. We could go to Idaho or to the rain forest in Washington. I know how to build a cabin and to hunt and fish. What do you think? Meet me outside our place on Front Street at 8 tonite.*
*Your friend,*

*Terry*

"'Our place'?" I said.

"He must mean the bar where I met him. What a loser."

"Has your dad seen this?"

"Not yet. He went to the feed store. What does he mean you shot at Wyatt Dixon?"

"Witherspoon has probably been eating mushrooms," I said.

But I didn't fool her. She put her hands on her hips, her eyes boring in on me.

"Have you lost your mind, Billy Bob?"

"Don't underestimate the value of mental illness. It makes life a lot easier," I said.

"I thought my father was uncontrollable. You two guys are beyond belief," she said. She shook her head despairingly, tapping her toe, her mouth screwed into a button.

BUT THINGS were just warming up. A half hour later I saw Nicki Molinari's maroon convertible tearing through the field behind Doc's house, the top down, with Molinari behind the wheel and his second baseman, the man called Frank, next to him. Frank looked like a seven-foot cadaver propped up in the seat.

Molinari got out of the car and left the door hanging open, the engine still running, and jabbed his finger at me.

"I'm about an inch from creating one less lawyer in Missoula, Montana," he said.

"Oh?" I said.

"I'm eating breakfast in a café this morning and this rodeo psycho, what's-his-name, Wyatt Dixon, comes in and stands there, leering down at me with this twisted smile on his mouth. I go, 'You got a problem?' He goes, 'I've got it on high authority your friend Mr. Holland took some shots at me. Could it be you was involved with a cowardly action like that, sir?'

"I go, 'What are you talking about? And stop calling me sir.'

"He says, 'I seen one of your men bird-dogging me. Which made me wonder if you and Mr. Holland is working together. All these people is waiting for your response, sir.'

"I go, 'No, I don't know nothing about people shooting at you. So get away from my table, you crazy fuck.'

"He goes, 'You are a war hero, sir. I have driven by your home many times. I have seen the batting cage in your barn and the beautiful women that swims in your pool. I would like to model my life on yours but I am only a humble cowboy. You, sir, are a credit to the Italian race.'"

I waited for Molinari to continue.

"Are you listening?" he said.

"Yeah. So why are you out here?"

His face blanched with anger.

"You're playing with this guy's head. I'm a businessman. I got this shitkicker meltdown 'fronting me in public. I don't need that kind of publicity."

"Why did he put you and me together?"

"He's con-wise. He knows we've both been involved with the skank. Hey, bottom line, my man, he's nuts."

"Nice of you to come out," I said.

I walked away from him, into the trees, into the cold air rising off the river in the shadows. Molinari followed me and scooped up a pinecone and threw it at my head.

"Don't turn your back on me, Mr. Holland," he said.

"Your problem is not with me, Nicki. It's back in Laos, on that helicopter skid."

His hands opened and closed at his sides. His hired man followed us into the trees, his silhouette gargantuan against the sunlight. Molinari turned and said, "Everything's cool here, Frank. Take a smoke. I'll be along in a minute." I started to speak but Molinari shook his finger.

"You got no right to stick that information in my face," he said.

"Hell is a place you carry with you. I hope you get out of it one day."

"Save the shuck for people who are easily impressed," he said.

But he didn't leave. He stared at me, the veins in his forearms pumped with blood.

"Say something," he said.

I shook my head and walked around him, out into the sunlight, into the glory of the day and the humped blue-green chain of mountains that lined each side of the Blackfoot Valley. Frank, the hired man, looked at Nicki, waiting for instructions.

"Leave him alone," Nicki said.

I WAS BY MYSELF that evening. The sky was blue, the sun glowing like a red spark through a crack in the hills. The Blackfoot had dropped, and the rocks along the bank were white and dry and etched with the skeletal remains of underwater insects. When the wind gusted I could smell a meat fire in a neighbor's yard and the cold odor the river gave off inside the shade.

It was an evening to put aside thoughts about Nicki Molinari and Carl Hinkel and their minions and all their nefarious enterprises. I called Temple Carrol at her motel.

"How about dinner and a movie?" I said.

"I guess that could be arranged," she said.

"Thank you," I said.

"Don't be smart," she replied.

Well, that's a start, I thought, and went into the bathroom to shave.

A minute later the phone rang.

"Hello?" I said.

"We need to talk," the voice said.

"Cleo?"

"At least you haven't forgotten the sound of my voice."

"I'm going to ring off now," I said.

"Come on, stop pretending you're a victim. I apologize for my behavior at the Joan Baez concert. Can't you show a little humility?"

"Have a good life," I said.

"I'm turning off the dirt road right now. It doesn't look like Doc's at home. That's good.

You and I have a lot to talk about," she said.

I hurriedly put on a fresh shirt and my hat and headed out the door for my truck, just as she drove around the side of the house and parked by the porch. She wore a yellow sundress and a pink ribbon in her hair. But for some reason that had no exact physical correlation, she looked sharp-edged, aged, her eyes intent with an animus that would never allow her to acknowledge any perception of the world other than her own.

She walked toward me with a box wrapped in satin paper.

"A little present," she said.

"This isn't good for either of us, Cleo."

"If you won't open it, I'll do it myself."

She tore away the paper and the ribbon, her hands shaking slightly. The paper blew away in the wind when she folded back the top of the box.

"There's every kind of bass lure here," she said. "That's what you fish for in Texas, isn't it? Bass? Do you like the lures?"

"I appreciate your thoughtfulness. I'm headed out right now. I wish perhaps you had come out at another time."

"Stop being cute, Billy Bob. Southern charm doesn't work too well after you bed a woman and drop her."

"You have a lot of qualities, Cleo. You're

devoted to your work. You obviously have compassion for the poor. Any guy would be lucky to have a lady like you."

"I want you to come out to my place. It doesn't have to be tonight. But this has to be worked out."

"It's not going to happen."

"I'm sorry to hear you say that," she said.

"Let me be straight up with you. Nicki Molinari told me your husband and son were murdered by gangsters, not by Lamar Ellison's biker gang. The sheriff believes the same thing. Why don't you give Molinari and his friends the money your husband owed them and be done with it?"

"You quote Nicki Molinari to me about my son? You worthless piece of Southern garbage," she said.

"Adios," I said, and got into my truck. While I ground the starter I could feel her eyes pulling the skin from my bones.

THAT SAME EVENING Sue Lynn Big Medicine drove her uncle's pickup truck into the Jocko Valley and onto the Flathead Indian Reservation. She passed the rodeo and pow-wow grounds and followed a dirt road into the hills, climbing higher into trees and deep shadows and outcroppings of gray rock that were marbled with lichen.

She pulled off the road into a flat, thinly wooded area by a creek. The remains of an abandoned sweat lodge stood next to the creek, the concave network of shaved willow limbs hung with strips of rotting canvas. She cut the engine and walked down to the water and leaned against a rock and smoked a cigarette and waited. It was not long before she heard a four-wheel-drive vehicle grinding in low gear up the road.

The man who had told her where to wait for him got out of his vehicle and walked toward her. He wore slip-on, half-topped boots and khakis and a long-sleeve blue cotton shirt and a bill cap. His hair was neatly clipped, and even though it was evening he was freshly shaved and smelled of the lotion on his jaws.

"Did I keep you waiting long?" Amos Rackley asked.

"I wasn't doing anything else," she said, inhaling her cigarette, her chin raised, her gaze averted.

"Where's your uncle's race car, the one with numbers on it?"

"It doesn't have lights."

He seemed to look at her kindly but for just a second his eyes would focus on her mouth and drop to her throat and breasts.

"I have a folder here with some pictures of guns in it," he said. "I want you to look at the pictures and tell me if you've seen any of these guns inside Carl Hinkel's house."

He opened the folder on top of the rock she was leaning against and shone a tiny flashlight on a series of glossy prints. She felt the hair on his forearm touch hers.

"I don't know anything about guns," she said.

"A gal from the Res? Who grew up around hunters? That's hard to believe, Sue Lynn."

"I don't know what kind of guns Carl Hinkel has. They're guns."

"I see. We need you to go back into Hinkel's house," he said, closing the folder.

"They're on to me."

"I don't think that's true. They're just a suspicious lot by nature. Call up Wyatt and tell him you had a fight with the Holland boy and you want to see him again."

"I don't want to ever be alone with Wyatt again. You don't know what he—"

"We'll be close by," Rackley said, interrupting her. "You'll be wearing a wire. Your job's almost done." He moved his hand slightly and let his fingers cover the tops of hers.

"I can't do it," she said.

"Do what? Can't do what, Sue Lynn?"

She wanted to pull her hand away from his but couldn't. She could feel her own heart beating, her chest rising and falling inside her shirt.

"I hate you. I hate all you people," she said.

She felt his hand leave hers. The wind was cold on the back of her neck and she felt her hair feathering on her cheeks. She wanted to turn and stare him down but all she could do was fix her eyes on the desiccated remains of the sweat lodge and the discarded heat stones that had been blackened by long-dead fires.

"I'm disappointed to hear you say that, Sue Lynn. I'll call you very soon. You're going to be a big help to us. You'll see."

After Amos Rackley was gone, she sat on the creek bank with her knees drawn up in front of her, her hands clasped on her ankles. The light was gone from the sky now and she heard animals moving about in the woods, deer certainly, perhaps black bears and cougars, perhaps even a moose, and she hoped if she saw the latter she would not be afraid, even though the moose was considered a man-killer. She wanted to believe the animals represented the spirits of her ancestors, people who lived in harmony with the earth and sky and wind and the water in the streams and all the winged and four-footed creatures and the salmon who swam all the way back from the sea to lay their roe where they had been born, that maybe the animals she heard in the darkness came bearing an omen of power and resolution and courage that daily eluded her and translated her sleep into a prison filled with grotesque shapes she could not control.

She rose from the ground and waded into the stream and felt its coldness swell over her ankles. She walked up the opposite bank, across small stones that hurt her feet, and entered the tree line. Again she heard the noise in the brush and she walked farther into the woods until she entered an old clear-cut that was dotted with toadstools and tree stumps that had gone gray with rot. A bull elk reared its head out of the grass, its rack clattering with moonlight.

For a moment she thought she had found the totem that spoke of the power her people could pass on to her. But instead she stared at the elk's rack, the ridged texture and hardness of the horn, the curved points, and all she could think of was Wyatt Dixon. And she knew she would not sleep that night.

# Chapter

## 24

❦

IN THE GRAYNESS of the following dawn I sat by Lucas's fire on the riverbank and listened to Sue Lynn tell her story. The wind blew ashes out of the fire ring and they settled on her shoulders and in her hair like snowflakes. While she spoke she squeezed one hand on top of the other and her eyes seemed to look into a place that neither Lucas nor I occupied.

"Are you going to wear a wire?" I asked.

"No, not around Carl. He scares me. Even more than Wyatt does. He's a lot smarter than Wyatt," she answered.

"I think it's time you got out from under these guys, Sue Lynn," I said.

"Why did Mr. Rackley want to know about the guns?" she said.

"If you saw automatic weapons in Hinkel's house, Rackley could get a warrant and hit the place. You didn't see any heavy stuff in there?"

"There's a rack of guns in the basement. Bikers call them 'pogo sticks,'" she said.

"Those are either M-16s or AR-15s. The AR-15s are legal. The others aren't. You're not sure which they are?" I said.

"I think that gun stuff is for dipshits," she said. She stood up from the rock she was sitting on and looked into the mist that shrouded the trees and at the river that flowed like satin over the boulders in the deepest part of the current.

"Lucas, I could never drink coffee without a little milk in it. Do you mind?" I said.

"Since you put it as subtle as a slap in the face with a dead cat, no, Billy Bob, I don't mind," he replied, and rose to his feet and walked up the bank and across the porch into Doc's house.

"Your little brother was abducted and murdered, wasn't he?" I said.

She stood above me, one foot resting on a rock, her thumbs in her pockets. I could see the pulse beating in her throat.

"Who told you that?" she said.

"The night Lamar Ellison died, he was marinated on beer and weed in a tavern up the Blackfoot. He had a blackout of some kind and said something that made you very angry."

"I don't remember that," she said.

"Doc goes on trial in a couple of weeks. Do you think he should be on trial, Sue Lynn?"

"I came here because Lucas asked me to. Stop questioning me. You're not a policeman."

"Doc's inside. Come on in and talk with him."

Her eyes were watering now. She stepped away from the fire and pretended that smoke had gotten in them. She wiped her nose on her wrist.

"You know what it's like to have no choices, to be used by everybody around you, to have nobody care when your little brother is killed? Have you ever lived like that, Mr. Holland? Tell me," she said.

LATER, I sat with Temple Carrol at a picnic bench in a city park fringed with maple trees and read through the material she had amassed on Carl Hinkel.

"Where'd you get all this stuff?" I said.

"It's not hard. There're a half-dozen organizations that track people like Hinkel. Besides, he can't wait to get in front of a camera or a microphone," she said.

His record was one of failure on every human level: he had been a low-level operator in the Vietnamese black market; his three marriages had ended in divorce; he had been denied tenure as a communications professor in a South Carolina community college; the state of Georgia had put him out of business for operating a scam that involved selling fraudulent home warranty policies to working-class people.

But he was to discover the enormous potential of the Internet. Not only could he create an electronic recruiting magnet for racists and psychopaths, his self-published books and pamphlets inculcating the hatred of the government and Jews, homosexuals, blacks, Asians, and Hispanics found a huge mail-order audience. The more grim his perspective became, the more his constituency became convinced his voice was the one they had waited to hear all their lives.

He held televised news conferences in front of his ranch and claimed the CIA was making nocturnal flights over his home with black helicopters and that Belgian troops, working for the United Nations, were being trained in the Bitterroot Mountains for a takeover of the United States.

The fact that he obviously had symptoms of schizophrenia did nothing to dampen his newfound success. He actually addressed the Montana state legislature and went to Washington and was welcomed in the offices of at least two U.S. congressmen.

But Hinkel's history was a predictable one and was of little help to me in my preparation for Doc's defense. It was an entry at the bottom of a report and an attached news article sent to Temple by a Klan-watch group in Atlanta that caught my eye. A pedophile who was wanted on state charges had been arrested five years ago in Hinkel's yard. Hinkel had claimed he didn't know the man and in fact thanked the authorities for arresting him.

I circled the entry on the page and pushed it toward Temple.

"Does anything else about child molestation show up in this guy's past?" I asked.

"None that I know of. Why?"

"I'm not sure."

In the center of the park was a cement wading pool and a fountain and children were playing in it, and out on the street a man was selling ice cream out of cart with a blue umbrella on top of it.

"There's something else on your mind you're not telling me about, isn't there?" Temple said.

"Quite a few things."

"Start with one."

"Early yesterday I tried to bushwhack Wyatt Dixon."

"Say again?"

"I got downwind from him while he was running a chain saw and put four rounds past his head. He didn't see me but Terry Witherspoon did. Those ATF guys know about it, too."

She propped her head on her fingers and looked at me with her mouth open. Then she took her hand away from her brow and her eyes searched mine.

"Why?" she said.

"A guy like that deserves it."

"Don't lie," she said.

"Come on, I'll buy you a Popsicle."

"You thought I was going to do it. That's why, isn't it?"

"You think too much, Temple," I said, and began putting away her papers and file folders into her nylon backpack.

She was standing next to me now and I could smell the sun's heat on her skin and the perfume on her neck. There was a flush in her cheeks, a different light in her eyes.

"Look at me," she said.

"What?"

She pushed several strands of hair out of her face, a smile tugging at the edge of her mouth. But she didn't speak.

"Would you say what's on your mind?" I said.

"I guess I'll just have to keep an eye on you, that's all," she replied.

THAT EVENING Lucas borrowed my truck to go to work at the Milltown Bar. When he picked up Sue Lynn at her uncle's house he didn't make it out of the driveway. Amos Rackley and the agent named Jim pulled their car at an angle across the entrance, their brights burning into Lucas's face, and approached both sides of the truck.

"What's with you guys?" Lucas said.

"We just need a minute of Sue Lynn's time," Jim said, and reached through the window and turned off the ignition.

"Maybe she doesn't want to talk to you," Lucas said.

"Trust me, she does. Step out of the truck. I'll give you a cigarette. Would you like that?" the agent said, and winked. He squeezed the handle of the door and eased it open.

Lucas stepped down on the gravel, feeling belittled, unsure why, unsure what to do about it. The sun was down, the sky purple, the air cold and bitter with the smell of diesel off the highway. Jim wore jeans and a beige sports coat and had a blood blister on the bridge of his nose.

"Walk over here with me," he said, turning his back, clicking on a pen light with his thumb and focusing the beam on some photographs he held in one hand. "This will interest you."

Lucas stared down at the photos of Sue Lynn and himself coming out of a supermarket, sitting in her uncle's car, entering the Milltown Bar, undressing on a blanket by a stream.

"You guys are real shits," Lucas said.

Jim put a filter-tipped cigarette in his mouth but didn't light it.

"I heard you play at the Milltown Bar. You want some advice? Lose the Indian broad. It's a matter of time till she goes into the system. Number two, I don't blame you for being pissed off. Nobody wants a telescopic lens focused on his bare ass while he's getting his ashes hauled. But you're taking your old man's fall, kid."

"You're talking about Billy Bob?"

The agent blew his nose into a Kleenex and looked at a drop of blood on it.

"He messed up his career. He's got a storefront law practice in a shithole. You think it's a mystery why he runs around trying to fuck up a government investigation? I'd use my head," the agent said.

"Billy Bob's got a nice office on the town square. People respect him. That's more than I can say about some folks," Lucas replied.

"You see *Treasure of the Sierra Madre*?" the agent said. "Humphrey Bogart plays this worthless character named Fred C. Dobbs. He's always saying, 'Nobody's putting anything over on Fred C. Dobbs.' What do you think that line means? I never really figured it out."

But Lucas's attention was now fixed on Sue Lynn and the other federal agent, Amos Rackley. Rackley had opened the back door of his car for her and Sue Lynn was getting inside.

Lucas started toward them, but Jim stepped in front of him and spread his fingers on Lucas's chest, pressing slightly, his face only inches from Lucas's. In the headlights of the car the shape of his head seemed like a manikin's.

"She's coming voluntarily. Don't mix in it," the agent said.

"Sue Lynn?" Lucas called out.

But she didn't answer. Jim backed away from Lucas, one finger pointing at him.

"Keep in mind what I said. Hey, stop squeezing your Johnson. We're gonna bring her back," he said.

LUCAS RETURNED my truck keys the next morning and sat at the plank table in the kitchen and drank coffee and looked out the window at the frost high up on the mountain.

"Don't worry about her. She's a smart gal," I said.

"I went by her uncle's after I got off work. They hadn't brought her back," he said.

"She was involved with these Treasury guys before you met her, Lucas. She hung out with bikers. She was there when they stuck up a general store and post office on the Res."

"I don't like it when you talk that way, Billy Bob."

"Sue Lynn's history is her own. I didn't make it up."

"That agent said the same thing about you."

"Maybe you should listen to him."

Lucas got up from the table and threw his coffee out the back door. Then he washed the cup in the sink and set it in the dry rack.

"You hurt people when they try to stand up for you. But I don't hold it against you. It's just the way you are. You ain't never gonna change, Billy Bob," he said.

He fitted on his hat and went outside, past the side window, his head bent forward, his face as sharp as an ax blade in the wind.

# Chapter

## 25

KINGDOMS ARE LOST for want of a nail in a horse's shoe. I think perhaps lives unravel in the same fashion, sometimes over events as slight as an insult to the pride of a misanthropic young man from North Carolina who thought he was going to be a mountain man.

Lucas was playing that afternoon with a band at a bluegrass festival outside of Hamilton. The bandstand had been knocked together with green lumber at the bottom of a long slope that tapered upward into the shadows of the mountains, and thousands of people sat on folding chairs and blankets in the sunshine, while the electronically amplified songs of Appalachia echoed through the canyons of the Bitterroot Valley.

Doc, Maisey, Temple, and I spread a blanket in the grass, not far from a group of college kids who were red-faced with beer and agitated by a situation of some kind near the concession area.

"Somebody should rip it down. It doesn't belong here. This is Montana," a girl was saying.

"Ignore them. They're a bunch of losers," a boy said.

"There's a black man working at the hot-dog stand. How would you feel if you were a black man and somebody stuck that in your face?" the girl said.

"What's going on with the college kids?" Temple said.

"You got me," I said.

I looked past the crowd at a white camper with a tarp extended from the roof and supported on poles to shade the people who sat under it. On one side of the tarp was a staff that flew the American flag; on the other side, flapping like a red-and-blue martial challenge out of the past, was the battle flag of the Confederacy.

"I'm going to the concession stand. Y'all want anything?" Maisey said.

"Yeah," Doc said, and gave her a twenty-dollar bill.

"Like what do you want?" Maisey asked.

"Whatever you like. Just make sure everything is free of cholesterol and preservatives and none of it is made by Third World child labor and the vendors have sound political attitudes," Doc said.

Maisey made one of her faces to show her tolerance of her father's immaturity and walked off into the crowd, just as Lucas's band came on stage and went into Bill Monroe's "Molly and Tenbrooks."

The sunlight was warm on Maisey's skin as she stood in line, the wind balmy in her face, the timbered slopes of the mountains rising almost straight up into snow that still had not melted with summer. The fields were iridescent with the spray from irrigation wheel lines, and up the incline the aspens and cottonwoods along the drainages rippled in the shadows of the mountains that towered over them.

Then she felt a presence behind her before she saw it, and smelled an odor like a combination of hair tonic and chewing gum and layered deodorant, as though the person emanating it thought a manufactured scent was a form of physical sophistication.

"Bet I scared you," Terry Witherspoon said.

He wore a white T-shirt and black jeans and engineering boots and a skinning knife on his belt. He grinned at the corner of his mouth and pitched his head to get a strand of hair out of his glasses.

She turned away from him and moved up
with the line, her eyes fastening on a jolly fat
man frying burgers inside the concession
stand.

"Did you get my note?" Terry asked.

"No," she said, hurriedly, then felt her
cheeks burn with her lie. She turned and
faced him. "I did get it. Please don't leave any
more."

"I went way out on a limb for you. You
shouldn't talk to me like that."

"Leave me alone," she said, her teeth grit-
ted, her eyes shining with embarrassment at
the stares she was now receiving.

He didn't answer. A long moment passed
and she thought perhaps Terry had gone away.
But when she turned around he was looking
down into her face, crinkling his nose under
his glasses, his arms hanging straight down, as
though he didn't know what else to do with
them, one hand locked on his wrist.

"I'll pay for the burgers. Let's walk up the
canyon and eat them. There're grouse in the
pines. I've got a hand line we can fish with,"
he said.

But before she could reply she saw her father coming toward the concession stand,
pushing his ash-blond hair back over his
head, his gait longer than it should have
been, his shoulders slightly stooped. Perhaps
for the first time she saw the complex man

who would never be at home in the world, a
Mennonite farm boy who went to war as a
healer and became a killer in the Phoenix
Program, a recovered intravenous addict who
published poems and whose soft voice belied
the potential that burned just below his skin,
a father who mourned his wife and loved his
daughter and brooked no intrusion into the
life of his family.

Doc's right hand bit into Terry Witherspoon's arm, squeezing the muscle into the
bone.

"You're the boy who left that note?" he
said.

"I might have. Take your hand off—" Witherspoon said.

"Don't find any reason to get near me or
Maisey, son. Now, you get back over there
with your friends. While you're at it, you tell
them those are grand flags on their camper
and sonsofbitches like them don't have any
right to fly them."

"I don't have to do anything you tell me,
you old fuck."

Doc pulled Witherspoon out of the line and
marched him by one arm through the crowd
toward the camper. When Witherspoon
tripped and fell, Doc knotted the back of his
T-shirt in his fist and hauled him out of the
dust and pushed him through the crowd like a
rag doll.

In the shade of the tarp Carl Hinkel and Wyatt Dixon sat in canvas recliners, drinking canned beer, gazing benignly at the stage.

Behind them, Sue Lynn Big Medicine sat in the doorway of the camper, wearing shorts and a halter and no shoes, her face fatigued, her lipstick on crooked.

Doc shoved Witherspoon into their midst.

"Your man here got lost. Make sure he stays on a short tether," Doc said.

"Goodness gracious, sir, you behave like somebody just spit in your dinner plate. Sue Lynn, get Dr. Voss a cold drink. Terry wasn't rude to your daughter, was he? He got one sniff of her and ain't talked about nothing else," Wyatt Dixon said.

Wyatt Dixon turned his attention back to the stage, grinning at nothing, his body supine, one hand cupped on his scrotum, while Carl Hinkel puffed on his cob pipe as though the events taking place around him had nothing to do with his life.

I draped my arm around Doc's shoulders and walked him toward the concession stands.

"Wrong place to take them on," I said.

"If you're the voice of reason, Billy Bob, we're in trouble," he replied.

A HALF HOUR LATER Sue Lynn found Lucas behind the bandstand. He was kneeling on a blanket, replacing a broken treble string on his Martin, twisting the tuning peg until the string whined with tension.

"Where have you been? I went by your place three times today. Your uncle said you took his car and didn't tell him where you were going," he said, getting to his feet.

"I went back and got a few clothes. I'm staying at Wyatt's awhile," she replied.

"*Wyatt's?* Are you insane?"

"I have to, Lucas."

"Tell those government buttwipes to kiss your ass."

"Lower your voice."

"I mean it, Sue Lynn. Eighty-six this stuff. This is a free country."

"We can't be together again. You have to accept that."

He stared at her, then looked out at a deep, shadowed chasm that cut through the mountains.

"Don't tell me stuff like that. I'm not gonna listen," he said.

"I'm going to jail or I'm going to be killed. You want to be killed, too?"

"Come out to Doc's and talk to Billy Bob."

"Try to understand. I have to make a decision about something. It eats on me all the time. I might have to go away for a long time, for something you don't know about."

"Go away where?"

She gave up.

"Don't get around Wyatt," she said. "Dr. Voss just humiliated Terry in front of a bunch of college kids. Terry is Wyatt's punk. That means Wyatt has to hurt somebody so Terry can feel he's important again. That's the way they do things inside."

"Who cares what these guys do? They're scum . . . Stop backing away from me."

But she was running now, in her moccasins and halter and shorts that were dirty in the rump, and for some reason she made him think of a frightened doe bolting through a forest where the trees took no note of the wild beating of its heart.

TWO HOURS LATER Lucas, Temple, Doc, Maisey and I loaded up in Temple's Explorer, drowsy on beer and from sitting in the sun, the encounter with Terry Witherspoon pushed out of our minds, the summer evening still blue and pink and filled with promise.

As we snaked our way out of the parking area, I looked through the haze of dust and saw Wyatt Dixon in front of the white camper, dancing with Sue Lynn slung over his shoulder like a side of beef. When she tried to raise her torso erect, he slapped her rump and danced faster and faster in a circle, his knees jerking upward like an Indian's while the Confederate flag flapped over his head.

Lucas was sitting next to me in the backseat. His eyes started to follow mine.

"Look at the eagles up on the hill," I said.

"Where?" he said.

"They're flying right above the trees, right across the canyon," I said.

He looked at the canyon, then out the rear window of the vehicle.

"Was something going on back there?" he asked.

"Nothing that we can change," I said.

THE NEXT DAY was Sunday. That afternoon Sue Lynn sat on top of a boulder behind Wyatt's log house and watched him and Terry smoke home-grown gage and flip a hatchet end over end into a cottonwood tree. Wyatt had said nothing to her about her relationship with Lucas, nor had he tried to put moves on her last night or this morning. In fact, he gave her a blanket and pillow and told her to sleep on the deerhide couch in his house and said he would sleep in the bedroom. When she woke in the morning, he fixed coffee and eggs for her and whistled a tune while he did it, his bare triangular back turned to her, as though he were both indifferent to the coldness of the predawn hour and the presence of several loaded firearms that hung on antler racks which she could easily take down and discharge if she chose.

But she knew Wyatt and the way he thought, if "thought" was the proper word to use. He never did what others expected. Unlike Carl Hinkel and his shaved-head windups, Wyatt seemed to be possessed by no ideological passion. His war was not with the government or with people of a different race. His war was with humanity, or better yet, the normality that defined most human beings. Wyatt was like the virus that immediately recognizes the antibodies in an immune system as its enemy. He used and ingested people. He did it with an idiot's grin, eating his own pain, demeaning and degrading his adversaries in ways that often took them days to figure out.

From a good thirty feet Wyatt threw the hatchet into the tree trunk, thunking it so solidly into the wood the handle trembled with a sound like a sprung saw blade. He worked the steel head out of the bark and extended the handle to Terry, then jerked it back, smiling, when Terry tried to take it.

Then he repeated the maneuver, teasing Terry, jumping around sideways as though he had springs on his feet. But before Terry could go into a pout, Wyatt slipped the handle into Terry's palm and clasped his hand affectionately on the back of Terry's neck and pulled the roach Terry was smoking off his lips and took two hits off it, then pinched off the ash and ate it.

"Roll us another one, Sue Lynn," Terry said.

Roll it yourself, fuckhead, she thought.

But she didn't say it. Not with Wyatt there. He might bitch-slap Terry or force him to wear makeup and throw him from an automobile, but when push came to shove, with either Carl or any of the other lamebrains who hung around the compound, Terry was Wyatt's mainline bar of soap and nobody made remarks about him or put their hands on him except Wyatt.

So she rolled a joint from the home-grown marijuana in Wyatt's tobacco pouch and licked down the glue on the seam of the cigarette paper and crimped down the ends while Wyatt went inside the log house to use the toilet.

Terry pulled the joint from her fingers and put it into his mouth. He was bare-chested and his pants hung two inches below his belly button. Dirt rings clung to his neck like a necklace of insects.

"Light it for me," he said.

She ignored him and slid off the boulder and walked down toward the river, dusting off her rump, working a pack of cigarettes out of her jeans, sticking one into her mouth.

"I can have your ass if I want," he said behind her.

He traced his fingernail down her spine to her panties.

She tried to bite down on the words that welled out of her throat but it was too late. "Your mother must have thought she gave birth to a tumor," she said.

He took her book of matches from her hand and lit the joint, holding the hit deep down in his lungs, and bounced the dead match off her face.

"Have a nice day, Sue Lynn," he said.

LATER, she went inside the log house and lay on the couch, a blanket wrapped around her head, and tried to sleep. But it was no use. One of Wyatt's buddies was running a dirt bike up and down an adjacent hill, gunning the engine through the trees, scouring humus and rock and grass into the air, filling the softness of the evening with a sound like a chain saw grinding on steel pipe.

Why not eighty-six it, like Lucas said? she thought.

Because Amos Rackley told her she stayed

on the job until she found out what kinds of weapons were in Carl Hinkel's basement. Maybe she should have worn the wire, she thought. Now she had no umbilical cord to the outside.

What Amos Rackley could not comprehend, what he would not hear, was the fact that Carl Hinkel could look inside people's heads. He saw where they were weak, the thoughts they tried to hide, the flare of ambition in their eyes. He understood evil in others, tolerated it the way a father does an errant child, and used it for his own ends. His followers all knew they could deceive themselves or lie to the world and Carl would remain their friend. But they dared not lie to him.

He seemed to have no sexual interest in either women or men. His pastime was his absorption with the Internet. He sat for hours in front of his computer, his features wrapped with the green glow of his monitor, while he tapped on the keys and addressed chat rooms filled with his admirers.

But she had seen one peculiarity in his commitment to his computer. In nice weather he left the door open to his little stone office, and anyone in the compound could see him at his desk, puffing clouds of white smoke from his cob pipe, his back as straight as a bayonet, while his fingers danced across the keyboard. But sometimes he would shut the door and slide the wood crossbar into place, and everyone understood that Carl was not to be disturbed.

Once a new member at the compound, a jug-eared kid just out of the Wyoming pen, called Shortening Bread behind his back because of his dark skin, wanted to curry favor with Carl and made lunch for him and carried it on a tray to the office. Unfortunately for Shortening Bread, Carl had not quite secured the crossbar on the door, and Shortening Bread worked his foot into the jamb and pushed the door back and started to step inside the office without asking permission.

Carl rose from his chair and flung the tray into the yard. When Shortening Bread broke into tears, Carl put his arm over his shoulders and walked with him around the compound, explaining the need for discipline among members of the Second American Revolution, reassuring him that he was a valuable man.

Sue Lynn got up from the couch and washed her face and walked down the slope to the river, then wandered along the bank to a shady copse of trees and sat down in the grass and watched the spokes of white light the sun gave off beyond the rim of the Bitterroots.

Then she heard the dirt bike go silent and

the voices of Wyatt and Terry and she realized the two men were no more than twenty
yards above her, behind a boulder, and Terry
was sharpening his knife on a whetstone,
probably spitting on it, as was his fashion,
and grinding the knife in a slow, monotonous
circle.

"She's got a mouth on her, I'll 'low that.
'Birth to a tumor'?"

"It's not funny, Wyatt."

"You ain't got to tell me. An Indian woman
shouldn't be talking to a white man like
that," Wyatt said, his voice suddenly somber.

"What are you gonna do about it?" Terry
asked.

"Have a little talk with her."

"I want it to hurt."

"Oh, it will."

"Wyatt?"

"What?"

"I want to watch."

Sue Lynn sat in the shadows, bent forward,
her stomach sick. Even in the coolness of the
wind off the river she was sweating all over, a
fearful sweat that clung to her skin like night
damp. She remained motionless, afraid to get
up or turn around. Then she heard Wyatt
and Terry walking out of the trees toward the
campground upstream, where Terry sometimes worm-fished with a hand line behind a
beaver dam.

When they were out of sight she ran for her uncle's windowless stock car that had no headlights. She fired up the engine and fishtailed across the gravel driveway in front of Carl's house and roared up the dirt road toward the highway that led back into Missoula, her heart pounding, the reflected images of Carl Hinkel and three of his subordinates staring at her like painted miniatures in the rearview mirror.

SHE STOPPED at Lolo, ten miles south of Missoula, and used a pay phone outside a café to call the contact number the Treasury agents had made her memorize. An unfamiliar voice answered, then the call was relayed to another location and she heard the voice of Amos Rackley.

"I can't take it anymore," she said.

"Slow down. You can handle this."

"Carl *knows*."

"You're having a panic attack. He doesn't know. He's not that smart."

"They're out there."

"Out where?" he said.

A low-slung red car ran the yellow light at the intersection and she felt her heart stop. Then she saw the car was not Wyatt's.

"They're everywhere. They have radios in their cars," she said.

"Go to the meeting place on the Res. People will be waiting for you there. Now stop worrying. You did a good job."

"I never saw the guns."

"So fuck it," he said.

She drove on through Missoula and caught the highway west of town that led to the Flathead Reservation. The Clark Fork of the Columbia River looked like a long, flat silver snake in the twilight.

THE EVENING STAR had risen above the mountains when she drove up into the timbered hills above the Jocko River and pulled off the dirt road and parked by the abandoned sweat lodge on the creek bank. Twice on the highway she had seen cars pace themselves behind her, dropping back when she slowed, accelerating when she sped up. Then she had turned on to the Res and had lost them. But five minutes later, as she climbed into the hills, she had seen headlights down below, tracking across the same bridges she had crossed, following the same dirt roads she had driven.

The trees and hills were dark now, the sky like a bowl of blue light above her head. She got out of her uncle's stock car and waited by the stream, listening to the water that braided across the rocks, the thick sounds of bats' wings crisscrossing through the air, the animals that were coming down through the woods to drink at the close of day.

Where was Rackley? He had said people would be waiting for her. But once again she was alone, and now it was too dark for her to drive her uncle's car back home.

She saw the trees move on the ridge above her but she guessed it was only the wind. Upstream there was a clattering sound on the rocks, deer or elk or perhaps cattle crossing the creek bed.

She had to get it together, stop her hands from trembling, her blood from racing. If she could just think clearly, just for a moment, she knew she could figure a way out of this.

Rackley had said fuck it. That was a surprise. Was he letting her off the hook? Or did he plan to put moves on her, use her as his permanent snitch and part-time squeeze?

She saw lights coming up the road, a four-wheel-drive vehicle in low gear, and she folded her arms across her chest, starting to hyperventilate now, determined to stare down whoever it was, even if they killed her.

The agent named Jim and a second agent whose name she didn't know pulled their Cherokee onto the grass and parked next to her car and got out and walked toward her, dressed like trout fishermen, smiling easily.

"Amos says you had a rough day today," Jim said.

"Where've you been, you sonofabitch?" she said.

"Let's don't have profanity. That's not nice," Jim said.

"Somebody was following me," she said, trying to keep her voice from trembling.

"The road was empty. There's nobody out there," he replied.

"I want a plane ticket to Seattle," she said.

"I don't think that's in the cards right now," Jim said.

"You do it for people in Witness Protection all the time."

"We still got a lot of unfinished work. A lot of work," he said, shaking his head profoundly.

"Amos said 'fuck it.' He told me I did a good job."

"You shouldn't have boosted a post office, kiddo," Jim said.

"I got to take a leak," the other agent said.

As though she were not there, the two agents walked down by the stream and pointed themselves into a Douglas fir tree and urinated on the ground. She stared at their backs, listening to their banter, realizing finally how absolutely insignificant she was.

Screw you, she thought, and got into their

Cherokee, started the engine, and made a U-turn, the driver's door swinging back on its hinges. Their mouths hung open in disbelief as the Cherokee roared down the road in the darkness.

Jim took a cell phone out of the pocket of his windbreaker and punched in several numbers.

"A little problem here, boss man," he said.

"What problem?" the voice of Amos Rackley said.

"Pocahontas just hauled ass."

"So go after her."

"Can't do it, Amos. She took the Cherokee and left us her shit machine. The one with no lights."

There was a pause.

"Have you visited Fargo in the winter?" Rackley asked.

Jim clicked off the cell phone and set it on the roof of Sue Lynn's car and propped his arms against the metal and stared at the waning light on the ridgeline. The trees rustled in the wind and he thought he smelled rain. He fished in his pocket and removed a cheese sandwich he had wrapped in wax paper and handed half of it to his friend just as a solitary raindrop struck the hood of the car.

He and the other agent got inside and closed the doors and ate the sandwich, bored, irritated with themselves, wondering if Amos was serious about Fargo.

High up on the ridge a man wearing cowboy boots with sharply defined heels worked his way through the tree trunks until he saw the stock car parked down below in the glade, the orange numerals in bold relief against the gray primer on the door. He stuffed rubber plugs in his ears and got down in a prone position and steadied a rifle on a collapsible tripod in the softness of the pine needles, then pulled back the bolt and chambered a round.

He sighted down the slope and waited, working his jaw comfortably against the stock. The moon was up now and he could see clearly into the glade. A shadow moved behind the steering wheel; a cigarette lighter flared on a face. Perfect.

The shooter squeezed back the trigger and burned the entire thirty-round magazine, swinging the barrel on the tripod, the copper-jacketed .223 rounds pocking the door panels and the roof, gashing the seats, blowing glass out of the dashboard, popping the horn button loose like a tiddlywink.

When the breech locked open, the shooter rose to his feet and removed the rubber plugs from his ears, dropping one into the pine needles, and walked back down the opposite slope to his vehicle.

Down in the glade the driver's door of Sue Lynn's car swung open and Jim fell out on the grass, his mouth blooming with uneaten sandwich bread. He clawed his way up the side of the car and found his cell phone where he had left it on the roof, then collapsed on the ground again, his clothes soaked with blood, and pushed the redial button.

But when Amos Rackley answered, Jim realized that the sucking chest wound he tried to close with his hand had stolen his voice. He lay on his back in the grass, one leg bent under him, and used his fingernail to tap out a last message on the mouthpiece to Amos Rackley.

# Chapter
## 26

"YOU KNOW what he Morsed me? 'Sorry.'
*He* was sorry," Amos Rackley said.

It was the next morning, and we were
standing in front of Doc's porch. Rackley's
face was drained of color, his eyes smolder-
ing.

"Sue Lynn Big Medicine hasn't been here. I
don't know where your vehicle is, either," I
said.

"Is your son in his tent?"

"He took my truck to town. Leave him
alone, Mr. Rackley. He's not in this."

"He just porks her on a regular basis when
she's not getting federal agents killed?"

I looked at the fatigue and caffeinated tension in his face and knew it was only a matter of time before the anger in his eyes

focused inward and Amos Rackley found himself locked up with his own thoughts for many years.

"Come inside, sir," I said.

"What?"

"Have you eaten? I have some coffee and pancakes on the stove."

He took a breath of air through his nose, looking off into the distance, as though he were choosing between one of several insults to hurl at me.

"I should have been with them," he said.

"They were doing their job. Why not give them credit for it?"

"I made a wisecrack to Jim about Fargo. That's the last thing I said to him."

"It wasn't anybody's fault except the bastards who did it. These are the guys you hang out to dry. Not yourself, not a kid like Sue Lynn Big Medicine."

He rubbed his face with his hand. He had shaved so closely there were pink scrape marks on his chin. He seemed to take my measure as though he didn't know who I was.

"I'll take a raincheck on the pancakes. Could I use your bathroom?" he said.

AS RACKLEY drove through the field behind Doc's he passed Temple Carrol's Explorer. She parked in the yard and walked up on the porch, her backpack full of research materials slung from one hand.

"That guy looked like a fed," she said.

"He is. Two of his agents were killed on the Flathead Reservation last night."

"The ones who rousted you?"

"Yeah, one of them, anyway."

"Who did it?"

"Probably one of Carl Hinkel's people. Sue Lynn took the agents' vehicle and left them stranded with her uncle's stock car. The shooter probably thought she was inside."

Temple threw her backpack onto a chair and went into the house and came back out with a cup of coffee in her hand.

"Where's Sue Lynn?" she asked.

"I don't know."

"I checked out the background of Xavier and Holly Girard," she said.

"What for?"

"He's a writer and she's an actress, but they keep showing up where they don't have any business. Each time they have some innocuous explanation. Read this," she said, and handed me a manila folder filled with fax sheets from a private investigator in Phoenix, Arizona.

"By the way, Holly Girard didn't meet Nicki Molinari out here. Their families both belonged to the same country club in Scottsdale," she said.

I sat down and read through the sheets in the folder.

"Her mother's maiden name was Carruthers?" I said.

"You got it."

"Why is it I feel I've been had?" I said.

"I couldn't guess," Temple said.

WE DROVE to the Girards' house above the Clark Fork but no one was home. Then, because I was unconvinced of Xavier's sobriety, we tried the downtown bars. We found him playing pinochle in the back of a workingman's place on Front Street called Stockman's, a bottle of ginger ale by his elbow.

He gave me a tired look.

"What is it now?" he asked.

"Not much, a discussion of assets, family names, mining interests, that sort of thing," I said.

He grinned at the other players and shrugged his shoulders, as though saying "What can I do?" We went out the back door into the sunshine. A carousel was revolving on the riverbank, the hand-carved wooden horses filled with children.

"Your wife is a member of the family that owns the Phillips-Carruthers Corporation, the same guys who want to destroy the Blackfoot River?" I said.

"You're talking about Holly's mother, not Holly. Holly doesn't own anything," he replied, leaning against an iron rail, looking off at the river.

"That's a little bit disingenuous, don't you think?" I said.

"Hey, get out of our lives, Mr. Holland."

"You misled me. I think you've misled this community, too."

"About *what?*" he said.

"Your wife has a vested interest in seeing Doc hurt. By extension, so do you. That brings us right back to the rape of Maisey Voss and the murder of Lamar Ellison," I said.

"You're full of shit."

But he looked like a wounded animal, the hot glare in his eyes focusing on nothing, as if nothing in his range of vision would connect with the confused thoughts in his head. He had managed to combine the roles of cuckold, novelist, flamboyant drunk, Hollywood iconoclast, friend of the environment, confidant of gangsters, and object of pity all in one persona. I wondered when the day would come when he stuck a pistol into his mouth.

Temple and I started to walk away.

"If it's any of your business, Holly and I are busting up," he said at my back.

"Why?" I said.

"She's getting it on with Molinari again. I've had it," he replied.

But if he intended to elicit sympathy, he failed with Temple. She walked to within a foot of his face.

"You're going on the stand, baby cakes. Get used to it," she said.

LATER, Maisey got into Doc's truck with a shopping list and headed down the dirt road toward the main highway and the small, independent grocery store in Bonner. As she approached the log bridge over the Blackfoot she saw a low-slung red car in her rearview mirror. The bridge trembled under her as she rumbled across the wood planks and a dust cloud blew out on the water and disappeared in the current. When she swung out onto the highway she looked back briefly and saw the red car again and this time she recognized Terry Witherspoon behind the wheel.

He followed her all the way into Bonner, through the quiet stretch of tree-shaded, company-owned houses, past the sawmill and the piles of green lumber stacked next to waiting train cars, past the normal world that most people lived in, then around a bend in the road to the grocery store parking lot. She got out of the truck and started inside, then went back and locked the door, even though she left the window open.

Terry Witherspoon pulled in close to the store entrance and was now waving at her, as though the only problem between them was her failure to recognize who he was.

Then he got out of his car, smiling at her above the top of the door.

"Didn't you see me back there?" he said.

"Right," she said.

He was dressed in khaki slacks and shined loafers and a gold and burgundy University of Montana sweater.

"I was coming up to your house when you zoomed on past me," he said.

"You were hiding on the side road."

"I wasn't," he said, crinkling his nose under his glasses, waiting to see if she would refute the lie. When she didn't she could see the vindication grow in his face. "Your father attacked me in front of all those people at the concert. I took you home that night when the football players were going to hurt you. I got in a lot of trouble with Wyatt over that."

"You buried a woman alive. You're disgusting. Get out of here," she said.

"You don't know what you're saying. That Indian bitch caused all this."

"Caused *what?*" Maisey said, then realized she had stepped into the trap of arguing with a person who had probably never told the truth about anything in his life.

"She got those federal agents killed. They're gonna blame Wyatt or me. Everything's coming apart. I had a lot of plans," he said. Then he seemed to grow more passionate, more unjustly injured, his eyes magnifying behind his glasses. "I bought a camera. I want to take pictures of you. Down on the river."

The fact that he was speaking intimately to her, as though she were part of his world, made her stomach turn. She rushed inside the store and got a basket and pushed it down the aisle, trying to concentrate on the list in her hand.

Out in the parking lot Terry Witherspoon stood by Doc's truck, chewing on a hangnail, glaring at the traffic.

"Is everything all right, miss?" the butcher said. He was an Indian, wrapped around the middle with a red-stained apron.

"Yes. Fine," she replied.

"You know that fellow out there?" he asked.

"Not really."

"He was in here once before. That's why he's not in here now. You let me know if he bothers you," the butcher said.

Fifteen minutes later she wheeled her basket loaded with sacked groceries back into

the parking lot. Terry Witherspoon was waiting for her, tossing his head to clear a strand
of hair from his glasses.

"When I saw you through the window, in
the shower that night, you were as beautiful
as a movie star," he said. When she didn't answer he started to lift one of the sacks from
the basket.

"Don't touch that," she said.

"I want to help you."

"Don't put your hands on our food. Get
away from my basket."

The wind blew his hair across his glasses.
He continued to stare at her as though he
could not assimilate what he was being told.
Then he said, "Shit on you."

She loaded her groceries into the bed of the
pickup, trying to ignore the closeness of his
body and the smell of deodorant that rose
from his clothes. She got into the truck and
started the engine, but Witherspoon remained standing by her window.

"I can't see the street," she said.

"I should have let Wyatt bust you. You're
just a little whore. That's why you were
hanging out in that bar. You wanted more of
what Lamar and the others gave you. Lamar
said you gave good head."

She ground the transmission and tried to
swing out on the street, but the guards were
up at the train crossing and traffic had

backed up across the entrance to the parking lot.

Witherspoon got behind her and began blowing his horn and smashing his bumper against hers, much harder than she thought a low-centered car would be able to do. Then she realized pieces of pipe were overwelded, like gridwork or a battering ram, on the front of his car. Witherspoon snugged the bumper against the rear of the truck and slowly accelerated and starting pushing her into the street. His back tires burned black strips on the asphalt and spun circles of smoke under the fenders, but the truck was wobbling on the frame now, the back wheels losing purchase, Maisey's foot slipping on the brake. All the while Witherspoon kept his palm clamped down on his horn button.

Even if she made it out into the traffic without being hit she knew he would follow her all the way home, tailgating and cutting her off, trying to force her into the path of oncoming traffic.

Go inside and get the butcher, she thought.

Like hell.

She pulled into the street, glancing once in her rearview mirror. Witherspoon was looking right and left, waiting for an opportunity to floor the accelerator after her. He never realized the seriousness of his presumption until it was too late.

Maisey hit the brakes, shifted into reverse, and mashed on the gas pedal. The trailer hitch on the truck speared through the pipework on Witherspoon's grille, gashing the radiator open, tearing the fan so metal screamed against metal. She straightened the truck, then floorboarded into him again, this time crumpling a fender down on a tire, shattering the headlights, knocking his forehead into the windshield.

When she shifted back into first gear, the low-slung red car that belonged to Wyatt Dixon was bleeding green pools of antifreeze onto the asphalt, spokes of steam whistling from under the hood. An elderly woman with Coke-bottle glasses pulled in behind Witherspoon and began blowing her horn for him to get out of the way.

THE NEXT MORNING the sheriff called and asked me to drop by his office.

"The two ATF agents were killed by .223 rounds, all fired from the same rifle, probably an M-16. The spent casings were all clean," he said.

The sheriff was sitting behind his desk, his Stetson pushed up on the back of his head, his suit coat on, fiddling with his hands as he talked, as though he were concentrating more on his own thoughts than on his listener.

"Amos Rackley told you this?" I asked.

"The Flathead Reservation has patches of privately owned land on it. The ridge where the shooter was? It's owned by a white man. The government can't keep me out of this one," the sheriff said.

"I don't understand why you called me."

"The shooter dropped one of his ear plugs. He left a thumbprint on it. You know a guy named Clayton Stark?"

"No," I said.

"He don't have a record here, but three years ago he was picked up for questioning in a child abduction case in Pocatello. Does that ring any bells for you?"

"A pedophile was arrested in Carl Hinkel's yard five years ago," I replied.

"That's right. Your son's girlfriend, this gal Sue Lynn Big Medicine? Her little brother was abducted and killed, wasn't he?"

"How'd you know that?"

"I get paid to do my damn homework, son. You see a pattern here on this pedophilia stuff?"

"Yeah, but I don't know what it is."

"Neither do I," the sheriff said. He got up from his desk and began fumbling around in a closet.

"What are you doing?" I asked.

"There's a bull trout under the Higgins

Street Bridge that daily gives me a lesson in humility," he said, lifting a rod and reel from behind a raincoat. "Take a walk with me. I want to tell you a story."

THE PREVIOUS DAY the sheriff had been visiting a cemetery on the north side, a lovely, tree-shaded area on a knoll where the town's oldest families were buried. He saw Cleo Lonnigan sitting on a bench by her son's grave, leaning over, setting stem roses in a row by the headstone. She was talking to herself and did not hear the sheriff when he walked up behind her.

"You want company?" he asked.

"It's his birthday," she said.

"Oh," he said, nodding.

"On his birthday I make a wish for each year of his life that he would have had, then put roses on his grave," she said.

The sheriff sat beside her on the bench. It was made of stone and felt cold and hard under his legs. "I worry about you, Cleo."

"Why is that, J.T.?"

He looked down the slope, through the trees, at a maroon Cadillac convertible that was parked in the drive with the top up. The Cadillac had been waxed and hand-buffed with soft rags and the reflection of the leaves overhead seemed trapped inside the paint.

"You're here with Nicki Molinari?" the sheriff asked.

"We've let bygones be bygones."

"I have a hard time accepting a statement like that."

She rose from the bench. It was cool in the shade and she wore a silk scarf tied under her chin.

"I don't ask you to, J.T.," she replied, and walked down the slope toward Nicki Molinari's car. The wind blew the roses into crossed patterns on top of her son's grave.

"SHE'S ONE I can't read, Sheriff," I said.

"It's not hard. Her husband's crooked money got her little boy killed. Cleo says she didn't know where that money come from. When people got more than they're supposed to have, they *always* know where it comes from. So she's got to get up every morning, denying to herself that little boy's death is not on her. How'd you like to carry a burden like that?"

We were in the shadow of the Higgins Bridge now, and the sheriff had managed to fling his lure into a willow tree.

"Why'd you tell me about Cleo and Molinari?" I asked.

"It's just a warning. She'd like to see you hung from a meat hook."

"You can sure put it in a memorable way, sir," I said, and started to leave. "By the way, how is it you're so close to Cleo?"

"My son's in that same cemetery. He was killed in Desert Storm. That was rich men fighting over oil, Mr. Holland. My boy was too young to enlist on his own. So I signed the papers for him."

He began jerking his lure to free it from the tree, until the line broke in his big hand.


I BOUGHT avocado and creamed cheese sandwiches and frozen yogurt and cold drinks at a grocery by the university and put it all in an ice chest and picked up Temple at her motel. We drove through Hellgate Canyon, east of town, and out toward Rock Creek to eat lunch. I told Temple about the sheriff's encounter with Cleo Lonnigan in the cemetery. I thought I could simply mention it casually and get it out of the way and not call up unpleasant memories about past relationships. That's what I thought.

"What's God's gift to the Res up to?" Temple said.

"Taking Molinari over the hurdles. He's out of his depth," I said.

"Maybe it's the other way around. Xavier

Girard says Molinari is in the sack with his wife. But maybe our girl is asexual or a lesbian and doesn't care. What's your opinion?"

"I don't have one," I said.

"A little sensitive, are we?"

"No, I just wish I hadn't brought this up," I said.

There was no sound in the truck except the hum of the tires on the asphalt. We were in a long valley now and the hills rose up steep and green against the sky. When I turned off the interstate I passed a restaurant made of logs and entered another valley, this one traversed by a wide, pebble-bottomed stream that flowed out of the south, with both meadowland and high, wooded, sharp-peaked mountains on each side.

I drove two miles along the stream, past fishermen up to their waists in the riffles, and did not try to say anything else to Temple. But I could feel her looking at the side of my face.

"You're just going to turn to stone on me?" she said.

"No, I gave up."

"Pardon?"

"I'm tired of sackcloth and ashes," I said.

"You're saying I'm too heavy a burden to deal with?"

Farther up the road was a deep-green piney woods and a rusty turnstile that allowed fishermen to enter the woods on their way to the stream without letting cattle out on the road. Temple waited for me to answer her.

"You know how I feel about you. But you're unrelenting and unforgiving," I said.

She sat very still for a long time, her milky-green eyes filled with thoughts I couldn't guess at. She turned her head and studied my face.

"I don't know how much more of this I can take," she said.

"You want to go back to Texas?"

"After I nail the two guys who tried to bury me alive."

"That's the only reason you're here now?"

"That's a good question. Let me think very hard on it," she said, her mouth pinched with anger.

I pulled off the road into a stand of grand fir and pine trees and parked in a dry slough that fed into the stream. My head was splitting. I wanted to turn around and drive back to town, but Temple had already gotten out of the truck and slammed the door and walked through a clump of huckleberry bushes to the edge of the stream. The wind dropped and I could hear the heat of the truck engine ticking under the hood.

I got the food and a picnic blanket out of the truck and walked down the slough toward the bank. Through the trees I could see a huge dalles and the stream sliding over sculpted boulders the size of small blimps. The air was loud with the roar of the water, sweet and cool with the spray that coated the rocks.

I tripped on a root and looked down at a fresh, hoofed track in the slough, one as long as my foot. To my right the reeds and huckleberry bushes had been broken or mashed down into the moistness of the silt and gravel along the bank.

I set down our food and followed the hoofed tracks through the reeds. I worked my way through an overhang of willows and stepped across a cottonwood that beavers had cut down, then I saw the moose on a small promontory above Temple, its webbed rack the largest I had ever seen on an animal of any kind, its nostrils puffing with her scent.

She was standing on a sand spit, her hands in her back pockets, looking upstream, and she neither heard nor saw the animal behind her. I moved quickly along the bank, and the moose jerked its rack around, its eyes on me now, its weight shifting on the promontory, dirt scudding down into the water from its hooves.

Then I heard it whirl and turn in the undergrowth and I knew it was coming for either me or Temple.

I ran along the water's edge, yelling Temple's name. She looked at me, startled, then her face went white. I picked her up at the waist, locking my arms around her, and splashed into a side channel and came up onto an island. But the moose was right behind us, its hooves clacking across underwater rocks, its rack cracking a cottonwood limb in half like a twig.

I stumbled and fell, then rose to my feet and picked up Temple again and went over the other side of the island into the stream, into deep water and a fast-running, ice-cold current that swept us through a series of gray boulders that steamed with mist.

We floated around a bend, under an overhang of willows, into a pool that was deep in shadow. I felt the pebbled bottom under my shoes, and I pulled Temple toward me out of the current and we walked chest-deep toward the far bank, behind the protection of a beaver dam. But the bank had been undercut by the current so that it kept shaling under my weight as I tried to get out of the water. I grabbed the bottom of a willow and pulled myself up until I could find purchase with one knee, then I locked my hand on Temple's wrist and hoisted her up after me.

I heard the moose's hooves clatter once more on stone, then saw it lift itself, wet and blowing and magnificent, onto the opposite bank and disappear into the trees. Temple and I fell into the leaves, and I held her against me and kissed her face and hair and neck and covered her with my body and felt the firm muscles of her back and legs and gathered her against me with such force that I could hear the breath coming out of her chest. Her cheek felt as hot as a baby's waking from sleep.

I kissed her hands and mouth and the tops of her breasts and I unbuttoned her shirt and kissed her stomach and touched her breasts and thighs without permission or shame, then felt her hand begin loosening my belt. She peeled off her shirt and bra and threw them aside and put her tongue in my mouth and pulled my weight down on top of her. I rubbed my face in the wetness of her hair and kissed her eyes and sucked her fingers and put her nipples in my mouth, then I was inside her, inside Temple Carrol, inside all her pink warmth and the caress and charity and heat of her thighs. Her mouth opened and her breath rose against my skin with a smell and coolness like flowers blooming in snow, and she pressed me deeper inside her and held me tight with her arms and locked her legs in mine.

I wanted to raise up on my arms and kiss her again and look into the flush on her face and the mystery and beauty of her eyes, but I felt both of us rushing toward that irreversible moment that even memory cannot enhance, and I held her against me, my voice hoarse and weak and barely above a whisper, my poor attempt at a statement of affection lost in the roar of the stream and the creak of the wind in the trees and the rhythmic breath of Temple Carrol in my ear and the kneading of her palms on my spine. Then I felt a burst of light in my loins and a release from all the rage and violence that had fouled my blood for a lifetime. There was only the beating of her heart and the moist touch of her skin and the softness of her smile as I slipped out of her, exhausted and spent, and rested my head between her breasts while her fingers stroked my hair.

# Chapter 27

THURSDAY MORNING I drove down to Stevensville, then east of town toward the Sapphires and Nicki Molinari's ranch. It was raining in the south and dust was blowing out of the valley, and in the distance there were veins of lightning inside the dust and rain. When I turned into Molinari's drive his man Frank was trying to catch up a horse that was eating the petunias in the flower bed.

He ran at the horse with a rope, then threw dirt clods at it. He tried to whip it across the flanks with a fishing rod and instead tripped over the garden hose and was almost kicked in the face.

Nicki Molinari came out of the barn, waving his hands.

"Frank, Frank, wrong way to go about it," he said.

"He ate all your flowers," Frank said.

"We'll get some new ones. Look, give him these molasses balls. See, let him eat them out of your palm so he don't bite your fingers," Molinari said.

"He went to the bathroom all over the walk," Frank said.

"I'll hose it off. I'm gonna talk to my guest now. You did fine, Frank," Molinari said.

He watched Frank walk into the barn with the horse following behind him.

"You want a job in personnel management?" he asked.

"I hear you got over your objections to Cleo Lonnigan."

"What, you think she's working my joint or something?"

"It occurred to me," I said.

"Well, you thought right. It would be the smart move. Cleo gives me my money, I remodel your bone structure. Except the truth is I like you. Don't ask me why."

"What's the angle with Cleo?"

"Horizontal. It's the nature of the world, Counselor."

I looked away at his neighbor's property. There was a small white church by the road, and the neighbor was up on the roof, hammering down shingles. I looked back at Molinari. For some reason his face seemed different, the eyes sunken, the skeletal outline of his skull just below the skin.

"What are you staring at?" he asked.

"I think you're going to come to a bad end."

"You're a fortune-teller or something?" he said, and tried to grin. "Hey, Counselor, you need to get that look off your face."

"It's the way you use people. I think it's about to come back on you."

"I'm in a good mood here. But you're using up my patience."

"You're a victim, Nicki. You just don't know it."

"*I'm* a victim?"

"She's a physician. You're a graduate of Terminal Island. Who do you think is going to win all the marbles?"

"Frank, get out here!" he yelled at the barn.


I DROVE BACK to Missoula and parked at Temple's motel, and we took a walk down by the river and she put her hand in mine. The current in the river looked fast and green and coppery in the late-afternoon sunlight, and rafters were floating under the walk bridge that led to the university, splashing foam into the air with their oars. I told Temple about my visit with Nicki Molinari and felt her release my hand.

"Cleo Lonnigan again. What's this guy got that she wants?" she said.

"I'm not sure."

"Why'd you call Molinari a victim?"

I looked out at the rafters rolling and spinning through the riffle and wished I had not gotten into the subject.

"I smelled an odor I'd almost forgotten. At first I thought it was on the wind. Soldiers talk about it," I said.

"I don't know if I want to hear this," Temple said.

"I stuck playing cards in the mouths of dead people, Temple. I couldn't wash their smell off my hand. Like they'd breathed something on my skin. I smelled it on Molinari. I didn't imagine it."

"I'm not going to listen to this. No, no, not today. See you in the ice cream store," she said, walking ahead of me, shaking her hands in the air, smiling giddily at people passing in the opposite direction.

THE NEXT MORNING the phone rang in Doc's living room. Maisey answered it, then handed the receiver to me.

"That little puke Terry Witherspoon just left the department. He's filing a hit-and-run charge against Maisey Voss," the sheriff said.

"What are you going to do?"

"She deliberately smashed in the front of Wyatt Dixon's car."

"Witherspoon started it. She should have run over him," I said.

"I can't believe you're an attorney."

I waited in the silence. Then I said, "Did you call here for another reason?"

I heard him exhale against the phone receiver. "I drove out to Cleo Lonnigan's yesterday. She told me this ATF agent, this guy Rackley, was out to see her last week. Rackley says her son and husband were probably killed by outlaw bikers."

"How do you know he actually said this?"

"I called him up. He says Lamar Ellison may have been mixed up in it."

"Why are you telling me this?" I asked.

"Because maybe Cleo was right all along and I was saying otherwise. Because maybe other individuals had reason to set Lamar Ellison on fire."

"Did you tell that to the district attorney?"

"None of your business," he said.

"You're a good man, Sheriff."

"Tell my old woman that. Have you seen Sue Lynn Big Medicine?"

"No, sir."

"Where's your son?"

After a beat, I said, "I couldn't say right offhand."

"That's what I thought," the sheriff said. The line went dead.

I walked into the kitchen, where Doc was washing out three gutted rainbows in the sink and rinsing the rubber liner of his creel.

"Why would Nicki Molinari insist West Coast wiseguys killed Cleo's husband and son if somebody else did it?" I asked.

"People are scared of the Mob. He wants to hold a threat over her head without seeming to be involved."

The clarity of Doc's reply made me wonder about the depth and adequacy of my own thought processes.

TERRY WITHERSPOON did not have memories, not in the ordinary sense. The high school he attended had been a place he went in the morning and left in the afternoon, neither better nor worse for the experience. He learned that reticence ensured he would not be bothered by others; in fact, reticence in school was a way to purchase virtual invisibility. If pressed in a difficult situation, he just grinned at the corner of his mouth and flipped his hair out of his face and let others wonder what was on his mind.

Teachers pretended to believe in the importance of what they taught, art and history, save the Earth, respect your fellowman, but they shopped at Wal-Mart like everybody else, while their neighbors' businesses went under. His classmates sang in church on Sundays and Wednesday nights but somehow the girls got pregnant anyway. He wondered why they all spent so much time convincing themselves they were somebody else.

When he was a junior in high school his father, who fixed bicycles and sharpened lawn mowers, was seventy-two and his mother sixty. The three of them lived in a small house at the end of an alley, behind a loan agency, and did not own a car. Across the street was an empty lot where black people planted gardens in the spring. Terry's mother often cleaned houses with black people and made friends with them and worked alongside them in their gardens. When she came home at night, sometimes with a paper bag full of vegetables, she smelled of sweat and the dirt in her clothes. In fact, she smelled just like the black people she worked with.

A little girl broke her tooth on a BB that was inside a watermelon picked from the field. Terry was caught on the loan agency's rooftop a week later, air rifle in hand.

Aside from his two-beer visit to the VFW hall every Saturday afternoon, Terry's father spent most of his waking hours in his shed, which was hung with bicycle frames and wheels and narrow tires. He seldom wore his false teeth and his cheeks were collapsed inward on his jawbones so that his expression was wizened and severe, although in reality he appeared to have no emotions at all.

The night of the junior prom Terry went into the shed to tell his father supper was ready.

"What's your name again?" the father said.

"My name? I'm Terry."

"Where's my son? He's supposed to help me."

"I'm your son."

The father studied Terry's face. "Yeah, I can see the resemblance to your mother. Her people always had that pallor. Like they was shut up in a root cellar," he said.

Terry put on the new suit he had bought with the money he had earned at the grocery and walked to the junior prom and convinced himself he really didn't care about the prom one way or another; he was just going there to watch the jocks and snarfs and frumps and socials and sluts with their pushed-up boobs jerk each other around. He stood by himself for most of the dance, creating the illusion of activity, taking a smoke outside, walking down the emptiness of the corridor to the boys' rest room, constantly fixing his glasses on his nose, lifting the corner of his mouth in an expression that could be interpreted as either disapproval or interest.

Then he asked a girl to dance. Her father was a Mason and real estate broker who sold lakefront lots in the mountains to people from the North, and the family lived in a two-story brick house with a gazebo on the lawn, on a hill above the town. She was plump across the middle and chubby under the chin, but she looked cute with her Dutch-boy haircut, and she had always spoken to him in the halls, unlike most of the girls whose families had money.

"I'd love to dance, Terry," she said, then leaned close to his ear, her breath husky and cold and scented with raspberry from the wine coolers the jocks had been handing out in the parking lot. "I have to go to the bathroom. I'll be right back."

The girl walked with two of her friends down the corridor, the three of them looking back at him briefly and giggling. He went out the side exit and lit a cigarette in the shrubbery and looked up at the moon. Then he realized the window to the girls' rest room was right behind him, the top portion of the glass pulled down for ventilation.

"Did you check that suit? Neon blue with white socks. He must have gotten it at a black funeral home," the plump girl said.

"Don't knock those socks, Jenny. They match his dandruff," another girl said, and the three of them howled.

He stood a long time in the shadows, his cheeks tingling, the blood singing in his ears. Then he walked down the empty street, back into his own neighborhood, the music from the dance fading behind him. The sodium street lamps glowed like a gray vapor on the clapboard houses, the outdated cars, and the vegetable gardens that people grew out of necessity, not choice. He walked past his house on the alley where his parents were watching television, out to the lounge on the highway, where the vinyl upholstery was red and black and the bartender was built like a steroid addict and wore gold earrings and black leather, and the traveling salesmen stayed late.

The man who picked him up at the bar said he was from Raleigh but he had a Yankee accent.

"If I could buy you the best thing in the world, what would it be?" the man asked.

"Buster Bars at the Dairy Queen. I ate twelve of them once," Terry said.

"You're still all boy, aren't you?" the man said, and touched his hair in the car.

At the motel Terry ate the Buster Bars out of a paper bag, taking his time, enjoying each bite while the man tried to suppress the discomfiture his desire was causing him.

"There's a refrigerator over here. You can save some of them for later," the man said.

"I'll think about it," Terry said.

When they made love Terry realized for the first time in his life the power a female, or one taking her role, could exercise over a man.

Later, the man showered and dressed and began talking about a trip he was taking to Hollywood with his son, who went to a private college in Massachusetts. A neon sign glowed through the curtain and gave a peculiar purple hue and shape to the man's mouth, like a distorted flower. Terry could not remove his stare from the man's mouth and the way it moved against the pallor of his skin. He found himself becoming angrier and angrier, although he didn't know why.

"Why don't you stop talking? Why don't you shut up about your son?" Terry said.

"Beg your pardon?" the man said, turning from the mirror where he was knotting his necktie. When Terry didn't reply the man grinned in the mirror and continued knotting his tie. "I'd like to call you when I'm in town again. This evening was special for me, Terry. You make me feel young."

Terry felt a rage like someone kicking open the door to a furnace next to his skin. He drove the man's head down on the toilet bowl and smashed his mouth again and again on the rim until the porcelain was striped with red from the top of the bowl to the waterline. Then he emptied the man's wallet and ripped his watch off his wrist and his class ring off his finger and shook the wallet's contents into the toilet bowl and dropped the wallet in on top of them.

"There's still a Buster Bar in the fridge," he said, and jiggled with laughter.

NINE MONTHS in the state reformatory, then one day after his eighteenth birthday he was discharged and his records sealed. Not a bad deal. He got a GED inside and learned how to make prune-o, hot-wire a car, cook down diet pills and shoot them up with an eyedropper, and dive Dumpsters for people's credit card and phone and bank account numbers.

But the revelatory event that would change his life came about by pure accident.

He wandered into a gun show at the high school gym. The building was packed with hunters, collectors, Civil War enthusiasts, competition shooters, people Terry had never taken seriously and did not take seriously now. But at one display table was a group of four men who were different from everyone

else in the room. Their bodies had the hardness of professional soldiers, and they wore
neatly trimmed goatees and black T-shirts
and their arms were scrolled from the shoulder to the wrist with intricate tattoos. They
grinned at the people drifting up and down
the aisle, but there was no mistaking the
black electricity in their eyes, the dried testosterone in their clothes, the invasive look that
made other people swallow involuntarily.

Their table was spread with Lugers and
Nazi memorabilia. Terry picked up a pam-
phlet with a headline about a Zionist Occu-
pational Government.

"What's a Zionist?" Terry asked.

One of the men pushed a chair toward him
with his foot. "Have a seat, kid," he said,
then rested his arm across Terry's shoulders.

The man's arm felt heavy and thick across
the back of Terry's neck, a sensual heat and
power transferring from the man's body to his.
When Terry glanced out at the people in the
aisle, their eyes quickly turned away. Terry felt
his loins tingle like a swarm of bees.


IT WAS DUSK at the compound now, the
river streaked with the last gold light of the
day, the air cool and smelling of cut hay and
Carl's prize Angus, which were drinking in
the slough.

But it wasn't a good evening for Terry. Wyatt was still mad about Maisey Voss destroying the front of his car and had told him if he wanted to go anywhere, he could walk or hitchhike, because neither Wyatt nor Carl would give him a vehicle to drive.

Now Wyatt and Carl had gone to the drive-in movie in Missoula and left Terry to his own devices. Terry walked along the riverbank to the campground upstream from the compound and baited his hand line with a piece of corn and cheese and threw it into an eddy behind a rotted cottonwood. The mountains on the western rim of the valley were purple with shadow, lighted only on the high crests where the snow had not melted.

He heard a car door open and feet crunching on the silt and pebbles behind him, then he turned and stared into the face of the biggest man he had ever seen.

"Walk up there and get in the trunk of the car," the man said. The voice was flat, mechanical, clotted with rust.

"Fuck that," Terry said.

The man slapped Terry on the ear, so hard Terry thought the drum was broken. He jerked Terry's line from his hand and threw it into the river, and, by his belt, dragged him stumbling up the embankment and pushed him headlong into the trunk of a small car and slammed down the hatch.

A half hour later Terry was sitting in a heavy wooden chair inside a batting cage, his wrists roped to the chair, staring at an automatic pitching machine loaded with scuffed base-balls. The cage was located inside a closed barn, and motes of dust and wisps of hay floated in the haze of the electric lights that ran the length of the horse stalls.

The man who had kidnapped him had not spoken a word since removing him from the car trunk.

"You work for that doctor? Is this over Maisey?" Terry said.

But the man did not answer.

A side door opened and a man in a cutoff baseball jersey and blue jeans that were new and stiff from the box stepped inside the barn. His hair was black and combed, his skin olive-toned, his eyes brown like a deer's.

He leaned over in the shadows and picked up a remote-control button that was attached to the pitching machine.

"You did a one-bit in North Carolina?" the man said.

Terry ran the tip of his tongue along his lips. Don't give a smart answer, he thought.

"Not exactly. I was in the reformatory. I bashed a fudge packer who came on to me," Terry said.

"I can respect that. Now, all you got to do is tell me and Frank the truth about a couple of things, and we'll take you home. This machine pitches up to seventy miles an hour. You getting the picture on this?"

"No," Terry said, then realized he'd just given the wrong answer.

The man's right thumb moved and the mechanical arm of the pitching machine fired a ball into Terry's chest, then reset itself for another pitch. Terry felt as if someone had driven an auger into his breastbone.

"I know, it hurts. I been hit by it," the man said.

"You're Nicki Molinari," Terry said.

"What's in a name?" Molinari said.

Terry started to reply, but Molinari held a finger up for him to be quiet.

"Two years ago, on July Fourth, a man and a little boy were killed on the Clearwater National Forest. Who you think did that?" Molinari said.

"How am I supposed to know?"

The machine clanked and Terry leaned sideways, straining against the chair, but the ball caught him on the collarbone. He tried to eat his pain, but he couldn't bite down on the groan that welled out of his chest.

"Was it Lamar Ellison?" Molinari asked.

"*Lamar?* He was a snitch for the ATF."

"So?" Molinari said.

Terry knew he needed to provide an answer, but he couldn't think, couldn't sort out all the wise remarks and insults that he had always carried around like a sheaf of arrows.

"Ask Wyatt. He celled with Lamar," he said, and realized how afraid he actually was.

"The rodeo clown? You think I go to clowns for my information? That's what you're telling me?" Molinari said.

"No."

"You think anybody's-fuck from a state reformatory can lie and call me stupid on my own property, in front of a business associate, and just walk out of here?"

Terry was drowning in Molinari's words.

"I was fishing. I turn around and a guy who looks like Frankenstein locks me in his car trunk. I don't deserve this."

"I don't think you should call Frank names, kid. You want to apologize to Frank for that?" Molinari said.

Terry hung his head and shut his eyes and waited for another ball to hit him. But nothing happened.

"I'm gonna fix a sandwich. Then I'll be back. Search your memory about that deal on the Clearwater National Forest," Molinari said, and went out the side door of the barn.

It was quiet a long time, then Frank stood up from the sawhorse he had been sitting on and folded his huge palm around the trigger for the pitching machine. Terry remembered thinking his jaws looked like dirty sandpaper, his recessed eyes like those of a man whose moment had come.

A HALF HOUR LATER the side door opened again and Molinari entered the batting cage and reached down out of a red haze and lifted Terry's chin with one knuckle.

"You gonna make it?" he asked.

Terry's face felt as if it had been stung all over by hornets.

"Wyatt's gonna—" he began.

"The clown again?" Molinari said.

"Wyatt—" Terry said, but could not clear the blood from his mouth to speak.

Molinari looked at Frank, who shook his head negatively. Molinari chewed on the ball of his thumb and gazed thoughtfully into the shadows, then spit a piece of skin off his tongue.

"Spread some raincoats on the car seat and get him out of here," he said.

"He called you a dago and greaseball," Frank said.

"I've answered to worse. Call Phoenix and L.A. and tell them I want everything they got on this militia guy, what's-his-name, Hinkel."

He picked up a baseball that had rolled out on the floor and tossed it into an apple basket.

"This valley used to be a nice place. Now we got half the riffraff in the United States moving here," he said.

Just before 11 P.M. that night, at the end of what had probably been the longest day of Terry Witherspoon's life, he was stopped by a Ravalli County sheriff's deputy only two hundred yards from the entrance to Carl Hinkel's compound. The moon was high and yellow over the mountains, the upside-down American flag popping on the metal pole in Carl's yard.

Terry was almost home free. Don't wise off, he told himself. Turn into an ice cube. Tell him you fell off a truck. Let Wyatt deal with Molinari.

In minutes Terry had forgotten all his resolutions and was cuffed and in the backseat of the cruiser and on his way to the county jail.

# Chapter
## 28

❦

THE NEXT DAY was Saturday. A turnkey walked me down to the holding cell where Terry Witherspoon had spent the night.

"Have you been spit on lately?" he asked.

"Can't say that I have," I replied.

"Don't stand too close to the bars." The turnkey walked back down the corridor and sat at a small table and picked up a newspaper.

The cell was splattered with food from a serving tray that Terry had thrown against the wall. He stood under a barred window, wrinkling his nose under his glasses.

"What are you doing here?" he asked.

"The sheriff in Missoula told me you were in the slams. I thought I'd drop by for a chat," I said.

"I should be in a hospital. They put me in jail."

"You stuck your finger in a deputy sheriff's eye?"

"It was an accident. He grabbed my arm. It hurt."

Then I watched a phenomenon to which I had never seen the exception in dealing with sociopathic behavior. Terry threw a temper tantrum, his voice hissing with spleen. He was the victim, not others. It was he who had been wronged by the world, the fates, the cosmos, maybe even by his own genes. It was my obligation to be an attentive and sympathetic listener. Never mind the fact he had buried a friend of mine alive. Nothing was of consequence to him except his own pain and the unfairness with which he had been treated by a pair of greaseball humps like Molinari and Frank and now a bunch of Montana hillbillies with badges they probably got out of cereal boxes.

"I might watch what I said to these guys, Terry."

"Why?" he asked.

"They don't like you."

Then, as though I were supposed to fix the situation for him, he said, "Wyatt and Carl aren't home. I got a five-hundred bond. Somebody's got to go a bond for me."

"You think Wyatt Dixon gives a shit what happens to you?" I asked.

He pushed up his glasses and looked at me, uncomprehending.

"He might get around to going your bond but he's not going to take on Nicki Molinari. Nicki's a made guy, Terry, a genuine Sicilian badass. You think Wyatt wants to get into it with the Mob because you got hit with some baseballs?"

"Wyatt's my friend."

"Could be," I said, and leaned on one arm against the cell door and looked down the corridor at the turnkey, who was reading the paper.

"Somebody needs to take the weight for those dead ATF agents. The real shooter is probably up in Canada now. Think about it, Terry. Who's the most likely candidate in your bunch? Somebody who wanted to do Sue Lynn and didn't know the agents were sitting in her car? Somebody who never had a job except as a box boy?"

Then he did something I didn't expect. He walked toward the cell door and gripped the bars loosely with his palms, his weight on one foot, his hip cocked at an angle. He pursed his lips, as though he had reached a conclusion that would affect both of us. His eyes were strangely serene, the way dark water is, devoid of all light and moral conflict and perhaps, at least in that moment, any fear of mortality.

When he spoke his voice was suddenly feminine. A smile played around his mouth.

"Maybe you're right. Maybe I'm at the point I don't have any more to lose. Say hello to Maisey for me. You can do that for me, can't you?" he said. His breath touched my skin like vapor off dry ice.

THAT EVENING I took Temple to an Italian restaurant on Higgins called Zimorino's Red Pies Over Montana. The tables and bar were crowded with tourists and people from the university. In the back of the room, wearing a suit and tie, I saw Amos Rackley eating by himself.

"You feel sorry for him?" Temple said.

"Yeah, I guess."

"If Lamar Ellison was a snitch and the feds knew he killed Cleo Lonnigan's child, our man there deserves whatever pangs of conscience he has."

"Maybe."

"No maybe about it," Temple said.

I started to say something else, but let it go.

In the middle of our dinner a shout went up from the bar. On the screen of the TV attached high up on the wall was the face of Xavier Girard.

"That guy's on CNN?" Temple said.

"Looks like it," I said, and continued to eat.

But Temple's attention remained fixed on the TV screen, where Xavier was promoting his new book and being interviewed by the best-known talk-show host in the industry.

"Girard's talking about Nicki Molinari," Temple said.

I got up from the table and walked to the bar. Xavier had set aside a copy of his new book and was now expounding on his work in progress.

"Nicki is right out of Elizabethan theater," he said. "He volunteered for the Army and Vietnam to get away from his father. But he ended up in a godforsaken outpost in Laos, surrounded by oceans of poppy fields. He escaped out of a Pathet Lao prison camp by shoving his best friend off a helicopter skid at five hundred feet. He's a tormented human being, Larry. I like him, so does my wife, a little too much, to tell you the truth, but I've never underestimated his potential for violence."

The talk-show host propped his chin on his thumb and smiled slightly.

"You sure you want to be saying all this?" he asked.

"Oh, Nicki's become one of the family, so to speak. He put up a big chunk of money for my wife's new picture."

"I hear you're separating," the host said.

"Yeah, who'd believe it?" Xavier said, and laughed and looked knowingly at the camera.

I went back to the table and sat down.

"I wonder if Molinari watches much television," I said.

Later, we went to a movie in the refurbished vaudeville theater by the river. When we came out the sun had gone down and the moon had risen like a yellow planet over the Bitterroots. We walked down an outside flight of iron stairs to a parking area under the Higgins Street Bridge. There was a supper club below the movie theater, and the wide glass doors were open and an orchestra was playing dance music.

"You want to go inside?" Temple said.

"No," I said.

"Why not?" she asked.

"Because right here is good enough."

I put one arm around her waist and lifted her right hand in mine, but she dropped my hand and put both arms around my neck and we danced in the parking lot, under the great dome of heaven itself, surrounded by mountains that had changed little since the Earth was new, in a breeze that smelled of the river and all the trees and flowers that grew along it, to music that had been composed sixty years ago by Benny Goodman. An audience of college kids watched us from the bridge overhead and applauded when the song ended.

Maybe the Earth is better or more beautiful and life more wonderful in another place than it was at that moment. But I seriously doubt it.

LUCAS DID NOT RETURN that night from his job at the Milltown Bar. Just before dawn I heard a car out in the field and I looked out the back door and saw Lucas get out of the car and walk around the side of the house toward his tent. I slipped on my jeans and boots and a nylon vest and put on my hat and walked down in the grayness of the morning to the riverbank.

"Can I come in?" I said, pulling back the flap to his tent.

"Hope you didn't worry about where I was at," he said.

"Just because you're out all night? Not in the least. Who dropped you off?"

"An Indian guy."

"That clears it up. Do I smell perfume?"

"Lay off it, Billy Bob." He was sitting up on his sleeping bag, pulling off his boots.

"Where's Sue Lynn?" I asked.

"What are you gonna do if I tell you?"

"She's wanted for questioning in a double homicide. Use your brains, Lucas."

He threw one of his boots against the wall of the tent. "I knew you was gonna get on my case," he said.

"You want the ATF to find her first?" I said.

His face was fatigued, his hair in his eyes. He folded his arms around his knees and glowered into space.

"She says Carl Hinkel's people are looking for her. They think she knows stuff she don't," he said.

I didn't reply. I went out the flap and took his frying pan and coffeepot out of his grub box and built a fire and started breakfast. It was still cold and misty and the fire felt warm against my face. I heard Lucas behind me.

"Midway up Swan Lake," he said.

I DROVE UP the Blackfoot, through lake country and meadowland and ghost ranches and humped green foothills, then caught the two-lane highway on the east front of the Mission Mountains and entered the Swan Valley. John Steinbeck once said Montana is a love affair. If a person was going to make his troth with any particular place on Earth, I don't think he could find a better one than the stretch of road I was now on. Every bridge crossed a postcard stream, every mountain tumbled into one higher and a deeper green than itself.

Through the pines I saw an enormous, elongated body of blue water glimmering in the sun and I turned off the highway and drove down a shady driveway into a collection of cabins that had been built during the Depression in a stand of birch trees. On the far side of the lake the mountains were thickly wooded with ponderosa and larch and fir, and the only boat on the water was a red canoe from which a man was fly-casting along the bank. Out of the north, a gust of wind blew the length of the lake, wrinkling the surface like old skin, carrying your eye with it to the southern shoreline and, in the distance, the Swan Peaks jutting up over nine thousand feet, gray and steel-colored and snow-packed against the sky.

It wasn't hard to find the Cherokee Jeep Sue Lynn had stolen from the ATF agents. It was parked in a carport attached to the caretaker's cottage, where her cousin lived and took care of the grounds. I knocked on the front door and waited. When no one answered, I walked around back. Sue Lynn had created another prayer garden by placing a circle of stones around a birch tree, with a cross made from strips of red and black cloth that met at the tree trunk. She was sitting on the back steps, in pink tennis shoes and a sleeveless denim shirt and cutoff jeans rolled up high on her thighs. Her face showed no surprise when she saw me.

"Lucas told you where I was?" she asked.

"You'd rather Amos Rackley get to you first?"

"He's not all bad."

"Are you in contact with him?"

"I take whatever help people offer me. I don't have a lot of choices right now."

I sat down on the step below her and removed my hat. A family was grilling sausages on the cement porch of the cottage next door and smoke drifted through the tree limbs overhead.

"You going to let Dr. Voss go down for Lamar Ellison's murder?" I asked.

The surface of the lake shimmered with blades of light.

"Ellison told you something in the tavern the night he died. Something you couldn't deal with," I said.

She paused before she spoke, as though she were about to explain someone's twisted mentality to herself rather than to me. "He said he was sorry about my little brother. His words were 'I didn't know the kid was gonna get snuffed. I thought they'd turn him loose after a while. There's some real sick guys in the D.C. area, though.'"

I turned around. Her eyes looked like washed coal, bright and hard and filled with injury and an unrelieved anger that would probably never find release.

"Ellison kidnapped your little brother?" I said.

"He sold him to a deviate. On the East Coast. Him and some others."

"Who?"

"I don't know. Lamar was incoherent. When he finally stopped babbling he didn't know what he'd said."

"You followed him home?" I asked.

She rose from the steps and squatted down by the prayer circle and began rolling up the strips of red and black cloth that intersected at the trunk of the birch tree.

"I thought I could find an answer. But there's no answer. I read that book you told me about, *Black Elk Speaks*. You know the ending. For Indians the Tree of Life is dead," she said.

"You listen to me, Sue Lynn. The right lawyer can get you off. Ellison was a son-ofabitch and deserved what he got."

"I'm not going to say any more."

"You have to. Doc's going on trial for what you did."

"Somebody else was there. You leave me alone."

"Say again?"

"A guy was in the shadows. Outside Lamar's house."

"What guy?"

"I didn't stop to chat. But he could have saved Lamar's life and he didn't. Get that look off your face, Mr. Holland. Who hated Lamar as much as I did? Tell Lucas good-bye for me."

"*Doc?*" I said.

She bundled the strips of black and red cloth under one arm and went inside the cottage and deadbolted the door behind her.

I USED a pay phone on the highway and called the sheriff at his home.

"Sue Lynn Big Medicine killed Ellison," I said.

"How do you know?"

"I just talked with her. She's hiding out on Swan Lake."

"She confessed to you?"

"Not exactly."

"Here we go again."

"Pick her up, Sheriff. I'll give you the directions."

"It's Sunday. On Monday I'll think about it. In the meantime, try to enjoy life. Give the rest of us a break."

WHEN I GOT BACK to Doc's, he and
Maisey were raking manure out of the barn
and shoveling it into a wheelbarrow and
hauling it to a compost heap by his vegetable
garden. Doc was bare-chested and sweaty
and had tied back his long hair with a blue
polka-dot bandanna.

I walked out to the horse lot and leaned on
the top rail of the fence and watched the two
of them work. Maisey kept smiling at me, as
though I were being remiss in not helping
them. I hated what I was about to say.

"Got something on your mind?" Doc
asked.

"Yeah, if you can take a little walk with
me," I replied.

"Maisey's a big girl," he said.

"This one's private, Doc."

"We got no secrets here," he said.

"Sue Lynn Big Medicine torched Lamar Ellison. There was a guy outside Ellison's house
when she did it," I said.

Doc paused with his hands propped on the
inverted end of the rake and gave me a measured stare.

"No kidding?" he said.

"That's what the lady said."

"Maybe that'll help us at the trial," Doc
said.

"Could be. Was it you?" I said.

He brushed at his nose and watched a

hawk up in a tree not far from Lucas's tent.

"I saw that Witherspoon boy while you were gone. Out yonder in the trees," Doc said.

"Did you turn around on the road and go back to Ellison's place that night?" I asked.

"I guess you got to ask questions like that. Even though they might sorely disappoint an old friend. Well, the answer is—" he said.

But he didn't get to finish his sentence. Maisey threw down her rake in the dust and walked toward me with both her fists clenched, saying to her father, "Don't you answer that question." Then she turned her outrage on me.

"You listen, Billy Bob Holland. Don't you ever question my father's honor. He's your friend, so you by God had better act like it," she said.

I took off my hat and hit a horsefly with it.

"I can understand your sentiments, Maisey," I said.

"No, you don't. No matter how all this turns out, no one is ever going to question this family's integrity again," she said.

I raised my hands.

"You won't hear it from me," I said.

"You got that right," she said, and tossed back her hair and walked to the house.

Doc grinned at me.

"You look a little windblown," he said.

"I need to put you on the stand, Doc. That's not a problem, is it?"

"Not for me. What do you reckon Witherspoon was doing around here?" he said.

LATER, I asked Lucas to take a walk with me along the water's edge, through the trees, to a pool where you could see the shadows of trout hanging in the current just above the pebbles on the bottom. Under the canopy the ground and boulders and tree trunks were suffused with a cool green light and a tea-colored spring leaked down the lichen into the river.

"Sue Lynn has probably taken off. She wanted me to tell you good-bye," I said.

"Took off where? What for?"

"She killed that biker, Lamar Ellison."

The color drained out of his face. He stopped and picked up a pinecone and flung it at the stream and watched it float down the riffle and disappear under a beaver dam.

"She told you that?" he said.

"More or less."

He kicked at the softness of the ground with his boot. It was one he had worked on oil rigs with, steel-toed, scuffed, laced through metal eyelets with leather thongs. The whites of his eyes were filmed now.

"She didn't leave no note or anything?" he said.

"She's scared. Go easy on her, Lucas. Ellison murdered her little brother."

"Then he had it coming. Why's she letting Doc go down for it?"

I knew words could not lessen his anger or ease his sense of betrayal. Eventually he would forgive Sue Lynn, not at once, not by a conscious choice or arriving at a philosophical moment, but instead one day he would look back through the inverted telescope of time and see her as being possessed of the same moral frailties as himself and hence, in memory, an acceptable part of his life again.

But that day would be a long time coming and these are notions you cannot impart to someone younger than yourself, particularly when the individual is your son.

"What if I take you and Doc and Maisey to the Indian powwow in Arlee?" I said.

"I'm going up to the Swan and find Sue Lynn."

"She's caught air, bud."

He kicked a toadstool into a pulpy spray.

"I'm going to her uncle's and get the dog. I bet she didn't even take the dog," he said.

I walked back to Doc's alone.

I WENT INTO the barn and took down Doc's ax from between two nails and ripped stumps out of the pasture and weeded Doc's vegetable garden and sprinkled all his flowers and curried his horses and swept the stalls and hauled a truckload of trash down to the dump and buried it with a shovel and generally wore myself out, but I could not think my way out of the problems that seemed to beset me from every direction.

A sun shower was falling on the mountains in the west when I put my shirt back on and went into the barn and hung Doc's ax back on the nails. My skin was filmed with sweat and the wind was cool through the open doors and dust puffed up off the barn floor in my eyes.

At the far end of the barn L.Q. stood against the light, his face lost in silhouette, his coat open and his thumb hooked above the brass cartridges in his gunbelt.

*"What are y'all gonna do about that Witherspoon boy?"* he said.

*"I'd like to cap him and drag the body inside the house. But I've had a bad day and I don't need you to vex me, L.Q."*

*"If I recall correctly, you told the priest you wasn't gonna gun nobody."*

*"Maybe I'll have to adjust,"* I said.

*"I'm for it. I'd suggest a ten-gauge loaded with pumpkin balls. Start with Carl Hinkel and Wyatt Dixon and work your way on down. Remember when we caught that bunch coming out of the arroyo outside*

Zaragoza? They was passing around a bottle of yellow mescal. The first round blew glass right through one fellow's face."

"I stole your life, L.Q."

"I never held it against you. You're still my bud."

"Your words are a crown of thorns," I said.

He canted himself sideways and looked at someone behind me, then turned and walked through the barn doors, into the evening and the flicker of lightning on the fields.

"Temple just called. Should I tell her we're on our way to pick her up or you're too busy having a conversation with yourself?" Maisey said.

EARLY THE NEXT MORNING I drove into town and took Temple for breakfast. On the way back to the motel I saw Terry Witherspoon come out of a medical clinic and get into a battered car by himself and drive away. Temple did not see him.

"I'll drop you off and call you a little later," I said.

"You don't want to come in?" she asked.

"I need to take care of something."

She reached across the seat and ran her fingernail up the back of my neck.

"Secrets have a way of undoing a relationship," she said.

"I think Terry Witherspoon plans to hurt Maisey. Somebody needs to step on this kid's tether," I replied.

She squeezed her thumb and forefinger on my neck, then released the pressure and squeezed again, on and off, and tried to see into the corner of my eye.

"When Dixon and Witherspoon go down, I'm going to be there? Right?" she said.

"You bet," I said.

She leaned forward so I could not avoid looking into her face.

"Don't take what I say lightly," she said. Her milky green eyes held on mine and never blinked. I felt my truck tire hit the curb.

BACK AT DOC'S PLACE I borrowed Maisey's laptop computer and set it up in a sunny spot on a folding table down by the river, fixed a glass of iced tea, and began composing a letter to Wyatt Dixon. It read as follows:

*Dear Mr. Dixon,*
    *I interviewed Terry Witherspoon in the Ravalli County Jail after Nicki Molinari's goons dumped him in front of your ranch. Here are a couple of observations I would like to share with you.*
    *It appears Terry has made up a story*

*about my trying to shoot you in the back
with a pistol. I don't know if you believe his
account or not, but you might ask yourself
why an ex–Texas Ranger would try to pop
you with a handgun, on your own property,
when a man with a scoped .30-06 rifle could
punch out your brisket from a mile away.*

*Terry told me and several others at the
jail that you did not have the guts to take on
Nicki Molinari because he was Mobbed-up
and in Quentin you were a punk for two
greaseballs and had run scared of them ever
since. He said Molinari already made you
look like an ignorant peckerwood in a café
someplace but you were too stupid to know
you had been made a fool of. I'm not sure
what he was talking about. He just said
Molinari told him rodeo clowns risk their
lives for chump change, and that's why only
bozos from backwater Southern shitholes
are hired for the job.*

*In closing I'm obligated to inform you of
the following as a matter of social conscience. My associate has accessed Terry's
welfare and police and medical records back
in North Carolina. It looks like Terry has
AIDS. Has he been going for medical treat-
ment here? If I were you, I'd get tested.
There are ninety-nine strains of the virus. I
suspect Terry has most of them. By the way,
conclusive test results take four months.*

*To be honest, I have a hard time believing anyone who did time in Huntsville and Quentin could be reamed this bad by a box boy whose biggest score was rolling fudge packers. Maybe my perceptions are incorrect. If so, please forgive me.*
*Have a nice day,*

*Billy Bob Holland*

I went back into Missoula and had the letter delivered to the Hinkel compound by a florist, along with a cluster of pink and blue balloons.

# Chapter

## 29

THE NEXT DAY Temple and I walked inside the Montana State Prison at Deer Lodge and waited for a turnkey to escort a trusty gardener by the name of Alton Dobbs to an interview room. He had salt-and-pepper hair that was cropped short, workingman's hands with clean nails, square shoulders, and direct eye contact you do not normally associate with a pedophile. He wore horn-rimmed glasses and state blues, but the pants were creased, as though they had been pressed under a mattress, and his shirt was buttoned at the throat and the wrists.

He sat down across from us, his right hand resting in the center of the wood table. When I did not offer to shake hands with him, he removed his hand and put it in his lap. His

eyes narrowed once at the insult, then they
became totally devoid of expression.

"Your sheet says you've been down four
times on the same count, Mr. Dobbs," I said.

He inched a chrome-plated wristwatch out
from under his shirt cuff and looked at it.

"You're a lawyer for who?" he asked.

"Dr. Tobin Voss. He's charged with killing
a biker by the name of Lamar Ellison. Does
that last name mean anything to you?" I said.

"Never heard of him."

Temple looked at the first page on the clipboard she carried.

"How about the name of Billy Shuster?"
she said.

"The kid in Sioux Falls? I was three hundred miles away when that happened. I was
working in a bakery."

Temple's eyes shifted on mine. It was the
use of his vague reference to the event, the
lack of a noun or verb that would call up a
visual image, that gave us our first hint of the
manipulator behind the horn-rimmed glasses.

"He was thirteen. Pretty bad crime, don't
you think?" I said.

"I wouldn't know. Like I say, I wasn't
around," Dobbs said.

"Anyway, that's past history. But I think
you got a bum beef on this Montana deal," I
said.

"Run that by me again."

"You got nailed in Carl Hinkel's front yard five years ago. Carl told everybody he didn't know you and was glad the authorities had you in custody. I don't think you ever got to tell your side of the story."

"You see Carl Hinkel?" he said.

"With some regularity," Temple said.

Dobbs nodded and looked at a spot between me and Temple. "I never met him. I never had a chance to. So I'm not much help to you," he said.

"I hear you're quite a computer whiz. You've cataloged everything in the prison library," Temple said.

"It's a job," he said.

"It's funny you don't know the name of Lamar Ellison. He was in Deer Lodge when you took your last fall," I said.

"Could be," he replied.

"You were invited to Carl Hinkel's house. Maybe you had an appointment with him. Then you get busted in his yard and he calls you a pervert in print. Does that bother you, Mr. Dobbs?" I said.

He touched at the corner of his mouth and rubbed the balls of his fingers with his thumb. He straightened his cuffs on his wrists and glanced through the glass window in the door at a guard in the corridor.

"What's in it for me?" he asked.

"The feds have Hinkel under investigation.

You could be a big help to them. They can turn keys on state locks."

His eyes seemed to focus inward on thoughts that in all probability no else could ever guess at.

"We're finished here," he said.

"Fair enough," I said, rising from my chair. "I'll tell you what happened, though. You met Carl Hinkel through the Internet. Then you showed up at his house for a meet and got busted. He came off looking great and you're down on a short-eyes. How's it feel? By the way, I'll tell Carl we had a chat."

Dobbs got to his feet and banged on the steel door.

"What's the problem?" the guard asked.

"I want lockup," Dobbs replied.

AFTER WE GOT BACK to Missoula I dropped Temple off at her motel and drove down to Stevensville, then headed east toward the Sapphires and Nicki Molinari's ranch. I saw the next-door neighbor, the elderly preacher, raking out dead grass from the rain ditch in front of his church. I pulled my truck to the roadside and waved to him.

He wore bib overalls without a shirt and a coned-up straw hat. The choleric blazes in his neck and face looked like small tongues of fire on his skin. He leaned down to my window and I saw a raw knot the size of a duck's egg on his forehead.

"How are you doing today, sir?" I said.

"Cleaning up for our baptism services to-morrow evening. Back yonder in the creek. We do it the old-time way," he said.

"It's the only way to fly," I said.

"You're welcome to come," he said.

"I was baptized in a stream in the Winding Stair Mountains of eastern Oklahoma."

"I knowed it," he said.

"How's that?"

"River-baptized people got a mark. They look a person in the eye. Why you hanging around that greaser?"

"My work takes me into strange associations, Preacher."

"You carry a gun?"

"Sometimes."

"Stay away from that fellow, son. He's the devil's own."

The old man tapped my window with the flat of his hand and returned to his work.

I parked on the white gravel by the side of Molinari's house and started toward the front door. From the back I heard the spring of a diving board and a loud splash and the sound of women laughing. When I came around the corner of the house I smelled meat dripping into a hibachi and the drowsy, thick fragrance of a crack pipe and I saw

Molinari swimming toward the shallow end of his pool while three suntanned women in bikinis and shades watched him from reclining chairs.

He walked up the tile steps of the pool, dripping water, his sex etched against his bright yellow trunks. He rubbed his head and face with a fluffy towel, and a woman handed him a glass of iced tea with a sprig of mint in it. He pushed his feet into his flip-flops while he drank and took my measure over his upended glass.

"Where you come from, people don't call first before they drop by other people's houses?" he said.

"Has Wyatt Dixon been around?" I asked.

"No. He better not, either."

"I interviewed a pedophile in Deer Lodge this morning. He was busted in Carl Hinkel's front yard."

Molinari wiped water off his brow and pitched his towel over the back of a chair.

"Take a walk with me," he said, glancing back at the women by poolside. He put his hand on my arm. "Tell me in like three sentences."

"This guy was nailed in Hinkel's yard. I think Hinkel is behind the kidnapping and sale of children to child molesters."

"So I'm glad to know this. But I'm a little tied up right now. A little two-on-one going, get my drift? If you see Cleo or Holly, don't be mentioning what you saw here. Anyway, come back tomorrow when I have more time."

"Fuck you."

"I can't believe there's a person like you standing on my property. You want me to re-model this guy, but you tell me in my face to get fucked? You know what I do to people who use that kind of language to me?"

"Tell it to your biographer."

"I'm glad you raised that subject. Xavier Girard just got the shit kicked out of him. Why is that, you ask. Because he shot off his mouth on a certain TV talk show."

"What happened to the old man next door?"

"I put a knot on his head."

"You did what?"

"He was firing a nail gun into his church till six this morning. Bam, bam, bam, all night long. I was in a bad mood. He picked the wrong time to wise off."

"I made a mistake coming here," I said.

When I turned to go he grabbed my fore-arm again. I felt his nails scrape on the skin.

"Come here," he said.

"Your kind are always the same, Molinari. On the surface you seem to have a certain de-gree of élan, but under it all you're a real bum. Go back to your whores."

His mouth twitched slightly and the skin under one eye puckered as though my words had cut across a nerve ending in his face.

I DROVE BACK to Missoula and parked downtown and walked under the shade of the maple trees into the courthouse. I met the sheriff on his way out.

"I need to talk," I said.

"Why don't you rent an office down the hall from me? Cut down on your gas costs," he said.

"At what time did Xavier Girard call 911 the night Lamar Ellison was killed?"

"I don't remember."

"Let's find out," I said.

He sucked his teeth.

"Come inside," he said.

A minute later, he tossed his hat onto a rack in his office and sat down heavily in his swivel chair and fixed his eyes on me. They were as blue and intense as the flame on a butane burner.

"Get to it, Mr. Holland," he said.

"Lamar Ellison vandalized Xavier Girard's vehicle just before he died. Girard and Ellison fought on the side of the road and Holly Girard pointed a gun at Ellison to keep him from stomping her husband into jelly. Then Holly and Xavier went inside a friend's house and dialed 911. The question is when did they make the call."

"What are you driving at?" the sheriff said.

"Sue Lynn Big Medicine claims she saw somebody outside Ellison's place when she fled, someone who could have saved his life."

"Wait here," the sheriff said.

He went out into the hall and returned five minutes later and sat down in his chair and studied two computer printouts in his hands. He laid them down on his desk blotter and balled and unballed his fist on top of them.

"Holly Girard made the call. At ten-o-nine P.M.," he said.

"What time was the fire at Ellison's reported?" I asked.

"Nine forty-one."

"So they waited at least a half hour to report their vehicle being vandalized?" I said.

"That's what it looks like. You're saying the guy Sue Lynn saw was Xavier?"

"Ellison had smashed out the windows in Xavier's Cherokee and sliced the seats and cut his tires and humiliated him in front of his wife and friends. Maybe he took his wife's gun and decided to square things with Ellison, but Sue Lynn beat him to it."

"Maybe the guy Sue Lynn saw was the same fellow who reported the fire. You think of that?"

"The 911 on the fire was called in by a trucker on his CB," I said.

The sheriff rubbed his forehead and widened his eyes.

"I'll question Xavier Girard. But there's no evidence to put him at the crime scene, so I don't think this is going anywhere," he said. "By the way, I had the sheriff in Flathead County check out that resort on Swan Lake where Sue Lynn was hiding. Her cousin says Sue Lynn has bagged out for parts unknown."

I DIDN'T WAIT for the sheriff to pick up Xavier Girard or ask him to come in. I drove directly to the Girards' house out on the bluff above the Clark Fork. A moving van was backed into the driveway and a half-dozen men were trundling furniture up the loading ramp. I walked through the open front door of the house, into a bare living room with a cathedral ceiling that echoed with the sounds of the movers' work shoes. The sanded and lacquered pinewood interior of the room glowed with light, and Holly Girard stood in the middle of it all, dressed in oversize khakis and tennis shoes and a paint-splotched pink T-shirt, a baseball cap on her head, swearing, scolding the movers, but never quite crossing the line into direct insult.

She turned and studied me as she would a bird bouncing against a window glass. Then she walked toward me, her face tilted upward, touched with light, bemused, a bit vulnerable. She stood inside my shadow, the confidence in her sexual appeal undiminished by her appearance, the color in her eyes deepening.

"I hope Xavier hasn't hired you to sue me," she said.

Before I could reply she turned on a workman walking down the staircase and said, "You break that lamp and I'll own your salary for the rest of your life. That's a promise, Ed."

"Where's your husband, Ms. Girard?" I asked.

"Try detox or AA or any bar on Higgins. Or maybe he's in the sack with one of his twenty-year-old groupies. Each of them thinks she'll be the girl who changed his life and career. Oh, boring, boring, boring. *Here,*" she said.

She wrote out the address of a townhouse on the river, then turned her attention back to the movers.

"You posed as Doc Voss's friend," I said.

"Excuse me?"

"Y'all let him go down for a murder you knew he didn't commit."

"I'm sure what you're saying will make

sense to Xavier. But it doesn't to me. Now, good-bye, good luck, God speed, God bless, ta-ta, all that kind of thing."

"Y'all could have cleared Doc. Instead, you kept quiet and let him twist in the wind."

She had started to walk away. But she turned demurely and stepped close into me again, one of her small feet touching mine. She took off her cap and shook out her hair and gave me a long, deliberate stare. There were two white crystals on the rim of her left nostril.

"Contact my business agent at Creative Artists. He'd love to help you. Really he would," she said, and jiggled her fingers in good-bye.

"Watch yourself with Molinari, Ms. Girard. If you're tight with Cleo Lonnigan, you might share the admonition," I said, and went out the door.

When I started my truck she was standing in the yard, staring at me, her face disjointed with the wounded pride of a child.

WHEN I RANG the bell at Xavier Girard's townhouse, he yelled from the back room, "The door's open. Fix yourself a drink in the kitchen and don't bother me till I come out. If you don't drink or if you're a friend of my wife, get the fuck out of my life."

I walked to his office door and looked inside. He was hunched over his computer, framed like a bear against the window and the broad sweep of the river and the spires and rooftops of the town and the green hills beyond.

His eyes were washed out, pale blue, the pupils like burnt match heads, his face manic and tight against the bone and ridged with bruises along the jaw. An odor like unwashed hair and beer sweat filled the room.

"I'm working now. There's vodka in the icebox. There're magazines by the toilet," he said.

"You came out to Doc's and complained to me that your wife wouldn't help with a fund-raiser for Doc's defense," I said.

"Man, you just don't fucking listen. That's yesterday's chewing gum, Jack," he said.

"You saw Ellison burn to death. You also saw an Indian woman flee the scene. All this time you could have cut Doc loose."

He pushed the "save" button on his keyboard.

"Here it is, straight up. I don't know who did what at that scene. I had no way of knowing Doc wasn't there first. But if I understand you correctly, you think I should have put it on a Native American woman who's probably been dumped on all her life?"

"I see. You were protecting Sue Lynn Big Medicine. Did you go there armed?"

"None of your business."

"Accept my word on this, Mr. Girard. I'm going to do everything in my power to see you charged with obstruction and depraved indifference."

"Indifferent? You're calling me indifferent?"

I looked at the bruises along his jawline. "I'm not calling you anything, sir. How's your book going?"

"Which book?"

"Your biography of Nicki Molinari."

"Guess," he replied.

As I left I heard what sounded like a metal trash basket tumbling end over end across a bare floor.

THE NEXT MORNING was white with fog that boiled off the Blackfoot River and hung wetly in the trees and gathered like damp cotton on the hillsides. I walked down to Lucas's tent and watched him fix a fire and start cracking eggs and laying out ham strips in the oversize skillet he cooked in.

Minutes later I picked up the spatula and started to shovel some food onto my plate. Lucas gently removed the spatula from my hand and went to his tent and picked up a plastic dog bowl. He began shredding pieces of white bread into the bowl while his dog, now named Dogus, watched.

"Remember what you told me Great-Grandpa Sam wrote in his journal? 'Always feed your animals before you feed yourself,'" Lucas said, and scooped a fried egg out of the skillet and chopped it up in the bread.

Later, we ate in silence. The trees along the river were dark and wet and black-green inside the fog, and I could hear a hoofed animal clopping on the rocks on the far side of the water.

"I know what you want to ask me," Lucas said.

"My head's totally blank," I said.

"Sue Lynn didn't call. I don't blame her. She tried to tell me all along she was in over her head. It don't seem right, though."

"What's that?"

"She's on the run and all them other people—that fellow Wyatt Dixon and Witherspoon and the people who killed her little brother—these guys just go on hurting folks and nobody does anything about it."

"Eventually they'll go down," I said.

"It sure does take a long time," he replied.

He got up from the rock he was sitting on and rinsed his tin plate and cup and fork and meat knife in the river, then scrubbed them with sand and rinsed them clean again and put

them into his grub box. He poured the coffeepot on the fire and refilled it with water and
doused the fire a second time while steam
boiled off the stones in the fire ring.

Both our fly rods were propped against his
tent, the dry flies snugged into the cork han-
dles, the tapered leaders tight inside the
guides. He picked both rods up and handed
me mine.

"Come on, there's a fat rainbow up yonder
that wants to add your flies to his underwater collection," he said.

"You're growing up on me, bud," I said.

He looked back over his shoulder at me,
not quite sure what to make of the remark.

WHEN THE LETTER for Wyatt Dixon arrived at the compound, delivered by a nervous florist gripping a handful of pink and
blue balloons, Wyatt was out in the equipment lot, barefoot and bare-chested, his jeans
on so tight they looked like they'd split,
working on Carl Hinkel's tractor engine. Wyatt paused a wrench on a nut and stared over
his shoulder at the florist, then walked to the
fence and took the letter and clutch of balloons from the florist's hands.

"Sir, you look like you're fixing to piss your
pants," Wyatt said.

"No, sir. I wouldn't do that."

"Good. Get out of here," Wyatt said.

He thumbed open the envelope and read the letter inside, the wind blowing the paper, the tethered ribbons on the balloons tugging in his hand.

Terry watched Wyatt's face. Wyatt had only two expressions. One was the idiot's grin off a jack-o'-lantern. The other was a nonexpression, a total absence of any feeling or thought or content whatsoever, at least not any that could be seen. It made Terry think of a clay mask that a sculptor might have molded on an exhumed skull, with prosthetic eyes stuffed into the sockets.

Wyatt finished reading the letter, then folded it and stuck it inside his belt, against his skin. His left hand opened and the balloons rose into the wind and floated out over the Bitterroot. He turned slowly toward Terry, the clay mask transforming itself, cracking into the idiot's grin again.

"I got to run to town. By the way, what's the name of that clinic you go to sometimes? I got to get me a flu shot," he said.

What did Wyatt mean by "go to sometimes"? Terry thought. He'd gone to the clinic only because he'd been beaten up by either Wyatt or that greaseball Nicki Molinari. "The one off the Orange Street Bridge. Anything wrong?" Terry said.

"In a country like this?" Wyatt tilted his face

up toward the heavens, his palms lifted as though he were requesting grace, his shaved underarms white with baby powder. "Ain't no place like the U.S.A. Don't ever doubt it, either." Then he aimed one finger at Terry, a nest of veins rippling over his shoulder.

Wyatt drove away in his low-slung red car, with its exposed new radiator and hammered-out fenders bouncing through the dust. He returned two hours later and pulled off his shirt and strapped on his tool pouch and went back to work on Carl's tractor.

"I didn't think you could get flu shots in the summer," Terry said.

"A dumb fellow like me had to drive all the way to Missoula to find that out," Wyatt said, grinning from under his hat.

Terry went up to the dining room and put three dollars into the tin can on the steam table and ate lunch with Carl and the others. He glanced out the back window just as Wyatt stopped work on the tractor and threw his wrench down and climbed through the railed fence and took a shortcut across the pasture to his log house.

Except Wyatt was now in the pasture with a young bull that did not willingly share its territory. It began running the length of the fence, then it whirled and headed for Wyatt, blowing mucus, its horns lowered.

Wyatt could have made the fence and

vaulted across it with time to spare. Instead, he pulled his wadded-up shirt from his back pocket and slapped it across the bull's snout and eyes, then dangled it in the dust, working it like a snake, charming the bull to a standstill.

Wyatt inched his hand forward, then grabbed one horn and pivoted behind the bull's angle of vision and grabbed the other and twisted the bull's neck until it fell to the ground in a puff of dust and manure that had dried into fiber.

Everyone in the dining room had risen to his feet and was now watching the scene in the pasture. Wyatt continued to twist the bull's neck, his boot heel hooked hard into its phallus, the tendons in the bull's neck popping against its hide like black rope, the one visible eye bulging from the socket as though it were about to hemorrhage.

Carl Hinkel dropped his fork onto his plate and ran out the back door to the pasture, tripping over the bumps in the ground, waving one arm at Wyatt.

"What in God's name are you doing? You know how much that animal cost me?" he shouted.

Wyatt rose to his feet and threw a small rock at the bull's head and kicked it in the rectum. Grass and grains of dirt were matted on Wyatt's naked back.

"I think I'll bag me up a lunch today and eat on the river," he said.

"Is something bothering you, boy?"

"Ain't no man calls me 'boy,' Carl." Wyatt picked up his hat out of the dirt and fitted it on his head and straightened the brim with his thumb and forefinger. He grinned at Carl, then inserted a pinch of snuff inside his lip. "No-sirree-bob."

The men standing around Carl dropped their eyes to the ground.

FOR THE NEXT HALF HOUR Terry paced about on the slope of the river, while down below him Wyatt ate his lunch out of a paper bag and drank from a quart bottle of buttermilk. Wyatt's back was a triangle of muscle cut with scars from a horse quirt. Wyatt had never told Terry who had used the quirt on him or why. That was Wyatt's way. He recycled pain, stored its memory, footnoted every instance of it in his life and the manner in which it had been visited upon him, then paid back his enemies and tormentors in ways they never foresaw.

Now Terry was afraid to talk to him. Should he stay or hitchhike home? What was in that letter? Had he done something disloyal, made a careless remark that someone else had reported to Wyatt? Was this over

Maisey Voss? Or maybe Molinari or that damn lawyer was behind it.

But before Terry could find an answer to any of his questions, Carl Hinkel sent word he wanted to see him in his office.

Terry entered the stone hut by the side of the main house and sat down next to Carl's computer table. It was the first time he had been invited inside Carl's office, and he realized his palms were sweating. Carl's beard was freshly trimmed, his suspenders an immaculate white against his dark blue cotton shirt, his cob pipe cupped regally in his hand.

"I've been watching you. My staff has, too," Carl said, and fixed him with a dead stare. Terry shifted in his chair and looked at the framed photo of Carl in a paratrooper's uniform and felt his mouth go dry.

"If I did something wrong—" he began.

"You have what soldiers call fire in the belly. It's the fire that burns in every patriot. It's in your eyes. It's in the way you carry yourself."

Terry felt his cheeks burn.

"It's a great honor to—" Terry began.

"I'm promoting you up to the rank of lieutenant, with duties as an information officer. That means you'll be representing us at meetings in Idaho and Washington State. Of course, we'll be paying all your travel expenses."

"I don't know what to say, sir." For a moment Terry could feel tears coming to his eyes.

"We don't wear uniforms or wear gold or silver bars here. But I have a gift for you," Carl said.

He opened his desk drawer and removed a chrome-plated, double-edged dagger with a gold guard on the blade and a snow-white handle that had been inset with two red swastikas.

It was the most beautiful knife Terry had ever seen. He held it in his palms and started to slip the blade from the white leather sheath but first lifted his eyes to Carl's to seek permission.

"Go ahead," Carl said, and fired his pipe, cupping the match flame as though there were wind in the room.

Terry turned the blade over in his palm. He could see his face in the oily reflection and feel the coolness of the steel like a kiss against his skin.

"Later you and I will bust some clay pigeons out over the river. How's that?" Carl said.

"Yes, sir," Terry answered.

Carl puffed on his pipe and gazed reflectively into the smoke, his brow furrowing slightly.

"You notice anything different about Wyatt?" he asked.

"Wyatt's a mite moody sometimes." That was the right answer, he thought. He was giving Carl what he wanted without saying anything Wyatt could use against him. His statement even sounded sympathetic. Way to go, he told himself.

"I'd like to think he's just off his feed. But we can't have loose cannon on board our ship, Terry."

"Yes, sir, I know what you mean," Terry said.

"You're a fine young man," Carl said, and held out his hand. Carl's grip was meaty, encompassing, the skin warmer than it should be.

"Carl, my rent's due on my place above the Clark," Terry said.

"Yes?"

"I wonder if I could move out here. Work for room and board."

"I don't see any reason you shouldn't get the first vacancy," Carl replied.

# Chapter

## 30

❦

IT RAINED just before dawn, then the sun rose inside the mist on the hills and through my window I could see the pale green shapes of cottonwoods swelling in the wind and a lone black bear running past Lucas's tent, as though the pinkness of the morning had caught it in a dishonest act.

Doc came into my bedroom and set down a cup of coffee for me on the nightstand and pulled up a chair next to my bed.

"That ATF agent, Rackley, the one who was hassling you?" he said.

"What about him?"

"He called while you were still asleep. He left this number," Doc said.

"He must be an early riser," I said.

"Why you been sleeping with L.Q.'s gun

on your nightstand the last couple of nights?"

"I sent a letter to Wyatt Dixon and told him a few things about Witherspoon, including the fact he had AIDS."

Doc nodded reflectively. "Where'd you come by all this information?" he asked.

"Temple got ahold of Witherspoon's welfare and juvie records. I made up the stuff about AIDS."

Doc got up from his chair and propped his hands on the windowsill and stared out at the morning.

"I thought *I* had an iron bolt through both temples," he said.

I SHAVED and brushed my teeth and dressed and called the number Amos Rackley had left.

"Meet me inside the University of Montana football stadium in a half hour," he said.

"What for?"

"I have something for you. You bring anybody with you, I'm gone."

I drove through Hellgate Canyon and took the university exit and parked by the stadium. A half-dozen hang gliders were floating on the breezes high up on Mount Sentinel, their shadows swooping across the green slopes beneath them. I walked into the great emptiness of the stadium and saw Amos

Rackley sitting twenty rows up on the fifty-yard line.

He wore shades and a brown rain hat and an open-neck checkered shirt and khakis and sandals with white socks. He could have been an academic who had strolled off for a moment's respite from his summer classes. For the first time I noticed a religious chain around his neck.

"Open your shirt for me, would you?" he said.

"That's a little silly, isn't it?" I said.

"So you don't have to be offended," he replied, and waited.

I unbuttoned my shirt and pulled it out of my trousers and turned in a circle.

"Sit down and let me explain something, although you probably already know the drill," he said. A manila envelope rested on his knees. "All federal law enforcement agencies use informants. A good agent flips the right guy and puts a lot of nasty people in the gray-bar hotel chain. But once in a while an agent gets too jacked up on a case and forgets he's allowed a sociopath to run loose with a baseball bat."

"You're talking about Lamar Ellison?"

"As time went by we became more and more convinced he and some other bikers tried to kidnap Cleo Lonnigan's child. The father probably showed up and the bikers killed them both. We couldn't prove it, though, so we gave Ellison a long leash and used him."

"Except you didn't nail anybody and Carl Hinkel probably had other children kidnapped and sold to perverts, including Sue Lynn's little brother?"

Rackley looked out at Hellgate Canyon and the wind bending the ponderosa along the edges of the cliffs and the hang gliders that hovered and dipped against the immense blueness of the sky.

"I quit the Bureau," he said. "There are two signed and notarized affidavits in this envelope. One is from Sue Lynn Big Medicine, admitting she set fire to Lamar Ellison. The other statement is from me, describing her role as an informant for the ATF. If anyone wants to question either her or me, I wish them good luck, get my drift?"

He placed the envelope in my hands.

"They'll come after you," I said.

"Could be. I doubt it. A stock brokerage doesn't prosecute the employees it fires for embezzlement." He got up from his seat and removed his hat and ran his hand through his close-cropped hair, then replaced his hat and looked at the panorama of mountains that enclosed the city.

"I hear the Canadian Rockies are great this time of year," I said.

"I've always been a flatlander. Stay away from Carl Hinkel's compound, Mr. Holland, unless you want to end up on a recording."

"You finally got a wire inside?"

"Put it this way. I've got the sense somebody unscrewed Wyatt Dixon's head and spit inside it. You don't happen to know anything about that, do you?"

"Not a thing," I said, my gaze fixed straight ahead.

He walked down the cement steps to the exit. He didn't look back.


WYATT DIXON had a simple vision of life. You ate your pain, you shined the world on, and you accepted inequity as the natural state of man. The only unforgivable sin was personal betrayal.

The paling of the sky at dawn, the place the sun occupied at noon or twilight, the rain or ice or drought that wore away the surfaces of the earth had nothing to do with a man's fate. You took your first breath with a slap. If you were lucky, your mouth found a teat before you starved. You grew out of your own excretions and ate what you were given, carried slop to hogs, shucked chicken feathers in scalding water, split smokehouse wood, chopped and picked cotton, punched and dehorned cows, shot mustangs and wild burros for dog food contractors, and maybe put your seed in a Mexican girl inside a bean field. Then, one morning, at age fifteen, you walked past the waiting school bus to the train tracks and climbed aboard a freight that carried you all the way to Big D and an Army enlistment center.

Wyatt liked the Army. He liked the food, the good clothes, the PX beer, the access to fine guns. The problem was the Army didn't like Wyatt. Or at least the black mess sergeant didn't after Wyatt asked him if he had a tail tucked inside his pants.

The base psychiatrist said Wyatt had antisocial tendencies. The mess sergeant probably agreed after Wyatt broke his nose with a bottle behind a bar in San Antonio and cut his stripes off and stuffed them into his mouth.

While he was in the stockade waiting for his uncle to show up with a birth certificate, Wyatt tried to figure how to avoid getting himself jammed up like this again. He finally figured it out. Stay off the computer.

He traveled the country as a roustabout for a tent preacher, milked rattlesnakes for a veterinarian in West Kansas, slaughtered cattle below the border, daily pumped a hard rubber ball five hundred times in each palm, and by age twenty-one was a full-blown rodeo clown, fearless, twice hooked and slammed into the boards, able to knock a horse unconscious with his fist or snap a steer's spinal cord with his bare hands.

Beer-joint women kissed his fingers and men feared them. He chewed cigars like plug tobacco, sewed his own wounds, asked no favors, drank tequila like water, borrowed no money, carried all of his possessions in a cardboard suitcase, read a new comic book every night, wore two-hundred-dollar hats, and stitched an American flag as a liner inside the duster he wore in rainy or cold weather.

But it was the greasepaint grin that bothered his rodeo cohorts. When Wyatt wiped the grease off his face, the lunatic expression was still there, accentuated by eyes that were full of invasiveness and light that had no origin. A female barrel racer claimed he raped her. The board members of the RCA tried to ban him from the circuit.

So what? The good life was always there, sleeping in a bedroll under the stars, sometimes shacking up in a trailer, carrying plenty of cash, drinking beer and eating Mexican food whenever he wanted and grilling steaks in roadside parks up in the high desert. Everybody loved a cowboy. This was a great country, by God.

The only problems in life came from disloyalty. That's what Carl Hinkel didn't under stand. A man who claimed to be a patriot and should have known better. But Wyatt knew that under the pose of the Virginia gentleman Carl was weak and dependent. That in itself was forgivable. But ingratitude and disrespect were a form of betrayal, and that was not.

After Carl had called him "boy" and Wyatt had rubbed Carl's nose in it, Carl had tried to straighten it out in the dining room, in front of a half dozen others. Big mistake.

Wyatt was at the steam table, bagging up a lunch to eat out on the riverbank.

"I can't abide a soldier sassing me like that, Wyatt," Carl said.

"Is that right?" Wyatt said, without looking up from the sandwich he was making.

"You were out of line, son," Carl said.

Wyatt filled the side of a butter knife with mustard and layered it on his sandwich bread, nodding, as though digesting a profound statement.

"Would you hand me those 'maters, Carl?" he said.

Carl gestured to a boy behind the steam table, who picked up a platter of sliced tomatoes and tried to give them to Wyatt. Wyatt ignored him.

"You got what some folks might call a serious character defect, Carl. You cain't cut it on your own. That's why the airborne run you off. That's why you got to surround

yourself with a bunch of sawed-off little pissants don't know their own mind. Now get
the fuck out of my face."

AT DAWN Friday morning Terry woke in
his shack above the Clark Fork and saw Wyatt standing against the window, inside the
shack, the blue-green softness of the pines
and the mists off the river rising up behind
him. The fire in the woodstove had gone out
and the room was cold, the air brittle. Terry
hugged the quilt around him and sat up on
his bunk. The German dagger Carl had given
him lay on the table in the center of the
room, the swastikas on the white handle as
bright as drops of blood.

"I knowed a preacher who used to say,
'Fool me oncet, shame on you. Fool me
twicet, shame on me,'" Wyatt said. He wore
a heavy long-sleeve crimson shirt, with his
purple garters on the arms, and tight jeans
and his flat-brimmed black hat with the Indian band around the crown.

"I don't know what I did wrong, Wyatt. I
don't know why you're mad at me."

Wyatt picked up the dagger and eased it
halfway out of the sheath. The chromed blade
clicked with light. Why hadn't he put the knife
under his pillow? Terry thought. Why did Wyatt have to put his filthy hands on it?

"Carl promoted you?" Wyatt said.

"I'm information officer, if you want to know."

"Going over to Idaho? Meet all them groups at Hayden Lake?"

"Maybe. If Carl tells me to."

Wyatt sat down in a chair and fiddled with the German dagger, never removing it all the way from the sheath. Then he tossed it to Terry.

"I noticed you been coughing a bit. I'm gonna introduce you to a woman used to be a whore down by the railway tracks," Wyatt said.

"Why do I want to meet *her?*"

"She thinks she might know you from the clinic. You call to mind a woman looks like she was just dug up from a cemetery?"

"I don't know what's going on, Wyatt."

"I'll pick you up at seven. Maybe we'll check out the Voss girl again. Or maybe that female private detective. I told Mr. Holland he'd know when it was my ring."

"Carl says it's a bad time for stirring anything up."

"Seven o'clock," Wyatt said.


THAT SAME MORNING Temple and I ate breakfast together in a café across from the train yard, then walked down Higgins toward the river. Two city police cars had pulled up in front of a saloon, their flashers on, and two uniformed officers had gotten out and were approaching a man who sat like a pile of wet hay on the curb. The officers slipped their batons into the rings on their belts and leaned over and tried to talk with the man on the curb.

It was one of those moments when, if your life is fairly sane and you're able to greet the day with a clear eye and enjoy the simple pleasure of reading the newspaper over a cup of coffee and a bowl of cereal, you thank the Creator or Yahweh or the Great Spirit or the Buddha or Our Lord Jesus you are not the wretch whose fate seems so awful that no reasonable human being could deliberately choose it for himself.

Xavier Girard's clothes looked as if they had been stolen off a washline. His face was puffed, his eyes like sliced beets; his mouth hung open as though he had just witnessed a train wreck. He vomited between his legs, then stared stupidly at the splatter on his tennis shoes.

But even from across the street and in his drunken state Xavier recognized me and pushed himself out of the policemen's grasp and stumbled into the traffic, where he was almost hit by a milk truck.

He came toward me, waving his arms, a

vinegary stench welling up from his armpits.

"Molinari's goons ripped up all my disks. These fucks won't do anything about it," he said, swinging one arm backward to indicate the two policemen who had followed him into the street.

"They look like decent guys. Talk it over with them later," I said.

"Fuck 'decent.' Tell Molinari my new book is titled *The Cuckold Shoves His Horns Through the Greaseball's Heart*," Xavier said.

The two policemen got him by each arm again and walked him back across the street, then one of them recrossed the street and stepped up on the curb.

"You know this guy?" he asked.

"Yep."

"We got a full house. You want to take care of him?" he said.

"Nope," I said.

"I had a feeling you might say that."

Later, Temple and I went back to her motel. I sat in a stuffed chair and turned on CNN while she went into the bath and brushed her teeth. When she came out I noticed she had taken off her earrings and her gold watch and the barrette from her hair. The blinds were closed but the sunlight glowed around the edges of the slats and touched her face and accentuated the girl-like quality of her mouth and the mysterious beauty of her eyes, which I had never understood, no more than you can understand the strange hold a tree-shaded green river can have on you, the way that its depths, the thickness of its color, and the warmth of its current can swell above your loins and arouse an undefined longing in you that makes you feel you do not know who you really are.

I stood up from the chair and removed a small blue velvet box from my pocket.

"What's that?" she asked.

"I happened to be passing by the jewelry store yesterday and this caught my eye."

She looked up at me, and I saw the color grow in her cheeks and her face become smaller and her eyes fix mine in such a way that I could hardly look back at the box in my hand.

I opened the top against the stiffness of the spring and removed the ring and lifted her hand and put the ring on her finger and slipped it over the knuckle and folded her fingers down into her palm.

"You can take it back if it doesn't fit. Or, if you don't want it, we can just return it and get a refund," I said.

"Get a refund?"

"Yeah, I sort of did this without taking a vote."

She pushed one loafer off, then the other,

and stood on top of my feet and tilted her head sideways and closed her eyes and placed her mouth on mine. Then her arms were around my neck and she tightened her stomach and breasts against me, and when she took her mouth away from mine her eyes were open, as though she doubted her power to take my heart. I kissed her again and ran my hands down her back and breathed the fragrance of her hair and skin and the perfume on her neck. I took off her blouse and unbuttoned her jeans and pulled back the bedspread and laid her down on the sheets and removed her socks and worked her jeans off her legs and sat beside her and kissed her breasts, her nipples, her throat, her eyes and cheeks, her baby fat, her back, her hair, then I stroked the inside of her thighs and traced her sex and the smooth taper of her stomach and hips and the perfect lines of her breasts.

"Billy Bob?" she said.

"What?"

"Do you want to take off your clothes?"

I undressed and lay beside her, then I looked once more into the green mystery of her eyes and I finally knew what it was that made her eyes different from any other woman's on Earth. Their depth had no bottom; they went straight into the soul, and they contained no guile, no fear, no regret, and no doubt about the intentions of her heart. I leaned over and took one of her nipples into my mouth and worked my palm under the small of her back and entered the space between her thighs, where her hand received my sex and placed it inside her while her mouth parted and only a whisper of sound came out. Then I was inside Temple Carrol again, the feathery touch of her breath against my cheek, her fingers deep into my back, and I felt the two of us slip as one into a valley of buttercups and green grass and sun showers that she had created for both of us simply by widening her thighs and raising her knees and turning her face like a new flower up to mine.

AN HOUR LATER, while Temple was in the shower, the phone rang on the nightstand.

"This is the front desk. Was Ms. Carrol expecting a guest?" a young man's voice said.

"Not that I know of. Is something wrong?" I said.

"A man cruised through the lot twice. He stopped by your door. He backed up and down, like he was trying to see through the window."

"What kind of car did this guy have?"

"You can see for yourself. He's parked across the street. In a red car with the radiator showing."

I went outside and walked to the edge of the street and looked through the traffic into the parking lot of a fast-food restaurant. Wyatt Dixon stared back at me from behind his steering wheel. His face was mirthless, the idiot's grin gone, his features like dried putty. He threw whatever he was eating out the window, onto the pavement, and started his engine and rumbled into the street. He turned his head and stared at me for only a second, but I think I saw the real Wyatt Dixon for the first time. The downturned mouth, the hollow eyes, the sensual flesh that had hardened against the facial bones, were like a Stygian image from a dream suddenly released into daylight.

Temple walked up behind me and glanced up and down the street.

"Who was that?" she asked.

"A guy who's been looking for a bullet a long time," I said.

ON THE WAY HOME, passing through the little town of Victor, Wyatt Dixon saw Carl Hinkel's truck parked in front of the barbershop. Wyatt Dixon pulled into the grocery down the street and bought a half-gallon container of ice cream and sat bare-chested on the high sidewalk in the shade of a tack and feed store and ate the ice cream with a metal spoon. It was a fine day, the mountains shining in the sun, the breeze cool on Wyatt's skin. But he couldn't enjoy it, not even the ice cream that slid in cold lumps down his throat. One obsession had haunted all his thoughts, ruined his sleep, woke him in the morning like a vulture on his bedpost, and tainted every moment and pleasure in his day.

The woman at the clinic had given him both an oral and a blood test. But it would be three weeks before he could receive even tentative assurance that he was not HIV positive, and the nurse had said something about an incubation period that would delay any certain knowledge of his status for another three months.

Wyatt wanted to tear Terry Witherspoon apart. But that was too easy. Terry expected abuse, got high on it, and used it to feed his bitchiness. Wyatt had special plans for Terry, a date with destiny that'd make him wish his mama had stuffed him hot and smoking down the family honey hole. But in the meantime he had plenty of substitutes to do a number on. Mr. Holland and his girlfriend were ripe for some fine-tuning and that war hero, Dr. Voss, could use straightening out as well. But right now Wyatt's mind was on Carl, who had convinced all his neighbors he was a stomp-ass paratrooper. Right.

Carl came out of the barbershop, his boots

shined, his seersucker slacks pressed, a Stetson at a rakish angle on his head, his western-cut coat puffing open in the wind.

Wyatt cleaned off his spoon in his mouth and dropped off the high sidewalk into the street and stuck the spoon down into the side pocket of his jeans. Carl stood in the shade of the nineteenth-century brick-front buildings and gazed at the Bitterroots rising up out of pastureland into the sky. Always posing as the patriarch, Wyatt thought, the gentleman rancher who turned no patriot from his door, the prophet who gave voice to folks who'd had their rights stolen by the government.

Maybe it was time Carl got a lesson in humbleness.

Wyatt squeezed his scrotum and started toward the barbershop, when a maroon Cadillac convertible and a tan Honda pulled up on each side of Carl's truck and four greaseballs got out and approached Carl with smiles on their faces, like they were all old friends. The greaseballs formed a circle around him, a couple of them glancing over their shoulders to see if anyone had taken notice, Carl flinching in the middle of the circle like one of the greaseballs was about to pop him in the face.

Well, ain't this a pistol? Wyatt thought. He removed a toothpick from his hatband and leaned back against the coolness of the elevated sidewalk and cleaned his fingernails while Carl was bundled into the Honda. For just an instant Carl seemed to look between two of the men pushing him into the back-seat and see Wyatt watching him. Wyatt laughed to himself and slipped the toothpick into his mouth and walked up the cement steps into the grocery store, past the sign that said NO SHIRT, NO SHOES, NO SERVICE, and pulled a six-pack of beer from the cooler and paid the clerk.

Outside the store window, one of the greaseballs got into Carl's truck and started it up, then the truck, the Honda, and the maroon convertible pulled onto the highway and caravanned toward Stevensville.

Wyatt walked back outside and ripped the tab off a can of beer and drank the can half empty, leaning over so the foam would not run down his bare chest. The mountains were a deep blue-green now, the valley floor as golden as the inside of a whiskey barrel. Wyatt stepped aside for an overweight woman and removed his hat.

"Howdy do, ma'am. Would you set out here and drink a beer with a rodeo cowboy that has been blown away by your beauty?" he said.

"Excuse me?" she said.

He squeezed her bottom and left her stunned and outraged on the sidewalk.

But Wyatt's mind was already on other

things. He crushed his beer can in his hand and tossed it into the street and fired his car up. A man shouldn't have to die if he loved the world as much as Wyatt did, he thought. Brought down by a piece of queer bait who couldn't pick a half sack of cotton without a diagram. He wanted to rip the steering wheel off the column. Instead, he drove slowly down the street, waving good-bye to the woman he had violated on the sidewalk.

IT TOOK ME several hours to get the sheriff on the phone.

"Say all this again," he said.

"Dixon was cruising the parking area in front of Temple Carrol's room. Then he stationed himself across the street so he could watch the motel. He left when I went outside."

"Seems a bad time for him to be making a move," the sheriff said.

"Dixon doesn't consult with a psychiatrist before he hurts people."

"Something else is going on, ain't it?"

"He thinks he might have AIDS."

"I hate to even ask how you know this."

"I wrote him a letter and gave him a few speculations to study on."

There was a long silence.

"You know anything about Carl Hinkel being kidnapped?" he said.

"No."

"He went to Victor to get his hair cut. A fellow with him went inside the bar to shoot pool. He says when he come out a little boy told him a bunch of men threw Hinkel in a car and took off with him."

"Boy, that breaks me up."

"You been putting glass in these people's heads, Mr. Holland. Now it's done turned around on you. I don't want to listen to your whining."

"You left Dixon on the street, Sheriff. If he comes around me or mine, I'm going to kill him."

"Oh, I'm sure you will. You stay home today. You stay away from these people. And you stay out of my business," the sheriff said. His voice was like a heated wire when he hung up the receiver.

TERRY WITHERSPOON had taken two showers that afternoon but couldn't get clean. As soon as he dried himself and put his clothes on, a smell like soiled kitty litter rose from his armpits. He tried to eat a can of Vienna sausages and vomited in the backyard.

He had never been so frightened in his life.

Wyatt had said seven o'clock. Terry wiped his face and mouth with a soiled towel and looked at the slanting rays of the sun through the pines, the flecks of gold on the river's surface down below, the bats that were already flying through the evening shadows.

If he had a car, he would run. If he had a phone, he would ring Carl. But he was trapped in an eighty-buck-a-month shack that was worse than the shack he grew up in, at the mercy of Wyatt and his craziness. Where had everything gone wrong? Why had Maisey treated him the way she did? Why did a Mobbed-up guy like Nicki Molinari, a real player on the Coast, want to beat the shit out of him over a kid and his father getting killed on the Clearwater National Forest?

Terry's head throbbed.

He went out into the railed dirt lot behind the shack and stood listening to the sounds of birds in the trees, the crack of a stick under a deer's hoof, the tumble of water in the river down below, the muttering of an owl up a larch that was shaggy and black with moss.

Nobody could be this alone, he thought. These feelings would pass. Maybe it was just a stomach virus. He wasn't a coward. Ask the queens he'd beaten cross-eyed with a sock full of sand.

Down the road he heard Wyatt's car com-

ing hard, the engine roaring, rocks ricochet-
ing like bullets under the fenders. Terry's
throat trembled when he took a breath. If
only he had the .22 rifle. But that damn lawyer had splintered it across a tree trunk.

He faced the road just as Wyatt turned into
the yard, a cloud of cinnamon-colored dust
drifting across his car into the light that
slanted through the pines.

Wyatt cut the engine and stepped out on
the ground in a new pair of striped black
trousers, a hand-tooled belt with a gold
bucking horse embossed on the huge silver
buckle, a heavy, long-sleeve, snap-button cotton shirt, a new white Stetson with a gray
feather in the band, a shined pair of oxblood
Tony Lamas powdered with dust. He had
just shaved and rubbed talcum on his neck
and cologne on his cheeks, and for some reason he looked more handsome than Terry
had ever seen him.

"You ready to ride?" Wyatt asked.

"You say an Indian woman knows me from
the clinic?"

"Don't worry about that now. You know
ole Carl disappeared? Too bad that happened
just after he promoted you."

"Disappeared?"

"He'll probably turn up. I got a chore for
you tonight."

"What?"

"You're gonna do the Voss girl. Then we're both gonna do that lawyer."

"No, sir," Terry said, shaking his head, one hand on the top rail of the fence, his eyes averted.

"Say that again."

"The ATF and the FBI are all over the place, Wyatt."

"That's when they least expect it. I got it all planned. Get in the car."

Wyatt removed his hat and combed his hair and waited, his manner casual, the setting sun pink on the taut surfaces of his face. Then Terry knew, without any doubt, that if he got into the car with Wyatt, he would be driven to a place in the woods from which he would never return.

"I'm staying home tonight," he said.

Wyatt grinned and approached him.

"Terry, you never could figure out when good things was happening in your life. That Indian woman I was talking about? I showed her a picture of me and you just a little while ago. She seen you in the clinic, all right, but you was in there to get fixed up after them greaseballs stuck you in the batting cage. It's time to have some fun."

What Wyatt had said to him made no sense at all. Wyatt was walking closer to him now, rolling an unlit cigar in his mouth with his fingers, his eyes possessed of a curious gleam, as though he were both amused by Terry and enjoying a fantasy about Terry's immediate fate.

He pinched Terry's sleeve, tugging slightly on the cloth.

"Don't wrinkle your nose at me, boy. Hop in the car. You're gonna like it," he said.

"I got to go to the bathroom first," Terry said.

He walked down the fence line toward the shack, tapping his hand on the top rail. His single-bladed pocketknife was stuck at a forty-five-degree angle in the corner post, where he had thrown it that morning. He reached out and grasped it by the wood handle, hefted it once so that the blade dropped across the calloused cup of his fingers, then whirled, whipping his arm backward, flinging the knife into Wyatt's chest.

Wyatt stared at him stupidly, then grabbed the top fence rail with one hand and fitted his other around the knife's handle. His lips formed a cone and he sucked air in and out of his mouth, as though a piece of dry ice were burning his tongue. He tried to pull the knife from his chest, but Terry pushed it in deeper, bending it sideways to widen the wound, hammering the flat of his fist on the knife's butt like a man driving a spike into wood.

Terry felt the blade snap off at the hilt, felt himself lose balance, then realized he was only inches from Wyatt's face now, staring into Wyatt's eyes, the broken handle of the knife clenched impotently in his palm, his fingers warm with Wyatt's blood, his whole life laid out behind him like a railroad track that had brought him to this particular moment and place, his heart bursting with the terrible knowledge that he had only seconds to remove himself from Wyatt's reach.

Then Wyatt's left hand seized his throat and lifted him up into a vortex of sunlit pine needles and blue sky and mountain peaks that were so high no air existed on their slopes.

# Chapter

# 31

THAT NIGHT Temple stayed at Doc's and I gave her my bunk bed and slept in the tent by the river with Lucas. During the night I heard rain on the canvas and the pop of lightning on the ridges, then the dawn broke clear and cool and deer were grazing in the pasture behind Doc's barn when I opened the tent flap in the morning.

Lucas had already built a fire and made coffee. He squatted down and filled a tin cup for me and added canned milk to it and handed it to me, then looked thoughtfully at the smoke drifting out on the water.

"You can make a fellow nervous sleeping with that dadburn gun," he said.

"Next time I'll leave it somewhere else," I said.

"Doc's gonna get out of his troubles?"

"I think so."

"Then let the law take care of all them bad people out there."

"It doesn't work that way, bud. When you're the victim of a violent crime, most of the time you're on your own."

"I ain't gonna argue. You're a lot smarter than me. Can you loan me two thousand dollars?"

"What?"

"I signed up at the University of Montana for the fall semester. I got to pay out-of-state tuition."

"If it's for your education, it's not a loan. You know that."

"Thanks, Billy Bob. Me and Dogus are going upstream. I'll catch you later," he said.

He picked up his fly rod and creel and slung his fly vest over his shoulder. He and the mongrel dog walked through the trees to a white, pebbly stretch of shoreline where the water had receded and Lucas could back-cast without hanging his fly in the trees.

If indeed I was smarter than my son, I thought, why did I feel I had just been had?

When I walked up the slope, Doc opened the front door and tossed me the portable phone.

"Tell this guy to work on his speaking skills. He's a little incoherent," he said.

"Which guy?"

"The sheriff."

I put the receiver to my ear.

"Hello?" I said.

"What'd *he* say?" the sheriff asked.

"Sorry, I wasn't listening," I replied.

"Then you'd better listen to this. We just pulled Terry Witherspoon out of a tree. He's alive but that's about all. His back's broken. Guess who did it to him?"

"Wyatt Dixon?"

"Witherspoon left a knife blade in Dixon's chest. He says Dixon has plans for you and the Voss girl and Ms. Carrol."

"Thanks for telling us."

"You're responsible for all this bullshit, Mr. Holland. I hope you can sleep at night."

"Like a stone. Good-bye, sir," I said, and clicked off the phone.

But my lie hung in my throat.

AN HOUR LATER Holly Girard drove a hand-waxed, fire-engine-red Corvette across the field behind the house and came to a stop two feet short of the front steps and got out and slammed the door behind her. Her hair was blown into a tangle on her head, her face red with windburn around her brown-tinted aviator's glasses.

"Has Xavier been here?" she said.

"Not to my knowledge," I said.

"Go inside and ask Doc and Maisey."

"Pardon?"

"Do I have to say it more slowly so you understand? Go inside and find out if that drunk idiot has been here."

"No, he hasn't. I can't think of any reason he'd want to come out here, Ms. Girard."

"He went up to the set of my new picture and accused the director of being a money launderer for Nicki Molinari. He had a gun with him. He starting screaming about protecting the river. I may be fired off my own picture."

"A gun?"

"Oh, you *are* listening."

"I'd appreciate it if you'd take your anger out on somebody else."

"You twerp," she said, and went past me and into Doc's house.

Doc was reading in a chair by the window, his granny glasses down on his nose. His eyes lifted up into Holly Girard's.

"Eventually the poor, self-deluded weakling I married will be out here. That's because you've been stoking him up ever since you moved to Montana and he can't pee in the morning without first praising the noble Dr. Voss. If you don't call the sheriff the minute you see him, your troubles with rapists will be the least of your problems," Holly said.

Doc folded his book and removed his glasses and dropped them into his shirt pocket and gazed at her face.

"I'm really sorry to hear you take that point of view, Holly," he said.

"You and your friends are so smug, with your books that nobody reads. Did you ever have to make a payroll or tell people they were laid off because of a revolution in Malaysia?" she said.

He started to reply when Temple came out of the kitchen.

"Doc and Billy Bob are gentlemen. I'm not. Get out of here, you stupid bitch," she said, and shoved Holly Girard through the door.

I WALKED down in the trees by the river and sat on a pink and gray rock above a pool filled with cottonwood leaves that had turned yellow and sunk to the bottom. I had lied to the sheriff about my peace of mind. The fact was I got no rest, not with L.Q.'s wandering spirit, not with the anger and the thirst for blood and vengeance that was like a genetic heirloom in the Holland family.

Witherspoon and Dixon deserved whatever happened to them, I told myself. Their violence lived in them like a succubus; I wasn't the catalyst for it. The law had failed Maisey; it had failed Doc; in a way it had failed Sue

Lynn Big Medicine. Sometimes you had to shave the dice or be consumed by the evil that society or government, for whatever reason, allowed to exist.

My carefully constructed syllogism almost had me out of the woods.

But a strange sense of guilt and depression seemed to settle on me, and it had nothing to do with Dixon or Witherspoon. For the first time I knew with certainty why L.Q. Navarro's spirit haunted me.

I had broken the troth the preacher had described to me when I was river-baptized in the Winding Stair Mountains of eastern Oklahoma. While I was still shivering inside my father's old Army shirt, the preacher had leaned his long face through the truck window and had told me I never needed to be afraid again, that there was no mistaking the significance of the green-gold autumnal light that had broken like shattered crystal across my eyes when I was lifted gasping for breath from the stream. The burning in my skin was like no sensation I had ever experienced, as different from prior association as the landscape had become, the way the leaves of the hardwoods fluttered with red and gold, flowing for miles like a field of flowers, all the way up the slope to the massive blue outline of the Ozarks.

But fear that L.Q. and I would not prevail,

that we would not be vindicated or avenged, got L.Q. killed in an insect-infested arroyo over amounts of narcotics that were minuscule in terms of the larger market, that probably did not change the life of one addict or put one dealer out of business. What a trade-off, I thought.

"I make you mad up there, throwing Holly Girard out?" Temple said behind me.

"No, not at all. You were eloquent," I replied.

"So what are you thinking on?"

"Carl Hinkel's gone missing. I know where he is."

"Oh?"

"I made sure Nicki Molinari knew about Hinkel's connection to the murder of Cleo Lonnigan's son. Molinari's going to use Hinkel to get his money back from Cleo. I think Molinari might let Cleo pop him."

"It's their grief," Temple said.

"Maybe."

"Where you going?" she asked.

"To pull the plug on this if I can," I said.

But there was no answer at Cleo Lonnigan's house and her message machine was turned off. I went back outside and took L.Q.'s revolver and a box of .45 rounds from Lucas's tent and found Temple down by the river.

"Want a ride home?" I said.

"No. But I'll go with you wherever it is that you and I need to go together," she replied.

WE DROVE out to the Jocko Valley and Cleo Lonnigan's place, but she wasn't home. I left a note inside her door that read:

*Dear Cleo,*
   *Do not go out to Nicki Molinari's ranch, regardless of what you might consider the necessity of the situation. I'm contacting the sheriff and informing him I think Molinari is involved with a kidnapping. Eventually Carl Hinkel's fate will probably be worse than anything you or I could design for him. I wish you all the best,*

*Billy Bob Holland*

I got into the truck and used Temple's cell phone to call 911. A dispatcher patched me in to the sheriff. Once again I had caught him on the weekend. I told him what I believed had happened to Carl Hinkel.

"You're telling me it was Molinari grabbed him in front of that barbershop?" the sheriff said.

"Yes," I replied.

"And you set it up?"

"Not exactly."

"No, you set it up."

"Okay."

"I'll pass on your information to the sheriff in Ravalli County."

"When?"

"When I get hold of him. In the meantime I'd better not hear from you again till Monday morning," he said.

I clicked off the cell phone and started the truck.

"I have a feeling the sheriff isn't sweating the fate of Carl Hinkel," I said.

"What do you want to do?" Temple asked.

"I have to go out there. I'll drop you off at your motel."

"Forget it," she said.

We drove into the Bitterroot Valley, into its meadowland and meandering river lined with cottonwoods and canyons that were like dark purple gashes inside the green immensity of the mountains in the west. Up ahead I saw four or five cars and a wrecker on the side of the road and a highway patrolman interviewing two people and writing on a clipboard.

One of the interviewees was Cleo Lonnigan. She seemed to recognize my truck as we sped past her. In my rearview mirror I saw her hand raised momentarily in the air, like someone trying to flag down a bus.

"You think she'd shoot Carl Hinkel?" Temple said.

"Maybe. It's not easy to do when you have to look the victim in the eye."

"Hinkel and Wyatt Dixon aren't victims. I wish I'd been there when Terry Witherspoon was taken down from the tree. I had something I would have liked to say."

"What?"

"He would have remembered it."

We turned off the highway at Stevensville and drove through town toward the Sapphires. I pulled into the entrance of Molinari's but stopped when I saw the preacher from next door standing on top of his church, an electric saw in his hand, staring at Molinari's stucco house.

I got out of the truck and walked to the fence that separated the preacher's and Molinari's property.

"Anything wrong?" I said.

The preacher draped his saw across the crest of the roof and climbed down a ladder and walked toward me.

"There was a drunk man around here last night and again this morning. I think he was looking for that greaser. But he couldn't raise nobody," he said.

"What was he driving?" I asked.

"A Jeep Cherokee. He knocked down the mailbox."

"Where'd he go?" I said.

"He come back a little while ago. That's why I was trying to see what went on."

"I don't understand," I said.

"I heard about fifteen pops. They sounded like they all come from the same gun."

I got back into the truck and started the engine and Temple punched in a 911 call to the Ravalli County Sheriff's Department.

"Y'all going in there?" the preacher said.

"Yeah, I think we'd better."

"Wait a minute," he said, and went into his church house and came back out with a Bible. He climbed up into the bed of the truck and scrunched down like a squirrel and hit the cab with his fist.

We drove up to the stucco house and parked behind Molinari's convertible and a white Cherokee. When we got out of the truck, our footsteps seemed as loud as rocks on slate. Out in a field an unmilked cow, its udder hard and veined, bawled in the wind. I picked up L.Q.'s revolver from the seat and let it hang from my right hand. We walked through the arcade that fronted the house, past the ceramic urns spilling over with passion vine, around the side to the heated pool that looked like a chemical green teardrop.

"Good God," Temple said.

A fat woman in a dress floated stomach-up in the pool, her face goggle-eyed beneath the surface, her blood already breaking up in the water. The man named Frank sat in a lawn chair, a cigarette burning in his lap, a small bullet hole above one eyebrow.

A second man, one I didn't know, with a pink face and thinning blond hair, lay on the grass, as if he had curled up and gone to sleep, an exit wound in his neck. There were bees in the clover where he lay, and one of his hands twitched involuntarily. When I felt his throat he opened his eyes and tried to breathe and a hard piece of chewing gum fell out of his mouth.

The preacher squatted beside him and stared into his face. He patted the man's chest with the tips of his fingers.

"You ain't got to talk. I'll say the words for you. You just pretend in your own mind they're your words. 'I commend my soul into the hands of the Lord.' The prayer's that simple, son. Don't be afraid. Ain't nothing bad can happen to you now," the preacher said.

Temple and I walked on into the backyard. The barn door was open and I could see Carl Hinkel tied to a chair inside the batting cage. The area around his feet was covered with scuffed baseballs. Hinkel's face didn't look human.

Xavier Girard sat on a plank table, drinking from a huge red plastic cup that rattled with ice and smelled of mint leaves and bour-

bon. His face was gloriously happy. A Ruger
.22 automatic and two spare magazines lay
next to his thigh.

"Where's Molinari?" I asked.

"In the shower. He almost made it to his
clothes. He might have been trouble," he
replied.

"Did you kill Hinkel?" I said.

"You bet. In the ear. Twice."

Xavier leaned forward and peered out the
door at the preacher bending over the man
on the grass. Xavier smiled fondly, then
looked up at me and Temple, his eyes full of
expectation, as though somehow he had lib-
erated himself from all the baggage of a dull
existence and he waited for us to usher him
into his new life.

"Why'd you kill the woman?" Temple
asked.

"Frank's wife?" Xavier seemed to review a
scene in his head. "Yeah, she got it, too,
didn't she? It's hard to put the bottle down
when it's half full. What a rush. I'm still
high."

The wind fluttered the barn doors. The air
was cool and filled with the smells of horses
and alfalfa and distant rain in the mountains.
I didn't want to stand any longer among the
creations of Xavier Girard's alcoholic mad-
ness.

Xavier picked up his .22 and rested it on

his thigh, the balls of his fingers rubbing the checkered grips.

"Molinari left you a message. He said, 'Tell the counselor I'm square.' What do you think he meant by that?" he said.

"You going to do anything else with that Ruger?" I said.

"I haven't decided."

"Yeah, you have," I said. I gave L.Q.'s .45 to Temple and wrapped my hand around Girard's pistol and removed it from his grasp and pulled the magazine from the butt and ejected the unfired round in the chamber and sailed the pistol by its barrel into the barnyard. I stuck his spare magazines and the ejected round into my pocket and poured his booze and ice into the dust and set his empty cup next to him, then Temple and I walked back into the wind and sunlight and the rumble of thunder out in the hills.

"Don't quote me about the rush. That was off the record," Girard called out behind us.

TEMPLE AND I had to go into Hamilton with the Ravalli County sheriff, then we drove back to Doc's place on the Blackfoot. Fires were burning in Idaho, and the western sky was red with smoke, but a sun shower was falling on the Blackfoot Valley and the light was gold on the treetops along the river and there were carpets of Indian paintbrush and lupine on the hillsides.

I wanted to scrub all the sounds and sights from Molinari's ranch out of my mind. But I knew I would dream about dead people that night and the collective insanity that caused human beings to kill one another and justify their deeds under every flag and banner and religious crusade imaginable. Any number of people were probably delighted that Carl Hinkel and Nicki Molinari were dead, and each of them would find a way to say a higher purpose had been served. But I've always suspected the truth of the human story is to be found more often in the footnotes than in the text.

Carl Hinkel would be lionized in death by his followers, then replaced by someone just like him, perhaps someone who had already planned to assassinate him. Molinari was a passing phenomenon, an ethnic gangster caught between the atavistic bloodletting of his father's era and Mob-funded gaming corporations in Chicago and Las Vegas that now operate lotteries and casinos for state governments.

If Nicki Molinari's life and violent death had any significance, it probably lay in the fact that he had volunteered to fight for his country and had been left behind in Laos with perhaps four hundred other GIs, whose names were taken off the bargaining list during the Paris peace negotiations at the close of the Vietnam War.

But those are events that are of little interest today.

The only real winner in the mass murder committed by an Edgar Award–winning novelist was an individual whose name would not be reported in a news story. The man responsible for killing Cleo Lonnigan's child had not only been tortured and executed, but Cleo now could keep the seven hundred thousand dollars her husband had stolen from Nicki Molinari and almost no one, including Xavier Girard, the shooter, would ever know the enormous favor the fates had done her.

Doc fixed a late supper for all of us and we ate in the kitchen, then I took a walk by myself along the river, through the lengthening shadows and the spongy layer of pine needles under the trees. The air was heavy with the smell of damp stone and the heat in the soil as it gave way to the coldness rising from the river. But I couldn't concentrate on the loveliness of the evening. I listened for the sound of a car engine, the crack of a twig under a man's shoe, strained my eyes into the gloom when a doe and a spotted fawn thudded up the soft humus on the opposite side of the stream.

Then I saw a track, the stenciled outline of a cowboy boot, in the sand at the water's edge. It was too small to be either mine or Lucas's, and Doc didn't wear cowboy boots. I picked up a stone and cast it across the stream into a tangle of dead trees and listened to it rattle through the branches, then click on the stones below.

But there were no other sounds except the rush of water through the riffles and around the beaver dams and the boulders that were exposed like the backs of gray tortoises in the current.

The sky was still light but it was almost dark inside the ring of hills when I walked back to Lucas's tent. He had built a fire and had turned on his Coleman lantern and was combing his hair in a stainless steel mirror that he had hung from his tent pole. His guitar case lay by his foot.

"Is Temple staying up here tonight?" he said.

"That's right."

"He's out there, ain't he?"

"Maybe. Maybe he holed up in a canyon and died, too. Maybe nobody will ever find him."

"Doc propped his '03 behind the kitchen door," Lucas said.

"Then Wyatt Dixon had better not get in his sights."

"You aim to cool him out, don't you?"

"I wouldn't say that."

"You can go to church all you want, Billy Bob, but you don't fool nobody. You get the chance, you're gonna gun that fellow."

"Would you hold it against me?"

He slipped his comb into his back pocket and picked up his guitar case and removed his hat from the top of the tent pole and put it on his head.

"You mind if I borrow your truck?" he asked.

"You didn't answer my question," I said.

"Like you say, maybe he holed up and died in a canyon somewheres. See you later, Billy Bob. It don't matter what you do. I love you just the same," he replied.

SUNDAY MORNING Temple and I drove up the Blackfoot into the Swan Valley to look at property. The lakeside areas and the campgrounds along the river were full of picnickers and fishermen and canoeists, and we walked with a real estate agent along the shore of Swan Lake and I stood in a copse of shaggy larch that was cold with shadow and cast a wet fly out into the sunlight and watched it sink over a ledge into a pool dissected by elongated dark shapes that crisscrossed one another as quickly as arrows fired from a bow.

Something hit my leader so hard it almost jerked the Fenwick out of my hand. The line flew off my reel through the guides and the tip of my rod bent to the water's surface before I could strip more line off the reel, then suddenly the rod was weightless, the leader cut with the cleanness of a razor.

"What was that?" Temple asked.

"A big pike, I suspect," I replied.

"We have to get us a place here, Billy Bob."

"Absolutely."

I looked at the severed end of my leader. The air seemed colder in the shade now, damp, the sunlight out on the water brittle and hard.

"What's wrong?" she said.

"I don't want to leave Lucas alone," I replied.

BUT MY ANXIETIES about my son seemed groundless. When we got back to Doc's he was sitting on the front porch, the belly of his Martin propped across his thigh, singing,

*"I wish they'd stop makin' them ole pinball machines.*

*They've caused me to live on crackers and sardines."*

"Everything okay, Doc?" I said in the kitchen.

"The sheriff called. He said Wyatt Dixon's car was found in a ditch the other side of the Canadian line. No sign of Dixon," he replied. He was washing dishes, with an apron tied around his waist, and his arms were wet up to the elbows.

"What's your read on it?" I asked.

"I think Dixon and General Giap would have gotten along just fine. When the NVA drew us into Khe Sanh, Sir Charles tore up Saigon."

"Maybe Dixon's not that smart," I said.

"Right," he said, and threw me a dish towel. Outside the window I saw a flock of magpies rise from the top of a cottonwood and freckle the sky.

LATER we would discover he had boosted the skinned-up brown truck outside a pulp mill in Frenchtown, west of Missoula. How his own car ended up in Canada no one would ever know. But during the night Wyatt Dixon had crossed the Blackfoot above us and slept in a campground, dressing the wound in his chest, from which he had extracted the knife blade with a pair of needle-nose pliers, eating candy bars and drinking chocolate milk for strength.

He had snaked his way across Forest Service land and parked in a low spot sheltered by trees on the river and watched the front of Doc's house through binoculars, a .44 Magnum revolver on the seat, waiting until he could assess who was home and who was not.

He watched me and Temple leave and return. Then he saw Doc and Maisey come outside together and walk past Lucas and get in Doc's truck and drive through the field in back and return a few minutes later with a horse trailer they had bought from a neighbor.

Wyatt Dixon could feel himself growing weaker, see the inflammation in his wound spreading beyond the edges of the bandages on his chest. He pulled the tape loose and poured from a bottle of peroxide into the gauze. He watched the peroxide and the infection it had boiled out of the wound seep down his stomach.

Time was running out, he thought. All because he had let a jail bitch like Terry get a shank in him. Maybe if he was that dumb he deserved to be cooled out. He shook his head in dismay and finished a carton of chocolate milk and pitched the carton out the window.

Then the moment came. Raindrops ticked on the canopy overhead and sprinkled the surface of the river with interlocking rings, as though hundreds of trout were feeding on a sudden fly hatch. Lucas stood up from the steps and put his Martin inside its case and snapped down the latches, then carried the guitar in its case down to his tent on the riverbank and got inside and pulled the flap shut. A moment later Dogus scratched on the flap and went inside, too.

Wyatt Dixon fired up his truck and floored it out of the trees, snapping the wire on a fence, scouring dirt and pinecones into the air. The steering wheel spun crazily in his hands, then he righted the truck and bore down on the tent, shifting into second gear now, the truck's body bouncing on the springs, the cleated tires thumping across rocks and driftwood.

The truck tore through Lucas's tent, splintering the poles, crushing Lucas's guitar case, blowing cookware and fire ashes and camp gear in all directions. But Wyatt Dixon's efforts were to no avail. While he had come powering out of the woods, he had not seen Lucas exit the opposite side of the tent with Dogus and walk down to the water's edge to cast a spinner into the riffle.

Wyatt Dixon braked the truck and stared through the back window at Lucas, who had dropped his rod and picked up a piece of driftwood the thickness and length of a baseball bat. I was out on the porch now and I saw Wyatt Dixon shift into reverse, the front of his beige shirt stained as though he had left an open bottle of Mercurochrome in his pocket. I cocked L.Q.'s revolver and fired at the truck without aiming.

The round cut a hole in the back window and exited the windshield and whined away in the woods. I gripped the revolver with two hands and steadied my arm against a post and sighted on the side of Wyatt Dixon's face, then squeezed the trigger. But the shot was low and must have hit the steering wheel. Dixon's hands flew into the air as though they had been scalded.

He shifted into first and drove into the field, headed for the dirt road and the log bridge that would take him across the river. I walked into the yard and fired until the cylinder was empty, the recoil jerking my wrists upward with each shot, my ears almost deaf now. The entry holes on the truck cab looked like dented silver coins embedded in the metal.

I watched the truck grow smaller in the distance and I thought Wyatt Dixon had eluded us again. Then the truck swayed out of the track and cruised through a long swath of Indian paintbrush and came to a stop six inches from the trunk of an aspen tree.

I went back into the house and removed a box of hollow-point .45 rounds from the kitchen table and shucked out the spent shells from L.Q.'s cylinder and began reloading. Temple and Doc were out in the backyard, staring at the truck in the distance. Doc worked the bolt on his Springfield rifle and ejected a spent cartridge in the dirt and locked down the bolt again. The keys to his pickup were on the table. I picked them up and dropped them into the drawer I had taken the box of .45 rounds from and closed the drawer, just as Doc entered the room.

"Where you going?" Temple said.

"I'll check on our man. Y'all call the sheriff's office," I said.

"He's alive in there, Billy Bob. The truck stopped because Doc hit the engine," Temple said.

"Really?" I said, and went out the front door before they could say anything else and drove into the field.

Through the rain I could see Wyatt Dixon moving around inside the cab of his truck. The wind had grown cold and torn pieces of cloud hung in the hills, like smoke rising out of the trees. In the rearview mirror I saw Doc and Temple and Lucas standing in the yard, like three figures trapped inside an ink wash.

I cut my engine just as Wyatt Dixon opened the passenger door on his truck and half fell into the weeds. He raised himself to one knee and reached for the .44 Magnum that now lay on the floorboards. I grabbed him by the shirt and pulled him away from the cab, and was surprised at the level of his physical weakness. He tried to get up but fell again, then pushed himself up against the rear tire, his face bloodless, his eyes blinking against the rain.

"Are you hit?" I asked.

He shook his head and breathed through his mouth, as though he were trying to oxygenate his blood. His eyes looked up at the revolver in my hand, then at my face.

"I told you, you'd know when it was my ring," he said. His teeth showed at the edge of his mouth when he smiled.

"I got a problem, Wyatt. I'm afraid you'll be on the street again one day."

"Folks love a rodeo clown. They don't got no love for lawyers."

"Why'd you bury Temple?"

"It made me feel good."

I squatted down next to him, L.Q.'s revolver propped across my thigh.

"You a praying man?" I asked.

"My daddy was. I never took to it."

"Your clock's run out, partner."

He nodded and looked out into the rain.

"Give me my hat."

"Pardon me?"

"My hat. It fell on the floor. I want my damn hat."

I reached inside the open passenger door and picked up a white Stetson with a gray feather in the band and knocked the dust off it against my thigh and handed it to him. He pulled it down on his head and stared out under the brim into the field of flowers. His shirt was buttoned at the throat, and the flesh under his chin looked old, wrinkled, peppered with white whiskers.

I knelt on one knee, three feet from him, and pointed L.Q.'s .45 at his jawbone.

"My notion is nobody knows what goes on inside a man like you. But all your life you look for a bullet. If need be, you make the state your executioner," I said.

He turned his head slowly toward me, the pain rippling upward into his face.

"I ain't afraid of no man. Do it and be done. I'll live in your dreams, motherfucker," he said.

I removed a hollow-point round from L.Q.'s revolver and dropped it into his lap.

"That's why you're going into a cage, Wyatt, where somebody can study you, the way they would a gerbil. We plan to have a good life. You won't be part of it, either."

I stood up and felt the bones pop in my

knees. I steadied myself against the side of the truck, kicking the stiffness loose from one leg, like a man who knows he's a little older, a little more worn around the edges, a little more prone to let the season have its way.

I got into my truck and drove through the rain toward Lucas and Temple and Doc and Maisey, who were walking toward me under a huge red umbrella, indifferent to the lightning that split the sky.

# Epilogue

WYATT DIXON'S .44 Magnum proved to be the weapon that had killed the biker and rapist Tommy Lee Stoltz. The death of the third rapist, the one who was found drowned in his chest waders, was written off as accidental. But I suspect Carl Hinkel ordered the attack against Maisey as a way of hurting her father, then, after Lamar Ellison was killed, had the other two men murdered in order to hide his own culpability.

But we'll never know the entire truth of what happened. Wyatt Dixon went to trial and gave up no one, even though he was facing a capital sentence. Oddly, the jury seemed to like him. At least two female jurors couldn't keep their eyes off him. When Dixon was sentenced to sixty years in Deer Lodge, he drew himself to attention and saluted the judge and called him a great American.

Terry Witherspoon confessed to burying Temple alive, not out of remorse but to incriminate Dixon and pile as much time on him as he could. The irony is that while Witherspoon was hospitalized in a body cast, his bloodwork came back HIV positive. Dixon may leave prison one day but Witherspoon will not.

I received a letter from Xavier Girard, written from the same penitentiary where Dixon and Witherspoon were being held. It was short and did not contain either the litany of grief or the self-pronounced redemption that is characteristic of most people who have made a holocaust of their lives. It read:

*Dear Mr. Holland,*

*I wanted to apologize for making a nuisance of myself. You seemed like a nice gentleman and I'm sure you had more to do than put up with a lot of grandiose and silly behavior from an expatriate coonass.*

*I've given up fiction for a while and have gone back to writing poetry. I think some of my new poems are pretty good. I can't say I've learned very much in here, unless an old truth that I knew as a young man and forgot as I reached my middle years. A writer's art is only as good as his devotion to it. I forgot that I didn't do anything to earn my talent. I burned my own kite but I hurt a lot of other people as well.*

*Come see me anytime in the next few decades. I'll be here.*

*Please consider this letter an apology to Ms. Carrol as well.*

*Best to you both,*

*Xavier Girard*

After the charges against Doc were dropped, Temple and Lucas and I drove back to Texas through the northern tip of New Mexico and stopped for the night at Clayton, a short distance from the Texas state line. We walked from the motel at the end of what had been a scorching day to a nineteenth-century hotel named the Eklund and had dinner in a dining room paneled with hand-carved mahogany. The hotel was three stories, built of quarried stone, anchored in the hardpan like a fortress against the wind, but the guest rooms had long ago been boarded up and the check-in desk and boxes for mail and metal keys abandoned to dust and cobweb.

On the wall of the small lobby was a framed photograph of the outlaw Black Jack Ketchum being fitted with a noose on a freshly carpentered scaffold. Another photograph showed him after the trapdoor had collapsed under his feet. Ketchum was dressed in a black suit and white shirt and his face showed no expression in the moments before his death, as though he were a witness to a predictable historical event rather than a participant in it.

Most of the patrons entering or leaving the dining room were local people and took no notice of the photographic display.

Temple and Lucas and I walked outside under a turquoise sky that was turning yellow with dust. The streets were empty, the air close with the smell of impending rain and a hot odor blowing from the stockyards west of town. We walked past a movie theater called the Luna, its marquee blank, its thick glass doors chain-locked. At the end of the main street a long string of grain cars sat idly on a railway track. The only sounds we heard were a shutter banging and a jukebox playing inside a stucco tavern.

Northwest of us was Raton Pass, a steep, pinyon-dotted canyon that leads out of the mesa country into the old mining town of Trinidad and the beginning of the Rocky Mountains, where the glad of heart come on vacation to rediscover the American West. In the morning we would cross the Texas line and drive through the remnants of the old XIT Ranch and into the industrial vastness of the twenty-first century. One city would not be different from another, its petrochemical plants burning as brightly as diamonds at night, offering security and prosperity to all, its shopping malls and multiplex theaters a refutation for those who might argue the merits of an earlier time.

I looked back over my shoulder at the stone rigidity of the hotel and its scrolled-iron colonnade, a huge cloud of orange dust billowing up behind it against the sunset, and I wondered if cattle and railroad barons had hosted champagne dinners in the hotel dining room, or if cowboys off the Goodnight-Loving Trail had knocked back busthead whiskey in the saloon and shot holes in the ceiling with their six-shooters. Or if the town had never been more than a dusty, wind-blown place on the edge of a stockyard where the most memorable event in its history was a public hanging.

But I think it was all of the above, truly the West, unappealing to those who have seen only its facsimile, found in no tourist brochure, the old buildings creaking with heat and decay, awaiting the arrival one day of those children of John Calvin who saw down forests and poison rivers with cyanide as votive acts and reconstruct the very places they have just fled.

"Why so quiet?" Lucas asked.

"Was I?" I said.

"We thought maybe we should take a pulse beat," Temple said.

"It's been a hot day," I said, and wiped my forehead on my sleeve.

"Time for some ice cream," Lucas said.

"That's a fine idea," I said.

The three of us walked on down the street to a small grocery store. The bell on the screen door rang when we went inside. An elderly Mexican man was reading a newspaper in front of a television set with a cracked screen. His skin was creased and brown as chewing tobacco and his eyes pale to the point of having no color, like those of a person who has spent most of his life outdoors in harsh light. He folded his newspaper loosely on a chair and walked behind the counter and looked at us expectantly, bemused by our presence in his store, perhaps embarrassed by the paucity of his goods and the little he might have to offer.

It's funny the places you end up.